W9-ABN-713

WITHDRAWN

TARGETED

Center Point
Large Print

Also by Stephen Hunter and available from
Center Point Large Print:

Game of Snipers

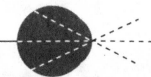

**This Large Print Book carries the
Seal of Approval of N.A.V.H.**

TARGETED

A Bob Lee Swagger Novel

STEPHEN HUNTER

CENTER POINT LARGE PRINT
THORNDIKE, MAINE

To beautiful Franny and Alice,
for renewing hope,
and all the brave men and women
who'll keep them free and secure

TARGETED

We're poor little lambs who've lost our way,
Baa! Baa! Baa!

—*Rudyard Kipling,*
"Gentlemen-Rankers"

CHAPTER 1
Mordor

I t was just July, and Northern Jersey was crud-luscious. Petroleum by-products in the form of iridescent goo accrued on all surfaces, leaving them slippery and gleaming. Vegetation of no species or color known to earth rioted and crept everywhere. Three-foot-long bull crickets, albino and pink-eyed, chirped in the marshes as if meat was on the menu for tonight. It sounded like saws on radiators. Brooks burbled, rivers gurgled, sewers clotted, algae mutated. Superheated sea zephyrs floated in over the swamps and town-ships, bearing the fragrance of small, dead mammals or large, dead Italians.

The rust was general except on wood, where rot was general. To the north, in the refinery zone just below Newark, various vapors and gasses drifted to the ionosphere, forming a plate on the industrial entities below, trapping an atmosphere full of carcinogens and other poison fogs. Here and there spurts of flame lit the clouds, giving the landscape a wondrous satanic cast. It looked like Mordor.

A few miles off the turnpike that bisected this

slough of despond and connected Philly to New York, Ace's Truck Stop addressed the darkness with flickering fluorescent lights—those that weren't out, that is—and eighteen pumps of diesel and only four of gas. It was strictly for lower-tier trucking companies, not the big boys closer to the big road, on tighter schedules. If you wanted fuel and state troopers, you stayed on the turnpike; if you wanted fuel and discretion you came here.

Around 4 a.m., a high-end Peterbilt hauling sixteen wheels' worth of van slid into the station, though not progressing immediately to the pumps. The truck—it was a huge beast, definitely the King Tiger of cross-continent haulage—kept its options open for a few minutes. In time, the doors popped open, and a lean figure debarked and quickly disappeared under the van. In a few seconds he emerged, and to watch him move was to know him. He was lithe, slim, quick, attentive, perhaps more lizard than man. A high-capacity pistol clearly nested under the shoulder of his otherwise unnecessary coat, and a Tommy Tactical baseball cap sat atop his crew-cut crown. He moved with a kind of unself-conscious precision, still the schoolboy athlete. He looked like he knew what he was doing. And he did, which is what made him different from most men: formed by Texas high school football, Ranger School, Special Ops, and nine years with

Combat Applications Group Delta, then ten years in service under contract to various alphabet-lettered entities the world over, some of which were even legal. Now in service to only himself, he sold boutique security to those who could afford it, and was known to have never lost a shipment. He got $8,000 a day, all expenses and all ammo; of the latter, he'd used up quite a bit as a variety of dead caballeros the nation over could testify, if the maggots ever cleared out of their throats. Call him Delta, after a onetime employer. Everyone else did.

He finished his security run-through on Ace's. No other vehicles inside. The pumps deserted, needing only credit cards to open them to commerce. A small convenience store supervised by a sleepy Nigerian studying thermodynamics in a glass booth, amid racks of candy bars, salty fried chips, antacids, condoms, off-brand soda pop ("Rocket-Kola"), and suchlike. In shadows, nothing. No discordant notes, no anomalies. More important, Delta got no vibes from those weird little twitches tuned to the subtlest whispers of aggression that had saved his life many a time.

He turned, waved, signaling the tractor-trailer inward for $500 worth of diesel. It kicked into gear, issuing sounds like a Jurassic apex predator clearing its throat of phlegm and blood after a nice sit-down of Thanksgiving bronto, and edged ahead. Its shiny paint scheme of red, white, and blue magnified the wan beams that came from the overheads so it seemed to move in its own penumbra of sparkles and neon, and someone expertly guided it to the trough, clearly a trucker of mature and assured skill.

Delta watched it come. Then the lights went out.

Anzor slithered to the edge of the canopy that covered Pumps 18 through 22, and shot the security man in the head. He used a rifle called an AK-74, the 74 designating, as had the previous model's 47, the year it was adopted by Soviet bloc forces. The Soviet bloc has long since disappeared, but the rifles may be found in abundance the world over. The 74 distributed a .22-caliber bullet at 55 grains, designated the 5.45 X 39, smaller, lighter, faster. The point is to allow soldiers to carry more man-killing ammunition for the same weight, following the principle adapted in 1966 by the Americans in Vietnam with their M-16 round, the 5.56mm.

The Nigerian, lost in the nuances of mechanical statistics of perfect gas, did not hear the sound of the shot, because the rifle was suppressed. The tube at the muzzle takes the snap, crackle, and pop out of the gunshot by running its excess gasses through an obstacle course of switchbacks and arroyos inside, and it slows as it negotiates, so that when it finally emerges it has lost energy and does not shatter eardrums and windows but instead resembles a loud burp.

In any event, that's why the Nigerian did not look up when Anzor entered the store. So he did not see a bulky man in dark sweat clothes and a watch cap pulled low to his ears. Neither did he see him lift the rifle, acquire a sight picture through a Sovbloc red dot. If the Nigerian saw anything at all, it may have been a peripheral of the burst of gas that emerged after the bullet, which penetrated the glass booth, leaving an almost perfect image of a spiderweb, and struck him above the left eye.

Meanwhile four other men, equally dressed, equally armed, had descended from other canopies. Like Anzor, they were immensely strong, formed by long, sweaty hours in the gym in pursuit of gargoylesque muscle mass to make their tats gleam more menacingly in the sunlight when an opportunity for such display came. These four also knew what they were doing. They moved quickly to the cab of the Peterbilt and poked at the windows with their AK-74s.

The drivers understood that they were taken. They did not expect mercy nor did they receive it. They were marched back along the body of the van, and the executions proceeded without much ceremony at the doors. One muffled shot each, behind the ear. That was the business they were in.

Again things went according to plan, their bodies then heaved by two of the raiders through the open van doors. No clues would be left for law enforcement to discover who had employed the drive team and what the probable highjacked cargo might have contained. The victims would know, of course, but too late to react intelligently. They would thrash about and beat, torture, and kill in their immediate sector of the jungle, but they would not solve the mystery until the criminals wanted it solved.

Two men used a stolen credit card to pump the four hundred gallons of diesel into the beast while the one among them who had more or less mastered such a sophisticated and gigantic piece of machinery climbed into the still-warm driver's seat, familiarized himself with a panel, and turned to await the go signal.

Meanwhile, Anzor had returned from his sanitation responsibility in the store, just as the men were climbing into the rear of the van.

"Anzor," Uncle Vakha said in his native language, "go check the security. Make sure he's dead. Bring his wallet and weapon."

Anzor, the youngest of the cousins, ran to his task. He was eager to please the patriarch, and quite excited at the way things were going. He had not fought in the war, and his kills were limited to drug shootouts and beatings in back alleys, here in America and in his homeland. He wanted to prove to his uncle and his brother and cousins that he was up to the task.

He approached the facedown man, placed the muzzle of the suppressor against his neck.

The only impression he had was of speed. The man beneath seemed to enter another dimension, and Anzor found himself in a chokehold from an extremely practiced martial artist, a wrist of death pressing hard against his larynx and the muzzle of a large Glock against his skull.

Why was Delta not dead? Part of it was luck, since men of his disposition somehow discourage bullets from finding a lethal spot; they always just miss or only slightly wound him, concussions knock him down but not out, he comes back to operational reality fast, and he figures out the next option without losing a lot of sleep over the failure of the last. But part of it was tactical too. The black ball cap, which seemed to mark him as just another wannabe mall jungle operator in a world full of them, actually concealed a net of overlapping Kevlar disks that shielded the Delta brain. Though it was only Level II, suitable to stop pistols alone, it had in this case, aided by a slightly acute angle of fire, managed to deflect the bullet off into the Jersey night. It could do nothing about the impact, however, which downloaded full-force into the brain.

It conked Delta out, hard. He had no memory of falling to the pavement and opening a laceration along his cheekbone. Besides unconsciousness, it filled his brain with images of porno-blondes from Texas strip clubs doing interesting things to himself and each other. Thus he awoke several minutes later with a headache and hard-on and a deep curiosity about what was going on.

The world was now horizontal as he was flat on the asphalt. His head felt like someone was clog dancing on it. He could see the boots of the raiders as they conferred near the rear of the truck. Now it came back to him. He presumed that Cy and José, the drive team, both good guys, slept with the fishes. In any event, his job was not to save them but to save himself first and the shipment second and, failing that, gain as much operational evidence as possible from the event, to help the inevitable track-down that had to happen next. But then he saw the commander—whoever, as they were all in black watch caps and sweats—indicate that the conference was over and sent each to his next job.

Delta saw one pair of boots detach and head his way. He knew instantly what for, and he knew as well whoever it was had no deep well of experience, or he would have already head-shot the fallen man.

The boots approached and ceased to move; he waited as the shooter bent to press the suppressor

18

against his neck and then ripped him down with a move that is known to only a few of the warrior elite, and involves pain, leverage, and totality of will, all at light speed. The next time the world stabilized, he had the Glock 10mm against the fool's temple and his neck in a vise grip ten ounces from unconsciousness and twelve from death.

What now?

First instinct, as always, was to kill. Pop this motherfucker and go to strong isosceles on the four silhouette targets forty feet away. But he had no full-auto capacity. Though a superb shot, he knew the boys who faced him were too. He'd get two definites before they got their 74s into play and pegged him and went on with the job, figuring on a much better split for the swag. So that was a no go, both for professional and personal reasons.

He yanked the boy to his feet and turned him to orient toward the others, who by this time were aware of the emergency.

"Guns down, motherfuckers, and kick 'em away or I toast this punk and take as many of y'all to hell as I can."

Whether they understood his Hill Country patois or not, they complied. The guns went to the asphalt, and were further removed from activity by strong shoves at boot end that sent them skittering away.

"Stay put and this kid lives. Otherwise he's breakfast."

Using the boy's throat as his control point, he edged backward, out of the zone of light. He could see the four men tensing, coiling, building in rage and energy, as the distance increased. It was a slow drag through perdition, the boy hard against him, their legs moving in syncopation, the long backward walk seeming to take an epoch.

But then the darkness had them.

"You tell Papa that if he has the guts or time to go on a bug hunt in the swamp for me, I'll kill him last and slowest. Now it's nap time, Junior."

With that he clipped the boy hard with the butt of his pistol, right under the left ear, and sent him folding to earth.

He turned and melted into the black.

Ibragim and Khasan were first to the rifles, but Uncle Vakha's command voice froze them.

"No!" he screamed. "You stay put. Let him see you do nothing."

"Uncle, he—"

The young, so stupid. It was Khasan, the smartest, voicing dissent.

"Let him go. We will not spend hours in the dark trying our skills against his. He is too good, we do not have the time."

"Anzor—"

"—is all right. See!"

And indeed, Anzor, hand cupping his head under the ear, stumbled back into the light, caught himself, fell, and struggled to regain footing.

"Get him. Now. We must leave."

Ibragim and Khasan ran to their youngest brother or cousin (it varied), got him by the arms, and half guided and half carried his addled body back to the scrum.

"I know I did not miss—"

"Shut up."

"Now what, Uncle?"

"Into the truck."

"To Coney Island?"

"Coney Island is dead. Or we are dead if we go to Coney Island. The guard will bear witness, the Russ will put one plus one together. The Cossacks will be on the streets with guns in their hands and blood in their eyes tomorrow, and all snitches and rats at full alert. No force on earth can save us in New York."

"But it wasn't—"

"No, it wasn't. But who could guess they'd have a superman guarding. We counted on cartel shooters, not whatever that fuck was. We guessed, we lost."

"So?"

"So, the truck is full of fuel, the highway is clear. We get in, we drive. Always under the speed limit, always moving west. Too much Russ in LA. We will go north, perhaps to Seattle or

Portland. It's very simple. Flee or die. It is quite possible we may flee *and* die, but that is for the future to tell. A few hundred miles out, you will call your loved ones and explain the change in plans."

CHAPTER 2

Cascade, the Porch

Bob Lee Swagger liked everything about being famous except for the being famous part.

Fame had befallen him following two inevitable mandates in human behavior: no good deed goes unpunished, and there are always unexpected consequences.

He had taken a shot, under official auspices, on a known terrorist who was himself about to launch a shot. Both men had hit. The terrorist was permanently shipped onward, while Swagger had his left collarbone shattered and his thoracic cavity shredded. That was the business he was in.

After near death on the operating table, he had mostly recovered over a long winter in Walter Reed, and was now at least partially ambulatory, in Idaho, on the porch, in the rocker, where the days passed, the chair bobbed forward and back, the temperature turned, the clouds cleared, the earth thawed, the grass greened. Soon it was summer.

In the public sphere, however, things over which he had no control were happening. Various politicians and government bureaucrats had seen much to be gained from public attention to the event. That's what they did, it was to be expected, and so indeed, an anonymous source told key big media players about the FBI team that had brought down Juba the Sniper at the ultimate moment, emphasizing the brilliance of the manhunt, the last-minute breakthrough that allowed the man hunters to arrive at the shooting site and the unidentified FBI marksman to take a three-hundred-yard shot from a helicopter, saving everybody's marbles.

That, again, was to be expected. What happened was government publicized its triumphs. Not just this government, but all government, all the time, since government began. Swagger was fine with it. He mended in peace, oblivious to the general hubbub the incident had spawned about the "mystery shooter." He had no inclination to be the solution to anybody's mystery; he just wanted his old simple life back, rocking on the porch, going for a ride on this or that horse, working on eccentric wildcat cartridges in his shop, and ambling to the range for test shoots. The best thing was kids, especially since his son Ray had just presented him with a squiggly caterpillar of a granddaughter, a wrinkled pink blob of beautiful protoplasm, Frances Evelyn, whom they called Franny. She filled old Bob, who'd seen and done way too much in the shitholes of this world, with faith and optimism. If the world could produce a little creature of perfection like a Franny, maybe the old joint was worth saving after all.

Time passed, life seemed good. Family regularly, friends occasionally, good nights of sleep (fewer nightmares), most ghosts buried and forgotten, the hallowed dead (so many of them!) remembered and respected. Who could want more?

But it all fell apart when he received an email from old friend and collaborator Nick Memphis.

"Bob, it seems some *New York Times* reporter is nosing around on the issue of 'mystery shooter.' He has sources. Stay tight."

This was upsetting but not so much as another email arriving a day later. Yes, the genius had cracked the case. In fact, David Banjax had been on the Swagger beat before, having covered the aftermath of several Bob adventures that had occurred under government sponsorship. It appeared also that he knew, or at least knew of, Kathy O'Reilly, a *Washington Post* correspondent with whom Bob had adventured in Russia some years back. She had mentioned Bob in the acknowledgments to the book she had written on the event, providing any snooper with a link.

Anyway, the fellow said, "I have two solid sources identifying you as the helicopter shooter who took out Juba the Sniper. I'd love to talk with you about it. I am aware of your reluctance to do press after previous encounters, but I felt it only fair to reach out. If I don't name you, someone else will. I will give you a great platform in the *Times* and all good things that you have deserved will come your way. Please consider this. I should warn you that I am ahead on this story but only by a few days. It will come out. Better via someone who knows and respects you and lets you frame your story than some hack from the yellows.—David Banjax, *New York Times*"

Bob reached out immediately to O'Reilly, for advice. But she was out of the country with her husband.

He emailed back: "No comment."

The story broke two days later.

"The unknown marksman who took the shot last year that terminated the terrorist called 'Juba' has been identified by several sources as retired Marine Corps Gunnery Sergeant Bob Lee Swagger, the *New York Times* has learned.

"Sergeant Swagger, a decorated sniper in Vietnam, has been involved in several shooting incidents over a long career under contract to both the FBI and CIA, including last year's event. He was seriously wounded by the terrorist's bullet but is now recovering.

"Additionally, sources continued, he has advised the Justice Department on several cases involving high-tech ballistics and long-distance shooting issues, on which he is an acknowledged expert.

"Swagger, 74, lives in Idaho. He declined to comment for the *New York Times*."

It went on in Banjax's dry style, unvarnished by emotion or attitude, factually accurate, thorough, and relying on the information it contained to communicate the emotion.

That was not to be the case for long. By three in the afternoon, eastern time, the *New York Post*, under the headline "MASTER SNIPER SNIPED BY NYT," opened with "If it absolutely, positively must be killed today, get retired Marine Gunnery Sergeant Bob Lee Swagger. He's the only man for the job."

Thus began a relentless campaign of hustle, genuflecting to the hero while at the same time pushing him toward specific commercial enterprises, which some, not Bob, might have seen as opportunity. There was money to be had, if only he would reach out and grab it. Publishers, agents, movie and TV producers, both Netflix and HBO, reached out. Slick lawyers, unctuous executives, women with husky voices—they all tried their best, leaving a message list jammed like a beaver dam, and Swagger dumped that phone, got a new one with a new number. His Arkansas lawyer, Jake Vincent, was in the public record as his representative in a real estate deal, and it took the hustlers but days to move on to him. Poor Jake became besieged. Then there were the veterinarians. Every one of them that

Bob had done business with as the owner of eleven lay-up barns in five states was equally sought out and turned to for entertainment media possibilities. Several movie stars and several big-name directors called to discuss the various possibilities, hinting of the Big Movie that all could collaborate on. The implication was that just by saying yes he could join the cool kids in Beverly Hills. They didn't know: he hated movies almost as much as he hated cool kids.

And a few days after the news broke came the backlash. It was as if the Juba thing was situated perfectly on the fault line between two Americas. On one side stood those who believed in use of force, who believed society needed protectors in the form of strong men armed, and who believed that under certain circumstances, the state had the right to authorize killing for the sake of the larger society. But others disagreed, sometimes ferociously. They felt that the state had no right to be involved in a killing game. They believed that the warrior, particularly the subspecies sniper who shot wantonly without warning, was an obsolete archetype, an emblem of patriarchy. They noted that many of the sniper's targets were people of color and felt that the sniper was in some sense a custodian of white supremacy. In the case of this Juba, he was not only of color— they so considered an Arab heritage—but also of Islamic faith, and therefore, they charged, an "outsider," a subhuman whom it was easier to kill than to treat with equality and justice.

That was how these things worked and it didn't hurt or surprise him, but it did astound him how much hate could be whipped up so fast.

Somehow, at least for one day, his email address became known, and he received literally hundreds of messages, most of which were death threats, a few of which were earnest well-dones. There was no sense letting such poison into his life, so that account was quickly abandoned and a new, friends-only one emplaced. And of course it was not all media. The incursions had physical manifestations: copters buzzed the place, news SUVs parked on the perimeter, even drones reconned, getting some long-lens stuff of Bob on horseback, Bob on the shooting bench, Bob walking from shop to barn to house. Gone, perhaps forever, were the occasional early-morning breakfasts in Cascade amid cowboys and ranchers, whose banter he enjoyed and who knew enough not to bother him otherwise. So too the odd trip into Boise for an upscale meal and a walk around the civilization he had defended so intensely he'd never had time to learn much about it. Such episode would have meant an ordeal by iPhone camera, perhaps even demonstrators on the other side of the issue, if they could flash-mob it together fast enough.

"I just wish it would go away," he told Nick.

So he sat and rocked, orienting the chair anew each day to see the least amount of media hubbub at the fence a quarter mile away. Thank God for that fence.

The wind changed directions, the temperatures moseyed upward. The midsummer grass had greened up nicely and the yellow thatch of winter's dehydration had largely vanished. Northbound fleets of geese vectored overhead for the fatlands of Canada. Occasionally herbivore mamas and their spindling newborns ambled into vision, the kidlings still of shaky legs but assured of at least a few summer months in paradise before any serious predation was brought against them, which began in fall. If you squinted hard, you could convince yourself that things were as they had once been. The only annoyance in this was his left hip. It was still a bone ball, unlike the right one, titanium and three times replaced. But the lubrication had finally worn too thin on the left one and it grated when it functioned—it was called arthritis—and soon it would have to go, but not, doctors advised, until he had fully recovered from the more grievous bullet wound.

Rock, rock, rock, ache, ache, ache, breathe, breathe, breathe, remember, remember, remember. His iPhone tingled. He moaned, wanting no interruption of his privacy. He pulled it out, saw the call came from Bud, the day gateman, who was under instructions to turn all visitors away unless previous arrangements had been made.

"Yeah, Bud?"

"Sorry to bother, Mr. Swagger. Federal marshals are here. Say it's official business. Two of 'em."

"Oh, Christ."

"You want me to ask 'em the nature of their visit?"

He thought. Maybe something about an environmental impact statement his lawyers had just filed for the construction of a new barn on one of his Wyoming properties. But why wouldn't they go through those same lawyers?

"Let 'em in."

He watched the government car ease up the road from the highway, a black Ford sedan of no distinguishing feature, and pull into the yard. Two linebackers in boots and fifteen-gallon hats got out. A jacket fell open, exposing a pistol, but that was of no importance.

"Sergeant Swagger?"

"That would be me. I'd get up, but I have a bad left hip and a bad left shoulder."

"Not a problem, sir. I'm U.S. Marshal Gary Watson, this is my partner Jack Kleck."

"Come on up. How are you boys today?"

"Sir, we're fine. Both wanted to say, duty aside, it's an honor. They don't make 'em much like you no more. You done some great work."

"Kind of you to say so. Now what's this here about?"

"Sir, it's my duty—we take no position on the meanings implied herein—to serve you with this."

He pulled a wad of papers from his breast jacket, handed them over.

Bob unfolded them.

It had the fancy look of a peace treaty from the age of steam and bayonet.

Across the top, emblazoned in serious-looking caps, ran the heading "UNITED STATES CONGRESS," and beneath in smaller print, "HOUSE JUDICIARY COMMITTEE," and below that, "SUBCOMMITTEE ON CRIME AND TERRORISM."

Then the killer word: "SUBPOENA."

"YOU ARE COMMANDED," the document continued, "to appear at time, date and site to be named later to testify concerning events taking place under federal auspices on—" and it gave the date of his shot on the terrorist.

"YOU ARE FURTHER COMMANDED," it continued, "to surrender all documents, electronic transmissions, physical objects, and other items having direct reference to that day and to further permit inspection of premises in the same reference."

Several laws were cited by federal code, then the warning, "Failure to Comply could lead to prosecution for Contempt of Congress."

CHAPTER 3
East of Boise

A citizen called it in, and Trooper First Class Boynton, in the Whiskey 41 unit, was closest. He'd just come on duty out of the Fairmount Barracks when the call crackled off the speaker. He realized his position in relation to the complaint and signaled HQ he'd take it.

He was young, in great shape, not dumb, and completely committed to the ethos and mores of the Idaho State Police. He nudged the pedal on his Charger, and the lively engine kicked in. Everything got blurry fast except the perdurable Boise Mountains, that snaggle of dragon's teeth which lay above the capital city. No need for siren or gumball; traffic was light, the weather clear, folks saw him coming in rearview and moved into 84's slow lane, and in a matter of a minute he was on location. He saw it.

It was a Peterbilt tractor-trailer hauling the biggest of all vans (sixteen wheels), all shiny in the sun. Red highlights on the cab, and a little chrome for splash, three plates, Texas, New Mexico, and Ohio. He settled into a two-hundred-foot follow, went on radio, called in the plates. The answer was swift.

"Whiskey 41, no action on the plates. They're clean, all three of them, Renson Haulage out of Waco, no outstandings."

"Got it," said Boynton.

It was almost enough to peel off and look elsewhere for provocation. But not quite enough. The issue wasn't speed, but lack of speed. These big guys made their living fifteen miles over the limit, a fact that was not recorded anywhere but was universally known. So this sucker could have been pounding along in seventeenth gear at ninety, no problem, and he'd have made it to Portland before midnight.

But he wasn't pounding at ninety, he was in fact somewhere between sixty and sixty-five.

Boynton called in again, requested a re-run on the license check, as well as a look into the Federal DOT numbers on the rig. Again, clean as a whistle, again the temptation to let it slide.

But letting it slide wasn't in the vocabulary of Idaho State Police.

He went to gumball but not siren, indicating in the language of the professional road that this was administrative, not a speed-limit stop.

It took a few more seconds than it should have—another indicator of weirdness afoot—and the big guy began to ease on down the gears as he decelerated to pull over. He missed eighth

34

though, jumping from ninth to seventh, and the thing lurched just a bit.

Boynton thought: This guy is too tired to be on the road. He ought to pull in at one of the big Boise truck stops, get himself some shut-eye.

Magomet saw the police vehicle slide in behind him and just hold there.

"Cop," he said to Uncle Vakha, who dozed next to him.

Vakha stirred, his mind worked the word, he recognized it, and he came alert.

"What? Where?"

"He's behind us. He's just inside my mirror, holding steady, probably to check us out."

"Fuck," said Vakha. "You're not speeding?"

"No, not at all." They spoke in their native language.

"All the paperwork is right, all the licenses up-to-date. What the fuck could he want?"

"I don't know. What should we do?"

"There is nothing we can do. Just hold steady, do not panic."

"But Uncle, if he pulls us over, he understands foreign men in sweatshirts are not usual truckers. Then he demands to see the cargo and encounters men with machine guns."

"I know all this. You tell me nothing."

"Yes, Uncle."

"I will talk if that's what happens. What

bothers me is that one of your cousins might do something stupid. The young one, Anzor, he is not experienced."

"By a long shot," said Magomet, who was blood to Anzor but no admirer.

Vakha pulled his phone out, called Ibragim in the van.

"Yes, Uncle."

"Policeman shadowing us. You keep them calm. No guns, no violence, nothing stupid. We are not at war. If he pulls us over, I will try and talk him out of any difficulties. If he opens the van, I want the three of you down low, quiet, deep inside, no shooting, nothing, do you hear?"

"Yes, Uncle."

Vakha got the papers out of the glove compartment, scanned through them. Bills of lading for furniture imported from China and delivered in Galveston, meant for delivery in Brooklyn, the receiving outfit called Skyway Furniture Distribution—all false, of course, but impenetrable at this level.

"Is it good?" asked nervous Magomet.

"I'll tell him we got last-minute change-of-delivery call, had no time for paperwork," said Uncle Vakha.

The police car veered out from behind them, the red light flashing, but no siren.

"Oh, shit," said Vakha.

• • •

More strangeness. Instead of, as usual, sliding to the shoulder, the truck continued even under the duress of the red pulse. Eventually—much too slowly—he slowed, again dropping gears, and then glided to the side of the road, ripping up a shroud of dust from the shoulder, coming finally to a halt in a cloud of gray particulate.

Danger, danger, danger, signaled all of Trooper Boynton's cop antenna. He went to radio.

"Six, Whiskey 41."

"Go ahead, 41."

"I want backup on this deal. I'm eastbound halfway between Exits 11 and 12. But something's not right and I don't want to get caught with my pants down."

"Roger, 41. All eighty-four units, all eighty-four units, proceed to Mile 144, back up Whiskey 41 on traffic stop, Peterbilt hauling sixteen, odd patterns noted."

Boynton reached down, removed his Glock .40 from the holster, did a slide check, not because he thought he might not have chambered but because it ate some time until more cars arrived.

Seeing it was ready, he eased the pistol back into its holster but did not button the strap. He could draw and shoot with anybody.

Behind, he saw Moore pull up in the 55 car, and Charley Rankin in the 51 pulled in behind him. Across the highway, Hatch and Bogardus, coming in from Boise, pulled aside on the median, and each got out of his unit and set up a stern observational posture close to the unlatched trunk, where he carried an M4 with a thirty-round clip and lots of spare ammo.

Boynton—it was his stop after all—got out, adjusted his hat so that it sat square across his brow, and approached the truck. He signaled roll-down to the driver, who was another surprise, a blunt man with dark eyes, slightly Asiatic, not the good-old-boy type in a baseball cap you usually found behind the wheel of a big rig.

"Sir, may I see your license please."

He heard a man say something in a foreign—Russian, perhaps?—tongue. He backed off a bit, saw the second guy hunched close to the driver.

"Mr. Policeman, he does not speak English. I translate."

"That's fine," said Boynton.

The driver handed down the license, and Boynton judged it real—that is, Class A Commercial, which legally qualified him to drive such a rig. It was from New Jersey.

"Thank you, sir," he said. "May I ask, what's your heading? It says here Coney Island, New York."

"Last-minute change by phone. We divert west, to Portland. The paperwork will catch up there."

"Happens all the time. But the reason I pulled you over was that you were going too slow, some of the other drivers were complaining you were causing congestion. You've got to maintain a consistent speed out here."

"He is substitute driver," said the translator. "The original got sick, this man was called in from labor pool. He said he had correct license. We don't want no trouble."

"There won't be any trouble. If everything checks out, I'll have you on your way. Also, I have to say, this man—" he checked the driver's license—"Mr. Rugisov, he looks tired. You may be best to book a night in a truck stop, get some sleep, then push on tomorrow. A vehicle like this takes full concentration to drive and I'd hate to have y'all get involved in some kind of accident. Let me just check your cargo manifest and we'll consider it handled."

The manifest seemed all right, even if shipping Chinese chairs and sofas to Portland didn't make a lot of sense, since Portland was already a big port city. But in fact Boynton was somewhat hamstrung by the new rules, which meant that unless there was clear evidence of felony, he was not allowed to play hunches, guesses, rogue suspicions. It may have smelled to high heaven, but he had no other course of action. He was thinking mainly about how to get these morons off the road or at least out of Idaho. A 16-wheeler was a beast and an out-of-control 16 was death to any and all who got in the way. Not on his watch.

"Fine, seems okay," he said. "Let me just take a quick look into the van, make sure it's packed up solidly. The cargo gets to shifting and it can make problems happen fast."

"Yes, sir," said the translator, while Mr. Rugisov looked down on him with uncomprehending eyes.

As the translator got out of the cab on his side, Boynton spoke into the radio unit pinned to his Sam Browne diagonal.

"All units, no obvious derelictions or infractions, I'm going to take a look in the van, I want you guys in backup alert now."

Boynton followed the translator around back. The fellow was older, in hoodie and sweats. He had a watch cap pulled over his ears and wore wraparound sunglasses—expensive Magpul or Oakleys—but even under all that he had the same kind of "foreign" features, a broadness of face, a bluntness of nose, perhaps some Tarter exoticism through the eyes, and every muscle under the sloppy-fitting cotton boasting of endless strength, convict strength built up in a regimen of heaving iron in the yard day after day, year after year.

They arrived in back, and the older man threw the grip—Boynton noticed the rig wasn't locked from the outside—and various rods and bolts pulled free or unlatched, and the twin big doors swung open.

Boynton looked. It was about half-full. Sofas, clearly wrapped in heavy plastic, filled the far end of the space. They appeared to be strapped in solidly. Professionally stacked, and of no safety consequence in their arrangement. He didn't see anything he could hold them on, much less run a search. Best move now: get 'em on the road to Portland, let Oregon worry about them.

"Okay," he said, "looks fine. You can close it up and—"

Somebody inside coughed.

Boynton froze, not sure he'd heard what he heard.

"Sir, is there someone in the van?"

"No, no, no passengers. That was just some furniture settling or shifting."

"Sounded like a cough to me."

"I swear to you, Officer, there is nothing—"

The bullet hit Boynton in the left lung, being small and fast, and was a total through-and-through, deflating the air sac, opening a dozen minor veins, delivering the kick of a mule, and he spun and fell backward even as he heard the old man screaming "No, no!"

CHAPTER 4

She Who Must Be Obeyed

Charlotte Venable, the chairman of the House Judiciary Subcommittee on Crime and Terrorism, was widely admired, beloved even, not only in her own district and state but nationally as the consequence of a storied career. She had been a congresswoman for the last sixteen terms: She had followers, acolytes, and even worshipers, in the millions. Media adored her. Her press conferences were always well attended (as were her hearings), her op-ed pieces (ghosted, of course) were well read, and she had acquired after so many years on the Hill a staff of extraordinarily talented and loyal people. She was no stranger to either magazine covers or Sunday talk shows.

But Representative Venable was also widely hated. National politics in America had of late become more of a kick-ass rampage, sometimes so savage and ruthless in its slaughter that age-old traditions of courtesy, forbearance, and genial collegial affection transcending party lines had been destroyed. Now it was crush or be crushed, and she was herself facing a reelection drama.

Not far enough left, it was said; her polls were down and she was being primaried—probably—by someone much younger, much more radical. So she had to go left or perish.

Thus her haters on the equally febrile right steamed and seethed with anger. They didn't just hate her. They. Hated. Her. She hated right back. She especially hated this president, and therefore the sniper who seemed to be his favorite killer.

Thus, to her many enemies, no insult was too squalid, no snub too abrupt, no comment on her appearance too mean, and that was fertile ground for creativity. She appeared to be a genetic blend of Attila the Hun and some twitchy urban bird. Had she hatched from one of those brown-gray species that congregate wherever garbage and scraps fester in heaps, singing squawkily of riot and mayhem? She had the avian's glittery eyes, forever moving, forever on alert, forever in mid-dart, but also the Hun's empty stare at that which he was about to slaughter, be it human or animal. Her face was sharp-featured, composed of galaxies of wrinkles cranked tight by surgical genius, her hair lit from within by Clairol, a fifties pageboy of mathematical precision; it might even have been her own, but probably wasn't. Who would ask? Her chin was sharp as a katana's cutting edge—probably from surgery, but again who would ask?

Moreover, these legions of enemies conjured vile nicknames to evoke her powers and menace, as if in naming the beast they could slay it. Perhaps the best would have been "Attila the Wren," but nobody thought of it. For a while it was "The Bag," owing to the weekly face-tightening that wore thin by Thursday and caused her features to droop somewhat, as if gravity's pull had increased its claim. Then there was "The Wicked Witch of the West," as played under green paint by Margaret Hamilton in *The Wizard of Oz*, sunk deep into every generation's collective subconscious. Many staffers of the other party deployed exquisite imitations of the green witch's ripsaw cackle to liven drinking sessions in Georgetown. The other half of Hamilton's great performance as Almira Gulch, Kansas's meanest church lady, did not go unmemorialized. Representative Venable was also "Madam Almira" or "La Gulch," foreclosure whipsnake and Toto kidnapper/would-be executioner.

All these colorful descriptors came and went. Two seemed to last, however. First runner-up was "Lady Macdeath," but it broke down when someone pointed out that the original never got her hands wet. The winner then, severe in its minimalism, was "Mother Death."

And on this day, Mother Death sat in her corner conference room on the third floor of the House office building, less than a mile by

Tomahawk glide path from the great chamber itself. In attendance were two shrewd men who owed much to Mother Death: the lead majority congressman of the Subcommittee on Crime and Terrorism, Ross Baker, and her very own Bud Feeley ("He has no feeley, only hurty" went the barb), who served as her press secretary. She owned them both and they loved her for it.

"Representative," the PR flack said, "I just heard from Idaho and yes, he was served at two thirty-five local time."

"Gratifying," she said. "What time's the presser again?" she asked.

"Five. Make all the national news. Any later and we're stuck in *Action Cleveland* or *Goodnight Topeka* with the weather and tonight's dead kitten story."

"So he didn't pull a gun, blast anything, curse, start a fistfight, do anything John Wayne to express his anger?"

"No, ma'am. They said he sort of shook his head. And chortled. They say that in his old age he's developed a sense of humor. He wasn't exactly a laugh-a-minute guy when he was professionally killing people for the Marine Corps and the FBI."

"I love a witty mass murderer," she said. "We haven't had one since Hannibal Lecter."

"Madam Chairman, it took some horse trading but I managed to get Banjax in the *Chicago*

Tribune's front-row seat, and of course the regular *Times* gal will be in hers, two seats down."

"Which one is Banjax? Is he the blond guy with the smelly little goatee? His mouth looks like a vagina."

"No, that's Roy Finch, of the *Post*. Banjax is crew cut, lanky, nondescript. You would notice him because you didn't notice him. He's your basic child-molester type of anonymous wretch. Generally he writes enterprise features out of DC, profiles, the occasional lightweight thumb-sucker. He's made a career out of Swagger. He's the ranking Swagger expert. He's the guy who tipped us that this little alleyway might bear exploring. He heard from a Bureau source who's not a fan of the president."

"So that means I have to pretend to like this guy? Really, they're all such syphilitic goats."

"Yes, ma'am. But Banjax has been and will be quite useful."

"Okay, I'll pretend to like him. All right. Congressman Baker. What have you got today?"

"I thought we ought to go over the talk points for the presser. You know what happens when you're not briefed and don't stay on message."

"Baker, it's not really on you to notice such things. If it gets around, people might realize I'm a senile alcoholic."

"Yes, madam."

Baker's picture was in Webster's in the "ambition" definition. To see him was to feel it. He was unconsciously odd, with a long neck and an ovoid head, with a thinning thatch of blondish hair atop. He looked like an egg that had just reached puberty. But the oddest thing was his eyes, which, normal enough at most times, had a distressing tendency to bulge, and his preternaturally tiny pupils stood out like pinballs on frosted cake. These eyes were particularly weird in photos. He was aware of this, but he could not help it, and he always ended up on front pages looking like a guy born to play Raskolnikov in dinner theater. He was beloved in his district because his one real talent was sucking up; he made his many million and billionaire donors feel like Olympian deities.

He summed it up dryly: No shame on the heroic Sergeant Swagger. He is not a "target" in any sense. But this event has been exaggerated and celebrated so excessively we feel it ought to be looked at critically, to see what knowledge can be gained. The BLM outbursts and the tragedy of George Floyd had finally brought these issues the attention they deserved. Perhaps new regulations for use of force are required. Or perhaps in examining a "successful use of force," we learn how to prevent unsuccessful or botched situations. Perhaps our criterion for deciding whom to let the snipers or SWAT people handle should be looked at and brought into federal uniformity. Blah, blah, and blah.

"And the subpoena?"

"Again, Madam Chairman, don't interpret it as disrespect or hostility to the hero. Instead, it's a way of emphasizing the seriousness of the hearing. I'm sure the sergeant would have happily testified without it, but we wanted to make a statement."

"Fine, let's call it a day. There's a bottle of vodka with my name on it."

"One last thing," said Congressman Baker.

"If you must."

"I was going to say, I would not mention the field-hearing plan until later. Let 'em think we're bringing Swagger here. It's an angle the right will freak on, and the louder they get, the more they alienate themselves. Elder abuse, disrespect to wounded heroes, contempt for the military, all those drums they love to beat. And then when you announce it, the love that will flow onto your robes—"

"You make it sound like ejaculate!"

"It's just as thick and gooey. We have to pretend to take his purity of motive, skill, steadiness, and heroism as a given."

"Show me a hero, I'll show you a fraud."

"One other thing," Baker said. "Certain people have paid millions for that genetic research. The whole issue is lost, no matter the outcome, if we don't get that in."

"Maybe leak it to Banjax?" said Feeley, who, as another ex-*Times* guy, was actually quite good at his job. "Or leak part of it to him, and the second part to Milt Zane, the *Trib* guy who gave up the front-row seat for Banjax today? I promised him a scoop in trade."

"They're like diamond merchants, aren't they? Little hustlers, little dealers, little masters of tats and tits. Anyway, let me ponder the genetics-by-leak scenario. I think you're right, it makes more sense coming from outside the tent than inside, and we can take it up, pretending to be totally innocent. I love pretend."

CHAPTER 5

The Famous I-84 Shootout

Boynton bled out, getting dizzier and dizzier as his life swirled down the drain faster and faster. He hoped he'd done all right. He hoped he hadn't let the fellows down. He wished he'd told his dad how much he loved him. And then it was over.

Meanwhile, across the median, Hatch and Bogardus were fast to the M4s. Each dumped a mag into the side of the van, shooting high to frighten, not to kill. That much was a hoot. Nothing like a few seconds of full-auto to clear the sinuses. The mechanism is at full sensual nourishment, all its affects assuaging the pleasure centers: the muzzle flash leaches the light and sharpness from the day, the recoil is easily controlled by strong hands and becomes mere steady pulsation, the ejected casings spew from the breech, catching the reflection of the sun in a pleasing arc to the right, and through the hardly moving Eotech hologram sight it's easy to see the silver sides of the van vibrating spastically as thirty .223s rip diagonal punctures in neat furrows across, up, down, and everywhere.

Inside the van, where Anzor—he had fired, the young dope!—Khasan, and Ibragim lay flat on the floor, the environment turned viciously hostile in a half of a second. They could hear the bullets whizzing through just inches above their heads and the sound of a moving bullet, as distinct from the sound of the whang-clang-bang rupture of the aluminum walls when pierced, had an especially terrifying zing to it. Meanwhile, from the rear, Moore in 55 went fast to handgun, drawing clean, dropping to kneeling two-handed isosceles, eyes on front sight. His .40-caliber mag dump wasn't as spectacular as the M4 carnage, but as satisfying. Three shots whistled by his head and hit his windshield, turning it to a galaxy of fracture, but he didn't even notice it. He too held lower, and his bullets hit plastic-shrouded cheap Chinese furniture, sending billowing clouds of processed wood, synthetic fabric, and Styrofoam filling aswirl through the air. Meanwhile, Rankin, in the last car, got to his trunk, got his M4 unleashed, set up a solid shooting position off the slightly canted front left wheel well of his unit, found the dot of his Eotech right smack on the same wall of plastic shrouding that filled the back half of the van, and thought not to go full-auto. He just popped off his thirty, looking for crevices, shadows, irregularities that might have signaled the presence of a gunman.

While all this shooting was going on, Uncle

Vakha had gone prone on the highway, covering his ears. He cursed the gods for giving him such morons for nephews. But then they were of idiot stock; an idiot brother, father of two of them, had gotten himself killed in an idiotic terrorist attack that, in the end, changed nothing and brought no money into the then barren family coffers. Then his other idiot brother had done the same idiotic thing in *another* terrorist attack. Death by politics had always struck Vakha as the idiocy beyond idiocy.

The shooting stopped not out of mercy or rationality, but out of ammo depletion. Each automatic and semiautomatic weapon came up dry at almost exactly the same second. Anyone whose eardrums had not been shattered by the ruckus would have heard an anvil chorus of clicks, snaps, slams, curses, and chunks as, momentarily drained of IQ, the troopers decided that if they *pulled real hard* the guns would start shooting again. Then reality dawned and each got in a fast combat reload, by which time enough IQ had returned to the lawmen that they ceased to shoot without clear targets.

In the silence, Uncle Vakha rose to his feet, hands raised stiffly.

"No, no, no shoot. No, we surrender, please, sirs, no kill us." Then in his own tongue he yelled, "You stupid motherfuckers, put the guns down or these Americans will kill you this very second."

As soon as he was up, he was commanded to get down to his knees again, and to put his hands on his head. He complied.

Bogardus ran to the cab, pulled open the door to find Magomet prone across the floor.

"Please, please," the man shrieked.

"Hands, show me hands," screamed Bogardus and knew he had enough for probable cause as it was now—no compliance, no hands displayed—and could legally face-shoot the motherfucker. But he didn't.

"Out, god dammit, out!"

Something in his tone communicated to Magomet and he cranked upright, hands now high and open, and began to creep out slowly.

Meanwhile, Moore had gotten to the fallen Boynton and saw that it was over. The officer lay in a lake of his own blood, eyes sightless and open, but otherwise the same decent plugger he'd always been, even as recently as that morning's roll call. Moore's rage erupted, and he spun to see the black forms of three men, hands high, pick their way toward him through the van.

"No shoot, no shoot, please, Mr. Policemen," someone was saying.

Moore almost shot just out of pure fury, but didn't, and neither did Hatch, behind him with M4.

"Out, god dammit, get the fuck out!"

The old man—no one thought to cover him—was translating.

"Tell 'em to jump out and go flat or we will cook their asses here and now," Rankin screamed.

The three surrendered. They were not treated gently, as two troopers had guns ready and trigger fingers set, while the third put a knee hard into the small of each back, yanked the arms back and got the flex cuffs as tight as they could go, then a little tighter.

"It's all big misunderstanding, sirs," the old man yelled. Rankin turned his attention at last to the old guy, and with it, his gun muzzle, prodding the old man hard in the guts and gesturing him to his knees. The old man obeyed, and was flex-cuffed as well, even as Bogardus perp-walked flex-cuffed Magomet to the group of prisoners.

Just at that point, three more black state Chargers—they'd been roaring down the shoulder under full siren and light display—pulled up, spilling officers. Then the ambulance, whose medics got straight over to poor Boynton, saw that he was gone, but still got plasma into him and an oxygen mask on him.

"Any pulse?" asked Rankin.

"Nothing, Sarge," said the medic.

"Keep trying, god dammit," said Rankin.

CHAPTER 6
Presser

Jack Hitchens—Dr. Jack Hitchens, DVM, an extremely decent man who had a large-animal practice in Colorado and sent all sorts of ailing creatures to board at one of Bob's facilities in that state—hit Bob with an email before he could think what to do with the subpoena unfolded on his lap.

"Hate to tell you, Big Guy," it ran, "but I'm watching C-SPAN and their coverage of the exciting Corn Fructose Subsidy Bill Hearings, and they just put a crawl across the bottom that said 'Bob Lee Swagger subpoenaed. News Conference at 5:30.' "

That was 3:30 his time. He got up, dragged his aching hip through the house and into the kitchen, and made himself a ham sandwich. Lunch, on pumpernickel, lettuce, sharp mustard, not bad, washed down with a Diet Coke. He checked his watch to see if it was time for another tramadol; no, it wasn't. He could get through it until the surgery, but it still wasn't much fun.

Speaking of not much fun: the press conference was coming up.

Watch or not? Absurd question. Be insane not to, even if he just felt like going out to his shop and working on his current project, a load for a long-range 6.5 Creed. He would find it, that sweet spot where all the elements were in perfect harmony with one another, and the shooter did his part, he might come up with something extraordinary. Why? Because ballistics.

But reality cremated his fantasy. It has a cruel way of doing such things. He found the C-SPAN channel—he only knew it was there out of random channel surfing—and settled in for what looked to be an hour's worth of 1950s television. One camera, no announcer, the setting the podium of some DC media room. The podium bristled with microphones, each bearing the imprimatur of its owner, and now and then a flashbulb popped.

Dull print crawled across the scene, announcing "SENATE BRIEFING ROOM 4G, NEWS CONFERENCE CONCERNING UPCOMING JUDICIARY SUBCOMMITTEE ON CRIME AND TERRORISM HEARING ON USE OF FORCE" over and over.

A crew assembled behind the podium, and Bob saw several faces he dimly recognized, including, in her trademark blazing red jacket, Representative Charlotte Venable, the committee chairman, chairperson, chairwoman, whatever. To him, she was a horror movie thing, all bands of artificial elastic tightness, blots of rouge like a clown's polka dots, lips red with virgin blood. So much corrective work she looked like a trampoline with breasts. So much vitality she all but sucked the air from not only her room but his as well. She would be, he could tell, formidable.

She began, giving a recital of goals of the event scheduled in the next month. Reading telepromptered script was not her best thing, and she flubbed several lines, to no one's surprise but no one's remark, and finally came to Q & A, her cackling forte.

This was the real her, batting the lofted softball pitches from court ringers out of the park with disdain.

"Mr. Banjax?"

"Congresswoman, is it politically wise to subpoena Sergeant Swagger, who after all is a national hero and who was wounded gravely in defense of his country?"

"I'm sure Sergeant Swagger would have happily agreed to testify without the formality of the subpoena. We chose, however, to serve him to make the broader point that we were looking into all aspects of use of force and that even heroes have to be held accountable for their decisions."

The man with the salacious goatee, from the *Washington Post*, whose name she had forgotten, asked, "But isn't this really just a political gesture of defiance aimed at the right? After all, they singled out Swagger and praised him as the kind of American, et cetera, et cetera. Or rather they singled out 'the shooter.' It was the *New York Times* that made the man known and famous."

"They have their agenda, we have ours. We have never had an in-depth hearing on the difficulties of force, particularly as our population diversifies and becomes more complex and recent tragedies haunt us. That is an issue we have to look at."

It went on and on like that for exactly thirteen more minutes, and at the stroke of six, she stepped back—why, it was almost as if this was *planned!*—and ended the eunuch tea party. Timing perfect. Couldn't have done better to get onto the major news shows and—

"Madam," said Banjax, and she broke precedent by turning back from parading out the door to acknowledge him.

"Yes, Mr. Banjax?"

"One last question. Sergeant Swagger was gravely wounded in the action you are examining. Do you think it medically sound or even prudential to require that he make the arduous—"

So Swagger at last got a recon on his ancient nemesis from the *New York Times*. Somewhere between thirty and sixty, lanky in a jock-gone-to-seed look, hair unattended to in years. The suit, dumpy, was unevenly distributed across his shoulders and revealed an inch of gap as it uncertainly circled his neck; his glasses were too big. He had a perfect face for newspapers.

Then his moment-in-sun was over as she seized the means of communication back from him.

Without batting a polyurethane eyelash, she said, "You anticipate me. Indeed, we are mindful of his situation. That is why we have planned a field hearing—that is, not here, in Washington. Rather, out of deference to Sergeant Swagger's condition, in Boise, Idaho, not far from where he lives. That should ease physical strain on him considerably. The details are not final yet, which is why we haven't mentioned it in our statement, but I will tell you that we are arranging to hold the hearing at the recently built Frank Church High School auditorium-gym building in suburban Boise."

With that, she dialed her eyes to communicate "I'M ON MY BREAK" and, led by blocking-back Feeley, exited.

Bob was stunned. He knew the building, as its opening last year had passed for big news in sleepy Boise. It pleased him, but it also removed a possible health dodge that was at least an option until that second. Boise was an hour by good roads; more likely, however, he and Julie would take a room in one of the fine new hotels the city was attracting, and as a physical ordeal, the difficulties had just been reduced significantly.

Boy, does that old lady want my ass, he thought.

CHAPTER 7
Coney Island

Late afternoon, sunny weekday, summer-crowded but not weekend-crowded, and still suffering COVID fear, even if hot weather had driven the bug underground for a bit. Still, masks. Most of the big rides operated, producing thin screams and yelps, but only half the shops and hustles were open. The broad beach was therefore more desertlike than overpopulation crisis, with lots of social distancing except for those too stupid to catch on, and even the sludgy Atlantic looked dazzling in the sun.

At a Nathan's on the boardwalk, he entered and appraised through Ray-Ban's high-end Aviators. The place had a clean, medicinal look to it, yet stunk of chili and some kind of orangey sweet tomato sauce, upon which the hot dog chain rested its traditions and history.

Delta made out Mr. Abrusian immediately, for his size, the out-of-style wefts and woofs of curly hair, and the expensive drape of his black suit, even if he wore it without tie and with shirt unbuttoned to the third one, to show off a Midas treasury of gold loops and chains. Dark glasses, rings all over his fingers, lots of matted chest hair, and a few grim-looking soldiers at other booths, eyes open, hands not far from concealed weapons, completed the portrait of modern American gangster, born in Sevastopol or Minsk or in the lee of the Urals.

Abrusian saw him in the same instant, and gestured him over.

None of the guards made a move.

"You don't search me?" Delta asked, sliding in.

"Nah, you are friend. How head?"

"Head fine. No longer see four of you. Now, only two."

"You not going to die on us? We will tell you when you can die, and it's not yet."

"Thanks, but I plan on at least another fifty years of shit-kicking and prisoner-shooting,"

Abrusian laughed.

"You American cowboys! Such bold ones! Such heroes! You want hot dog? Good here. I own the place, you not get one that fell on floor."

"Life's dangerous enough without hot dogs."

"Fair enough. Up for job?"

"Easy job. Concussion still might cause black-outs, the doc says. Headaches most of the time. Can't get quite into the sharp focus mode I need for good shooting."

"This one easy."

"I hope it involves those fucks who jumped us. I don't like running away without leaving a pile of smoking corpses."

"Yes. Here, from *Post* yesterday."

He handed over a carefully trimmed-out news story.

"Trooper Slay in Idaho," went the headline. The body of the text explained that state cops had pulled over a big semi on 84 in the potato state, and found themselves under fire. One died, but other troopers returned fire and took all five bad guys alive.

"Sounds like my truck," said Delta.

He finished the brief, which concluded, "Authorities have been unable to identify or communicate clearly with the suspects, but say they doubt terrorism is the motive."

"We know what motive is," said Abrusian. "We just don't know who these motherfuckers are."

"You must have ideas."

"Very true. One of several minor groups, who live off of us but hate our guts and if they could, would replace us in a single evening's slaughter."

"Why not just kill 'em all? I think I shoot well enough to go all M-249 on their asses."

"Sure, fun, maybe not so smart. We have to get this right, you see? Our bargain with the Mexicans is now somewhat shaky. They not sure if maybe we stole from ourselves and refuse to pay them second half due for the merchandise. We do not want to fight them, they do not want to fight us, but such things sometimes cannot be avoided."

"I do not want to get stuck between you and the Mexicans."

"You won't. Here's the deal. Me, Abrusian, I cannot send any these guys"—he gestured to the cone of big-shouldered gunmen sitting around him—"because if suddenly ten Russ thugs with skulls and Orthodox crosses tattooed on their chests showed up in cowboy city like Boise, demanding vodka and borscht, everybody would know and things would get complicated. Complicated enough now. Need simplicity."

"So you want a cowboy?"

"Yeah, from Texas, better. Nice-looking boy, no one looking at the great Delta would know how many kills he got."

"Or how many concussions. Broken bones, reinflated lungs, hearing shot all to hell."

"You could ride in from the range, ha ha."

"I'll make sure to smear some cow shit on my Tony Lamas."

"Yeah, you get it. You go out, nose around, see what you can see. Probably not much, but a good man like you, you could surprise us."

"What's the goal here?"

"We have to kill them, if it's them. If it's not them, we have to go away and find real guys. So first thing is, yes, confirm, these are our guys. Best way is to get a look at that truck the cops confiscated. You would know that truck."

"I spent three days in that truck."

"Yah, good. Then, if it's them, you develop a plan. I don't mind losing people, sure, that's what they're paid for. But it can't be some huge crazy movie John Wick bullshit."

"Keanu charges way too much."

"Ha ha, he does. But also, way too much attention, too much newspapers go crazy. So what I need is a good Spetsnaz operation. You take team into—well, wherever they are. You take team in, no kill Americans or puppy dogs, but put these five cocksuckers on one-way slab ride to hell. Then you melt into night."

"I got it."

"Maybe you could even do alone."

"Seems too big for one guy."

"The point is, it has to be done soon. We have to show these Mexes this was legit robbery. We wouldn't kill five of our own kind as theater show. Not even we are that crazy."

"What about the stuff?"

"Another department. When they find it, they'll go ape shit, and that has its own problems. Maybe it goes into storage, some time down the way we get it back. Or it's destroyed. The governor throws it into furnace, after he's taken a life supply. If that happens, it's lost and that's the price of business. I just don't want it going back to Mexes, or to some LA Russ. But you let me worry about that."

"I'll fly out tomorrow."

CHAPTER 8
Sally

Nick didn't call until eight, which was ten in the east.

"Hoo boy," he said. "Someone's got some troubles."

"I think that would be me."

Swagger was on the porch, rocking in the dark. Forward, back, forward, back. The plains were a dark shroud, no mountains visible. Now and then came a call or squeal or grunt of some wild thing about to get laid or eaten, depending. Chilly now, and Swagger had an old Air Force A-2 wrapped around him.

"Sorry I'm late reaching out," Nick said. "But let's talk about keeping Swagger out of jail."

"Is it that bad? Did you see the press conference? They said I wasn't the target."

"I saw snippets on CNN. But right now, I don't know. Too soon to tell. They do lie, you know. The truth is just another resource to be deployed as needed. It's always been that way, it always will be."

"Great. I don't think I did nothing wrong."

"Nor do I. If you did, I did. I'm responsible. We may end up in the same cell."

"Just trying to think what this could be about."

"Don't waste your time. Lavrenti Beria, head of NKVD, thirties. Stalin decided to purify and murdered a couple million of his own people. Beria was executioner. 'Show me the man,' he said, 'and I'll find you the crime.'"

"Meaning somewhere, somehow, some way, they can find a crime?"

"Exactly. Some ludicrous reading of the law, some transparent sophistry, something taken out of context, an irony read literally, a joke interpreted as a confession, a coincidence seen as a conspiracy. They'll sift and sift and sift until they find it. A witness you never heard of who remembers something you never did. Then if that's what they want, that's what they'll get. Or at least they think it's worth the effort."

"So what's my move?"

"You only have one. Get a lawyer."

"You?"

"I never practiced. I never passed a bar. Law school is just a blur. I arrest guys, let others tidy up the details."

"Somebody in Boise? Some pretty good ones out here. I'm known and respected. I could get the best the state has to offer."

"But see, this is different. This is federal political theater, mainly for media. It's not about winning a trial, it's about coming off best on the idiot tube. It's about knowing how these big fish like Mother Death—"

"Who?"

"That's what they call her on the Hill. You know, the lady in red. The chair herself, Representative Charlotte Venable."

"Any idea why she hates me?"

"She doesn't. Politics, that's all. She sees opportunity, it's in her genes to go for it. So you need somebody familiar with her game, and do remember that a hearing isn't a trial. There's no standards. They set the rules, and whoever you have has got to react fast. The rules may change halfway through the hearings. The hearings may go in a strange direction. There's no way to outguess them on that. They'll stay up nights trying to outguess you. And there's no discovery. We won't know what they've got until they spring it. So you need the quickest gun."

"Agh," said Bob. "I'm already three steps behind."

"Well, let's look at another thing. I'm only telling you for your own good. Your interlocutor will seem to be a congressman named Baker. Harvard law, real smart, smiler, schmoozer, charm-bucket. Downside: cuckoo eyeballs. But he's her sock puppet. Mother Death is the real story here. She's looking for a way to cut you off at the knees. So I think your lawyer should be a woman. You don't want a cowboy lawman from Boise or a Little Rock genius in buckskins and ten-gallon screaming at a little old gal in a red suit. She wants that, and part of what she'll instruct Baker to do is goad, prod, poke, and twist. She wants to trick you into telling the truth. If she can get your goat, you're screwed. 'Yeah I killed him, he needed killing, and when I saw the crime scene photos of his brains on the ceiling, I allowed myself a pat on the back.' That's what they want."

"One problem," said Bob. "I'm guilty as hell."

"But keep it to yourself. It's a secret. So you have to tone it way down, and you have to have a softer advocate, a woman."

"So where do I find her?"

"Actually, she sleeps next to me every night."

"Sally! She don't even like me."

"No, she doesn't. But remember, she had thirty years as a federal prosecutor. She thinks like a prosecutor, meaning she knows all the tricks. And she knows the federal system forward and backward, and she's put some bad guys away over the years against big money geniuses from Harvard. Her values are dead-on. She works like a mule, she's sharp as a hypodermic needle, and she will not quit. No matter how late they stay up, she'll stay up later. She's not a part of the DC law culture, and she doesn't have secret entanglements, obligations, or enemies. I don't see how you could do better."

"Okay," said Bob. "I see the point."

"But you have to do your part. You can't go prima donna on her. You have to do what she says, even if it's against your instincts. You're in a different kind of jungle now, and all of a sudden your instincts aren't worth a damn. You'll be paying her for hers, not to let you have your way and good-intention yourself into the graybar hotel." Nick let a moment pass. "Now all I have to do is convince *her*."

CHAPTER 9
Tough Guys

They spoke to no one, not even their court-appointed attorneys. They simply glared in silence, sat in sullen stoicism, and took all that was dished out without complaint. They were observed chattering in a language nobody could identify, and observers could only draw certain conclusions. The young one was in the doghouse, for example. He was routinely smacked, ignored, chastised, and degraded. Most concluded that was because the forensic test proved he was the only shooter in the van, and therefore that he had killed Ted Boynton, not that they all weren't up for the rap.

All other avenues proved unfruitful. The driver's licenses turned out to be high-grade phonies. The fingerprints came back with no matches in the system. INTERPOL was also unable to ID, off the prints or mug shots. Their tattoos seemed related to Russian mafia symbology, but at the same time were clearly different in origin and tradition. No stars, as in Russian tradition; instead skulls, the universal symbol of the life-taker, and symmetrical Orthodox Christian crosses, all usually ensnared in barbed wire and done in a fine hand, way above the usual standard of prison tats. Their blood had been sent to the FBI lab for genotype analysis, which might prove of some aid, but it was a complex chemical and analytic process, and results wouldn't be ready for several weeks. It was as if they had beamed down from space, and were beyond earth science.

They were incarcerated in the Ada County lockup, in two cells in the isolation ward. They mingled with other prisoners only at exercise time, when they quickly acceded to the protocols of the yard. The cartel Mexicans, the toughest, most violent, and scariest of the inmates awaiting preliminary legal processing, controlled the exercise and weight equipment by right of biggest fish. The cycle gang boys, tougher than shit, had the east wall, in the shade during workout hours. The newbies and amateurs rested in the sunlight of the west wall, hoping that nobody would decide to fuck them. The only thing left for the mysterious boys of I-84 was the featureless circle of emptiness in the center of the space, lit by summer sun at all hours and without seating or rest.

They also obeyed the prison protocols, if listlessly. In all transactions, they obeyed without rancor or eye contact. They allowed themselves to be printed, blood-tested, photographed, searched without objection. A number of languages were tried on them; they either didn't recognize them or did a good job of pretending they didn't recognize them.

The first hearing, at a suburban courthouse, seemed to go without incident. Handcuffed and shackled, heads shaved, draped in the prisoner's bright orange cotton of ill-fitting jumpsuits, they stood before the magistrate, and a state prosecutor read off a litany of charges from first degree murder on down. Their public defenders testified that no contact or cooperation or even communication had been achieved, and the men themselves treated the whole thing as somewhat irritating but not worth serious attention. Still, more data could be gleaned. It was obvious that the older one was the leader, that three of the middle ones were the fighters or sluggers—they had the bodies for that kind of work—and the fifth, the driver, was more a technician, along for his skills but maybe not cut from quite the same cloth as the others.

But there was a moment, some noticed, when they were exiting the courtroom for the bus back to the lockup. It seemed to be more in the tradition of the listless existential theater they had perfected. One behind the other, they slouched out of the bright room, toward the back entrance and the bus, surrounded by armed men. At a certain second, the youngest one seemed to halt as if he'd just made a disturbing discovery. He looked into the seating, and there, far beyond the circle of reporters and cameramen documenting their exit, he fixed his eyes on a lone figure. He stopped, poked the guy ahead of him, and he too looked over and regarded the man. But then a guard said something, and the line hastened onward. And that was it.

Later survey of the videotape revealed a rather bland fellow in a Rockies baseball cap, a pair of Ray-Bans, some very nice Tony Lamas showing under his tight-fit jeans, and a hoodie. Maybe midforties, with a rangy, cowboy quality to him. But as the cameras were arranged to feature the prisoners and the court and security officers and not the civilians in the audience, the image could not be brought up for detailed study. And by the time anyone noticed anything, the man had vanished.

"You're sure?" said Uncle Vakha.

"Absolutely," said Anzor. "My face was ten inches from his when he tossed me."

They were alone in the isolation wing, well past midnight. The night shift guards were in their offices at either end of the empty, dark hall, and what passed for privacy was at last available to the prisoners.

"Goddamn you, Anzor," said Ibragim, always the angry one. "If you had done your job that night, we'd be the kings of Coney Island now.

73

We'd be getting blow jobs from every bitch on the street."

"I shot him square in the head. How did I know he'd be Captain America?"

"You missed the guard, you hit the policeman. AGGGGG!"

"Enough," said Vakha. "It's past, it's over, we are where we are and we had better deal with it."

"What do you think, Uncle Vakha?"

"The Russians sent him. He is the only one who can identify us. Now he has, now he's told them. Now they must move, that is sooner, not later. They have to. They have no choice. Their code requires such and the politics of the moment do as well. They have to demonstrate to the Mexicans their ruthlessness and the purity of their fury. Otherwise, the whole thing falls apart."

"Uncle, are we not safe, at least for a bit?" asked Khasan, who always saw ahead. "We are protected, after all."

"This prison holds us in, but maybe it does not hold them out. They have money. They will use it to buy leverage. Somehow, some way, they will find a path to get in here and kill us. We are the walking dead. We have to move and move fast, boys."

"Move how, Vakha?"

"This I do not know. I haven't figured yet. But I do know one thing. And that is, we are now the lowest of the low in this prison. Nobody fears us, nobody obeys us. We ourselves have no leverage. If we are to do anything, we must rule in here, and the guards and the other staff must fear us. So that when we command, we do so from a position of power, and nobody dares disobey us. Do you understand?"

"Yes," the boys answered.

"So tomorrow it all changes. By tomorrow evening, this is our prison, and all these men are our subjects. Now get a good night's sleep. You will shed blood tomorrow, perhaps much of it."

CHAPTER 10
More Sally

Julie picked Sally up at Boise International. That way the two women, who knew each other better than Sally knew Bob and vice versa, got their visit in, got caught up, probably had a few laughs at the expense of the men, got logistics set up, and more or less arranged what was to come. Now it was cleared for Sally to brief Bob, and for that relationship, whatever it might become, to begin its development.

She was a tall, grave woman, now sixty-six, her demeanor suggesting that she was somewhat disinterested in her own considerable beauty. She wore her still-blond hair tight and short, in a ponytail, though she could probably do something more interesting with it if need be. She wore jeans, running shoes, and a sweatshirt. She had no airs to her, but it was still clear that she was serious, not in anything for laughs or thrills or fun but just out of that iron sense of duty to get the job done.

"Okay," she said to Bob, "let's get through the shit first."

Swagger, in his living room, which was nicer than any room he ever thought he'd end up in, met her steady gaze with an even-keeled response of his own. He had never been a yeller, a moper, a crybaby. He didn't speak the language of tantrum or outrage. His had always been the practical, the necessary, the clear.

"I understand."

"First, do not rise to insult. Wherever they're going, you'll help them get there if you act out. They will good cop–bad cop you. Congressman Baker will probably be everything you hate: smug, insincere, morally superior, preening, seeking stardom, trying to rise off your ruin. But if he gets you hot and bothered, if, God forbid, he gets you to blow up, then whatever their destination is will be within reach."

"I get that."

"Then, vanity, hubris, pride, which goeth before the fall. You are a man with much to be proud of. You have done what these slithering reptiles cannot conceive of, and that is partly why they hate you so much. Again, they will pick at the scabs of ego. 'Shooting a man who doesn't know you're there through a telescope, how is that even fair? How is it even a challenge? Put the sight on him and pull that trigger. How is that heroic? Why are we calling you a hero? Aren't you really just a murderer?' You'll hear that baldly or you'll know that it's being implied. Here's what you have to do: nothing. You cannot let their attempts at diminishment rile you. You cannot be goaded into boastfulness. If you tell them how many kills you've made, particularly in a voice laden with satisfaction, you make their point for them—that you are a psychotic killer, with a need to kill, who only happened to find a nominal harness in the military. You had to kill anyway, and it's just our luck that you killed on our side of the fence, for our gain."

"I hear you."

"Do you know how many kills you have?"

"Of course I do."

"That's our secret. Officially, you have no idea. You simply did your duty."

Bob nodded.

"Okay, Marine Corps. I'm going to have an assistant go through your record very carefully. Are you all right with that?"

"I was a good Marine. I have no problem with that. But after the war, well, maybe there's some stuff I ain't so proud of. I was a drunk for ten years. I destroyed a marriage."

"Your first?"

"Actually my second. I had married a Vietnamese woman during the war. She didn't survive. It's a loss I ain't never quit grieving, and I would appreciate not answering questions about it."

"Any ugliness with the American wife?"

"Cops came for some yelling a few times. I

never hit a woman. No threats, no gun waving, nothing like that. Just a sullen drunk who wouldn't say nothing to nobody."

"Will she testify against you?"

"She died some years back."

"I've heard rumors about engagements with multiple deaths where the outcome was generally conceded to be favorable to the nation's security interests, or perhaps to justice, and a lot was let pass."

"Many times, people in your line of work have looked at the score and seen no advantage to opening certain doors, probing certain dark corners, asking certain dark questions."

"My hunch is they won't go there. They know the more gunfights you win, the more heroic you are to millions and millions. It might excite them, but they won't go there, assuming they have other places to go."

"Do they have other places to go?"

"I have to believe so. They wouldn't be running this game if they didn't think so. Okay, another tough one for you. That is your family. Meaning Earl and Charles."

"Great men."

"But killers."

"Of necessity, not need."

"Twisted certain ways, the law enforcement ethics of the past can seem close to murder on their own. A lot of killing, a lot of it."

"I'd hate to see that happen. My father and his father were better men than me and no calumny should be placed upon them at this late date."

"A sore spot. If you show your sensitivity, these people will come after it. That's what I would do if I was prosecuting."

"I'm beginning to think there ain't much difference between sniping and prosecuting."

"Both are blood games, to be sure. But I can see them doing something by which they tie you to generations of violent men (a) to get you to explode and (b), failing that, to make you the heir to generations of toxic masculinity. That would charge up their millions of constituents. I want you ready for it. I could run training sessions where I throw the ugliest shit in the world at you, so you won't be hearing it for the first time under oath. Interested?"

"I don't think that's necessary. I can get through it."

"Next, I want your family there at least at the start, when people are watching. And friends."

"We can do that. I can get big-animal vets from all over the West in the audience."

"Excellent."

"I can get little girls whose horses we've saved in the seats too."

"Again, excellent."

"Is that it? This is no fun."

"I wouldn't think too much about fun. There

won't be any fun for quite a while as this is going on. Now, one more thing."

"I'm a man. I can take it."

"See, you did it. As if on cue, exactly. That is—humor. Ha ha, you see the opportunity for a laugh and go for it. It's become second nature to you in your late years."

"I was too busy not getting shot to laugh at much earlier. Now I've got more time on my hands."

"Yes, and there you go again. It's a guy thing, I suppose. I've heard it my whole career, in police stations, law offices, prosecution meetings, in the press, on TV. You guys think you're so funny. Bob, you're not dating. You're not trying to get somebody to like you. You don't get points for smiles, giggles, even guffaws."

"Yes, ma'am."

"It has to be more than 'yes, ma'am.' It has to be concentrated on, focused on, rigorously committed to."

"I see."

"Maybe you don't. Even when they're smiling, these folks are not your friends. Even when they seem the friendliest, they mean you no goodwill. You are targeted. Words are bullets. Language is a jungle. They are very good with language—it's their culture. They know how to manipulate it, shade it, shape it, mislead with it. They can control their tone exquisitely. They will gull you."

"I see."

"Men, especially masculine ones who don't hang out in coffee bars or English departments, love to tease, to needle, to fake theatrical hostility. It's called irony. Define irony."

"I know what irony is. It's saying something you clearly don't mean in an exaggerated sort of way for comic effect. I might say to Nick, 'How's that rattlesnake you're married to?' He might reply, 'Looking for something to bite. She gets ornery when she hasn't bitten anything in a while.' We both laugh because we know you aren't a rattlesnake and that you don't have to bite something every week. And that the idea of you being a rattlesnake is so silly it's funny."

"Okay, that's pretty good. But here's where I'm going with that. What these people will do is play the irony game with you all day long until you trust them and you're all having a good old time. Then they might say, 'So when you kill somebody, do you celebrate with bourbon or scotch?' And you get the joke, and you say, 'Hell, Representative, I'm a champagne man.' It would be pretty damn funny, as a matter of fact. And that's when they change up on you. Suddenly they never heard of irony. Suddenly the *New York Times* is saying, 'Marine Corps humor is surely rough, but it goes too far when its champion killers laugh about champagne and murder, as Gunnery Sergeant Bob Lee Swagger did yesterday in sworn testimony.' Context doesn't matter, pointing out that it was all in good humor, pointing out that you meant it *ironically,* none of that matters. You've just hurt yourself bad and made whatever end they see for you more likely. Are you hearing me?"

"I am."

"Okay, one more. And you're really not going to like this one."

"I have to wear a dress? Oh, sorry, that was a joke, wasn't it?"

"Maybe you're not as far off as you think. No, no dress. But you have to be in a wheelchair."

"What?"

"Every day."

"You're kidding. I've had three hip replacements and I've never used a wheelchair."

"I'm not saying it's admirable, even honest. But it makes our strongest point: this man was severely injured in service to his country in an exceedingly dangerous situation. We need to remind America of that every day."

"Sally, I have pain in my hip. It has nothing to do with the gunshot wound in my shoulder."

"It doesn't matter."

"Christ, should I be in uniform too?"

"No, because that would be too much. That would be pandering and it would annoy the hell out of the blanketheads that are national correspondents. But the wheelchair—Nick will push you in and push you out each day. And you will be taken to and from by a car with a handicapped license. Then you can go dancing or mountain biking. But in that venue, you will be the wounded man."

CHAPTER 11
Mother Death

The day before the hearing, Representative Venable sat in the wholesome sunny-as-eggs-up restaurant that dispensed vittles in the Boise Hyatt, with a little girl's smile on her face and with PR genius Feeley at her side, chitchatting with the appalling Banjax of the *Times*.

"So, Banjax," she asked, "what the hell kind of name is Banjax, anyhow?"

Well, no, she didn't ask that, even if it's what she wanted to ask. Was he from the future? Should his actual name be Banjax-411Bpq or something, and shouldn't electrodes in his temples be blinking green for go?

No such luck. Instead, neglect had turned his crew cut into pasty fronds of too-pale-to-be-called-blond hair, which hung at the lank end of a lengthy comb-over construction too hideous to be examined. It fell like shit from a flock of diarrhetic geese from the thinning crop up top, his glasses had fogged, his eyes, as usual, were weepy, and he was so well informed it seemed like a loss to waste 150 IQ points in such a drear skull. Had he been the one whose mouth looked like a vagina, it would have been an improvement.

"Madam Chairman, don't you think Sergeant Swagger should have hired a DC power lawyer instead of a recent retiree from Justice?"

"Mr. Banjax, Sergeant Swagger and all the others should hire lawyers with whom they are comfortable. That is the important thing here. This is not a trial, it's a hearing, it's very casual. As chairman, I will allow everyone a good deal of latitude. The point here is not to scramble people's lives but to examine a troubling phenomenon and to come up with recommendations for new policies by which use of force is deployed."

"Some say the real goal is to come up with recommendations by which it is deployed never."

"Yes, our friends on the other side of the aisle fear such an outcome because they do seem to enjoy it when people get killed, don't they? No, we understand that human nature being the ghastly thing it is—go to a PTA meeting or a *New Yorker* staff conference if you want to see it at its ugliest—there will always be a tragic necessity for the state to kill. But that is the highest of all state responsibilities, at least on a domestic front, and therefore it ought to be liable to the most intense of all scrutiny. It's an issue we have gotten wrong too often, the goodwill of our police officers and soldiers notwithstanding, and we have to do better."

She thought: I wish Sergeant Swagger would put a bullet in your cream puff. She deeply enjoyed imagining the ker-splash such a development would entail. Splish, splash, splatter, the pitter-patter of little brain globs on the ceiling!

"Wouldn't it make more sense then to choose as a framework for the hearing an event in which it was widely conceded law enforcement failed? Nearly everyone says this particular case represented the system working at its most efficient."

"That is why we must look closely at it. Perhaps we will end up redefining what 'most efficient' or 'successful' means. If a man dies, even a jihadi assassin, maybe that's not a success but a failure. Tragedy. Loss. Maybe capture and rehabilitation should be the product, not the by-product."

"I must say, it does seem like you're looking at bigger fish to fry. It seems like you're looking at, and using, Swagger as a fulcrum to get at the whole notion of the state's right to kill, or, more generally, the right to apply force across a broad spectrum of issues."

"We will examine what we will examine, and it's up to others to find deeper meanings to it. That's not my business. My business is to ask how, and from how maybe get at why."

"I don't think anything like this has been tried. Can it be any coincidence that elections are coming up? Can it be that a finding in a certain direction as opposed to another direction might rile up a certain base and get more of them to the polls?"

"Politics? Why I'm shocked, *shocked,* that you would say such a thing, Mr. Banjax. May I call you David?"

"Of course. May I call you Charlotte?"

"Of course not."

"Yes, ma'am."

"Anyhow, there are always going to be elections coming up, and so any enterprise of the House could be called 'political.' We can't let that partisan bias stand in the way of the people's work."

"Yes, ma'am."

"Now, David, I think we have a little treat in store for you? Don't we have a nice dessert in store for David, Mr. Feeley?"

Upon hearing his name, PR whiz Feeley popped to life, after several seconds of gurgling, coughing, rearranging the phlegm distribution deep throat, lip-licking, and gum-flapping.

"Yes, we do," he said.

"Why don't you explain the career break we're about to give Mr. Banjax then. I hate to be around when the gimme-this/gimme-that of the game is so baldly played out."

"Absolutely," said Banjax. "That way you can deny any knowledge of whatever it is you're about to pitch, which obviously violates all principles that you've spent the last half hour laying out."

"Isn't he a bright one, Feeley?" And with that, and one of her brightly insincere smiles, she rose, bowed, flickered her bird eyes around the room for owls, cats, and poisoners, did not offer a hand to shake or kiss, turned like the Miss Dayton Auto-Brake she had been in 1958, and walked out majestically.

"Time for her morning vodka?" Banjax asked Feeley.

"We've got her down to nineteen a day, and they don't start until half noon."

"How disciplined she is! What a pro!"

"She's still got some kick-ass in the tank. Okay, are you up for this?"

"All ears."

Of course they'd done a little business before, but since Banjax wasn't the regular *Times* Joe— well, make that *Times* Jill—on the house beat, it wasn't a transaction well greased by mutually destroyed brown bottles over the years. It helped that back when he had morals, Feeley had done a spin on the *Times*.

"We do want to go deeper on this. No one has really ever looked hard at it. But some other folks are working in the same area and they've pitched in, so we have some assets we might not have had before."

"I like what I'm hearing," said Banjax.

"Look at history. We're in the history biz, we hardly ever look at it, we're so busy making it."

"Yep."

"History shows us a certain kind of man. All history shows us this man. He stands apart. Call him *Homo violentia*. He is responsible for all the bad shit that's been happening for five thousand years."

"Yeah."

"He's the sniper. He can kill. He has no problem killing, it doesn't haunt or ruin him. In malevolent form, he's Stalin. In benevolent form, he's Swagger. Yes, a good guy. But there's something in him that lets him do the stuff he does."

"So—"

"So. Here's the deal. Suppose we ID the behavior characteristics and trace them back, via DNA, through the years. Just one family, a family of killers. Maybe if we look hard enough we can find a marker or something."

"Genetics?"

"Yes. Suppose we did an in-depth genetic test on Swagger and tracked him back. And from that we learned what was inside him. We find that he wasn't required by the times to be what he was, he was required by his nature."

"He'd never cooperate."

"That's the beauty of it. He doesn't have to. He's left DNA everywhere. It was easy to harvest, easy to test."

"Which you've done?"

"Someone has. Someone with a lot of money because this stuff is very expensive. The upshot is that we know far more about Sergeant Swagger than he himself does. And we've made some remarkable finds."

"But you can't release it. Ethical issues, all that."

"Exactly. However, we can arrange for someone to leak the findings to you. We can decry the invasion of privacy and lead the condemnation of your newspaper, but the point is, we've got evidence at the DNA level that some men, that very tiny percentage, are natural-born killers. We can trace that proclivity back through time. We can explain who Swagger is and why Swagger is. Does this interest you?"

Banjax didn't have to be asked twice.

CHAPTER 12
Ada Lockup

U ncle Vakha and Khasan moseyed through the dust into the workout area of the yard, where Mexicans of various sizes and shapes pumped iron, their muscles bulging and gleaming. Others sat on benches and lawn chairs, all talking in high amusement, sharing their domination of the lockup and by extension the yard. A few sound machines belted out Spanish rap. Tattoos were abundant, and there were so many crucified Jesuses and weeping Madonnas in animation on biceps and chests it was like a cartoon festival at the Vatican.

Smiling innocuously, Uncle Vakha approached the biggest of them, and said in his best English, "Where boss man?"

This in itself was a radical breach in yard ethics. No one entered Mexican space without invitation, no one made direct eye contact with Mexicans, no one addressed Mexican leadership without permission, no one pretended that he didn't acknowledge *la raza* as the ruling force in the universe without consequence. Consequence ultimately included every form of degradation from homosexual slavery to instant death by dumbbell weight applied to center of face. There were no warnings, no second chances.

Immediately the guards in the towers perked up. They saw that something interesting might develop. In a few seconds more guards joined them, and some came to the fence to observe the drama about to unfold. Perhaps wagers were made as to how long the mystery meat from the I-84 shootout would continue to enjoy oxygen on this planet.

The Mexican returned Vakha's eyeball-to-eyeball, shot a glance at Khasan, then broke into a richly amused smile.

"You want to see the boss man?"

"Yes, we must have a chat."

Again: naive audacity or death wish? Hard to tell. But all would be settled in a matter of seconds.

The Mexican looked back at the boss man—presumably the senior chap reclining on a chaise lounge under the shade of the yard's single tree, surrounded by subservient factotums—and passed a WTF? expression to his leader. The older man nodded, as if to say, "Business as usual, Pedro."

Pedro looked back to the interlocutor. The old man was stumpy, knobby, grizzled, exotic in the Eurasian construction of his features, eyes almost Chinese, body broad, strength radiant from underneath the goofy orange jumpsuit that covered him.

The other was of similar materials, as if constructed by the same firm, from the same design specifications, except younger and broader. He too was built of prison-sculpted muscle, he too had a look of bemused calm as if he'd recently bitten a *Tyrannosaurus rex*'s head off, chewed it, spit out the skull frags, and enjoyed the tasty brain as one would enjoy the green meat of a pistachio. His jumpsuit was half-open, displaying a pie slice of tattooed chest. You didn't have to know his culture to suspect that such inkings were not free for the taking but must be earned in the commission of certain dangerous activities. He glowed with strength. Everything about him was strong, even his ears. He looked like a man who gargled anvils, after juggling them, along with chain saws and machine guns.

"It's not possible," explained the Mexican. "You must have appointment. Very hard to get."

"So regrettable," said Uncle Vakha. "My nephews would like to use the equipment now. So if your boss would tell the boys to move aside, that way troubles can be avoided and all will be happy."

"Sir," said the Mexican, "I believe I speak for *el Jefe* when I say that we are the owners of the equipment and it is not possible at this time for us to vacate. Perhaps you and your little monkey boy here would care to exhibit some homosexual perversions for our comedy use and then remove yourselves."

And with that, a squad of bruisers picked themselves up from various positions of languor and ambled over to form a semicircle of muscularity, backing up Pedro.

"I would hate to see anyone get hurt," said Pedro, and with that, he leaned forward and gave Khasan a shove on the shoulder, "but it is you who must—"

Khasan hit him, fist landing next to the solar plexus. It wasn't just any punch. It was an atomic-powered piston of irresistible force for which there was no such thing as an immovable object. Khasan, as did his uncle, cousins, and brother, had very large hands, and the contact surface against the vulnerability of his enemy was consequently sizable. Thus he broke four ribs with his blow, shattering one so fiercely that it spewed bone shrapnel into spleen, kidney, spinal connectors, and lower colon. Each of these wounds commenced to bleed copiously.

In the first second, the Mexican did not realize how bad he'd been hurt, and he puffed his muscles for combat—he was a crusher, not a puncher, having chased the life from many a poor man by sheer application of arms to body, turning diaphragm into frozen potpie—and then his brain got the message as the blood pooled in his thoracic cavity.

He stepped back, depuffed, a look of weary regret on his face, and sat down hard on his rump. He rolled over, vomited blood and breakfast, then flopped nose-first into that pond of scum, and breathed his last.

Khasan smiled like a happy puppy. He knew he had done well.

Three Mexicans came at him simultaneously, fists flying. He absorbed the blows manfully, with grimaces of annoyance, then moved tight on one of them and unleashed a one-two, again to the rib cage. Again the blows were far off any human behavioral spectrum, and they did unprecedented damage in unprecedented time. The recipient yielded to gravity and he collapsed, his knees having melted, and to eternal stillness.

Khasan pivoted, ignoring for a second the man who had gotten behind him, and hit the other fellow with one in the face. Imagine sledge-hammer vs. Dresden china dinner plate. Breakage total, the zygoma—it surrounds and protects the eyes like an opera mask—pulverized into fragments, the concussion an overwhelming dynamic that simply occluded the poor man's brain, permanently exiling him to the land of night and fog.

Now Khasan faced his third antagonist, but only briefly, for that one, who'd spent his strength fecklessly rabbit punching Khasan in the kidneys, saw his own death manifest itself in the uber strength of Khasan and in a split second had vanished.

Silence attended the ceremony of violence. All the Mexicans stood, but their body language communicated the idea that they had decided today was not a good day to die.

"It is unfortunate that this had to happen to such fine young men," said Uncle Vakha, putting his foot on Pedro's face, "but you see, *señor*, that my boys would like to work out."

And so it passed that the Ada County lockup had a new ruling class.

CHAPTER 13
Color

It came so much faster than Swagger had anticipated. The days blew away like leaves in the breeze, and suddenly it was August and the last meeting before the hearings opened. Sally—on Swagger's dime—had rented a suite of rooms in a nearby hotel, and with several interns from conservative law schools, all three of them, she made her prep for battle, sometimes with Bob on hand, sometimes with Nick, sometimes with only interns.

He sat with them in the meeting room, Nick at his side, his son Ray Cruz, his son's wife, his son's new daughter, his own two daughters, and his wife there for support. Only the dog was missing, and the horses.

"Thank you all," said Sally. "It is important, very important, that we show a family solidarity behind Bob. My guess is these folks will try to portray him as some kind of crazed gunman, a loco loner. We have to show him as a member of community, municipality, state, and above all, nation. Your presence is important for that image. Any questions?"

It was a dull room full of lively people. Outside, Boise's skyline showed against the Boise Mountains, those grave old sky-touchers capped still in hot August with a frosting of snow. The mountains, the town, the sky, the street: all outside. But no one paid any attention to outside, as from now on, there was only inside. Lots of chatter and squabble, lots of arguments and anti-arguments. Stale coffee in the stale atmosphere. Conditioned air, unnaturally chilly. Gray fluorescent light, giving everyone the complexion of a corpse.

All knew what was coming.

"They expect it to run a week, no more than two," said Sally. "It's their hearing, their rules. We don't get to call witnesses. Sergeant Swagger will be the only witness called, because he is the fulcrum of the story and therefore the fulcrum of the issue they mean to pursue. So mostly it's the Swagger show, as hosted by a congressman named Ross Baker, Harvard '05, very smart. He'll be the prosecutor. No cross-examination. I don't get to ask Bob Lee any questions. It seems unfair, and it is, but that is the way of power. Bob may ask me for clarifications, advice, amplifications, and I can answer. But mostly it's going to be Congressman Baker on the mound and Bob Lee Swagger in the box. Again, complain all you want, but that is the way of Charlotte Venable. And as the committee chairwoman, she controls everything. She understands power and isn't afraid to use it, give her that."

The baby made a noise. She was a blob of pure life and abundant energy at seven months or so, illuminated as if from within, putting out a steady pulse of existence even if still largely cue-ball bald. Her natural affect was squirmy and alert. She seemed to miss nothing, and anytime something new swung into her frame of vision, she fixed her baby blues on it, draining it of interest, until it no longer registered. Then she smiled, toothless yet, wet everywhere without shame, and went back to conducting with an energetic baton the orchestra only she could see. She had a bow on a ribbon around her globe-like head, showing red against the pale purity of her skin.

"That baby is worth a million bucks," said Sally.

"She'll do her part," said Molly. "We'll have her there every day."

"I must say," said Sally, "when they were handing out cute, she was at the head of the line."

Franny issued one of her famous smiles, made a policy declaration of gibbery noises, and promptly fell asleep against her mother's shoulder.

"Okay," said Sally. "Any questions?"

There seemed to be none, until finally Julie asked the only one that really mattered.

"Why is this happening?" she asked.

"I asked Nikki"—the Washington bureau of Fox, after all, said Sally—"to make some calls. She has the contacts, she knows the town. That information is very important to me, and now I'd like her to share it with you. Is that all right, Nikki?"

"Yes," said Nikki. "It doesn't make sense to us, because we live in a sane world. Good, evil, right, wrong, all clear to us. But not so in today's Washington. Everything is conditional, arguable, up for grabs, and must be parsed for advantage. Leverage is the name of the game, leverage, that is, in gathering votes for the next election. You've already seen that in the procedural rulings. It gets worse.

"Let's leave the big stuff out and begin with the assumption that all politics is local. They need to invigorate their party base, and they know that its demographics are changing. It is becoming heavily ethnic, rather fragile and insecure, and not without resentment and grievances. They know, therefore, that they will benefit if they can demonstrate that, at some level, law enforcement is more interested in shooting people of color than people of no color. The fact that Dad shot an Arab, ostensibly a 'man of color' and demonstrably a man of different faith, is the sort of shibboleth they can demagogue on. They will never ask, 'Is there a conspiracy to murder

Muslims, blacks, Hispanics, Filipinos, and central Europeans that you are a part of, Sergeant Swagger?' No, of course not. Nevertheless, being extremely clever people, they will find a way to make that point, if only implicitly. The point isn't to wreck Dad, it's to motivate all the ethnic and of-color stay-at-homes to go to the polls. Stop the murder of Albanians by electing Roosevelt Bowie alderman of District 7, that sort of thing."

"I don't like this one bit," said Bob.

"But it will happen, Dad. I'm warning you. Race is going to come into this. Not class, not nationality, not ideology. But pure and simple—color."

Swagger was under oath. He was also under bright TV lights, the gaze of hundreds in reality and still millions more in virtual reality, under pressure from his opponents and from his own sense of code, which was the most unforgiving of all.

He sat in his best suit, freshly arrived from Dodgeville, Wisconsin, and a black knit tie, in his wheelchair, behind a table. His unlubricated, real-bone hip ached because he didn't want to take the tramadol in case it slowed him down. Nick had wheeled him in, once hitting a cable that sent a rocket of pain up from the hip to the head.

He sat in front of six microphones, Sally to one

side, Nick to the other, Sally's interns farther out. It was at the brand-new gymnasium/auditorium of Frank Church, as it was called, made up as if for *Mr. Smith Goes to Washington: The Clinically Insane High School Remake*. An audience of journalists and locals filled the place to the rafters, and photographers, scruffy amid all the coats and ties and tailored pantsuits, crouched under the committee, which sat behind an arc of desks on a riser, to give them the elevation. Masks, at this point in the hot summer, had become optional, therefore random.

Baker turned to the panel of congressmen, eight of them. Chairman Venable sat there with the characteristic starved wren look on her face. Her glittery eyes danced about, searching for food, danger, shelter, something of interest at any rate. Her arched eyebrows looked like the black worms her eyes couldn't see. Nothing impressed her, and she hadn't smiled in public since Obama won the second time. Her jacket was red, her cheeks were red, her lips were red, all so bright that other colors were more or less vaporized by their intensity.

The others in attendance—men, women, their only true gender was "politician"—had that zombified look that Bob had come to believe was a result of too much time spent in DC, particularly in buildings of political purpose. Pink skin, glossy as if enameled, hair perfect, as if painted on, suits fitting full to shoulder and buttoned without a wrinkle showing anywhere, unlike his garment, from Harbin Industrial Textile Facility No. 427, by way of Dodgeville, which looked like it had been dry-cleaned in gravel.

Baker had an air of apology about him this day. The congressman wore woe like a shroud over his features, saddened by the tragedy he bore on his shoulders and yet at the same time ennobled by the truth he brought before the people. He concentrated on avoiding his peripheral glances, because that's what seemed to set his eyeballs off and turn him into psycho puppy-cruncher from outer space.

It was nearly a week into the thing, same as it ever was. Same gymnasium/theater. Same jam-packed audience. Same occasional R95s. Old buzzards sitting in their same glossy suits and skin and hair. Mother Death seemed especially perky today. She smelled blood and she cogitated on it in unseemly ways. She chatted animatedly with her colleagues of party and her colleagues not of party, but whom she also so virtually owned.

Congressman Baker cleared his throat, like Hamlet about to unload to-be-or-not-to-be on an audience of royals.

"Sergeant Swagger, it has become time to discuss certain realities of your profession. I mean you no disrespect, but in this case, the truth is more important than any sense of emotional privacy. You are a soldier, a leader, a ballistics expert, a detective, a patriot, a man of honor, courage, and conviction. No one can contest your heroism, your body bears the marks of the countless times you have put it in harm's way for your nation's benefit. But, sir, you are also a killer. You have slain many times in many circumstances, not industrially by pushing a button, but individually, by pulling a trigger. You have seen your targets die. I imagine that is a lot to bear."

"I don't talk about 'bearing,' " said Swagger.

"Yet the load must be immense."

"Maybe so, maybe not. It's not for discussion."

"Fair enough, Sergeant. So let us do the numbers."

Swagger said nothing.

"Third tour, Vietnam, sniper, official kills ninety-seven, according to Marine Corps records. Fair?"

"I never counted. That wasn't my job. If someone counted, it was to prove the efficiency of the program. They weren't trying to make me look heroic, but the program look effective. It was an officer's road to promotion."

"Ninety-seven. True or not?"

"Maybe, maybe not. More, less, not sure. That's a rough business, stuff happens fast, the situation changes in seconds. You can't really get a true picture of it because when you get around to the counting, everything's changed. Man you thought was dead crawled away. Man you thought you missed is found in the brush. The officer wants more, not less. He sees what he wants. I never got in that game."

"And there have been other kills too. There are rumors—I won't go into them—but for the Bureau alone you have been involved in shootouts."

"Yes, on some occasions, I have had to shoot."

"You killed two men in Bristol, Tennessee."

"I did."

"You killed a man driving hard at you in Dallas, Texas."

"I did."

"You killed two men in Litchfield, Connecticut."

"It's true."

"Any idea what a lifetime total would be?"

"None at all, sir."

Bob squirmed in discomfort.

He was drowning. This was material long buried. It was all duty, it was all right, it was all for the good. Yet watching a man squirm into the dust while spurting oceans of blood soon loses any sense of accomplishment. It's just death, squalid and permanent.

He wished this was over, he hated the people

who demanded it of him, he felt invaded, violated, penetrated. These pink zombies sitting in judgment. He could feel the blood throbbing through his veins. His hip ached like hell.

"Just one more question, Sergeant Swagger, on a subject I can see makes you uneasy. But this goes to policy, not individual action. From this we can see who our government sees as enemies and how it disposes of them. Of the killings, how many of them have been men of color?"

"Madam Chairman," said Sally, breaking the rules, "has the congressman no decency? Nowhere in the record or in the informal oral remembrances or even in legend has Sergeant Swagger done a thing that could be considered racist. He did hard but necessary duty, ask the young men who came home alive instead of in a box about it. To imply now that there was some kind of racial animus behind it is unconscionable."

"Madam Chairman, may I remind Mr. Swagger's counsel about the procedural rules. But I will answer. I imply nothing about Sergeant Swagger, only about the policies he was trained to express. I think we have to know if the United States government or its military took the killing of certain people less seriously than the killing of others. A racial imbalance of one highly successful professional sniper would confirm that tendency, or dismiss it entirely. We do not mean to impugn him, but perhaps the mindset that enabled him, the mindset of men in suits in offices in our town, not out in the bush where life and death is a fragile thing, should be looked at hard."

Madam Chairman ruled.

"My fellow representatives, as has been said, those who do not remember the past are condemned to repeat it. Congressman Baker is engaged in an act of forced remembrance. We furthermore have a right to know what was done in our name, and what steps were taken to assure that such a policy was fairly administered. I believe we do have to address these issues, to come to terms with them. You may proceed, Congressman Baker."

"I repeat, then, Sergeant," said Baker, ablaze with the weight of the immense tragedy it was his duty to bring to America, "how many of those you killed were men of color? Then, what percentage of the whole would that represent?"

"All of them. One hundred percent."

That caused a stir. The press people got all wee-weed up, started murmuring among themselves. Cameras clicked and digital motor drives buzzed. Then, silence returned. You could hear a tick breathe.

"All of them? Surely, Sergeant—"

"All of them," said Swagger. "And the color was gunmetal gray. That is, all of them had weapons, every last one of them, and every one of them was gunning for Americans in general or me in particular. Pick up the gun and you are gunmetal gray. Maybe some brown in there from the wooden stocks of the AK-47. Those are the only colors I saw. If you hunt my people, I will hunt you."

CHAPTER 14
Shop Talk

She was on her third martini. Two lesser aides had chatted with some other House staffers and got good takes on what their bosses were thinking, PR whiz Feeley summed up the immediate focus group response.

"Just what you expect. In the white group, over seventy-five percent were appalled, and thought race should have not been brought up. In the black group, the positive was over fifty percent, but that's not as high as we had hoped. We thought that one would light 'em up, but it doesn't seem to have done us that much good."

Mother Death didn't respond. She savored the last drops of No. 3, feeling the astringent bite of the vodka. Nothing beat cold vodka, plump olives, and a pinprick of vermouth after a hard day in the pits, saving democracy from its own worst enemy, democracy.

Finally she spoke.

Here it comes, Baker thought.

"Congressman Baker," she said, "where did you graduate in your law school class?"

"Number two."

"Harvard, correct?"

"Yes, Madam Chairman."

"Who graduated number one?"

"A Chinese woman, though she was from Singapore. Very bright, very, very bright. Her name was Cynthia Wen. She seemed to never sleep. She was either in class or in the law library studying. She lived on candy bars and Diet Coke. I never saw her smile, tell a joke, lighten up. Boy, she was something."

"Where is she now?"

"I believe Cynthia was elected state's attorney for Rhode Island last year. As you might imagine, she's one of the best prosecutors in the country. Still works like a demon, I'd bet."

"Here's what I want you to do. You call her tomorrow and offer her a job at four times your congressional salary, plus a million-dollar house in Kalorama, near the Obamas. She is to be the committee's guest prosecutor. Do you hear me?"

"Madam, I—"

"The only eccentricity is that on her first day, in front of all the congressional members of our party plus all the reporters and correspondents sympathetic to our cause, plus janitors, window washers, floor waxers, Capitol policemen, and those guys who sell hot dogs in those trucks on Constitution Avenue, she wears her best pair of Louboutin heels and she kicks your ass for an hour. With each blow, you shout, 'Thank you, Madam Wen.' Is that clear?"

Baker's eyes resembled black raisins on vanilla pudding. He looked as if the Mean Lady was going to hit him again and again and again. He yearned for a bed to hide under.

"I want severe bruising," said Mother Death. "Not little bitty red abrasions but big billowing smears of blue and yellow and black, both buttocks."

More silence.

Finally, PR whiz Feeley broke the silence.

"Madam," he said, "maybe Congressman Baker isn't really at fault. This Swagger is very smart. He's not a country rube. He's got a sophisticated mind, he's widely read, self-educated if you will, he's been around smart, educated people his whole career since he got sober, he learns in a flash, and he doesn't make mistakes."

"Unlike overeducated pea-head Baker here."

"I was consciously avoiding the word 'race,' " Baker said. "We all agreed on that. I used 'of color.' The difference, of course, is that 'color' has multiple meanings, and it can be turned against me easily enough, as Swagger did. I didn't see it coming."

"That sound bite and your marble-eyed expression will lead every news program in the nation," said Mother Death, into No. 4 'tini by now. "By the way, can't you have those eyes fixed? They just make people want to slap you!"

"I've tried. Short of new eyes from a fresh corpse, no."

"Ross, consider it. Please! Steal a body from the coroner's if you have to! Anyhow, we look like idiots, shamed by the Zeitgeist of the old masculinity."

"Madam Chairman," said Feeley, "it really doesn't hurt us. The issue will remain when the laugh is forgotten. The issue is that snipers specifically and cops and soldiers in general kill a lot of black people, yellow people, red people, brown people, and not as many white people. That point was made. It will settle and grow. They'll still be thinking about it when they've forgotten that 'gunmetal gray' comeback."

"All right, we'll forget it, and I won't transfer boy genius here to the Tubas and Dildos Sub-committee of Interstate Commerce. Not yet, at any rate. But Ross, read up on dildos. It would be a good career move."

In the other strategy meeting, things began on a somewhat gayer note.

"Bob, that 'color' business was brilliant. The look on that jerk's face! If you could bottle it and sell it under the title 'Been Had' or 'Just Got Took,' you'd make a fortune," said Nick.

"Old dog has some tricks left," said Ray.

Even tiny Franny was happy, and she invited

113

her orchestra to play yet faster and faster, her tiny fists a blur at the end of her tiny, pounding arms, and her smile seemed to radiate the warmth of a thousand suns and balmy winds forever. She burped but didn't spit up, a rare enough miracle for her, and looked around the room, her eyes eating up and cataloging everything.

"Yes, it was great," said Sally, but something in her tone announced rain in the immediate forecast.

"But?" asked Bob.

"Well," said Sally, "it seems to me we have a tough decision to make. You, particularly, Bob. But your family and loved ones too. Now that I see where they're going, we've got to decide where we're going."

"They're going to the room marked 'Here lie the fools who tried to hustle Bob Lee Swagger,'" said Nikki, "'where their tears will be many, black and bitter.'"

"Par-tay," said his stepdaughter, Miko, in just that morning from the British Eventing Circuit.

"Here are the choices, Bob," said Sally. "Number one, we defend our narrowest possible front. That is, we disconnect ourselves from any larger meaning, we deny it, we flee it, maybe we disavow it. You are just a poor innocent victim, guilty if anything of getting poor advice from a possibly racist entity in a probably racist culture. You did what you were told, trusting in them. You had no agency. My dear husband Nick, in this scenario, becomes the villain. They'll never go after him because he's not well enough known, so he's probably safe, though it will make him even grumpier."

"Do I get to defend myself?" said Nick.

"Sure. Write a book." Sally said. "In other words, we surrender on all issues that are meaningful to them, and we slink out of the hearing diminished but intact. You might have to read a speech of contrition. You might have to disavow the rifle, duty, your country, the sacrifices of your fellow warriors, and all those wounds. You beat them by joining them. Is that what you want?"

"Doesn't sound like much fun," said Bob.

"I could go to them, and seek a deal. I'm getting signals that's what they'd prefer. They don't cage or degrade you, you walk home free. But, you've acknowledged the moral superiority of their view, you've acknowledged the wrongness of your beliefs, you've come to abhor the act of killing—even, maybe particularly, the wicked. That's God's business, not yours. You're part of the general modern movement away from use of force in favor of a more congenial approach, in which you attempt to understand everyone's point of view, and your empathy enables you to talk. Everybody goes home alive and happy."

Silence reigned.

"What's the other way?" Bob asked.

"We embrace your symbolic meaning. We acknowledge your values to millions of Americans. You are the Sniper. You are the man with the gun, of the gun, and therefore implicitly for the gun. You take on the mantle of the sacred killer for the benefit of society. In the day when heaven was falling, when earth's foundations fled, you followed your sniper's calling, took your wages, and shot him dead. You stand for the most noble kind of masculinity, the kind that protects, that ensures the future, that fights for all, without complaint and in spite of what 'advanced' and 'superior' folks, your betters, may say. You embody what they hate."

Bob made a noise somewhere between a grunt and a snicker.

So did Franny.

"It will cost you. They will, they have to, they must, destroy you. Whatever, it may be your toughest fight yet."

"It's going to affect you too," Bob said to his family. "All your lives, forever and ever. So you'd best think on it, and tell me what."

"Do it," said Ray. "You are Bob Lee Swagger."

"They can't take that away from you," said Nikki. "It makes me sick that they think they can."

Miko said, "You can't live without your code. Without it and the belief in the decisions it led

116

you to make, I see you wandering between the winds. The door closes, and you are out there, exiled, on your own."

"Julie?"

"I signed on for the whole ride. No complaints here."

"Baby Sister?" he asked Franny.

"Gurghhh," she said, which all took for yes.

"Let's do it," said Bob.

"Maybe they think they're hunting him," said Ray. "Actually, as many have found out, he's hunting them."

CHAPTER 15
Possibilities

It dragged on and on. Decision to kill, as in: Was it discussed? Interference from politicians, did it happen? If your only tool is a hammer, does every problem look like a nail? Was there a destination, an endgame, a judgment to be reached? No sign yet. The second week—the first one had only taken three geological epochs—loomed beyond the weekend.

"When is this going to be over?" Bob asked Sally after the Friday session. "Or is it going to last forever?"

"I do see an end in sight. They have to find some thing—note I said *some thing* not something—real and tangible to hang the case on. They haven't found it yet and they're groping."

"What would that be? Something totally insane that can nevertheless be argued in a court?"

"Pretty much. I don't know what. Do you?"

"No idea. Maybe something so absurd we can't begin to imagine it."

"It's possible," she answered. "The deal here is that they want a *unanimous* approval that validates it beyond mere partisanship. That's what a thing would get them, rather than an opinion, an interpretation, an analysis. That would be victory. Then it's referred to the Justice Department. That would cause the Justice Department to open a case, mandate an investigation, assign a prosecutor and possibly convene a grand jury in a federal court district, I suppose. I just can't figure out what it could be."

"I can't either. But when they drop the trap, I can guarantee you one thing: our reaction will be unanimous. It'll be, 'What the fuck?' "

CHAPTER 16
Mr. Abrusian

They spoke by phone long distance. *Really long distance:* Boise to Manila to Bogotá to Johannesburg to Coney Island.

"Good news, bad news," said Delta. "Pick your poison."

"Bad first. Always. It makes the good seem better."

"We'll see," said Delta. "The bad news is that you can't kill them. They're in too tight. It's a county lockup, but these Idaho people take their locking up seriously. Triple razor wire on the cyclone, TV everywhere, all kinds of checks and choke points and ID inquisitions, all linked into a central computer, cross-checks and anomaly notifications everywhere. Nobody goes fast, it all moves slow and careful. I watched for an hour from a plane until I almost fell asleep and died."

"No raid?"

"You'd have to go all Navy-SEALs-on-Osama to get them that way. Sound like fun?"

"No fun," said Abrusian. "Can it be penetrated by an agent, under false flag?"

"Maybe, but not tomorrow, or the day after. You'd have to get a guy inside first of all to map the joint. I guess he'd have to be a lawyer, or a head doctor that a lawyer had hired. So first you'd have to steer them into hiring someone who actually worked for you, and that won't happen fast. Then you've got to manufacture top-level, computer-proof fake documents for the guy. Then you've got to get him a weapon by which he could do them all, and a way for him to get out, unless he's going kamikaze. Whatever, it's a bucket of sharks."

"I see," said Abrusian. "Interesting yes, but it does us no good. They have to die or the next several decades will be quite complex."

"I've been working on it. This is where the good news comes in."

"Go ahead."

"Only way I see it," said Delta, "is that you've got to catch them on the road. The prison system uses armored school buses. You figure the route, plant thirty-five pounds of C-4 under the pavement and command detonate from two hundred yards away when they pass over the package. Instant shredded passengers. Little evidence, all of it hard to track and demanding intensive forensic examination. Easy egress for the team, minimal civilian casualties, go home by airline, have a drink, fuck a gal, go to bed without bad dreams."

121

"Yes, fine. But how do we get them on that bus just when our surprise is ready?"

"That's more good news. But it comes wrapped in bad news."

"The bad news?"

"It'll cost you twenty-five million dollars. *Before* you hire one man."

"Ouch," said Abrusian.

"Think of the billions and jillions you'll make if you can repair the badly strained relations between yourselves and the Mexicans and the riches that come from it. And here's the good part: you've already paid it."

"I am lost."

"It's the twenty-five million in drugs in the truck. The truck is sequestered in the Ada County impound lot. It would be an easy takedown, but no possible getaway. Looks simple, is pure suicide. Instant death trap. They'd have every machine gun in the state on you before you got twenty miles. It would make a cool ending for a movie."

"I have heard nothing about a huge drug recovery. Surely it would be all over the news."

"Now you're catching on. The locals haven't found it. They did a once-over, came up with nothing. The boys themselves said nothing. Ergo the killing of that cop is filed under 'Screwball foreign nationals' and there's no pressure to fast-lane it. So here's the play. Find some way to leak to the DEA that there's a lot of dope in that truck. Watch 'em jump. They'll get high-speed forensics teams out there in a day and take the tractor-trailer apart. Bingo! Jackpot! That's when you get your big news stories, that's when Uncle Vakha and the nephews Huey, Dewey, Louie, and Larry suddenly become of big interest. That's when the heat is turned up, everybody sees profit in one of the biggest drug recoveries in history, major blow to whoever sponsored it, and it won't take long for them to work sources and see who did it and why and what it portends. Vakha suddenly has cards to play; they'll want to know for who, and why, and how. They'll talk deal and the feds will overrule the pissed-off Idaho State Police. The cards won't be played in a county lockup, so the feds will move him and the boys, maybe to an Air Force base, maybe to the federal courthouse, maybe to the nearest federal joint. But we will have already been there, the demolitions genius you're going to hire has already worked his magic, and when the bus takes the boys—I'm betting they'll be quite well dressed, instead of in those ridiculous orange jumpsuits—they'll roll over our surprise, and *ka-boom!*"

"Ka-boom!" said Abrusian.

CHAPTER 17

Genetic probe suggests sniper is descendant of Revolutionary War figure—a famous Redcoat
BY DAVID BANJAX, *NEW YORK TIMES* STAFF

Research by an independent DNA research team has found a genetic link between the former Marine sniper Bob Lee Swagger and a famous British officer who led troops against American soldiers during the Revolutionary War and was reputed to be "the best rifle shot in the Eighteenth Century."

Sergeant Swagger, currently under subpoena for the House Subcommittee on Crime and Terrorism and the central figure in ongoing hearings, is directly descended from Patrick Ferguson, a colorful and heroic British officer who led loyalist troops during the American Revolution.

Sergeant Swagger did not respond to emails or phone calls regarding the information.

The data was uncovered by the Artex Genetic Laboratory, of Dulwich, England, and involved comparing samples from Sergeant Swagger's DNA with that of known descendants, currently living in Scotland, of Major Ferguson.

The flamboyant guerilla was finally killed by Tennessee volunteers in the Battle of King's Mountain, when he and his Tory unit were trapped, on October 7, 1780.

Ending a series of colonial defeats in the bitter war, the Battle of King's Mountain marked the end of British aggression to the west in the war's final period, when fighting had moved south and west from its original New England beginnings.

"He was a remarkable man," said Professor Dilman Schiner of the University of Alabama and author of the book *1780: The Trap Closes*.

"You might call him the Green Beret of the American Revolution," Professor Schiner noted. "His skill at arms, his natural leadership abilities, his bravery, and his tactical creativity made him a massive thorn in the side of the colonial efforts wherever he opposed them. His ability to recruit, train, and lead loyalist troops into battle was legendary.

"Moreover, he had a visionary quality. He understood that the days of the short-range smooth-bore musket were limited. He developed a breech-loading rifle for military usage a hundred years before they became common on battlefields. The rifle increased both the accuracy and the rate of fire for its users."

Major Ferguson is also at the center of

a piece of folklore that has remained conspicuous from the revolution. Early in his service in America, in New Jersey, he claimed he was scouting beyond the British lines and he had a clear shot at a high-ranking American officer, denoted by the brightness of his tunic. Ferguson aimed his rifle and had but to pull the trigger to kill the man, but at the last second decided not to fire, as the man was clearly not directing operations, completely unaware, and presenting only his back as the target.

Legend has it that the target was General George Washington.

Though many historians dismiss the account, suggesting that the target could have been a number of other high-ranking officers, the speculation that Ferguson was the man who let Washington live persists until this day.

Another "what if" is also appended to the Ferguson story. He originally came to America under the sponsorship of the British supreme commander, Lord Sir John Howe, to command a specially recruited troop of riflemen. But political intransigence as well as bias in the British command structure against a Scotsman may have doomed the effort. It was clearly sabotaged by other elements in the early part of the war, and its demise is another tantalizing "what if" for countless researchers of the war.

That same intransigence and bias may also have contributed to his death on King's Mountain, where another flamboyant British major, the cavalryman and alleged war criminal Bannister Winston, claimed confusing communications prevented him from riding to the rescue of Ferguson's besieged Tory forces at King's Mountain, as had been the original plan.

Some British memoirists suggest, however, that enmity between Winston and Ferguson had long been brewing, partially because of Ferguson's Scottish heritage, partially because of differences in waging wars.

Ferguson advocated a more enlightened campaign while Winston embodied the concept of total war. Indeed, a phrase that emerged from the campaign, "Winston's Quarter," denoted the Winston approach. It meant "no quarter," meaning all prisoners were to be executed on the site.

When the Tennessee militiamen, called the Over-Mountain Boys, defeated Ferguson, killing 350 of his 600 men to losses of only 23 on their own side, the defeat was catastrophic for British efforts in a part of South Carolina that is now in North Carolina, on the border of Tennessee.

After uncovering the connection last year between the Swagger family and Ferguson, the Artex firm, which specializes in genetic research for aristocratic families, hired an American professor who concentrates on the period to uncover more about the actual happenings in South Carolina in 1780.

What events, the question was, resulted in Ferguson's possibly genetic shooting talent being passed on to an Arkansas family named Swagger, which has produced besides Sergeant Swagger a number of other noted gunmen, including a Marine medal of honor winner in World War II and a sheriff hired by J. Edgar Hoover for the FBI in 1934 to combat the heavily armed bandits of that year? As of now, the results are still a mystery, but the professor, Neal Hughes of Northwestern University, remains in Great Britain, hunting for the answer. He was not available for comment.

"Isn't that something," Swagger said. "Old Ferguson. He was quite a boy, as I recall."

"You knew of him from your family?" Sally asked.

"Not a damn thing. Only thing I knew was by family legend, a married couple called Swagger come over the mountain in 1780, claimed some land, and started a family in what became Polk County, Western Arkansas. We always speculated on them. Who were they, why'd they come? Where'd they get the name Swagger? Who were they fleeing? Why were they on the hunt for a new beginning? We guessed it had something to do with the war in the east, but nobody knew anything solid."

"But you knew of Ferguson?"

"Anybody who knows rifles knows of Ferguson and his rifle. He came up with a breech-loading mechanism. Spare you the details, but the upshot is more fire faster, more accurately, faster on the reload. If he was the first Green Beret, this was the first assault rifle."

"Sounds like a relative you should be proud of, not one over whom you should feel any guilt," Sally said.

"I am," said Swagger. "But Sally, how could this help them? It's interesting, but what happened so long ago has no bearing on events of the last year. Unless they know something we don't."

"It's just something they want in the air. It might be called 'genetic tendencies toward killing.' It's a way they can frame and color the debate without making any possibly incendiary accusations. What they're saying, in the release of this material, is that there's a gene for killing, just as there's one for blond hair or blue eyes. Everybody knows it, nobody talks about it, but the Swaggers have it. Beginning with genius Patrick Ferguson, with his ability and willingness to kill anything he sees. Well, not General Washington, that would be the exception. Anyhow, that 'talent' goes on down the line, and the Swaggers, generation by generation, are equally drawn to killing."

"We were drawn to shooting," Bob said. "The killing was our duty."

"Maybe in some way this hooks up with what comes next. This sets it up. I guess the argument, again unstated, that your DNA, as much as any external realities, demanded that you kill Juba. That need trumped all rational considerations—"

"Such as he was trying to kill me?"

"Yes, such as that. That need trumped everything, and therefore cannot be seen as heroic and necessary but only as psychotic and therefore fraudulent, possibly illegal. Of course they don't have the guts to say that straight out, but only to slide it into the conversation by the back door."

INTERLUDE: 1780

From the Memoirs of Major Matthew Kavanagh
8th October, the Carolinas

The first portent of disaster on the way to the cantonment arrived the morning of October the 8th, when a savage emerged from the woods, screaming, bedraggled, clearly insane. I reached to my pistol to put the man down, but saw in the next second that he was not of tribal origin. He was, or had been, some kind of dragoon, and had come into his present status by virtue of immersion in catastrophe. My sergeant quieted him—rather forcefully, as such was required—and I dismounted to examine and consider disposition. When he stopped gibbering, we examined him for wounds, to discover two of ball and one of bayonet. None were life-endangering but each must have delivered a woeful message of mortality, enough to tip the applecart of his soundness. In this stage, he could only repeat "Massacre! Massacre!"

Scarce had I decided to allow him a taste of brandy for the journey that lay ahead but another chap emerged. Less bedraggled yet not quite of sensible presence, he issued sacraments of thanks and rejoicing at such mad rate one could not keep up with, nor decipher meaning. As we progressed, we gathered two more, all shaken, all fuddled as to recourse. I had seen it before, for it is common to battlefields—the shock of much death, the concession to one's own, the freak survival; it all leads to a state of general palsy to the brain.

At last as we were putting up for the night, still half-day out from our destination, a fifth refugee of battle put in, and as a sergeant he had retained a bit of wit.

He identified himself as Kirk, of Ferguson's Horse, and stated that he and the others were of but a few survivors of that unit, which had been trapped atop a peak called King's Mountain by a Rebel force and all but wiped out. Worse still, they had been abandoned, or so said Kirk, by a supporting detachment of cavalry that was, by plan, to assault the assaulters from an unexpected direction, and thereby put the rout to them. The point of this initiative was to drive them back to the other side of the mountains to lick wounds and heal minds after the humiliation, and thereby free Cornwallis to move his army north from Raleigh into the Virginias without harassment.

I felt it my duty as the ranking officer of His Majesty's forces to piece together an account of what had transpired, while it was still fresh and hot in the survivors' minds. I spoke at length that night to each, and then invested subsequent time adjusting both the sequence and the discrepancies of the fight and Ferguson's fate. I now assay my account, while it is still hot and fresh to my own mind.

(Editor's note: Mr. Swagger, there follow several pages in which Major Kavanagh relates Ferguson's maneuvers in the hills of the Carolinas as he seeks to find a position visible to Major Winston's lurking company of dragoons, whose arrival he anticipated in relief to his own stand. I elide as it could only be of interest to military historians of the sort who produce incomprehensible maps adorned by flags, lines, arrows, and other uncertain symbols. Instead I leap to a moment well after his decision had been made, when it became clear that Winston would not arrive in time, if at all, and that he and his men were therefore doomed. —N.H.)

King's Mountain has been described to this correspondent as a scab of rock atop a scab of hill in a scab of region in a scab of country. It may well be that Major Ferguson chose poorly, for the boulders spread about the gently sloping hardscrabble afforded a determined enemy solid cover to move and fire, as did the numerous wind-gnarled trees. Meanwhile, those atop, returning by volley from kneeling as proscribed, lacked any protection whatsoever. Perhaps it would have been to the better had the Major elected to lead his men eastward at full quickstep to the Waxhaw cantonment from whence they'd come, a position too strong to allow attack. On the other hand, to do so would have then abandoned Winston to his circumstances, and it would have been the dragoons massacred. History will never be able to judge his decision; it must stand in some degree unfathomable, of the sort that no amount of second sight will reveal the elusive proper answer.

In any event, running low on ball and powder, many of them wounded, dying, or dead, exhausted from repelling attacks, the survivors rallied to the highest point and made what fight they could, amid a consistent application of shot, the effects of which turned their peak into a cauldron of battle-dust, ricochet, and the infernal percussion of miss against stone. It was a hell come to earth. The enemy riflery fell upon them as pepper from a shaker. But if they lacked ball and powder, they did not lack spirit or leadership. Atop his mount—only a Mr. Fielding could so invent, but it does seem indeed his horse was white— Major Ferguson ranged his position, shouting encouragement, promising relief, refusing surrender. Was this heroism or insanity? No one can say which of any well-turned war deed. But atop the white, he was for certain target to all, and the balls must have whizzed upon him as would pelting sleet. He did not flinch; it was not in him.

Reports put him here, there, and everywhere, rushing to a segment of his defensive wall wherever break-through seemed imminent, and there charging fully engaged into the attackers, slashing with sword, firing with pistols, ramming into them, breaking their formations apart, one against the many. His only cover the choking vapors of battle, he remained through the endless fusillade horsed and unperturbed, his green-checked shirt and bright red neckerchief visible to any under his command and any who would destroy that command.

"Steady on, boys, they'll fall back soon," he would yell or "I see Winston's dust, lads, and smell victory on air," or "You damned heroes, you're showing them how a Loyalist may fight." His final call, as his own guns ran silent, their marksmen either dead or wounded, was "Rally on me, boys. They'll not break our square this fine afternoon!" Again, it is reliably reported that the man seemed happy, alight with glee. He represented the British officer at his finest.

And then, fini. Exit. Parade's end. A ball, then another and finally another smashed into him. Battle is cruel. It afforded him no dignity. Hit so many times, he lost purchase on his mount and slid from saddle, untethered but for one ankle trapped in stirrup. One hopes he knew he had bled the partisans so badly that they were themselves finished as a military force and would not, could not, mount further campaigns against Cornwallis. That was the legacy of the man now dragged harshly downhill over the pocked slope by his panicked animal, raising a pall of dust and leaving perhaps a dash of gallant blood.

CHAPTER 18
89 Delta

Not much to look at. No SEAL or Spetsnaz man-beast, bursting with muscle and tattoo, big-handed, big-armed, able to leap tall buildings in a single bound. Instead, a squirrelly-looking apparition. He was lean to the point of emaciation, hair a mop, face half-hidden in the bush of unruly beard. But Delta liked the eyes, which were secretly watchful, and the body language, which was twitchless, without tremor. He was dressed in millennial slop, jeans so faded they may have been original to the California gold rush, work boots, a hoodie over a black T, and a Texas Rangers cap backward on his head.

He slid in across from Delta at the Boise mall's Panera.

"You're Delta," he said. "They said you looked Green Beret to the hilt. I'm—"

"No names. Better that way. I am Delta and we'll figure out what to call you soon enough. Tough drive?"

"Up from Texas, yep. Nonstop. Is there rack time in the program?"

"Conk out tonight, sure. I want you sharp. We'll look at the site tomorrow. Can you work in the dark?"

"Check. I have night vision gear. PVS-7, passive infrared. Real good out to fifty-sixty yards. It helps to know a supply sergeant or two."

"What's your maximum on-command detonation?"

"If it's within cell phone distance, I can make it go boom in one second."

"Not good enough. I need it on the dime."

"Tougher, but doable. Has to be wired up then. How far depends on how much wire I've strung."

"Maybe two hundred yards."

"I can always get more. It's cheap."

"See, it'll be a moving target. Best if you can blow not the bus but the back end of the bus, cut down on collateral."

"I can do it."

"But can you get out afterwards?"

"Mos def. After an event, it's crazy time. Everybody is all fucked up. It's minutes before they start paying attention."

"You sound like you know what you're doing. But just because I'm the nervous type, run your CV by me so I know what I have."

"Sure," said the guy. "Grew up dirt-poor in a dying Texas town, no athletic talent to get a ride to State U, no daddy to pay for nothing. Joined the Army to see something except cattle and derricks. Did a tour in Baghdad on an 11-Bravo ticket, and while I was over there trying to not get killed, I saw the explosive ordnance guys working the streets. Military Occupational Specialty 89-Delta, and they were the coolest guys I'd ever seen in my life. I knew in the first second I had to go to explosive disposal school and become an 89-Delta. So I re-upped to get that school. I did six tours, two back-to-back, in my ten years as an 89-D. You name the place, I defused shit there. Of the ten guys in my MOS class, I'm the only one who's still got a face, arms, and fingers."

"So you must be good."

"I didn't make no mistakes. Not like that guy in the movie, not crazy brave, but I had a gift for figuring out how they thought, and it turned out I was always a little smarter."

"And then?"

"Knew I was pushing my luck and got out. Went to work in the oil fields as a blaster, on the theory that if you knew how to fuse 'em down you could figure out how to fuse 'em up. And I was right. Was making good dough, getting real solid at the craft—blowing shit up isn't rocket science but it takes a knack—and someone asked me to work off the books on something a little shady. One thing led to another and I figured out that there was a lot more money on the dark side. I was the go-to guy for anything anybody needed blowed up real good in the Southwest. So that's where I'm at now."

"Is there any paper on you?"

"Nowhere. The feds know that theoretically there's a number one guy in the business, but so far, nobody's ratted on me. Plus, I work clean, so I don't leave little telltales for some genius to figure out. Never the same fuse twice, never the same timing mechanism. I like to mix up different brews of stuff, depending on what the target is. So the money's good, the job's interesting, and in another coupla years I figure on having enough to retire on, maybe get married, have some kids, go to baseball games."

"What shit have you got?"

"Fifteen pounds of C-4 in tubes pinned inside my wheel wells. That's enough to bring down any building west of the Mississippi. Some micro-thermite—that'll burn a hole in anything except the sun. RMT when you need to pack a lot of blowup in a little package. But I horde that stuff, it's so hard to come by."

"Okay, check into a motel—don't tell me where—and meet me here at eight a.m. tomorrow. Fast food only, no sit-down restaurants. No cell calls. No credit cards. You probably already know all that. Here's some more: Don't go out of the room after you're in. Watch TCM until you fall asleep. *West Side Story* is on tonight."

"That's a good one."

"Cool?"

"Cool. 'To-night, to-night.' What's my name, by the way?"

"I'll call you Niner, for 89-D. You can't be Delta because I'm Delta."

"Yes, sir."

"And don't call me sir. I wasn't an officer when I matriculated, I was an E-8, MOS 19-Bravo. But don't call me Sergeant either. Just Delta is fine."

"I had you figured for a snake-eater. Good guys. Worked with a lot of 'em."

"Then consider me your new best friend."

CHAPTER 19
Bad News

Vakha was thinking hard. He'd already cracked the essential theoretical of the place, and now moved on to specifics. Everything had to be planned. If you were improvising as you proceeded, you would die, because sooner or later something would go wrong. For example, witness the unanticipated professionalism of the security man on the tractor-trailer, whose agility had set this whole dismal thing off. Who could have anticipated that the Russians would hire such a resilient, capable fellow?

So he tried to work each last detail out, plus keep it simple because some of the nephews weren't exactly the brightest of fellows. He had to be realistic about what they were capable of doing, what not. Certainly most could accomplish anything physical, including any kind of violence. He knew they would kill on command and without remorse, but only Khasan was clever enough to make consistently right decisions. Ibragim less so, angry Ibragim, always ready for a fight. Anzor was so young he could only be guided, not trusted. Magomet was the mystery.

He seemed clever enough, and as the only one capable of driving, he was the lynchpin on which all things turned. But he had no fire in his belly. In a fight, he might shoot, but Vakha remembered him trembling under the wheel in the gunfight on the highway with the state troopers. It was doubtful he could kill with a knife, certain he could not kill with bare hands. It was thus appropriate to keep him far from the bloodiness of the actual violence, as he had to be clear and sharp in his driving for what—

Spider senses still keen, he sensed a presence. He looked up from his deep concentration, to see a guard standing awkwardly at the bars of the cell, as if afraid to interrupt. The guard swallowed, clearly overmatched. Odd, the boys were usually left alone from lunch through dinner, to rusticate as they wanted. Thus all were outside lifting weights in the yard, under the sullen eyes of the deposed Mexicans—all, that is, except for Magomet, who was probably writing poetry.

"Sir," said the guard, offering fealty to the boss con, "sir, you have a visitor."

Vakha said nothing, as he had yet to speak to a captor, an interrogator, a guard, a defense attorney, a prosecutor, even the trustee janitors.

"I have to—you know."

Vakha knew. Prison protocol demanded that he thrust his wrists through a rectangular gap in the bars, to be handcuffed. He complied, turning as the guard went on to encircle his waist with chain and locked it at the back. Thus ensnared, Vakha was no threat to anybody; he didn't have the freedom of movement, say, to reach a shiv in his sock or loop the cuffs around the guard's throat and choke him dead in a minute. Not that he would have—today he was obedient. Sometime next week, maybe not so much.

Clanking, he was released from his cage, and the guard guided him to the elevator, then down two flights to the main floor, then through two levels of security. At each way station, he picked up another guard, was electric-wanded for contraband, double-checked in foot and mouth. At least he didn't have to reveal his rectum, not out of humaneness or even hygiene but because unchaining him would be too much effort.

The small parade eventually reached the visitors room, where ten chairs in booths faced ten barred windows to an outside revealing ten more chairs. At three of the stations, men chatted with doughy, dreary wives or earnest attorneys, over phones provided for just that purpose. By this time the phones were dirty, perhaps unsanitary, from all the scum that had used them. And the windows bore the scars and stains of usage by the lowest of the low, being equally squalid and filthy, two or three cracked, all smeary and hazed, perhaps melted by the shedding of so many tears, the wails of much forlorn bravado, the desperation of the often-raped or the beaten-for-the-fun-of-others.

Vakha made a brisk gesture with his chin, meaning, "Get these assholes out of here," and no guard felt like making a big deal out of it with the boss con and risking retaliation on the yard, and so the three convicts were cut short of their ten-minute chat time with the outside world. As they were led by, each kept his eyes downcast, as they too feared retaliation from the chief of the mystery meat gang.

They led Vakha to a booth where he took a seat, turned, and faced through the blurry triple-paned glass a crew-cut American in a rumpled suit and a loose tie. He looked both overworked and over-abused, a whipping boy for all who felt like whipping a boy, which turned out to be a surprisingly large number.

His name was Jerry something, Vakha couldn't remember or perhaps hadn't bothered to learn in the first place. He was the hapless public defender assigned to the gang of foreigners, and his job had been made existentially more desperate by their utter indifference to him. He held the phone in his hand.

Vakha stared at him with dead eyes. What could this asshole want? He picked up the phone.

"Sir," he said, "as you know I have been appointed your defense attorney, in lieu of any request on your part for someone specific. Jerry Locklear, remember?"

Vakha said nothing, just continued to lay the weight of his disinterested gaze upon the young man, who was certainly not up to the rigors of eye contact. Indeed, Jerry looked away, swallowing, but then came back.

"Even though you have not cooperated with me, I am duty-bound to represent your best interests. It is in that regard that I am here."

More weighted silence from Vakha did not make this any easier on Jerry, who looked on the verge of a collapse. He seemed to think Vakha might be interested enough in him to smash through the windows and crush his skull like a grape.

He came back again to the phone.

"Sir, Mr. X, Mystery Man, whatever, I heard something you should know. No place is as leaky as a courthouse; the walls have ears and so do the floors and the lighting fixtures. Nothing is ever secret for long. I got this from a guy who knows a guy who in turn—well, on and on."

This brought no response from Vakha.

"Anyhow, I have it through this means of communication that a highly trained forensics search team from DEA is headed in tomorrow. Their job is to go over your tractor-trailer with a comb of fine teeth. They are said to be the very best. Evidently, somewhere in whichever organization you are affiliated with, there has been a leak. It suggests that far from being an expensive trailer jammed with cheap Chinese junk furniture, it's laden with narcotics, all hidden so professionally that no rube Western law outfit could hope to penetrate. But these new guys will find whatever is there, so again you should be prepared."

For the first time in his career in America, Vakha acknowledged an unarmed American. He nodded. This prompted Jerry to lurch onward.

"I don't know what's in there, but DEA wouldn't be sending its best team if it didn't think it was something big. If it is, that changes everything. First, you will be indicted by the feds, and that indictment will take precedence over anything local. You will be transferred to one of the big joints down in Kuna, doesn't matter which one because all of 'em are state-of-the-art. That'll be for your own protection, they'll say, but the real point is that you will be investigated furiously and pressured remorselessly. They will get your secrets from you and they will learn who you were working for and who you were working against. They will separate you, play each against the other four, and break you down. You will be offered deals to rat out your employers, and while it might get you out in fifty years instead of seventy-five, you know as well as I that your identities cannot be kept hidden in all this and there will be retaliation against you, even in prison, and against your families. I don't know about the Russians, but the cartel people are extremely vengeful. If you are involved with them—again, I have no information—things could turn dramatically ugly in very short time. They are not nice people."

For the first time in his incarceration, Vakha spoke to an American.

"Is good work, Mr. Jerry."

CHAPTER 20

Scandal

More fast-breaking news from the eighteenth century," Sally said, moving into the room where Bob, Julie, and Nick sat.

Sally pushed the morning edition of the *New York Times* over to them. Right-hand column, below the fold, but still on the front page, by David Banjax.

Sniper family origins traced to 1780 scandal at British outpost

"Now what the hell is this?" Bob said. "Can't they leave those old bones lie in peace?"

"They're the *New York Times*," said Nick, looking over his shoulder. "The news is what they say it is, and they don't want anyone to forget that."

The story told a sordid account.

A university professor working in London has located documents that indicate Bob Lee Swagger, the former Marine sniper currently at the center of a House hearing for his actions in slaying an alleged terrorist last year, has a family connection to a mysterious British army scandal that may have resulted in a cover-up.

Spies, desertions, official diversions, massacres, and dark secrets long buried are in play as Professor Neal Hughes, of Northwestern University, goes through records that haven't been touched in centuries.

Genetic research has recently confirmed that Sergeant Swagger is a direct descendant of Major Patrick Ferguson, a noted crack shot and anti-partisan expert who campaigned against the Colonials beginning in 1777 and ending with his death in 1780. Major Ferguson's marksman's talent has subsequently figured in Swagger family history, which has produced, beside the retired Marine gunnery sergeant, some extraordinary gunmen.

The documents reveal that the scandal followed almost immediately upon Major Ferguson's death at the Battle of King's Mountain, North Carolina, October 7, 1780.

"The proximity between events is too close to be viewed as coincidental," said Professor Hughes, who is now examining British records for context and clarification.

The newly uncovered data suggest that an unnamed British officer was reported to have disappeared from his duty station at a cantonment called Waxhaw in western North Carolina. Was he an American spy who had given up the location of the Ferguson column? Or was he was fleeing what might have seemed certain death at the remote mountain outpost, or gambling debts, romantic entanglements, or the ire of his peers? Or was there a more banal explanation?

The man allegedly had ties to intelligence organizations affiliated with the British army, and some have suggested he rejoined "the Spies" and that the scandal was manufactured to masquerade and justify his sudden and unexpected absence without raising alarm.

It was a singular event, nevertheless. Cantonment Waxhaw otherwise reported no deserters while in operation between June of 1780 to November of 1782.

"It might be significant," said Professor Hughes, by email forwarded to the *Times* on condition of anonymity of source, "and it might not. Typically those records were well kept but subject to the whim and preferences of commanding officers or other command influences."

What is not in doubt is that something unusual happened at the cantonment, from which Major Ferguson and his Tory Militia had set out to ultimately meet disaster at King's Mountain.

"It's a premature judgment, to be certain," said the professor, "but the vagueness with which it is recorded in the commanding officer's logbook is reminiscent of other attempts at deception in the era."

Professor Hughes, a specialist in eighteenth-century British army issues, is currently supported by a grant from the Artex Company, a British provider of ancestral history through DNA testing. He said that he had encountered the log in the files held at the Imperial War Museum in London. They were authored by or at least under the auspices of the garrison's commanding officer, Colonel James Bruxhall, who eventually became Lord Bruxhall after retirement from the service as a lieutenant general in 1791.

"This story is much more interesting than the one I'm in now," Bob said. "At least it's got some action. I hope he gets to the end. This one's just about a bunch of Washington hotshots playing pin the tail on the donkey with an old Marine."

"The donkey," said Sally, "still has some moves left."

"But what tail are they going to try to pin on him today?" Bob wondered.

INTERLUDE: 1780

There is no slough of despond deeper than that which swallows a garrison in the immediate aftermath of catastrophe. The cantonment at Waxhaw looked as if a plague had whirled through it, leaving mud, shite, and death. I could tell by the lax and demoralized aspect of the sentries, the torpor of those troops inside the log walls, the general sense of miasma that predominated. No one greeted my little party, nor raced to relieve our tired mounts of saddle and halter, nor take off the wounded survivors. No scarlet-dressed commanding officer awaited us with ceremony. Odd, as he was highly thought of as a capable officer. His name was James Bruxhall, I had been informed, a Colonel of some repute as a specialist in partisan warfare who had gathered under his tether both Ferguson and the officer named by all survivors, Major Bannister Winston. I actually had acquaintance with this man.

Finally a colour sergeant of the old school, still marginally dressed in proper kit and holding himself to posture appropriate, came to us. He was able enough to salute, then stand to.

"Colour Sergeant Stanley, sir. I shall see

Colonel Bruxhall is informed of your arrival on his awakening. What is it you'd be needing then? I shall dispatch men to see to your needs."

I told him of our needs and then, from a deep reserve of melancholy, said, "I cannot believe Ferguson is gone. He was a legend, and wherever he's served he's left nothing but grateful commanders and adoring rankers."

"It's a sad day, for sure, sir," said Colour Sergeant Stanley.

"Is there a man in fort who served as brother officer with Major Ferguson?"

"Lieutenant Grammercy, sir. He was the Major's adjutant, but the Major sent him back an hour before the battle to inform Colonel Bruxhall of the impending event, and to implore him to send Major Winston, standing by not far off, to ride in support."

"I understand," I said, and I did, as I knew too much of Winston.

He was of the sort that to their shame armies tend to attract. That is, his commitment to king and country, his obligation to duty, his ambition to serve well, all were suborned in his true nature which was to slake his thirst for violence. Where ere he'd served, he'd left bad blood in his footprints and the occasional corpse, for one of his specialties—it fits perfectly with the dark materials of his character—was the duel. I believe by now he had killed seven men, all by sword; one of them—and I had the misfortune to see it occur—was my brother officer Godfrey Scott-Browning, whose lungs he'd pierced and who died bloodily in the mud of the recruiting depot at Chatham, where our regiments had sent us for battalion-scaled drill, for a trifle, a joke that Winston contrived to take as a blood insult.

Between Ferguson and Winston there would be inevitable friction. Ferguson was known as a gentleman; he would warn well before raiding towns. He had, legend had it, probably true, declined a shot on a ranking colonial officer who may well have been General Washington himself. On the battlefield or in battle's aftermath, he had never been an executioner nor a hangman.

By contrast, Winston was a chap for whom carnage was métier, the medium of his artistry. His commanders always had to rein him in, not urge him forward, as if he had some deep-seated need to bring slaughter. I've never known anything like it, except for the odd butcher of whores who goes to the gallows at Newgate every few years.

I met Grammercy—his first name was Robert, I was to learn—that afternoon at two in the officers' mess, a rudely engineered replica of the well-appointed halls that enlightened the garrisons of all the fashionable regiments on the Pall Mall. Having no need of sumptuousness, nor of fashion, but only ordnance, I understood immediately that it would do.

The lieutenant turned out to be a rangy young officer nearing thirty, sharp of face, of superior peasant stock which included strong eyes and thick hair, all dressed, after the partisan method, in forest colors, that is a buckskin shirt with black neckerchief, dark, slim cavalry trousers booted almost to the knees and jangly with spur, and a curved saber in scabbard in descent from the green sash about his middle. He had leather bracelets of beaded array, artifacts from encounters with Indians, I presumed. He looked in toto rather more American than British, which I suppose was the point.

By this time I had met Colonel Bruxhall and, astonishingly, his daughter, a spirited young woman named Susanna, who had ventured to the cantonment on her own a few months back, her mother and aunt having grown boring and strident in London. She was, as was the Colonel, in a state of somberness, owing to the loss of the favored son within the week.

Thus I was astonished at the Lieutenant's deportment, which was quite the opposite of theirs. Rather than consumed in grief, as one would have expected given the circumstances, he seemed delighted.

"I say, Major Kavanagh, I am so happy to see you. I did indeed spend many a night by campfire discussing the rifle in battle with Patrick, and I shall try and recall our many conversations. He had me enthralled, and though a skeptic at first, I came to agree that Old Bess was antiquated and that a rifle which loaded from the breech, with its manifest superiorities in accuracy, distance, and speed of fire, was the path of the future."

We talked for about two hours, my man O'Brien taking copious notes, which formed the basis of my subsequent report to the Board of Ordnance, "On the Properties of Rifle in the Battles to Come," which resulted in my promotion to Lieutenant Colonel, even if it was otherwise ignored. I will skip my discussions with Grammercy and refer the curious reader to the report itself, on file in the Pattern Room of the Royal Arsenal as well as the Board of Ordnance headquarters in the Tower of London.

At the end, however, I felt I needed a greater sense of to whom it was I was in conversation. I said, "Lieutenant, our records being hard to maintain in the field, I have no acquaintanceship with your particulars. Briefly, sir, could you advise me. As I make my recommendations to the Board, it will be helpful to have knowledge of Major Ferguson's conduit and therefore his legacy."

"Of course, sir," he said.

He was from near Hereford and enlisted at fourteen, feeling both the call to arms and the need to escape a farm family with its near-empty larder and his twelve brothers and sisters to fight for scraps. He took to the Army immediately, and was within a year a corporal, and it was there his talent was discovered: the boy was a natural mimic, and could keep the barracks rollicking into the night with his imitations of sergeants and officers alike. Such a talent is one aspect that makes the private soldier's barracks life almost tolerable. But an officer—poltrooned in jest many a time by the young man—thought that such a gift might have further application. He decided to put the boy to the test by hiring him a tutor in Spanish, if only to prevent further damage to his reputation by the scalawag's jibes.

It turned out that the mimicry was the basis for Robert's gift for languages. *(Editor's note: Mr. Swagger, the major records here Grammercy's eventful life in some detail, the gist of which is that the young corporal was "talent spotted" and moved elsewhere. —NH)* Referred to the Intelligence Department, "The Spies," the language young Grammercy was required to acquire was not German or Punjabi or Senegalese but Cherokee. He was sent to the province of the western Carolinas and in the care of a trader who also reported to London, he was gently eased into the Cherokee towns, their ways, their standards and histories, and their language. As all expected, he quickly learned the language, he quickly earned the trust, he quickly became a tribal influence, especially in later years among the Indians of a splinter group of disaffected red men called the Chickamauga, who were led by a dark fury of a warrior named Dragged Canoe. Grammercy himself earned an Indian name: he was called, he said, *Ani-ja Nigan-guvna* of the Chickamauga.

"That's quite a mouthful," I said.

"Yes, sir, Cherokee is far more poetic than our rude tongue and in no rush to finish its words."

(Editor's note: Mr. Swagger, I summarize again. This young officer assisted the Chickamauga Cherokee in war against colonial interests. Much blood was spilled, including his own. A serious wound sent him back to Charlotte. It was then, in 1779, when Major Ferguson needed a man of such dash that he returned to action. Ferguson, who held some sway with Cornwallis, demanded that the spy be restored to regular Army status and promoted to lieutenant. Thus he was no longer Ani-Ja Nigan-guvna of the Chickamauga but Lieutenant Robert Grammercy of "Ferguson's Horse." —N.H.)

When we adjourned finally, he said to me, "Major Kavanagh, you will join our little party in the officers' mess tonight, I presume? It's the first time the command has been reassembled since the disaster."

"I had thought not, Lieutenant. I have a long

journey ahead and would leave before the sun rises tomorrow. I have what I came for, thanks to your cooperation and your colonel's good graces."

"Sir," he said, "as a personal favor to me I would request your presence. I plan a fitting tribute to the greatness of the man who has brought us to shelter and drink under the same roof, my friend and brother, Patrick Ferguson. Moreover, I have a diversion planned which I daresay you shall find quite amusing."

What soldier on earth could refuse such a summons?

CHAPTER 21
The Big One

T he timing is perfect," said Congressman Baker in another conference room, with another cup of coffee before him. "The last of Banjax's pieces appeared today. Unsaid in it all is a Swagger family rapacity for killing by firearm. From Major Ferguson onward, you can see the gene passed along, skipping generations now and then, but ultimately producing the three-of-a-kind in Charles, Earl, and Bob Lee. Now we lay today's surprise on him, and it all fits like a jigsaw puzzle. We'll get our unanimous finding, we'll sic Justice on Swagger, and we'll have discredited not only Swagger and the president but the whole macho shoot-first-ask-questions-later ethos that the Swaggers represent."

But his eyes, as usual, betrayed him. He couldn't keep the shiftiness out of them, and as he concluded, they rattled around in his sockets, first left, then right.

But Madam Chairman Venable didn't feel like smacking him today.

"Umm" was all she said.

She wore red today, as opposed to yesterday,

when she wore red, and the day before, when, just to change it up on everyone, she wore red. This one was a kind of smock over a camel's hair skirt, set off by a diamond necklace and some pricey Louboutin heels. Her hair and makeup were perfect, again as opposed to yesterday, when they were perfect. But on the day before that, they'd been perfect.

"Convince me you can handle the technical stuff as it comes up today," she finally said.

"I have studied it. I know it forward and backward."

"That's what Firpo said before he met Dempsey," she said.

"What?"

"Never mind. Anyhow, do we need to bring in that Chinese gal, the one who finished ahead of you at Harvard. Wang? Chong? Ling?"

"Cynthia Wen. No, Madam Chairman. Please, it's not necessary."

"I love it when you grovel, Congressman. You have such a talent for it. Anyhow, you know we're losing now, don't you? The ratings have gone south, the networks have bailed, it seems to be meandering and dithering and blundering. The focus groups are begging to be set free. They may stage an armed breakout. You're going to get it back on track today? And finish it with a bang?"

"Yes, ma'am. It's simple. The technical concept

is easily understood, and after that it's merely an issue of understanding timelines. What came when, and before what. Crystal clear. And once they see that, there's no choice but to go with us. I guarantee bang."

She turned.

"Come on, Feeley. Say something intelligent for once. Are we ready to get back in the bigs with this one?"

"Well," he said, "I've spoken to the network people. I've made the pitch that at last there's going to be fireworks, that it'll be a big day. I've twisted arms, called in favors, promised years of scoops, done every degrading thing my job requires me to—"

"No self-pity," said Mother Death. "You're getting the bucks, and the daily crucifixion is part of the package."

"Of course, Congresswoman. I merely—well, anyway, I'm waiting as various superstars of journalism try and convince twenty-three-year-old story editors who know nothing to get back out here and set up."

"I see a problem," said Congressman Baker, eyes wild with joy at finding an issue to bring against his good friend and worst enemy.

"I do too," said Feeley, intercepting the thrust with a nice parry. "The time curve. These guys don't like to rush. I call 'em yesterday, they decide this morning, they get here tonight. But by tonight, as currently scheduled, the show is over. So—"

"So postpone a day? I can't possibly—"

"Yes, you can," she interrupted, a keen display of her fabled decisiveness. "I'll announce that Baker ate some venison that didn't agree with the tum-tum. He's sitting on the pot shitting his guts out. Meanwhile, Feeley, get me some school or hospital to visit this afternoon or people will think I'm drunk again. No terminal wards, though. All those bald dying kids—God, that's depressing."

"Yes, ma'am."

"Now, before I let you worms slither away, I'm still waiting on Feeley's assessment of the plan, to dignify it with something it doesn't begin to approach."

"It's a good plan," said Baker.

"It makes sense," Feeley said, "and if Ross says he's got it nailed, I know that it's nailed. But . . . I do worry a bit."

"About what?" said Baker, miffed at the faint-praise murder attempt.

"To millions in the vast barren desert between the coasts, this guy is a hero. They *like* the fact that he's a killer. They love the 'Nailer' nickname. They love the Patrick Ferguson connection. They don't care that Ferguson was a redcoat. Most important, they're not ready to surrender the notion that when the cops blow away a brother, the brother deserved it, because he was guilty, dangerous, and, of course, a brother."

"They will understand the charge and they will see that he was wrong," said Baker. "Technically, legally, demonstrably, officially *wrong*."

"Fair enough," said Feeley. "I'm just saying that in a certain way, we are sowing the wind and may reap the whirlwind, and while it makes a lot of sense on paper and at meetings and among all those we know and trust, maybe it doesn't to the millions."

"I hate the millions," said Mother Death.

CHAPTER 22

IMSI

S o you think here?" said Niner.

They had parked about a quarter mile off the main road, just outside of Kuna, Idaho. Before them was a grim collection of brick barracks behind double-barbwire fences, in a style that might be called Brutalitarian Gothic. They examined it with naked eyes, because to go to binoculars was a dead giveaway, and highway patrol cars were much in evidence in this little sector of the state south of Boise. It was known as the South Boise Prison Complex, running down both sides of Pleasant Valley Road just outside of Kuna, and housed in total seven correctional facilities.

This one was called the Idaho Maximum Security Institute, "IMSI," rhymes with "whimsy," of which it had none. All the buildings—actually, they were much bigger than barracks—were low and themselves, though in the wider perimeter, in full enjoyment of their own private perimeter of double-barbed razor wire, guaranteed to cut to death anyone who tried to penetrate. An administration building lay in the center of the installation, and the five housing buildings were arranged around it. A cheerful batch of flags—one America's, one Idaho's, one the Bureau of Prisons'—flapped in the brisk wind. Mountains ringed the site, but mountains ringed everything in Idaho.

"Yeah," said Delta. "It's close, so transport won't be an issue. Hell, it's even in Ada County. State cops can convoy it, no problem. You can see the security. SEALs or Special Ops folks couldn't penetrate it, unless they raided in battalion strength with Warthog backup. In fact, it can't be raided, it can only be taken."

IMSI had 547 inmates, each in his own little cell, each in solitary twenty-three hours a day, with a Bible, a toilet, a blanket, and nothing else. Only men of exceptionally violent tendencies came here, having bounced out of other joints or committed crimes so horrific the public felt safer with them stored here until they died or were sent to an auxiliary building a few hundred feet away for a last lie-down before the big sleep.

"That's why we have to hit them before they get inside. Once inside, game over."

"I got it."

"So what are you thinking? Any inspirations?"

"Whichever way they come, they have to turn down that access road off of Pleasant Valley. I'll plant right at the turn, because he'll slow down taking the bus around the corner. Gives me a little more leeway."

167

"You going to detonate off a visual?"

"If you want it exact, I have to. My thought is tonight I'll gear up. You roll by and I'll slide out. Then go to an all-night diner or something."

"You can get it done on one shot?"

"Yeah. See, people think explosives only blow *up*. They see all the blasts from bombs and shit, all that Hiroshima stuff, they see a vertical rising cloud. But the cloud doesn't organize itself and go vertical for several seconds. I'll plant on the side of the road, and I'll shape the charge so it blows at a forty-five-degree angle. Fifteen pounds of C-4 angled at the bus will open it like a sardine can. It'll turn anybody inside into sardine hash. It'll look like a Hellfire hit it dead-on."

"How close are you?"

"I'll be about two hundred yards out. Any farther and the night vision gets shaky. I'm on the wire, and when I see the front tires hit the kill zone, I command detonate. The message gets through the wire in about one-tenth of a second, and the dets inform the 4 that it's time to dance. *Ka-boom,* as we say in the trade."

"How do you get out?"

"I cut through the trees, strip off my gear, put my night vision in a backpack and a ball cap on, and I amble out to the road. You make one pass, I hop in, and we're out of there. I'd go back roads to where we ought to go, no rush, nothing frantic, everything cool. You drop me at my truck, we shake hands, and it's goodbye until the next one."

"Sounds good. Now one other thing," said Delta. "In the bus, are there any survivors?"

"I can't make no guarantees. It's all in the breaks. If they get lucky, the guard crew is up front with the driver and the bad guys are back in the rear, and the good guys should have interesting stories to tell. That is, if they remember how they came to be sitting in the front half of a bus with their cargo spewed across Idaho."

"Finally, the stuff you leave behind. Traceable?"

"Nah. All of it's Radio Shack–grade stuff, nothing custom or fancy. Purchased from electrical supply houses in small quantities, no single big order to track. Who's going to put two hundred yards of number four copper wire from here together with three nine-volt batteries from there and six couplers from still another place? The C-4 is standard military explosive, unserialized, available in any quantity you want on any black market in the world."

"Anything else?" asked Delta.

"Yeah," said Niner. "I really enjoyed *West Side Story*."

CHAPTER 23
CNN

They knew when they pulled into the high school's parking lot. It was crowded with network TV trucks. Out front of the Frank Church High School, a couple of talking haircuts were prerecording their opening bits to front the developments that were set to come. Just beyond the trucks, journos milled and gossiped, sipping coffee from Styrofoam. TV guys handsome, newspaper guys scruffy, techies scruffier. But it was segregated by caste: the handsome dogs and smashing dolls didn't mingle with the beatniks, and the beatniks from out of town wouldn't mingle with the beatniks from in town. As usual they looked bored and disconsolate, to say nothing of tired, from the emergency changes-of-plan that had gotten them there. In all, only one rangy figure looked content and radiated heat waves of magnanimous goodwill. That was David Banjax, star of the *New York Times*, even bigger star of what had come to be known as the Swagger Show.

"Look at him," Bob said from the back seat of the Lincoln Town Car, driven, as usual, by

George, a decent guy from a limousine service. "Smug bastard."

"You know what this means," Sally said from the front seat. "They've got something big planned. That's why they canceled out yesterday, to let this horde get planes in."

"Oh, Christ, they've seen us," said Nick. "We're going to have to fight our way in."

The media broke into individuals, then clotted around the car.

"Bob," said Sally, as Nick got out to go to the trunk and recover and unfold the now completely unnecessary wheelchair, "I think I could get an adjournment from Mrs. Death. We could get a day or two off, figure out what angle they're going to ride and how best to prepare for it. Though I'm damned if I can think of something we haven't already figured on."

"Let's just do it," he said. "I don't know what I could come up with in a day anyhow. I'm as ready as I'll ever be."

"It's a different kind of war. But you're still a warrior."

But Bob was looking at his primary antagonist. "Look at him, the asshole. He's above it all. He don't even bother to jockey for position." Banjax, in a summer suit, his unkempt hair flipping in the wind, had positioned himself well back of the melee and adapted a rather blasé posture, as if he knew the attention would swing onto him soon enough.

"He needs a haircut," Swagger said.

"Actually I think he has one," Sally said. "You don't get that tussled, windblown look without a lot of time in the chair and a very good guy on the scissors. You don't see hair like that anywhere except New York and DC. Maybe LA. Nobody else has the time or vanity for it. And the suit fits through the shoulders nicely. That's no off-the-rack department store job. Somebody put some effort into upgrading Mr. Banjax."

"You want me to run interference through these folks, Mr. Swagger," asked George. He was large and black and, with high school football as an offensive tackle on his résumé, probably knew a thing or two about maximum leverage on a broad front.

"George, if you don't mind. Otherwise, I'm afraid they'll eat me up and spit out the bones," Swagger said.

George removed himself, powerfully inserted himself into the mass, cleared space with good inside moves, and opened the door.

"Bob, nothing for these buzzards," said Sally.

"Got it," he said.

Nick penetrated from another angle, the chair forcing the issue. Bob went through the pantomime of being helped into a contrivance he didn't need, though even as he moved, the arthritic hip flared, reminding him that he was far from 100 percent. The questions came at him like shrapnel.

"Did you kill Juba because you're Islamo-phobic?"

"Do you have a family gene for killing?"

"Why didn't you call for authorization?"

"What did you feel after you shot him?"

The accepted Marine-sniper response to this one had always been "Recoil," but he didn't rise to it. "Sniper boasts of only feeling recoil after kill," the headlines would read. He was learning.

"Were you happy when you saw the pictures of his head blown apart?"

"How can you be sure he would have fired? Could you read his mind?"

"If you're so good, why didn't you shoot to wound him?"

"Could you tell his faith from the helicopter?"

He willed the thousand-yard stare onto his face, something his three tours in Vietnam had never accomplished, nor any of the events afterward, and settled back as Nick pivoted the thing, and pumped up to ramming speed. The crowd parted, albeit reluctantly, and Bob looked both dead ahead and dead at the same time.

Nick pushed him briskly along, acquiring sidewalk smoothness, and Bob watched as the windowless exterior punctuated only by double-glass front doors and transom grew closer and closer. Two state cops in SWAT gear with M4s stood sentinel, and off to one side another crowd awaited entry, this being civilians who had sat through the thing's dull days and now wanted their climax. Idaho folks, some of the older still sporting the masks of the spring, they seemed to be on his side, not that it mattered, and for them he mustered a smile and a feeble wave, their answering cheers having enough force to somewhat dissipate and drive back the horde that trailed him.

Fortunately the building had been engineered to ground level, so there was no handicap ramp to deal with and he went in smoothly, feeling Nick's growing power after all the exercise pushing him about.

"Men's?" Nick whispered into his ear as the building swallowed them.

"Nah, I'm good," said Bob.

Entered, the auditorium yielded a basketball court with baskets on hinges cranked to the rafters and the space where the boys and girls had battled according to Dr. Naismith's rules now flooded in a tide of folding seats. He glided down the aisle on pure 100-octane Nick power, reaching the press zone, a crescent of a hundred or so folders set up on the lip of the stage. Two state cops, looking ceremonial in crisp uniforms except for M4 carbines held diagonally on straps across their fronts, flanked the stage.

Nick took a hard left, went to the handicap lift at the end of the stage. Bob nodded at the state cop, who nodded back. "Good luck, Gunny," he said.

Bumpily accessing the lift, Nick hit a switch and the thing raised Bob to stage level.

Perhaps it was a manifestation of how closely related are statecraft and theater craft, but the space had been tricked out as a mock House hearing room. No mahogany, no plush, no King George artifices, but the structure was parallel, with the big shots higher, their half circle of chairs on risers, and therefore able to look down upon the peonage with ironic detachment.

Nick steered him to his table, and parked him in his usual chair-less spot. Sally fell in to the right and Nick to the left, facing the inquisitors. Before the eight exalted high seats, staffers were assigned lower, ruder chairs and could easily scurry around to service their masters.

This area was now populated with the various minions who lubricated the process with their energy and ideals, mostly youngsters in their twenties, mostly well dressed and quite hand-some regardless of sex, all radiating energy and purpose. They now mingled and gossiped and paid no attention to Swagger and his team.

The favored press then appeared, and the inter-course between the two groups was immediate and electric. Everybody knew everybody, regard-less of affiliation or guiding moral principles or lack of guiding moral principles. Nobody paid any attention to the Swagger party until, inevitably, a rangy figure broke free and loped over.

"Sergeant," said Banjax, nodding affably.

"Mr. Banjax," Bob responded.

"Just wanted to tell you what a great job you've done so far, and wish you luck."

"Just trying to tell the truth."

"They say the truth shall set you free."

"Seems like these guys want to use the truth to set me in jail."

Banjax laughed.

"Glad you still have your sense of humor. Please do remember, if you want a fair hearing, if you want to get your side out direct to the public without the filter of the hearing, I'm your go-to guy."

"I'll bear that in mind," said Swagger.

With that, still wearing that little ironic whisper of a smile, Banjax sauntered back to his pals.

"Little bastard," said Nick.

"He wanted a good sniff of my blood before the kill," said Bob.

The new personality fit Congressman Baker better than the old. He was today sober, somber, filled with infinite regret. Melancholy haunted his face, and his eyes foresaw tragedy and never went googly. It was as if he were presiding at a deathbed wait.

Naturally, he fucked it up soon enough.

"Sergeant Swagger," he began, "we turn now to means and methods. We turn to decisions for means and methods. We turn to responsibility for means and methods."

It seemed the lights had been turned up a notch or two, and he heard the clicking and snapping not of bolts and magazines but of motor-driven digitals, of vid cams going hot with a snap, with scribes behind tensing as they leaned forward to catch it all, and the transcriber went into total concentration mode.

"What was the bullet you used in the Juba kill?"

"It was a Hornady .264 140-grain ELD, I believe," said Bob.

It was as if he'd slapped Baker in the face with a fresh, still flopping carp. The man's somber face melted into something like panic. You'd have thought he'd run out of oxygen. His eyes rolled like brown M&M's bouncing down a stairway.

"No, no, I mean *bullet*."

"I understand, sir. I answered correctly."

Baker turned back to Mother Death and sent her eye-lingo for "Help this drowning fool, I'm begging you!"

"Sergeant Swagger," she said, "I have to remind you that you are under oath. If you commit perjury, you can be indicted for that and for contempt of Congress."

"Madam, as I said, I have answered accurately."

Sally whispered, "What's going on?"

"This moron doesn't know the difference between a cartridge and a bullet. He asked me the wrong question, which I answered correctly."

Baker cleared his throat, adjusted his posture, tightened his face, de-googlied his psycho wife-swapper eyes, and confronted the big bad meanie Swagger directly. But not before swallowing and licking his dry lips.

"Sergeant, does the name '6.5 Creedmoor' have any meaning to you?"

"Sure it does."

"Isn't it true then, that you shot Juba with a bullet called a 6.5 Creedmoor?"

At least forty men in the audience laughed. Baker went eight-ball as if he'd just taken such a round right in his clockworks, looked around, swallowed some more, begged for help from anyone who would make eye contact with him, although few would.

"You asked me about a bullet. I answered you about a bullet."

"Could you explain then?"

"Sir, you really don't know enough about this stuff to be asking these questions," said Bob.

"Just answer the question please, Sergeant Swagger," said Mother Death.

"I did, ma'am. It isn't on me that this fellow doesn't know the difference between a bullet and a cartridge, much less how they fit together."

Everybody laughed. Baker seemed to deflate before their eyes. Googly, googly, googly.

"Explain then, please, Sergeant Swagger," said Mother Death. "We are waiting with bated breath."

"I'll make it simple for those that are having trouble keeping up with the class, ma'am."

Laughter, laughter, laughter. Googly, googly, googly.

"Sergeant, this isn't *Jimmy Fallon*. Please hold the sarcasm directed at Mr. Baker. That's my job."

Laughter, laughter, laughter.

"You two might have a future in stand-up," whispered Nick.

Meanwhile, Baker melted, shrunk, wilted, dissolved, dissipated, drained, miniaturized, and vaporized, all at once. His complexion had turned the color of yeast, his prim mouth the color of last week's flowers, assuming the maid hadn't thrown them out yet.

"All right," said Bob. "The whole thing you put into a rifle to make it fire is called a cartridge. That's what Mr. Baker means. Its name usually comes from the marketing department, designed to make it sell. It may or may not be an actual description. This cartridge—that is, a brass case, a certain amount of a certain kind of powder, a primer, and last of all a bullet, usually manufactured by someone else—was designed by a genius named Dave Emary at Hornady, the ammunition folks, a few years back. You see, cartridge development's all about finding some combination of elements, too many and too boring to cite, that make the end result into something special. What Dave was looking for was a round with exceptional long-range accuracy and wind-bucking attributes that was at the same time—contradictory, actually—both light in recoil and short in overall length, for mechanical advantages within the rifle itself. The closest anybody had come to it was the .308 Winchester, which has been the free world's sniper cartridge since the fifties. But it was never quite accurate enough and for years people have tried to come up with something better.

"So Dave combined a .308-like case—short—with a 6.5-millimeter bullet—long—and took advantage of the latest in propellants for energy without recoil in a small-amount package. The result was, at last, that special something. Light on recoil, so practice wasn't a burden, short in overall length for better mechanical function within the rifle, and the bullet itself, the Hornady 6.5mm 140-grain ELD, long so that the rifle's grooves get a better grip, imparting a faster spin which pays off in long-range accuracy. So when you asked me about the bullet, I answered about the bullet. Now I've just told you about the cartridge. Do you follow?"

"I do and I apologize for my mistake, Sergeant. But I do have the disadvantage of Harvard Law School," Baker said.

Laughter. It was a good move, because it showed he could poke fun at himself.

"Now, we have this brand-new super-cartridge, correct?" he continued.

"I wouldn't say super, I'd say highly accurate."

"Can you explain the peculiar name?"

"It's marketing, as I said, not particularly reliable. They call it 6.5, to identify the diameter, 6.5 millimeters being .264 thousandths of an inch. They don't call it a '.264' because that's a diameter—caliber, the proper term—that's never caught on. And they don't put in an 'mm,' abbreviation for millimeter, because that's a European designation, and American rifle shooters don't like European calibers or nomenclature. But they just can't call it '6.5' so they arbitrarily add the name 'Creedmoor,' which was a famous firing range in New York in the 1890s, back when shooting was the biggest sport in America. Calling it 'Creedmoor' was secret signaling that this was one designed for high accuracy. Plus, it was easy to remember and it was easy to say 'six-five Creed' in its casual form."

"And the accuracy is why you chose it?"

"Sir, I didn't choose it at all. It was Juba who chose it and used it to perform a previous three-hundred-yard murder in Wichita, Kansas.

He knew what an accurate, yet powerful and practical, cartridge it was. He was up-to-date in his firearms development knowledge. He must have been an *American Rifleman* subscriber."

"So it's a sniper cartridge?"

"It's just engineered to be accurate at ranges out to a thousand yards, pretty much no matter the conditions. The cartridge is useful to snipers, but it's also a match cartridge and a superior hunting cartridge. And as a consequence, it has been quite a hit for Hornady."

"Gee, you make the ammunition business sound like Hollywood, with all these big businesses employing creative people trying to put together a commercial smash."

"Now that you mention it—"

"Now, Sergeant, can you tell me if it has been adopted as a sniper round? I mean officially?"

Where is this going? Bob wondered.

"Well sir, military procurement is its own bag of worms. No military can just stop short and replace a system with a better system overnight. A few smallish, fast-moving, high-contact units have done so, but Big Army and the poverty-stricken Marines will be years behind. If they adopt it, it means re-barreling about twenty thousand rifles and surplussing millions of cartridges already procured, and rewiring a logistics system that's already more complicated than Russian history. They have to believe not that it's better, but that it's a *whole lot* better, to set that train in motion."

"Do you believe it's a whole lot better?"

"I've done a lot of shooting with it and my vote would be yes. It's not just incrementally better, it's radically better, particularly beyond three hundred yards, out to, say, a thousand. Our snipers should have the best." He caught himself from adding, "I wish I'd had it in Vietnam."

"Can you name the units that have adopted it?"

"Well, primarily the SEALs. They're very sniper-oriented, they get snipers and how tactically important they are. Chris Kyle, the great sniper in Iraq, he was a SEAL. There's another guy now writing fiction books who was a sniper in the wars. Started as a junior seaman, came out twenty years later a commander. I know his real name but I'm not going to tell you. He calls himself Jack Carr. As for the cartridge, I'm hoping the Marine Corps will follow the SEALs' lead. As for the Army, it's so big and slow and clumsy in its logistics and decision-making, that's probably a long way off. Maybe Special Forces will get going on it. Once that happens, it'll begin to infiltrate law enforcement, who are still pretty much in the .308 world."

"Do you think your enthusiasm for the cartridge informed your decision to use it?"

"Sir, as I have just said, I didn't choose it. Juba chose it. On the day of the event, a young FBI agent secured it for me because he could get his hands on it faster. It was in the FBI firearms lab on the fifth floor, the tactical gun vaults were in the sub-basement. Plus I'm sure he knew the people in firearms, whereas he didn't in the vault area. The vault people would have insisted on paperwork. The lab people accepted on trust his urgency, gave it to him without paperwork. The fact that I was able to hit Juba at exactly the last second is testimony to the wisdom of his decision. If he'd have gone through channels, I might still be on that roof waiting."

"Do you know what date the SEALs adopted it?"

"Not exactly, no. Sometime last year."

"I actually have the date here," said Baker. He read it aloud.

Then he said, "Do you see the significance, Sergeant?"

"I suppose you mean to point out it happened *after* I took my shot."

"Exactly. So at the time you took the shot, no American military or police units had officially adopted this 'cartridge,' is that so?"

Bob looked at Sally, covered his mike, and whispered, "What's this bird onto?"

"I'm not getting it either," she said.

Bob went back, uncupped the microphone.

"No sir. But later—"

"Sergeant, I'm not asking about later. I'm

asking about a particular time, a particular day, a particular minute. A second even."

Swagger could only nod.

"So the cartridge—and the bullet it fired—was unauthorized, unvetted, unsubjected to the rigors of an objective testing system?"

"It was being tested by the SEALs in—"

"But that testing was not complete. I have the records right here and will distribute them to the committee."

At that second, interns walked along the table that fronted the panel, handing out documents that would surely not even be opened.

Swagger said nothing.

"So officially there had been no finding on that bullet, wouldn't you say, Sergeant?"

"Officially no, but I had seen its effectiveness in Wichita and had shot seven antelope and one mule with it. All were one-shot kills."

"True enough, but that has no official significance. It has no legal significance."

"Madam Chairman," interrupted Sally, "I'm incredulous that Representative Baker would hold a technical detail against an American hero who saved one life for certain and, by implication of the plot, perhaps hundreds or thousands more. Under great pressure and at considerable risk to his own life, Sergeant Swagger performed a deed that should rightfully be remembered for years."

"Madam Chairman, this isn't a matter of

character or courage or any such thing. It's a matter of law. The sergeant has admitted that the bullet he used was not through its testing and recommendation cycle. Therefore it was unauthorized. What he knew or didn't know about it is immaterial. As long as an official finding had not been rendered, it was the government's legal position that anything could happen when he fired and no matter what, that position has the force of law."

"What is the congressman getting at, for goodness' sake?" demanded Sally. "As he's proven he doesn't know enough about this issue to ask reasonable questions. He's just stabbing in the dark."

"Well," said Baker, "for one thing the bullet could have been overly penetrative. At least seven people die a year, as near as we can tell, from bullets that pass through one person and hit another, killing the second one. He could have missed, and given the bullet's energy and speed, it could have passed through a wall and hit a child across the way. It could have exploded—"

"It didn't have no explosive charge," said Swagger. "Things don't just explode."

"Well, it could have hit something, a gas line, an electrical conductor, some wiring or transformers, and caused them to explode. It could have started a fire. If it's moving so fast, it's obviously hot, and if it hit something flammable, it could have ignited. If I'm not mistaken, when the FBI fired into the Waco commune, that started a fire that killed everyone inside."

"Those were tear gas shells," said Bob.

Baker went on.

"Perhaps it might have hit something hard and been moving so fast—remember it is unique in its perfect relationship between weight and speed, as the sergeant has testified—perhaps it would have hit and splattered and thrown lethal pieces of shrapnel, also at supersonic speed, and they would have harmed innocent civilians. Perhaps it might have struck a pipe at an angle, ricocheted, and reached street level and maimed or killed someone down there. I'm not saying all these things would have happened, I'm saying they could have happened and that the bullet was therefore not safe to use in a law enforcement context."

Sally could stand it no longer.

"Again, Madam Chairman, allow me to point out the ludicrousness of this. He mischaracterizes a cartridge that very shortly thereafter the elite Navy SEALs selected as the perfect midrange sniper round, safe to use by its shooters, safe to use among collateral targets because of its superb accuracy. Then he attempts to make a case based on the tiniest of technicalities, namely that when Sergeant Swagger, under great duress and in a zone of combat expediency, used it to prevent what could have been a tragedy with unknown social ramifications, he was in violation of the law. I should remind you that he was in turn hit by devastating return fire and almost died on an operating table and has spent the last year in recovery. You would besmirch his heroism on a charge of using an unauthorized bullet? It's a scandal."

"Whatever the circumstance," said Baker, "it is incumbent upon police and military agencies to employ weapons that have been rigorously vetted for safety issues. That is one of the fundamental concepts of governance. It *protects* the innocent."

"No innocents were hurt. No innocents came close to being hurt. The counsel is so eager to score his preposterous little point on the fulcrum of a minor technical infraction, which no prosecutor in America would consider for more than a single second, that he cannot see what he is doing. And what he is doing is besmirching the honor of a brave man."

"I am not questioning the sergeant's bravery," said Representative Baker. "I mean him no disrespect and am as thankful as anybody for his action. However, the fact remains that the law is the law and he seems to have confessed not to a technical infraction of arcane rules, but far more seriously to a felony called 'wanton endangerment.' "

CHAPTER 24

The Bus

I t was a superb plan and everyone executed it superbly.

Feigning nausea and urgent pain, the five mystery-meaters and three other convicts were loaded aboard the Idaho Prison Bureau's armored bus to the bigger correctional facility at Kuna a few miles away. The lockup doctor had been persuaded to sign off on this subterfuge when an emissary from Vakha reached him with the suggestion that he do so, or Vakha would spring one of his boys to eat the man's children's hearts with strawberries and chocolate sauce. It was a remarkably convincing argument.

The five were, as per security protocol, wheelchaired to the bus in shackles, helped up the steps, put inside the cage, and seated. Their shackles were further secured to one of the steel bars that ran down either side. Then the three other complaining, whining convicts were handled in the same fashion. The cage was locked before the driver and two guards came aboard, the last two heavily armed with 12-gauge shotguns (Remington 870 pumps, fourteen-inch barrels) and Glock .40 service pistols. The bus then took off for the anticipated short trip to the big house and its promised medical haven.

The bus itself was a beast. Olive drab in color, it was the standard GM school bus variant, but had been modified extensively to prevent those from inside getting out, with bars and cages placed at various choke points and steel mesh welded against the windows.

Two blocks into the run, a black convict named Jasper Wilmont, up for armed robbery and assault with a deadly weapon, began to howl.

"I'm dying," he screamed. "Oh, Lord Jesus, my gut is killing me, oh Christ, I swear to God I'm dying, oh help me, Jesus, help me."

In normal circumstances the guards would have laughed at the convict's health issues and gone back to, respectively, a Sudoku game and ESPN news on the iPhone. But these were not normal times, they were post–Freddie Gray times, and everybody in law enforcement had been wised up by the situation in Baltimore, where a prison transit official had paid no attention to the screaming convict in the back of the wagon, and arrived at the destination to find that he had smashed his brain when he had been slammed back by sudden acceleration and was now paralyzed and comatose. He died a week later, setting off riots whose consequences were still being felt.

Thus the senior guard, the ESPN fan, had to act as if he gave a shit. He ordered the bus driver to halt, and the bus pulled onto a shoulder. Once secure to move about the cabin, the guard tried to open a dialogue with Jasper Wilmont, who immediately produced some authentic puke and began to buck convulsively against the various chain systems that bound him.

"I'm dying," he screamed. "My gut is killing me."

There was nothing in the bus's medical kit for such an emergency but a pink bottle of Pepto Bismol, but the guard knew that it had to be on the record that he had reacted alertly and compassionately. Besides, what could go wrong?

He unlocked the cage and stepped in to examine Jasper Wilmont. The violence that followed was immediate, precise, and devastating. It had been well-thought-out: criminal craft at the highest level. It turned on the fact that as experienced convicts, the mystery-meat guys had sublime lock-picking skills, and when necessary they could disentangle themselves from prison chains quite swiftly, using ballpoint pen cartridges as probes.

In less than a second the guard with the medical kit was hit with a savage blind-side block by Ibragim, illegal in the NFL but not in the real world. He was smashed sideways against the far wall. Ibragim followed up with a punch so hard to the temple it rendered the guard instantly unconscious and he flopped floorward like a dishrag.

Even as that happened, Anzor flashed past him through the cage door and was on the second guard before he could finish adding up his left diagonal line. His eyes widened with horror as Anzor's hammer of a fist crashed into his face, and he too went elastic with the shutdown of his senses and dropped akimbo into the land of the unconscious.

There was no need to hit the driver, because, seeing himself overmatched as Khasan raced to him on fighting tiptoes, fists readied for delivery, he instantly put up his hands in surrender. He was unarmed, and treated roughly enough as it was, forced by Khasan to the back of the bus, where he was locked in the shackles that had recently restrained Uncle Vakha.

Since he was still conscious, he was the one to whom Vakha addressed himself, even as the guards were dragged back to the same area, stripped, dumped, then chained.

"You want to see your babies again, sir? Then you sit here and don't make a move. You tell this to these fellows as well. They sit, they make no bother, they say nothing, and maybe they get out alive. No other way. We will not hesitate to kill. It means nothing to us."

Vakha watched as the three convicts not of the

family were busy pulling on the clothes off the unconscious guards and the conscious driver.

"We drop you on way to airport," he said. "Then you're on own, just as deal said. If caught, you say nothing till our plane has left. We keep our word, we are honorable among our own tribe."

"Whoa, mama," said Jasper Wilmont, buttoning up his corrections officer shirt over his convict-orange jumpsuit, "you the man, you the man, motherfucker. Ain't never seen no shit like that."

He put up a hand for a high five, but Vakha had no idea what a high five was and walked past him to the front of the bus where the boys were going over the ammo and guns.

Ibragim announced the inventory.

"Two shotguns, seven rounds in magazine, twenty-five rounds in pouches. Two Glock pistols, each with fifteen-round magazines and two more fifteen-round magazines. Also in storage bin, medical supplies, some Fast Klot, disinfectant and bandages, and one hundred flex cuffs, plus two clippers for snipping them off."

"We could use more guns and ammunition," said Anzor.

"We'll take them from the policemen we kill."

The five of them hunched in the front guard's position, variously armed. Magomet slid behind the wheel of the bus, started it, and shifted gears. The bus lurched ahead, pulling back onto the road, and was soon up to speed.

All in all, it had taken less than two minutes.

"To airport?" said Magomet.

"Well," said Vakha, pulling out a recent copy of the *Idaho Statesman*—"Hearing Continues into Second Week" was the banner—"maybe little detour."

INTERLUDE: 1780

We gathered at 8 and given the circumstances, Colonel Bruxhall's cooks put on a passable imitation of the great meals served in the regimental halls of London. Much port was served, much port was drunk, and it had the effect of eroding the pain of loss all felt.

It was here that I saw Major Bannister Winston up close for the first time. I have to say, he was not an unimpressive man, and even the intimate distance of the mess revealed no otherwise unseen warts, pimples, or general flaws. Strikingly handsome, he had a quality of élan, as the French would say, meaning elegant but at higher velocity. No word in English exists that quite defines this phenomenon; people were simply attracted to him, as if he were powered by some form of animal enchantment.

He was of course older than when I had witnessed him kill my friend at Chatham, but he wore the added years well. A darker fellow, ruddy of face, white of teeth, of weight substantial through shoulder and chest, well groomed, he wore the green tunic of the light dragoon magnificently, its many decorations and its red piping merely magnifying the soldierly effect.

It was clear that his troops adored him, if the lieutenants of his "Winston's Dragoons" were any indication, for they looked upon him with both reverence and trepidation, as a word from him could send them to ecstasy or despond.

"I hope, sir," he said to me upon introduction, "that the young lieutenant's conversation was of aid to you. It would be not only shame but waste for you to venture so far and get no product for your effort. It is likewise appropriate that even in death, Major Ferguson was of use to king and country. A brave officer, his loss shall be felt." His crowd of fellows chimed in with emanations of agreement.

I did notice peculiarities within the seemingly amiable society that had gathered. He stayed among his own, after a few words of greeting to the Colonel and his daughter, and made no assay to sit at the Colonel's table, where I seemed to be guest of honor. Again, in conversation with them at the commander's table, I heard no mention of the battle itself, the loss of Ferguson and so many of his men, as if pretending it had not happened meant that indeed, it had not happened. I noted too on Susanna Bruxhall's part, a kind of imposed discipline, as if she would not let the pain of loss impair her father's attempts to restore morale to his people, even if the Legionaries, as they called themselves—thugees would be another term— seemed to need no morale uplift.

Others did not mingle either. Major Hancock, Bruxhall's adjutant, stayed at the Colonel's side, somewhat awkwardly. A Lieutenant Murray, in command of four squads of foot at the cantonment, kept to his side of the room, along with a Lieutenant Moore, freshly bandaged about the head, who had arrived as a survivor of the King's Mountain affair just that morning.

And where was Lieutenant Grammercy? He had especially conspired for my presence, yet he was not in evidence himself. I thought that passing strange. How could there be a "fitting tribute to the greatness" of Major Ferguson without the Lieutenant?

(Editor's note: Detailed menu of a fine meal, cut with regret. —N.H.)

It occurred then, by convention, that a last round of toasts would conclude the evening.

And indeed, they did. I was celebrated, even though no one knew much of me, and I could have been a Yankee spy for what little they knew. The Colonel was toasted, two of his lieutenants toasted Major Winston rather extravagantly.

"Does no one wish to toast Major Ferguson?" Hancock at last ventured.

"I do," came the voice of Lieutenant Grammercy. He stepped from shadows where evidently he had been lurking. Now splendid in the full dress green tunic of Fraser's Highlanders, his major's serving unit, his boots shined like anthracite, his face bold and alive, his hanger in its polished scabbard a-dangle on his broad black belt.

"May it please the Colonel?" he inquired.

"Proceed then," said Bruxhall.

"I come," he proclaimed, "not to bury Patrick Ferguson, but to praise him."

This caused a bit of stir, a loosening of unease, as it was a clear claim of antecedence, via Shakespeare, to the most famous murder in history, that of Julius Caesar.

"Let it be said that he rode hard to duty every day in every way, even to the end. We shall not dwell on his many campaigns and wounds, as all are known. Nor shall we mention his advances to the art of arms, hoping to make the British soldier paramount on the battlefield for years to come. But let it be acknowledged that even in death there came victory. He died and many of his men as well, but he so blooded the Overmountain Boys that they were effectively destroyed. Their claims of twenty-three lost may be believed by historians, but in truth it was tenfold that number and they retreated en masse. Lord Cornwallis's western flank is now secure at least through winter and the General may have his way in Virginia for another year. Let us hope the General uses that gift wisely."

"Hear, hear," said Colonel Bruxhall. "That has been the gist of my dispatches." His daughter

Susanna clapped, as did those of foot. Winston's Dragoons remained somewhat doltish.

"I do wonder," said Grammercy, "as to why it had to be so. After all, were not the famed Dragoons but an hour's ride away, and had they been released to the sound of guns, it seems certain that our most excellent light horsemen would have executed the Bruxhall plan, which was to trap the Tennesseans, and slay and capture them, ending the threat to Lord Cornwallis not for the season but for the war?"

No one said a word. This direct assault on a fellow officer's decision in battle was not of any tradition.

"Lieutenant Grammercy," said the Colonel, "this being neither appropriate to time nor place, I believe if you have complaint and charge, you must bring them to me, and they will be investigated and by turn adjudicated, according to Army regulations."

"I fear, sir," said Grammercy, "that Major Winston has his admirers throughout the staff and the facts would not be fair addressed."

"Be that as it may, Lieutenant, regulations are quite clear on what is permitted."

"Rather," said Grammercy, "I seek redress. I officially, by sanction of Code Duello of 1777, call out the Major and enjoin him to meet me and a second on the parade ground at dawn tomorrow. Death can be the only justice."

Of course the inevitable silence. Then, stirring amongst the British Legion officers, quelled by a hand from their commander.

"Code Duello specifically prevents junior officers from calling out seniors," said Colonel Bruxhall, seeking to halt the situation from its slide to madness. "Else our army would be an anarchy of death matches and all good military order would vanish, particularly on campaign, when it factionalizes the troops and breeds distrust and contempt, even more so enmity, between forces which must trust and coordinate with each other in battle. Therefore, by the wide authority granted commanding officers on campaign, I declare such an event forbidden and illegal. The sergeant at arms will enforce that decree."

"Sir, I make no military charge. Code Duello, on certain issues, is outside the reach of even the commanding officer, sir."

"Walk carefully here, Grammercy," said Major Winston. "No need to end up pickled on my sword point for a figment of imagination and an imagined insult."

"Thank you, sir, for your warning. But now I invoke Rule 10 of the code. 'Any insult to a lady under a gentleman's care or protection to be considered as, by one degree, a greater offense than if given to the gentleman directly and be regulated accordingly.' I charge that on numerous occasions Major Winston has referred to Miss Susanna Bruxhall, the commanding officer's daughter who graces this very room, as 'Ferguson's wench,' or 'Ferguson's whore.' ' "

"Leave us stop this nonsense here," said Winston, "unless this fool boy desires to lie in mud tomorrow morning. While I would of course regret and apologize for my untoward words, spoken under spell of drink and fatigue of battle, and will formally do so upon conclusion of this madness, there is no evidence that in any way Miss Bruxhall was 'under a gentleman's care,' the gentleman being Major Ferguson."

"Not so, sir," said Miss Bruxhall. "Indeed, my father married Patrick and me two months back. We thought it best to hold it private as to not introduce new species of concern among the troops, your dragoons included."

Hubbub in general broke out. But soon enough, Colonel Bruxhall put it to halt.

"I see you know your Duello, Lieutenant," he said. "But I fear you did not read far enough into it. There is still something of a codicil by which this affair must be halted."

Neither the Lieutenant nor the Major said a thing.

"I refer to Rule 14. 'Seconds must be of equal rank in society with the principals they attend in as much as a second may choose or chance to become a principal, and equality is indispensable.' I infer from that in this case, since Winston is a major, not only he but you must have a major as a second. Alas, gentlemen, with Ferguson's death we have a want of majors. While Major Winston will avail himself of Major Hancock, you have no major to call upon."

I saw exactly at that second why Grammercy was so pleased at my appearance. I was in fact the fulcrum upon which his whole campaign pivoted.

"Why, sir, at your very table is the distinguished visitor, a Surveyor of the Board of Ordnance, Major Matthew Kavanagh. An able veteran of war and campaigns, as well solidly vetted in administrative procedure and regulation and for all of that beyond reproach, he is the second no man could more desire. Major Kavanagh, sir, I humbly beseech you. Will you, sir, be my second at dawn tomorrow at the parade ground?"

I had doubts. I had no conception of what skill Grammercy possessed of blade, as his course into the officer's ranks had been via the spies, and he seemed likely to have missed the formal swordsmanship as taught at Sandhurst, where I had learned mine, much less the constant drilling on the regimental training fields. But on the other hand, such chances for just revenge come along seldom so neatly packed as this, and while I owed it to the Lieutenant, I also owed it to Scott-Browning, dead these many years at Chatham.

"You may be certain of it, sir," I said.

CHAPTER 25
Plans

A glum crew slid into conference room number four, where an assistant had provided the lunch break's menu of BLTs, fries, and Cokes from a nearby takeout. Nobody said a thing. Sally waited until another assistant slid a paper into her hand, then read, while the others ate silently.

" 'Wanton endangerment.' Usually brought in state courts, but the Justice Department can fold it into 'crimes of violence' statutes if it so desires. Rare, but it happens, and there are precedents to make it stick. Hardly ever done. I guess it's in there when the infraction takes place on federal property and local ordinances can't be applied. Usually the punitive disposition is a fine as applied by the court, or community service. There is a provision for not more than two years in prison. The formal definition is 'acts that create a substantial risk of serious physical injury to another person.' 'Wanton' is a step higher than its more usual form, 'reckless,' the implication being that the accused knew of the danger he was inflicting, but consciously decided to proceed. The accused person isn't required to intend the resulting or potential harm, but must have acted in a way that showed a 'disregard for the foreseeable consequence of the actions.' Basically anything under the sun. It's vague, so vague that I suppose it could be applied here and could ipso facto be forwarded to the Justice Department for investigation and recommendation to prosecute. I have to say, I never saw this one coming."

"Any police shooting could be called 'wanton endangerment,'" said Nick. "When you release a bullet into society, there's always that chance of unexpected consequences. They say, 'Every bullet has a lawyer attached.'"

"I think that's the point," said Sally. "In fact, I think, if they get their unanimous finding and referral to Justice, they don't give a damn what happens to Swagger."

"Dogs and cats living together, war is peace, two plus two is five, no cop can shoot back or even shoot," said Nick.

"It'll play brilliantly with their base," Sally went on. "The protocols will be so severe that cops and other agents are defenseless. The proposition is legal enfranchisement of the idea that the possibility of collateral damage trumped paying the perp down. It therefore implies the perp's life is more valuable than the cop's and is more worth protecting. It means that the policeman's duty is to die, rather than to kill. Great for morale. Bye-bye SWAT, bye-bye snipers. Bob, I have to apologize. I never saw this coming."

"Who could have?" said Swagger. "It's so crazy it seems impossible."

"And tactically it's brilliant," said Sally. "That little schmuck Baker, give him his due. He came up with something utterly simple as the fulcrum for the campaign."

"As politics, it's fucking dynamite," said Nick.

"And the worst part," said Bob, "is that I'm guilty."

"Of course you are," said Sally. "And if the great Bob Lee Swagger is guilty, then everyone is guilty."

"Okay, what's next? I mean, after I finish my sandwich."

"Well, I guess—" began Sally, but at that moment an intern from the committee chairman's staff knocked, was admitted, and came to Sally and whispered.

"All right," she finally said, "if that's what she wants."

The young man left.

"Yes, well, it makes sense. They want to strike now, when their little victory is fresh in everybody's mind. She has decided to call a vote this afternoon on a motion she will put forward that a finding be forwarded to the Justice Department that the shooting of Juba the Sniper, aka Sergeant Al-Aqua, on such and such date violated fair standards of wanton endangerment and therefore should be investigated for possible criminal intent."

"Ludicrous," Nick said. "It'll get thrown out in two seconds."

"But then she'll tailcoat revisions to the Crime Act of 1994 that will 'prevent this from ever happening again,' and she'll do it fast while momentum is high. She'll get it through because enough of the people who agree with us in the House don't want to inflame their own political enemies, with reelections coming up. The unanimity will make it 'bipartisan.' "

Nobody said a thing. The sandwiches seemed to have gotten cold fast, the French fries soggy, and the Cokes warm.

"Nothing we can do?" asked Bob.

"One decision remains," said Sally. "Before the vote is called, each of the teams will be allowed a fifteen-minute summation. Obviously Baker will deliver theirs. But the speaker isn't specified, which means that Bob, you could do it."

Swagger sighed.

"I don't like to explain myself," he said.

"But that's what America wants to hear. They don't want to hear someone named Sally. They want to hear Bob the Nailer, Patrick Ferguson's great-great-whatever-grandson, Charles's grandson, Earl's son who still worships the old gods. They want to hear from the sacred killer. We've got half an hour yet, we can put together some talking points."

Again, Swagger sighed. This was not his kind of war and he'd usually chosen to be eloquent only in his silence. But she was right. It had to be him.

In the other camp, victory fever ran high. Congressman Baker accepted flattery, pats on the back, high fives, handshakes, and the other accoutrements of success with a modest, if fraudulent, blush. PR genius Feeley told him he'd made himself a star in that one single moment. Someone read from the *Times* website the first and fastest account of the genius and his triumph.

"Sniper acknowledges shot was taken with 'unauthorized ammunition,' " read the headline, over the David Banjax byline.

Boise, Idaho—In a stunning admission, retired Marine Gunnery Sergeant Bob Lee Swagger acknowledged that the bullet he'd fired at alleged terrorist 'Juba the Sniper' in a highly publicized event last year had yet to be adopted by any armed forces or law enforcement agencies in the world.

Representative Ross Baker argued that the former sniper and decorated war hero is therefore open to charges of 'wanton endangerment,' which involves committing acts highly dangerous to civilians and bystanders. It does not require that such consequences occur.

"No one knew what could happen," said Representative Baker, who has been arguing his party's case against Sergeant Swagger on the use of force issue, the fulcrum of these hearings.

Representative Baker cited some possibilities, including explosive detonation, incendiary effects, electrical blackouts, or over-penetration, which could lead to physical harm in other apartments in the building which were occupied at the time.

In general, experts say, it takes several years for a piece of equipment or other potentially lethal addition to the federal arsenal to be analyzed and field-tested before it is found acceptable for such use. In this case, the bullet, a 6.5-millimeter Creedmoor, was undergoing testing in certain sniper detachments in Afghanistan, but no finding and recommendation had been released and no move was underway to acquire the ammunition and the rifles to fire it for federal service.

"The reviews are in," said someone. "The *Times* loves it. You've got a hit on your hands! Welcome to Broadway."

A corner TV pumped out images of some CNN

haircut eunuch reading the news over canned shots of Swagger and Mother Death and hero-congressman Baker, while beneath it a crawl informed all that "Sniper used illegal, deadly bullet."

But somebody was missing. Where was She Herself? She had not, as usual, headed into the base camp with the others, even though it had been made certain that the best takeout in Boise was freshly delivered. Last seen, she was heading into a special room, "Congressional Representatives only," just down the hall from the steps leading into the school itself.

And then she arrived, a swirl of energy and focus blowing through the door, all business, all death.

The place fell silent and she let the silence build. You could hear a tear drop as she went to a table and picked up a sandwich—roast beef, rare, the color of her jacket, with Dijon on fresh pumpernickel—and a soft drink and came to the table.

"I am *so* hungry," she said. "Good Lord, I'll be happy to get out of this town soon."

She finished eating in silence, and finally looked up.

"Baker, do you now understand the difference between a cartridge and a bullet?"

"I do, Congresswoman," he said. "But—"

"But nothing. Once again, he made you look

stupid. I was trying to figure out whether the Tubas and Dildo Subcommittee was your destiny, or perhaps Sewers and Port-a-Potties."

Then she said, "Oh by the way, we won. Unanimously."

"But there hasn't even been a vote yet," said Feeley.

"We won *unanimously*. To get our friends on the other side to go along, we needed a *thing*. 'Untested bullet,' perfect. Explosions, dead babies, school bus crashes, electrical blackout, airplanes falling from the sky, superb. So that, plus the thirty-five million dollars in aid I promised both Brandon and Weinberg for their districts—a new airport and an extension of suburban railway lines—got us over the hump. Congratulations."

So the party got happy again. The TV was turned up. Singing busted out all over the meadow and the dale. The staff girls started up a chorus of "On Broadway," even though Broadway was in Manhattan, not DC, because, alas, no one in the Brill Building had written a song called "On K Street."

"Goodbye to Boise," someone said, "town without deli."

CHAPTER 26
Speechifying

L et's start with this cartridge," said Bob. It seemed the lights were up so bright he couldn't see a thing except refracted fragments of glare. He made sure the wheelchair was locked tight so he wouldn't roll away from the microphone before him, and he tried not to notice the two cameras at either end of the representatives' table eating him up.

"I have to tell you I have been around guns my whole life, on ranges, on missions, on hunts, in competitions. I've never seen a .264 Hornady do any of the things Mr. Baker says this one might be able to do. It's not an artillery shell. It's not any harder or stronger or more destructive than any other like-sized bullets. It's just another bullet. But let's be honest. This isn't just about Juba and me, and what happened between us. It's about something bigger."

He paused, collecting.

"I'll start with Eric Blair, Englishman, wrote under the name of George Orwell. *1984*, *Animal Farm* are his famous ones. He said something— or maybe he didn't say it, maybe someone else

211

said it, and it got credited to him, it seems nobody's sure on this—but it says what I believe as well as anything. He said, 'Thousands of people sleep secure in their beds each night because rough men stand ready to do violence on their behalf.' "

He breathed in, tried to make solid eye contact with seven of the eight faces across the room and elevated from his position, figuring no eyeball-to-eyeball would help with someone nicknamed Death.

"I'm one of those rough men. I do the violence that more comfortable folks would prefer not to think about. I have killed, more than any man should have to, and what that's cost me is my business alone, nobody else's, except to say you wouldn't want my dreams. But I take pride nevertheless in being a rough man. There are people who need to be killed, and if that's the case, as most recognize, you need someone who's a professional to do the killing.

"It seems I come from a long line of killers. A Scottish soldier, an FBI gunfighter, a brave Marine who took part in five invasions in the Pacific in World War II and received the Medal of Honor for what I'm sure was the least of his heroic deeds in that war. He died in a cornfield in Arkansas, shot down by criminals. My grandfather went hell-deep into alcohol and died alone, and had few mourners at his funeral, none from the FBI. My great-great-grandfather was killed on a mountaintop in North Carolina, with most of his men. And in between, surely there were soldiers, lawmen, or just old civilian men with guns. I have a feeling their deaths were lonesome and uncelebrated too. They all ended up facedown in the dirt. The dirt always wins.

"So killers know what to expect: it ain't much.

"But that's okay. We know where we fit in. We're like a gun in the house. We make people nervous, nobody wants to know too much about us, and you-all shun the people like us who are enthusiastic about such things. But maybe there comes a night when the gun is needed, just as maybe there comes a day when the sniper is needed, or the commando or the cop, and in those moments you *love* us. We are your best friend, your long-lost brother, your comforting mother. You need us desperately, you yearn for us, at least for a few fast and dangerous moments. So we go and do what we have to do. We make the shot, we do the killing. You call it 'duty' and say we owe it to some code that you invented. But sure as rain falls and the wind howls, when it's over, you remember how uncomfortable we make you, and once again, you exile us.

"That's just the way it is. I do understand that Congressman Baker and the folks behind him clearly have a wider aim. They're not really trying to get this particular cartridge banned and they're not even trying to get me banned. It's simply that they don't like Mr. Orwell's rough men. So they're trying to get rid not just of me, but of *all* rough men. They think that rough men are the problem, not the solution. But I guarantee you, there will yet come a time when you need rough men, and if you think you won't, that is the true wanton endangerment. Thank you."

"Believe it or not, Sergeant Swagger," said Baker, goo-goo-googling him full power, "I understand your anger. I have no doubt you acted in good faith. I don't doubt your heroism as you proceeded, knowing that to make the shot you had to take the countershot. I applaud your stamina and life force in recovering from the ordeal, and I hope you're out of that wheelchair soon enough. Everyone here does. And I also understand why you might put this one in your 'No good deed goes unpunished' file.

"And you are right when you say that you're not really the agenda here. We mean you no harm or disrespect. We feel no hatred, we have no desire to destroy or humiliate. We wish we could just let it go.

"But we can't. We ourselves have a duty. We must do that duty no matter how onerous it seems and no matter that we know multitudes will hold us in contempt. It's the price we pay, and perhaps you wouldn't want our dreams either."

He turned to the congressmen and -women.

"As outstanding an American man as Gunnery Sergeant Bob Lee Swagger is," he said, "he is obsolete. He is an anachronism. He is a relic. He is the creation of a mindset that believed for hundreds of years, maybe thousands of years, across time and history, before history even, as it's not distinctly an American phenomenon, that it was his duty to kill those whose culture and vulnerability and pathos and genuine bad luck put them in the path of what was once conquest and then expansion and then colonialism and is now sustainment of an evil system. They did so under the delusion that their God ordained and encouraged it, and they did so because it was fun.

"It's not enough to say we didn't know. Or it was different then. Or nothing we did was illegal. Or it was the will of God. Or it was in defense of hearth, home, community, state, baseball, and country. In defense, if you will, of civilization. That was said by the defenders of slavery. It was said by the Ku Klux Klan. It was said by the Nazis. It was said by everyone, every nation, every creed that felt it had a natural entitlement to rule and dispense justice or the lack thereof from the barrel of a gun.

"We can only say to that: you should have known, and you should be held accountable. It doesn't matter how pure your heart was at the instant of killing or to what degree you followed the cues of your leaders, your education, and your culture. You must be held accountable in some way for the blood you have spilled.

"For there is a higher law at play here. It is the moral law of the universe. It holds that all people are equal and that none has the right to kill, invade, enslave, commit genocide, steal or loot, rape and pillage, slaughter and maim, and it's true of men and true of nations. I am happy to say that I represent that moral force in the universe and that I work toward a day when what I desire of men and nations will not be some distant utopian fantasy but a workable, practical reality. I know we will never achieve that if we see every problem as a nail and our hammer is only a 6.5-millimeter Creedmoor bullet or cartridge or whatever.

"As this distills itself into practicality, it mandates that moral law must be able to scrutinize every possible incident involving the use of force. It is clear that too often policemen shoot those they believe are criminals only to learn they are merely of another color. It is clear that too often snipers kill those they believe are guerillas only to learn they were teachers and that student papers, not bombs, were in those briefcases. It is clear that too often bomber pilots discharge their loads on enemy bunkers that prove to be hospitals or schools.

"We must instead morally discipline ourselves

to reach out to those who might be the object of force so that they understand where they are and who we are, and they must be afforded a chance at a sympathetic listener before—if ever—such force is used. In other words, we believe there is no such thing as 'righteous' force. Force is force is force, and it should only be used in a tiny, tiny, microscopic percentage of cases, and when that happens we should mourn, not cheer.

"This case is particularly resonant. It vibrates beyond its narrow confines. We must listen to what it is telling us, and we must answer.

"Sergeant Swagger has told no lies. Every night we pore over his testimony, seeking some evidence of malfeasance, untruth, manipulation of fact, omission of fact, all the tricks we'd feared his lawyers might have taught him. But if they tried, he didn't listen.

"But there is one fact he cannot change. At that time and that place, officially that bullet, cartridge, round, slug, whatever the jargon is, was illegal.

"Many will ask: Who cares? What difference can it make? Technicalities, nuances, gobble-dygook, the province only of pointy heads in ivory towers or politicians who have never held much less fired a gun in their lives.

"But here's the crucial point, maybe the point of the whole enterprise: use-of-force incidents must be held to the absolute highest standards of commission. There should never be any short-cuts, any technicalities, any evasions, any argued interpretations.

"And this is but one of the sweeping changes that must come to the tradition of force usage in America.

"Here are some others: Every attempt must be made to reach the possible victim of such action. If that is not possible, then law enforcement should withdraw until it can be achieved. Moreover, a psychiatric professional must review the case and sign off on its disposition. In most cases withdrawal is to be preferred over confrontation and execution. That shot must never be fired unless it is absolutely necessary.

"And what is absolutely necessary? Not incoming fire. Policemen must be prepared to retreat rather than return fire. Hostage situations? Almost all can be solved by time, not recourse to violence. Wait them out, don't shoot them down. Should police have access to sniper weapons, automatic rifles, grenades? No. Such implements should be under the absolute control of the federal government and a court order must be obtained to deploy them, and after the incident they should be immediately returned to federal lock and key. Eventually, police firearms should be replaced by nonlethal technology. That will take years. In the meantime, one of our policy recommendations is to defuse the kill-or-be-killed mindset. Police firearms training should be oriented not to the kill but to the wound. If you can shoot a man in the head, you can shoot him in the leg. If you can shoot a man in the chest, you can shoot him in the shoulder. And maybe getting shot by him is part of your responsibility to your fellow citizen and your fellow man. That is the true courage."

There was no stopping him now. This was his moment, and it came pouring out of him in perfectly formed sentences perfectly enunciated and timed, mellow, suave, convincing. He was at his apogee.

"And I'll take it one more step. For thousands of years human beings have been divided into those two eternally warring tribes, 'us' and 'them.' It is that division that enables, indeed requires, that we, us, our side, the guys, the team, whatever, kill them, the bad guys, the hordes, the minions, the insect people, the tidal wave. If we permit ourselves to turn people of a different class or creed or color into 'others,' we are halfway down the road to slaughter. We must stop the 'othering' of those we do not know and accept as our premise the idea that there is no 'other.' We are all the same.

"So we must end the theory and practice of the other. We must realize how just as Sergeant Swagger and Juba the Sniper are the same man, so are Americans and Nigerians, Brits and Chinese, Christians and Muslims, Russians and

Poles. There is no biological, no economic, no spiritual, no legal reason to kill. It will take time and strength, and the road is hard. We are just beginning it. But I am sure that the day of the sniper is over and the day of the brother has just begun.

"And that is why, my fellow congressmen and -women, in your wisdom and compassion you must begin this process so that—"

The universe disintegrated.

The crash of impact so loud it struck ears, vibrations like swarms of lizards everywhere, respiration jammed, a plague in an instant. A front of dust and debris riding suddenly released thermals of destruction, unfolding and enveloping. An atmosphere full of shrapnel and glass. Chaos, panic, raw fear, the screams of the crushed and mutilated. Everything went to blur, got faster and slower at once.

In a second the catastrophe organized itself to perception. A large green bus had smashed through the double doors of the building, shredding them, then plowed onward into the audience. It slowed at the impediments, human or otherwise, to its buzz-saw tires, progress reduced to lurch and crunch, yet still it came. When it ground to a halt, leaving a trail of maimed and murdered behind and the survivors stunned into paralysis, men in orange jumped out of it and began shooting.

CHAPTER 27
ZZZZZZZZZ

t was an interesting dream. His mother. A girl who had been in his homeroom in the seventh grade in Plano, Texas. Machine guns. Geishas, quite beautiful, pale and delicate. What appeared to be flying demons of some sort, possibly based on a memory of helicopters. An image from a seventies TV show starring somebody named Bill. Penny loafers. These themes repeated randomly, zooming in and out, pulsating. The plot was also random, involving congruencies between any two or three of the main icons. Music, also: "Deep in the Heart of Texas."

Ultimately, the music dominated, then predominated. It drove the other material away until he realized it was the ringtone of his cell.

He blinked awake. Nondescript motel room, off the interstate. Darkness. The sound of tractor-trailers racing by on the highway, outward bound. Where was he? Then it returned to him. He grabbed the phone, knowing that only one person knew this number, as it was a recently purchased cheapo, from Target.

"Yeah?" he said.

"Delta, have you seen the TV?"

"No, I was resting for later."

"Man, there may be no later. Check it out. I'll call back in ten."

He found the remote, clicked it to on, surfed through another dreamscape of random imagery and figures until at last he came to a local channel and made out an earnest reporter fronting what looked to be some sort of disaster from the pulsing gumballs in the background. The fellow's face wore an expression that was 90 percent fear and confusion and 10 percent Big Story ambition. Delta cranked up the volume as he noted the emblem "NEWS TEAM 11" in one corner and a crawl reading "Latest from hostage scene at Frank Church High School."

"—unknown at this time how many remain inside the building and law enforcement refuses to comment yet, but it seems certain that at least some of the eight U.S. congressmen, plus many media people, have been taken hostage by prisoners escaping from the Ada County Lockup in a Department of Corrections bus. No demands have been made, but the presence of so many ambulances suggests many casualties. Law enforcement has cordoned off the area. You can see over my shoulder the gaping hole in the building where the prison bus smashed through the doors and into the auditorium, which held the ongoing House Subcommittee on Terrorism hearings into an incident from last year. We have yet to get an official account of the situation, but there are many heavily armed law enforcement officers on-site"—the over-the-shoulder shot disappeared in favor of an image of a heavily armed and armored SWAT operator from the State Police moving into a covering position with his M4 at the ready, while another cop, this one a Boise municipal officer in standard duty rig, yelled at reporters and cameramen to keep back.

Delta watched, gathering it all in, trying to calculate the significance of it, wondering WTF is this. But the insight came almost instantaneously, and at that moment Niner called again.

"Are you thinking what I'm thinking?" asked the explosives expert.

"Yeah. Those have to be our guys. They somehow learned they were about to be outed, and once that happened, the Russians would come hard after them. Dammit, the old guy is smart. He outsmarted us, probably just by a day or two."

"Is it off? Do we break camp and head home?"

"No. Let me think on it. Oh wait, answer this. Can you rethink your package and come up with something you can remote from off-site that'll blow a hole in that wall?"

"Delta, you're not—"

"I just want to know what's possible."

"Technically it's easy enough. Yeah, I can

reshape so that the force is directed toward a single small point, and blow through it."

"Okay, let me watch for a while, and you go ahead and rebuild your charge. We have to recon, at least to the point it's possible. I also have to get some gear to make it all work. The fact that there'll be so many SWAT guys from so many jurisdictions is in our favor."

"Can you bluff your way in close?"

"Let me think on it. I'll call you back when I'm set to move and tell you where to pick me up. Hope you got some sleep. It's going to be a hard day's night."

CHAPTER 28

Inside

Vapors and rancid dust filled the air at a speed beyond light. Papers whirled in sudden typhoons of energy. The overhead lights, shaken by vibration, strobed as they swung, revealing and obscuring at random, as if God were blinking at what his creations had suddenly wrought. Noises beyond identification fought against each other, and more vibrations shook the foundations in ominous rhythms, as if a quake were about to ratchet open the earth and send everybody swirling to hell.

Some moved, some didn't. Some panicked, some froze. Some ran fast, dragging others. Some ducked, crawled, and prayed. Some didn't react at all. Some screamed, some reached for loved ones, some felt their hearts nearly explode in their chests and the air suddenly dryer than cotton in talcum powder. More than a few shat. Even more urinated. One had a stroke, another a minor heart attack. Some realized immediately what had happened. Some refused to believe what had happened.

Of those that understood one universe had been

destroyed and another reconfigured into a much harsher place in a single instant, Bob, with the most experience, reacted first. He stood, thinking of the weak—that is women, and how else had he been acculturated to think?—and reached to grab Sally and the female interns on the staff sitting behind her.

It was an ill-considered move, because he'd been sitting in the wheelchair for over seven hours, the tramadol had worn off, he had not made any kind of adjustment to the pain about to hit. So he stood up and collapsed in the same instant, dropped crazily to the floor and struck his head hard enough for the disorientation to scramble his mind. Blood ran down his face, pain bounced around inside his skull.

Nick bent to him, but he knew enough to yell, "Get your people out of here!"

And Nick did just that. Unarmed, aware that he was in the epicenter of lethal danger—a shot sounded, then another, people seemed to be finding it in themselves to achieve animal flight—he stood, grabbed Sally, and signaled to all interns, boys and girls, to get their asses up. It took him less than a tenth of a second to assemble a blueprint of the building from his mental files and another tenth to come up with a plan.

"That way, that way!" he screamed, a harsh father who would not brook disagreement, and got them up and moving. They faded back into the wings of the auditorium stage, toward an EXIT sign glowing in the dark. That led downstairs—they were the first to discover this route, but others clamored after, to a hall that took them back into Frank Church itself. He herded them along, but others, younger, faster, or more panicked, shot by and reached the first exit on the left, blew through the double doors and into the presumed safety of the outdoors.

"Everybody here?" Nick demanded in the sunlight.

"I saw Margie fall! She—"

"No, I'm here," Margie called out.

"What about Alex? I don't see Alex!"

"He was way up front. He's long gone."

"Sally, check them out."

Sally, frazzled, did a quick head count.

"All here, assuming Alex is out," she said.

"Okay, stick with me, we're heading to the parking lot, where we'll cluster at the van and see what's what."

"Shouldn't we help?"

"You'll just get in the way and get yourself killed. You can't help if you're dead. Law enforcement will have to handle this. Come on now, go! Tell them, Sally!"

"Go, go," said Sally.

The sound of a few more shots hastened them on their way.

Nick got them scrunched down behind the

car that had brought Bob, counted again, and concluded they at least were okay.

"You stay here until cops escort you to safety. Sally, don't let anybody go unless you see men in orange coming toward you. Then run like hell."

Then he pulled his iPhone, dialed a number he knew by heart.

"FBI, Night Duty Officer."

"This is Nick Memphis. Get me Emergency Ops, right away."

"Yes, sir."

The line went dead, a few clicks followed, and then he got the Emergency Operations office.

"Ops, McCallister."

"Yes, Memphis here. I'm in Boise—"

"Nick, we're suddenly getting crazy reports."

"Okay, here's what it is. You have to call in senior management, fast. It looks like four or five prisoners out of some Idaho installation jacked a bus. They crashed the congressional hearing at Frank Church High School. It's still unsettled, but I'm guessing the plan is to take the eight congressmen hostage—"

"Jesus—"

"Yeah, for some kind of leverage. I don't know their demands yet. It's still crazy here. But I do I know they've killed two Idaho State cops and maybe six or seven civilians crashing the bus into the auditorium. These guys are for real."

"Who are they?"

"No idea. I'm saying prisoners because all I saw were orange jumpsuits and the bus had 'Department of Corrections' on it. I'm headed over to what looks like incident command now, but nobody's organized, nobody's in charge yet. Get our Boise people out here. Get the director in. The president should be notified."

"It's already happening."

"Okay, I'll call back when I know more."

"Nick," another voice came on the line, Charlie Parks, head of Terrorism, "Nick, I just got in. Since its federal and looking like you're senior man on-site, you'll have to run the show."

"Roger that," said Nick.

Baker sat. His mind shut down. Nothing made any sense.

The bus had come to a halt less than twenty-five feet away, right at the edge of the stage. He was vaguely aware of men in orange coming out of the doors and firing rifles. The guns were so loud. He winced, becoming smaller at each percussion. He was aware that the reporters, clustered close to the stage, had enough time to spew left and right before being crushed. But he could see a lane of smashed and bent and tossed chairs tracking exactly the path of the bus through the crowd. Several people lay in it, some in the stillness of death, others screaming over legs that would never work again, or shoulders bashed toward the grotesque, or bloody rents or gashes, some spurting arterially, some merely copiously. It was a scene from Bosch's hell vision, an association his suddenly worthless education prompted him to make.

Someone shoved a pistol into his face. He looked up into a face not from Bosch but from Brueghel—that fucking education again!—a kind of ur-peasant of hideous bellicosity, features all knotted in action urgency, nose like an axe's blade, lips taut and bloodless, eyes dark and wide as saucers full of acid. The man was yelling, poking him in the throat. He channeled his hearing and made out, "Who bosses? Which are bosses?"

He gobbled for air, felt a dizzy swoon begin to swirl through him, but had enough smarts left to raise a finger and gesture toward the panel behind him, where all eight congressmen sat, too elderly, too shocked, stupefied, to do anything but watch in wide-eyed anticipation and dread as the world went eight-ball, that is, except for Congresswoman Venable, who was screaming *"Who are these motherfuckers?"*

Everybody had a job. It was not left to improvisation. Any plan was better than no plan, and this was a sound plan.

Anzor, best with guns, most experienced, shot one policeman from the door of the bus. His height gave him an angle over the still-frozen crowd near the stage; he held for the face, not knowing if his target was armored, and fired. No sights on a shotgun of course, but his hand-eye was superb and well practiced, and he sent a screaming swarm of #4 tactical shot into the face as the man struggled to unsling his M4. Results immediate, devastating, complete.

Anzor stepped off the bus, angling a step to the left, braced himself over the hood, and zeroed the second officer. The man had gotten his M4 unslung, but was struggling to insert a loaded magazine, having at least dropped the empty the weapon carried ceremonially. He was too far behind the curve and hadn't thought to move off the X. Anzor put a #4 blast into his head too, knocking him back, down, splayed wide, face a tatter of mess. Then Anzor pivoted and raced backward, cycling the shotgun as he went. His next task was the two guards who had been standing outside the double doors. Had they entered to bring war to the invaders or had they fled, or had they frozen? Anzor raced through the typhoon of fleeing citizens, looking for the uniforms that designated his targets. One was where he should be, in a crouch, rifle presumably stocked and cocked, red dot presumably activated, looking for someone to shoot but seeing nothing shootable as the screamers flooded by him. Unlike Anzor, he couldn't shoot through people, and so Anzor fired at him, hitting several with peripheral spray as the charge dispersed. They dropped, the officer dropped, people all around went to the floor. That let Anzor rush through them, kick the rifle from the cop, who had not been hit fatally but was in post-wound shock syndrome.

"Crawl and live," Anzor ordered, after plucking magazines from the belt around his waist and seizing his Glock.

He turned then. The other officer had either fled or raced inside, and Anzor suspected the former. He secured his treasures, racked the shotgun again, curled around the wreckage, and scanned the left sector of the auditorium as yet more folks fled by. He saw nothing.

Vakha, with a pistol, pulled himself onstage. People fled him. He fired a couple of shots to the roof to clear them out even faster. People seemed to be fleeing to the left, into the wings, where certainly there was an exit. But to the right, everyone seemed frozen. One man sat on the floor, away from the others as if lost in prayer.

Vakha closed in, poked him in the face with the pistol.

He looked up. Demon eyes! His eyes flashed and rolled, got very small, shrunken by fear as if they'd just been injected with something unpleasant. They looked like squirrel turds in goat's milk.

"Where are bosses?" Vakha demanded.

The man gibbered through a dry mouth and dry lips, unable to make words.

"Bosses?" Vakha demanded again, bringing the muzzle of the Glock to the man's madly jittering eyes.

No words. But he understood, pivoted timorously, and with a broad sweep indicated the eight old men and women sitting behind a panel on the highest tier, too old for rapid flight, all immaculate and beautiful in exquisite clothes. All were mortified solid, except for one old bitch in red screaming profanities in an anger so intense it actually gave Vakha a moment of pause. She must be insane.

On either side, Magomet and Khasan flanked him with pistols now leveled at the eight, while Ibragim, too busy for once to be angry, was collecting weapons and ammo from the two slain state policemen.

Vakha walked to the old lady, who turned to face him with a glare that could melt bank vaults.

"Who do you—"

He hit her hard in the face, an open-hand palm slap whose flesh-to-flesh smack snapped through the air. She fell sideways but not off her chair. It seemed her hair was fraudulent, and it fell off on the impact of the blow. But so important was it to her that even in this moment of maximum danger, she quickly snatched it off the floor and replaced it.

"You shut up, old bitch. Or I kill some people just to make you obey. It means nothing to me."

That quieted her down.

In fact, it seemed to have quieted everyone down, except the screaming wounded still on the floor. Otherwise, except for the bosses and several others corralled on the stage, the cavern was empty. The lights had ceased their vibrating and strobing, the dust had settled, the whirling paper and debris had fallen. Across the stage a man struggled to rise, got himself up, and planted himself in a wheelchair as Magomet went to him and pointed the gun at him.

My new kingdom, thought Vakha.

CHAPTER 29
Wardrobe

Delta had gone to three different outdoor places—a Sportsman's Warehouse, a Cabela's, and a local retailer called Bill's Hunting and Fishing—as well as a Target, and put together a kind of SWAT facsimile uniform on the fly. He had greenish camo pants, a greenish camo shirt, a black canvas utility belt with his Glock in a black flapped holster, a black commando sweater, and an OD hat with FBI emblazoned on it. He'd gotten similar stuff for Niner, who pulled the stuff on in his truck's back seat.

Now they were a block from the site and, with twilight closing visibility down, could see the riot of flashing red against the sky from at least fifty first responder vehicles clustered at the front of the high school auditorium. Sirens still bled noise into the air, a few helicopters orbited overhead, each offering its own constellation of illumination, and people streamed down the street, both to and from the site, some to see, some to escape.

"So what have you got?" Delta asked.

"I got the package in a knapsack. Function-wise, it's straight IED, wired up to my phone. If I call the number, it goes. Design-wise, it's shaped by a plastic shaper-thing, looks like a toilet plunger, you know, sort of cup-like, and that's the trick to direct all the force into one small area."

"Is it fragile?"

"I wouldn't hit anybody in the face with it," said Niner. "But it ought to hold together through reasonable transit."

"Brief on the NV package, again."

"Yeah, goggles. You pull them down, snap to on, and you've got good visibility. Not details, but shapes, silhouettes, targets, movement, that sort of thing. Best indoors."

"Now, about the blast, will I blow enough hole in the wall to get through?"

"The way I've shaped it, I'm thinking you should, but not having plans to the place, I can't guarantee. Anyway, how are you going to plant it? They'll have a tight perimeter."

"My thinking is that you have a smaller charge ready, and blow it somewhere else. Maybe blow a cop vehicle or an ambulance or something. They'll rush to that, and in the chaos, I can slip through the lines, low crawl to the wall, and plant it. Then I'll slip down the wall and hunker up. You blow it, and because I know what's going on, I'll get through and in. In the confusion, I ought to be able to ID and take down the bad guys. It'll be dark, I'm guessing, I'll have the NV goggles.

Anyone with a gun, I whack. After the blast, they'll have to assault. It'll be a mess, I'll have to improvise, but in the dark, with lots of panic and chaos, I should be able to put them down."

Niner handed over his suppressed Glock with a red dot 9 mil.

"Gold Dot 147-grain hollow-points."

"Perfect," said Delta.

"But how do you get out?"

"Good question," said Delta. "And the answer is, I have no idea."

CHAPTER 30
The Wounded

Vakha received Ibragim's inventory report: three M4s, select fire, each gun with three thirty-round magazines plus one empty magazine for display purposes. Three Glock .40-caliber pistols, each with three mags of fifteen rounds. With the shotguns and the already acquired pistols, he had enough to kill all the hostages and captive journalists if an assault came. He tried to think of problems. First, the doors.

He knew there had to be other entries into the building, or rather, other exits, in case of fire. He'd sent Magomet out to run a quick perimeter search, and indeed, Magomet reported back to him that there were three such doors. He ordered Magomet and Anzor to flex-cuff male hostages to each. Then there were the wounded.

They would not shut up. A woman whose legs had been broken by the bus screamed constantly. Another fellow, his hip crushed, begged in spurts, rested, then begged again. Several others moaned and quivered and occasionally blurted a scream of pure hurt. Another prayed so fervently he made everybody nervous.

Shoot them?

It would make a point.

But it would also require ammunition, which had to be rationed for full leverage purposes; it also might inflame the Americans, presumably as yet unorganized by discipline from security agencies, to react crazily, and the results would be a catastrophic gunfight.

He went to the old lady congresswoman, who was kneeling on the floor with the other august captives as someone tried to administer to her swollen face.

"Grandma," he said, "you come now. I need you."

"I will not comply with—"

He picked her off the ground by her shoulders, ripping her from the grip of the two who ministered to her.

"Old lady, you are not boss now. I, Vakha, am boss. When I say something, you obey. Otherwise I hit you again. You are old and frail, boo-hoo, it means nothing to me. I may fuck you if I get in the mood. I sometime like old, dry she-goat."

The old lady gave him a death glare, but did not otherwise resist.

"Oh, I see, you are 'old lady with spirit.' Americans like this type. It is in your movies and television. Ha! I spit on your spirit. It means nothing." But he didn't spit on her spirit, he spit on her face.

Gripping her frail wrist, he dragged her across the auditorium toward the smashed doorway that looked out into the yard, where, a hundred yards away, it seemed a thousand emergency vehicles had gathered, their red flashers going off spastically in the gloom, as night continued its inevitable advance on the drama.

The entrance through which the bus had bashed now looked like the mouth of a cave, jagged, raw, heaped with brick and glass frags and wood debris. Ibragim crouched in the lee of the opening, an M4 in his hand, keeping an eye on the ever-growing legion of policemen on the perimeter.

"They do not move?"

"No, Uncle Vakha, they are all afraid."

"Even with a thousand guns, they are afraid," said Vakha contemptuously.

He grabbed the old lady by the nape of her neck, and pulled her into the doorway. With his other hand he held a Glock against her ear. He shook her a few times and she responded painfully.

"Boss!" he yelled. "Send me boss now or I blow old lady's brains out."

A couple of men detached themselves, one in the uniform of the Idaho State Police, with brass enough on his collar to signify high rank, the other in a now-rumpled and dusty suit, though the tie was still cinched tight.

They approached, hands high to display their unarmed status.

"I'm Memphis, FBI," said the man in the suit. "I am in charge. What are your demands?"

"I, Vakha," he said, "will tell you. But pray I do not grow weary of this buzzard." He shook the old lady by her neck. "If she does not stop bothering me, I may kill her just to shut her up."

"That is a United States congresswoman," said the man in the suit. "You are not permitted—"

"I, Vakha, will decide what is permitted. Any attempt at attack, any disobedience, any pause or stall, I will kill them all—fancy politicians, pretty girls, scruffy boys. Bang, brains everywhere. Ha ha, heads like a teacup someone has stepped on. I tell you now, it means nothing to us. We are not like you, we come from hard land where every day is fight. We can kill, we can die. You understand?"

The two officials exchanged looks, then looked back.

"Six men in underwear and shoes. No socks. No shirts. Underpants, shoes. Send them in now, they are to remove wounded. They look only for wounded, otherwise eyes down or we will shoot them. Any spying, any keeping track, any noticing, we shoot them. They come in, remove the wounded, and go away. Ten minutes. At the end of ten minutes I shoot any wounded left. Get them out of here or I will kill a pretty girl or an old useless one like this one. Do you see?"

They nodded.

"Your ten minutes is begun," he said, and pulled her back from the doorway.

Magomet and Anzor, with M4s to assure compliance, took six of the scruffiest young men to the doorways under the bleachers and behind the stage. At each doorway, they flex-cuffed two of them to the locked-from-inside doors.

Magomet explained.

"If police try to come through these doors, they will have to blow them up. So if you hear them, you scream. Maybe when they hear you, they decide not, because it would kill you. So you have to hope they decide not to come. But if they do, that is okay, because it means everyone else will die too. All the old people, all your friends, even those pretty girls. And most of the policemen. Big, cool gunfight like in the movies. Ha ha, everybody dead, so you will not be alone wherever you go."

One of the boys started to cry.

"Do not cry," said Magomet. "If this is the night you are to die, that is because He has decreed it. You see? It is fate. It's all right. Maybe you come back in next life as someone rich, with lots of girlfriends."

"I'm a Baptist," said the boy.

"This thing I do not know," said Magomet.

"But it is the same. Live, die, all decreed, and life will go on. Maybe people remember you, maybe not. It really doesn't matter."

"How comforting," said another.

From the tone, Magomet understood he was being mocked. But it wasn't in him to hurt the boy. He just said, "Now come on, we have things to do."

"I have to go to the bathroom," another one of them said.

"Sir," said Anzor, "this is battle. In battle there are no bathrooms. If shooting starts or things are blowing up, you will not think of bathrooms. This I know. But piss now, before you are cuffed. All of you piss now, if it helps."

As the six volunteers stripped and departed quickly, Nick struggled to get his somewhat helter-skelter forces organized. He sent Boise municipal and other suburban municipality uniforms to establish posts on the perimeter, surrounding the gym/auditorium building, to drive civilians, if any there were, away and to prevent any single escapes by the hostage takers. This included monitoring the fire exit doors every two hundred feet—there were three—around the building's circular structure.

Another team tried to coordinate intelligence, both from the Bureau of Prisons and incoming from DC, and put together a meaningful portrait of who and what these hostage takers were. Others were tasked with close observation of the site for tactical purposes. A log-in desk was established as forces from farther-out police forces checked in, as did the Bureau of Prisons SWAT officers, and some guys from DEA. Then there was the press, which had to be cordoned off, kept updated and controlled. That task he assigned to Bud Feeley, Representative Venable's PR guy, who had made it out, while most of her staff had not. Feeley was legendarily good at this sort of thing and got press relations up and managed quickly. Two members of the Frank Church High School staff had been quickly located. They were working with the Boise FBI SWAT leader in charge of preparing an assault team, to be composed of Boise FBI's team, the State Police's, and the several other heavy-hitter teams that had shown up unbidden. The SWAT commander, Rich Hilton, was preparing a plan, although Nick doubted he'd use it. And that reality was officially confirmed shortly thereafter.

He grabbed Sally as well.

"You're with me, the whole way. You listen, raise any legal questions that come up, handle any inquiries, set any legal policies as needed, deal with DOJ if they try and get in on the game. Okay with that?"

"Nick, I can do that."

"I know you can. That's why I married you.

You're the best wife in America when it comes to advising SWAT entry teams!"

She threw him a bit of smile.

He was now in the incident command van of the State Police, designated headquarters, dealing with various officials who felt their input should be accommodated. This was listening patiently to idiocy such as helicopter assault plans, ingress through the hallway from the school, multiple attacks through the roof, and so forth, when a Boise officer interrupted to say, "Sir, DC on the phone."

That gave Nick an excuse to break off his discourse with the various chiefs who wanted a prominent place in the parade, but also wanted to make sure nobody from their department got killed. Plus airborne helicopter assault.

"Memphis."

It was the director.

"Nick, tell me what's going on and what you've laid out, please. I've got the whole team here."

Nick summarized quickly.

"How many?"

"Looks like five, out of the county lockup. Prisoners who never cooperated. They were taken by state cops a few weeks back after a gunfight on I-84. Still mysterious. Well armed. No demands yet, but the guy in charge allowed us to get the wounded out. We've got six cops in their underwear bringing folks out right now."

"Good. Any read on motive?"

"It's got to be an escape. My guess is that they realized just taking a bus and some guards wasn't enough leverage to get them what they wanted, namely a flight out of here. But the congressmen, especially Venable, ups the leverage times ten. Now we have to play ball."

"That's our thinking too."

"Yes, sir."

"Nick, I've decided that no assault is to be permitted. You only go if they start shooting. The key here is time, as I know you know. The longer, the slower, the more lies and excuses you can come up with, the better. If you confront, it's a bloodbath. We've got satellite imagery here and experts going over the building, and I don't see any scenario by which you can get people in fast enough to take these bastards down before they kill the hostages. And we don't think they're bluffing."

Nick knew all this, of course. To that purpose, he'd set up another SWAT platoon—several combined units—just behind the lights. They were armored and helmeted up, cocked and locked, and ready to go. If it seemed a massacre had convened, their task was to hit the front and shoot anyone in orange. Maybe in that way, some could be saved.

"They're not bluffing. They've killed over ten people already," said Nick.

"You have to hold the no-assault line, Nick. We've got stuff airborne now to reach you by morning, high-tech night vision, Delta experts, snipers and breachers, more body armor, explosive experts, all that stuff. But I'm so worried that some of these Idaho people can go off half-cocked. They don't give a damn about congressmen, they just want vengeance for the state cops that have been killed."

"I read you."

"Sorry this fell on you, Nick. You've done so much and deserve your rest, but you're the only one I've got there."

"Got it," said Nick. "Once their demands are made, and we figure out who and what they are, it'll be a lot clearer."

"Where's Swagger?"

"As far as I know, he's still inside. He fell, hit his head. We had to leave him."

The head had stopped gushing, but it still hurt. He could feel a slight swelling presence and smell blood on his face, a sting at the laceration itself, and if he moved his head it felt like glass fragments were loose to rattle around inside. Oh, and his arthritic hip hurt like hell. Plus he was seventy-four years old and he didn't feel a day over eighty. Other than that, he was fine. Well, the piercing pain in his elbow, which he had twisted when he hit the ground. And a dull ache from the steel hip, which always reflected his general body condition. And the steel collarbone, left shoulder. Not an ache, really, but an unpleasant presence, reminding him that a year ago he'd taken a major wound and was still not wholly recovered.

No one had paid much attention to him, old man in a wheelchair as he was. Who wouldn't make a zero-threat assessment? Now and then someone glanced at him, but they had so many higher priorities—inventorying the weapons, organizing the hostages under ready gunpoint, distributing and securing hostages at possible points of entry, reconning the site—it seemed unlikely that anyone would get to him for a bit. But watching, he couldn't help but conclude that the old guy knew what he was doing. He gave decisive orders in his native language, sensible orders, and his troops obeyed instantly, in good humor. In fact, the young guys seemed to find the whole thing pretty amusing. It was certainly more fun than sitting around in a prison cell. It was fun. Who doesn't love fun? And, moreover, it was clear to Swagger, from their easy postures, their familiarity with one another, that something bound them beyond mercenary interest. Family, probably.

Almost without willing it, his hand crept inside his suit coat. He waited for someone to race to him and butt-stroke him bloody. It didn't happen. In another few minutes he moved the hand up the inside of his coat and plucked his cell phone from the inside pocket. He held it, dead still, for what seemed hours. Still, no one came. Too busy, too preoccupied, maybe having too much fun. The only human being close by was poor Congressman Baker, who sat on his knees a few feet away, locked into a position of utter submission. Baker, he had realized, was trying to survive by aggressive weakness. It was a valid strategy. Many animals had used just such a coping mechanism to survive for millions of years and would overpopulate the world if not frequently chosen for lunch by slightly larger animals. If Baker could have willed himself to shrink to the size of a marmot, he would have done so. He seemed to be trying to compress his atomic structure, if such a thing were possible. Whatever, it kept him busy.

Swagger finally twisted his coat enough to see his iPhone screen. He plunked the phone icon, and when the screen came up he plunked the Contacts icon, which revealed for him the few people whom he admitted to his private world. He found Nick, pressed, and pressed again, the CALL designation, then slid the phone high up his chest and trapped it by pulling his lapel tight, though now both hands were visible.

"Swagger?"

He could hear Nick, if just barely. He assumed then that Nick could hear him, as he nonchalantly lowered his head, as if in pain, to bring his mouth closer to the receiver.

"Hear me?"

"Got you."

"Five of 'em. Older guy, four younger guys. Under the orange, all look like weight lifters. Lots of tats, so I'm guessing prison time. Very good with the guns. Look professional, maybe with combat too. Very relaxed, almost as if they're on a picnic."

"Firepower?"

"Plenty. They've got two shotguns, from the prison bus. They've got three M4s, from the two cops they killed inside and the one outside. Plus pistols, maybe five. I've seen magazines for everything but couldn't get a count."

"Congressionals?"

"All of 'em so far okay, although Mother Death is getting used hard. Her wig fell off."

"I saw her."

"She's spitting mad, I can tell. Anyhow, they're all in a circle, with their staffers, on the stage. All sitting, all under the gun of one of the guys. M4, full-auto, the youngest one. You come in hard, he will massacre them. I don't get a vibe of any hesitation or mercy. They don't see us as humans but just as targets."

"Psycho?"

"No. Just the business they're in."

"Other hostages?"

Bob described the twenty-five, particularly the six flex-cuffed to the fire escapes. "You can't blow the doors unless you want some dead kids before you even get inside."

"And you?" Nick asked.

"Fine, so far."

"Needless to say, guy, no Patrick Ferguson stuff, okay. This one's too big, too many moving parts. You stay in that chair until we come for you."

"Believe me, I have no ambitions to be Patrick Ferguson. I don't even want to be Bob Lee Swagger. Oh, and one more thing," said Swagger. "You know I spent some time in Russia. I got to know a guy who snipered in a war they had there, now a big gangster type."

"Yeah?"

"But he wasn't Russian. He spoke it, but he hated the Russians. He preferred his own language. I got used to the sound and the rhythm. I'm picking that up here."

"What was he?"

"Chechen."

"Oh, shit," said Nick, "Beslan. Moscow Theater."

"Uh-oh, he's coming for me."

He broke contact.

CHAPTER 31

Mr. Abrusian

Delta lay on the front seat, out of sight. Occasionally a Boise cop car came down the street, just on routine patrol near the incident zone, but each time it passed without difficulty. Delta had his phone.

He finally got through to Mr. Abrusian.

"You got news?"

"Have you seen the TV?"

"Some hostage thing out there."

"Those are your guys. They must have heard DEA was on the truck so they busted a move today to stay ahead of a transfer to a place they could never escape."

"Chechens! Cunning little pricks! The whole place should have been A-bombed, all dead, nothing but a huge ashtray. Bah, they make mischief everywhere. You never get ahead of them."

"I'm laid up just outside the zone."

"You have plan?"

"I'm not giving up. I can blow my way in with the explosive guy, roll in during the confusion, pop the guys in orange, and make my way out."

"Crazy," said Abrusian. "But so crazy maybe

good, Mr. Delta. Always thinking, always smart. But—"

"Yeah?"

"Forgive me, my friend. It occurs to me an easier way is to blow up the auditorium from afar. Police will then have to raid. Gunfight, lots of shooting. Everyone in orange is killed, for sure. Your job is done, you never even had to get hands wet. You just plant bombs, and detonate from Disney World."

Delta considered. He wasn't sure, but it made some sense. Let the FBI do the dirty work. They could wonder for years where the explosives came from, to no result. Rumors would circulate that someone else had been on the board, a thousand theories would gurgle out of the mulch, but nobody would get it right for years, until someone who knew finally leaked. But there were issues.

"Sir, what you're talking about is a massacre. The Chechens would spray-paint the hostages, then turn their guns on the cops. In the end, to get the five targets, you're looking at forty, fifty dead, maybe more, to say nothing of the uproar the dead politicians would cause. You're looking at scandal, investigation, task force, manhunt, and sooner or later someone on your team would crack. It would come back to you. Someone would talk and we'd be cellmates at a federal coop for the next ten thousand years."

"Risks must be run."

"If I can whack the Chechens with minimum collateral and get out clean, you're much better off. No scandal. In time, after the bullets are recovered and the forensics are done, after the explosive residue is analyzed, they'll figure out someone else was there. But they'll be so busy congratulating themselves for my work, they may not even go public with it. I'm sure the net will fill up on conspiracy theories, but nobody will ever know the truth except you and me."

"You can do this thing?"

"I've got advantages. Night vision, red dot Glock with can, easy to see the orange. I've got this genius explosives guy, he's building a charge that'll blow a new doorway in, and another one to distract the law enforcement types so I can get close to plant it. I'm in, bang bang, I'm out."

"I will have to pay you twice as much for this."

"And more for my buddy here, wiring up the C-4 in the back seat."

"Sure, sure. You do, you become even richer."

"In all things, you get what you pay for."

CHAPTER 32

Chitchat

They loomed, like the mountains. Three of them, faces darkened in the uncertain light. The older one observed him carefully, though Bob made certain not to get into an eye-lock contest with him.

The other two were less menacing. One wore a scowl that Bob knew signified the anger of the eternally aggrieved. There was one in every platoon. The other face was younger, unlined, earnest, stupid. The kid. There was always one of those in a platoon too.

"You are sniper?" asked the old man, genuinely curious. "Hero? Man-killer? Warrior?"

"I suppose," said Bob.

"Why they do this to you? Very strange. You kill Arab pig before he can do harm. And you end up here, like this, on trial? This I no understand."

"Don't know what it is myself," said Bob. "I guess it's just how it operates. Politics. These folks are politicians. They see some kind of advantage here."

"In our country, hero lives in big house. Has

255

gold Rolex, British car, gets all the pussy he wants, cocaine, any drug, has houses everywhere. Maybe owns football team. We like heroes. This place, what is?"

"Called the System. Rules operate a certain way. You get a paper saying you come testify, you come testify."

"Why not kill men who bring papers?"

"More would come next day."

"Kill them too. Kill for a week. Then no more come."

"People would get upset. Call me crazy."

"Crazy not to kill."

The angry one had a knife in his hand, some sort of American gizmo. He'd probably gotten it off one of the dead state policemen. He kept flicking it open and closing it, mastering the snapping wrist move that unleashed the blade in a split second.

He spoke in his language, made his pitch and failed to close the sale.

"Put the toy away," Vakha said. "This man is crippled. He fell to ground and knocked himself out. Don't be a silly child."

Vakha turned back to Bob.

"You have killed. I like, I wish to spare you. Boy here wants to cut your throat, but is no way for man like you to die."

Bob looked over at the angry one's dark face: he saw lethal idiocy, a sort of chronic bad-decision-maker's stupidity that would get everyone killed, himself first.

"Anzor," said the old man to the milder, broader boy, "put cuff on one arm to chair. Leave one arm free so he can scratch his balls."

He leaned forward to Bob, talking over Anzor's shoulder as the boy lashed him to the wheelchair arm, pulled the flex cuff tight until it snapped hard shut as far as it could go, leaving no play or twist, cutting into the left arm through the dopey suit.

"Look, sniper, I do not know how it ends. Maybe gunfight. It happens, no? Maybe have to kill all these peoples, all those old cows and goats in fancy shit, the cute girls, the filthy boys. Gunfire everywhere, you've seen it, no?"

"Too much of it," said Bob.

"Bullets go everywhere. You cannot say where. Bounce, go through, go wild, fired by dying man. Crazy-crazy. Maybe you get one. Too bad for you. As I say, man like you should not die here like this."

"What happens happens," said Bob.

"Is true. Is so true. Your cock okay? Still working?"

"Was okay last time I looked."

"So, maybe Sniper want last piece of pussy? In case dead by dawn? Bring girl, she could pull up dress for lap fuck? One last piece of pussy. Go out emptied, huh?"

"No," said Bob. "Let them girls be. They got enough to worry about."

"Okay. But if I die, you tell others like you, 'Vakha offer me last piece of pussy.' They will think, This Vakha, maybe not so bad."

CHAPTER 33
The Massacre

Beslan," said Nick to his commanders at a hastily called meeting. "Chechens. Ring any bells?"

"Town in eastern Russia. School hostage situation, 2004," said one of the officers. "Lasted three days. Lots of people got killed when the Russians finally assaulted. They even used tanks, as I recall."

"They did," Nick replied. "Thirty-three guys, Chechens, separatists, took over a school. Over a thousand hostages, half of 'em kids. But it was a royal fuckup, and in the end, thirty-two of the thirty-three were killed, but so were over three hundred of the hostages, again half of 'em kids. The next year they tried the same gag at a theater in Moscow. Took it over during a performance. This time one hundred and thirty hostages, and this time, after days and days, the Russians didn't use tanks, they used gas. Same results. All terrorists dead and again about half the hostages. Just so you know, that won't happen here unless these Chechens start shooting. Then we go. But nobody above wants us to go, and we only go if

259

we have to. No Beslan, no Moscow theater, and that's from the director himself."

"Do we know who they are?" someone asked. "Individually, I mean."

"Yeah, stuff is coming across from DC now. It's a maximum effort there, and they're grinding out the data. I have my wife sorting—she's a prosecutor and knows what she's doing. Sally?"

Sally came before the group, looking bedraggled. But there was nothing bedraggled in her briefing. It was one hundred miles an hour.

"We're dealing with a crime family named Shishani," she said. "The head man is Vakha, and he was brother to the two fathers of the four younger guys. It's an old criminal family, but it has nationalist leanings too. I should say, nobody sees jihad in this. They may be Islamic—we don't know yet—but basically this is straight crime. These guys have all sorts of reasons for wanting to get out and wanting to stay out, and hostage-taking seems to be the Chechen hammer for all sorts of problem nails.

"Anyway," she went on, "the boys' fathers died at Beslan. Vakha raised them. Very shrewd, tough guys, armed robbers, kidnappers, a part of Chechen organized crime, big rep. Maybe too big. According to INTERPOL, in 2013, Chechen authorities raided their stronghold. All were killed and burned to a crisp as the house outside of Grozny went up from the tracers.

"However—isn't this convenient?—no bodies were identified and no forensics are in the file. It was thought by some that the thing was a ruse, that five random corpses were burned, and that Uncle Vakha and the boys were secreted out of the country to America, which they entered with connivance from the Russian mafia. So that's why no names came up when the prints were run after they were initially busted for the I-84 shootout. As officially deceased, their fingerprints were removed from the INTERPOL index.

"DC now thinks that for the past few years they have been living in the Coney Island area, sort of as bad-boy enforcers and hit men for the Russians. It was a good deal for the Russians, because when they needed something done discreetly, they could go to Vakha and one of his boys would do the job, leaving no traceable prints or DNA, and thus no links to the Russian mob. So I'm guessing they did a lot of wet work, witnesses and snitches, recalcitrant debtors, criminal opponents with ambitions to move in on Russian territory."

Someone said, "Ma'am, if I may, I think I can shed some light on this."

Nick recognized him not merely from the DEA initials on his baseball hat but from an earlier hurried intro and handshake as he brought a team in.

"I'm Jack DeWitt, DEA senior agent on-site."

"Go ahead, Agent DeWitt," said Sally.

"You'll get this soon, but let me give it to you ahead of channels. When I'm not dressed in black and playing cowboy, I run a clandestine lab team. We find things. We know where to look, how to look, and when to look. We're pretty good at it."

"Go on."

"The reason my team is even here is that we got a tip that the I-84 shootout thing was narcotics-related, but that the locals had missed the connection because of the sophistication of the operation. We came out two days ago and spent all of yesterday and half of today in the Ada County impound lot, going over the truck. The van is a mule, and in a false ceiling is about twenty-five million dollars' worth of Mexican heroin."

A buzz circulated among the officers.

"Nobody locally could find it because it was welded into place, so the dogs couldn't smell it, no chemical sensors could pick it up, and X-rays revealed nothing. Whoever put it together knew what he was doing. Preliminary testing suggests that it's high-grade stuff. Stuff like that goes in transit in that quantity only when very high partners are involved. Other factors to be considered are the quality of the cover, including legit trucking papers and a high-end vehicle, plus the uncertain driving talents of the driver ISP pulled over, suggesting he was an untrained man, not the original driver, who would have been legit and highly skilled. He was also, I now see, Chechen, not Mexican or American."

"Do you have a read on this, Agent DeWitt?"

"I do. My agency believes that the Russians put together a big deal with one of the cartels. That would be a first because most Russian product comes from Turkey or the Caucasus. That would be alarming because the conflict between these two entities—Russian and Mexican—is one of the tensions that control the growth of the illicit trade and give us a chance."

"What's next?"

"Well, I don't know much about Chechens, but from what you've said, I'd certainly guess that they tired of their go-for roles, and even though they need the Russians and are affiliated with them in many criminal enterprises, they basically hate each other and have for centuries.

"Somehow the Chechens found out about the shipment. They decided to jack it, knowing that the Russians would suspect the Mexicans, the Mexicans would suspect the Russians, and in the confusion and suspicion they'd get away clean and could start dealing in small amounts. Then they'd begin to take over networks, and by the time anybody figured it out, they'd be too powerful to do anything about it."

"So what happened?"

DeWitt summed up the political dynamics of

the incident. Chechens highjack, but something goes wrong and cover is blown. They improvise, head west. Intercepted by Idaho state troopers, gunfight, capture. Russians find out about it. Chechens find out about Russians finding out, and realize they're going to get whacked if they don't split soonest.

"Hence, this thing. So what do they want now?"

A policeman leaned into the incident command van.

"Agent Memphis! The old guy is out now, and he's got Congresswoman Venable. He wants to talk."

INTERLUDE: 1780

I was awake when Grammercy knocked. He had with him two mugs of the coffee Americans had so recently found to their taste, and I could see from the light over his shoulder that dawn was still an hour away.

"I'm glad you're early, Lieutenant," I said.

"In truth, I haven't slept."

"I understand. I do loathe coffee, particularly in comparison with our teas, but it is said to carry some power of regeneration, so perhaps it will help us clear our minds."

"My idea exactly, sir."

I felt I might have some advice to give. I had— it is an occupational hazard of a life spent in the officer class—fought four duels. I had "won" all, won in the sense of, in the first, never having to retract or apologize for what had been taken as insult, and in the second, never having had to slay an opponent. I had endured multiple prickings, lashings, and bruisings, but at no point approached fatality. I therefore knew something of thrust and cut, of plunge and feint, of smash and butt. Moreover, I had witnessed far too many of such follies, a few, including Scott-Browning's at Winston's hand, of lethal variety.

"Tell me then. What is your acquaintance with the sword?" I asked. "You came to your lieutenancy by an odd path, and I assume missed swordsmanship at either Sandhurst or a regimental training regimen?"

"That is so. However, for the past year with Patrick, in many cavalry actions the saber has been our tool. I believe my presence is testimony to my efficiency. It helps too that among the Chickamauga, I used a hatchet of a sort called a tomahawk. That too is a blade weapon, albeit with shaft."

"Yes, but both the cavalry saber and the Redskin hatchet are chopping tools. The stroke is a broad sweep, where strength and angle to target are prized, to cut down the enemy's defenses and open a gash so wide that he must leave the field or perish *in situ*. The rapier, which you will be using for your life, is a thrust and parry weapon. It has but brief edge, and thus little meaning is attached to the sweep. If you sweep he will pierce you."

"I understand."

"It is incumbent on you to fight defensive in the initial confrontations. You must grow used to the rhythm of the fight, the motions of the sword directed at you. Your job is to parry and dictate space between yourself and your opponent. I take it you will not panic at the sight of your own blood?"

"I have seen much of it, Matthew. It comes with a belly split open or three Yankee balls scattered about, two still in place."

"You will see more today. You will be nicked and pricked and stung and poked. Many tiny rivulets will spring from your body. You must pay them no heed. It does not matter who gets the first dart in, but who the last. You must concentrate on the process, not the price."

"I will do my best, sir."

"Wait, there is more to come."

"I am rapt."

"How is your left hand?"

"In what meaning, sir?"

"Is it adept? Is it quick? Can you do things with it?"

"I have not made much use of it."

"I have seen this man fight. He never challenges, but goads the challenge, preserving for himself the choice of weapons. He will thus fight you *a Florentine*. That means with sword in one hand and dagger in the other, after the archaic fashion of the Italians. Your choice is of which rapier and which dagger, but his is of type. He chooses *a Florentine* because he is unusually adept with his left hand as well as his right. It gives him immense advantage."

"May it be countered, Matthew?"

"For a time, until fatigue sets in. You must always wheel to the right. In this way, you stay beyond reach of the shorter congress of the dagger and can reduce the fight to rapier versus rapier. You must not fight longitudinally, gone to thrust, but latitudinally, always on the circle, fast to the parry. The un-firm footing may be to your advantage also, as it will certainly reduce his speed."

"Excellent knowledge, sir."

"Do not force. Do not advance. Rotate rather than retreat, always to the right. Concentrate upon the parry. That is the true help of the dagger *main gauche*. Watch the point of his weapon, as it will still, possibly, withdraw slightly in the muscular preparation of his arm, like a firelock is cocked, before the thrust. When you see that, move swiftly to the right and set an angle with your blade that can intercept his. You will have no openings until he's fatigued, and thus it's pointless to spend energy on them. If killing there is to be, it should not happen until the fourth *quartam*."

"Excellent."

"There is a mystery I have no answer to. In the fight I saw, it was evenly matched until *quartam finali*. Then Winston enjoyed a sudden burst of energy, as if a new man. Maybe it is in his constitution to do so, but I doubt it so. It was this energy that fueled him to victory. He swelled like a cobra, then advanced on the quick time, unleashed a flurry of dazzlement and precision combined, and poor Scott-Browning had no answer and swiftly lay pierced and emptied, nose in Chatham's mud. That is why you must preserve your energy."

"So it shall be."

"You are an extremely brave young officer, Robert. No one can question that, nor your honor. I must say, though, that until the end, there will be a chance to survive if you can only swallow your gall and offer apology."

"I will not, Matthew. He is a blackguard and must pay for what he did to Patrick and our loyal horsemen atop King's Mountain."

"Then I will advise you but more helpfully I will pray for you."

CHAPTER 34

Ross

They moved Baker from his place of honor in the middle of the floor to the circle of august personalities. This was simply for better machine-gunning if Ibragim got the go sign and was ordered to ripsaw everybody. And, of course, they dumped him next to his superior.

In a way, she looked so much depleted it was hard to believe she was the same woman. The wig now rested like a dead racoon in her hands. Her natural hair, now revealed, was the gray of the Siberian tundra, held in place by a pin and afraid to defy her by coming loose. Her mascara and other eye makeup had streaked, turning her into one of those wraiths from the Kurosawa canon. Her stockings were seamed with runs and she'd taken her Louboutins off for comfort. Her left cheek bulged with discoloration, courtesy of the blow Vakha had landed when she first disobeyed him. Though it was now magenta fused with puce and lavender and the size of a small anthill or a bedknob, she didn't acknowledge it.

In fact, her eyes still glittered with that predatory keenness, as she glided, hunting for targets to snatch up and then to amusingly drop to the rocks below. Her lift had held, so face and chin— despite the lopsided swelling—were taut as drum heads, and if a denture had been knocked out, it didn't show, so she still had a mouthful of razor-sharp Chiclets between her narrow ruby-red lips.

"Well, Baker," she said, "another fine mess you've gotten us into."

"Representative, I assure you I had nothing to do with this."

"Of course you did. When you went into that idiotic slop about Us and Them, God decided to teach you a lesson and so He invented the Them of all Thems to come and machine-gun us. Don't you see, this is cosmic repudiation of your childish nonsense."

"Madam Chairman, you know that couldn't possibly be true."

"As I have many times said, He rules with an irony hand. If you defy Him with utter stupidity, you get to choose the form of your destructor. He will conjure your worst fear and deliver it unto you. And these nasty boys and their demented grandpa or whatever he is, are not Stay Puft Marshmallow Men."

"I'm glad you haven't lost your sense of humor."

"Is that what it is? I thought I was just spewing vitriol at another vulnerable creature to make myself feel better. It usually works. Now, you do understand, don't you, that if Thug One over there with the machine gun turns it on, your job is to lie across my body and absorb all the bullets meant for me?"

"I don't think I can do that, madam."

"I'll give you a better committee assignment. Say, Missiles and Bombs, or Welfare and Scams. You'll get very rich off that one!"

"I don't think I'd have time to cover you adequately. And although I don't know much about such matters, I suspect the bullets would go right through me."

"I should be fine unless they're shooting that famous super-bullet, the 11.7-caliber Creedville. If not, perhaps your flesh will delay them a bit so that Swagger can kill them. Oh, wait, first he has to warn them, then he has to get a psychiatric evaluation, then he has to try one last time to phone and email them, and then he gets to pull the trigger. What crap. Why did I even sign on?"

"If you recall, it was Feeley's idea. It made a lot of political sense. You know, you were losing the left, you were going to be primaried by a sixteen-year-old lesbian Chicana anarchist with beautiful teeth and legs, people were tired of you, rumors of your secretly monstrous personality and sense of royal entitlement were spreading."

"Yes, I suppose you're right. Sigh. What's a gal to do?"

"Now that we're in the fire instead of the frying pan, does this mean you've changed your politics? Have you had an epiphany?"

"Good God, no. Epiphanies are for jerks. If we get out of this without the pitter-patter of little machine guns, I'll go totally back to the woman I was, only more so. And once Swagger saves our lives, to get him out of the way and to keep his presence from reminding people how worthless we truly are, we'll put him in Alcatraz for ten years!"

"Excellent plan," said Baker, somewhat buoyed by the repartee, "but can you tell him to hurry up with the saving-our-lives part? I am getting anxious."

At that point, however, the Tracy-Hepburn chitchat was interrupted by no less than Genghis Khan himself, the burly boss of all scum and maggots, Vakha the Conqueror.

"Okay, old lady, time for go to work," he said, and grabbed her by the back of her wren-boned neck to pull her to her feet. "Put shoes on."

"Might we tiptoe over some crushed skulls?" she asked.

"No crushed skulls. Maybe broken bones or teeth. I want you to be comfortable. You, with the eyes, don't give me that bug-face look, I will have somebody cut your face off for you."

"He can't help it," said Mother Death. "It's just his face."

She slipped into her Louboutins, and Vakha pulled her off the stage and across the auditorium. Thank God the wailing wounded and the bloating dead had been removed. They were so depressing. Evidently the blood had been wiped up or perhaps there hadn't been much to start with, but the passage was easily enough accomplished without slippage or stumbles, as the bus had done a nice job of opening a passageway through the chairs. That vehicle seemed now like a dead green whale washed up on a littered beach after a picnic. They passed one of the other barbarians standing sentinel at the ravaged gap where once the doors had been.

She stepped into a new universe.

All the world's police forces had gathered at this one spot, plus half the world's lighting technicians, plus a quarter of the world's television and newspaper reporters. She saw Feeley looking at her from the front of the roped-off area where the reporters had been corralled, and next to him, in that expensive haircut and well-cut suit, the ever reedy Banjax, dressed more for a faculty tea or a Newspaper Guild meeting than a massacre. The line between them, *the safe,* and her, *the soon-to-be murdered,* was so slight; it was like the line between the jungle and the town, and yet it made all the difference. Both Banjax and Feeley tried to manufacture tragic commedia dell'arte masks as an apropos response to the situation, but both failed, because of course they were on that side of the line and she was on this side. They loved the fact they were not going to die. The abundant radiation of the survivor's self-satisfaction gushed from every pore. She hated them. "See those two," she wanted to say to the brute grandpa rudely shoving her along. "Kill them."

As they approached, two men stepped out from the mass presence—Memphis, of course, and that colonel of State Police who had yet to say a word. Both were dressed as they'd been, suit and uniform, but in keeping with the currently fashionable theme of massive gunfight, each wore a navy blue armored vest with "POLICE" stenciled on it and a little green helmet. "Boys," she wanted to say, "you really do look silly. Please, find another game to play, this one has grown so tiresome."

But then she was before them in a cone of piercing illumination so intense it hurt her eyes as lights from a hundred sources blasted them with radiance for the TV cameras, and she realized that about half a billion people were watching or would watch on time delay. The footage would become iconic to the first half of the still-young century. It annoyed her that she didn't have time to work on her makeup for her date with Forever. Then she felt something pull her hair tight and yank her head back even as it collided with some kind of metal prod, which had to be the barrel of the gun Vakha held.

"No sudden moves," he said. "Anything happen, lady, the first shot goes through your mushroom and there is no more for the fancy old bitch."

"Can you point the gun away from the congress-woman's head?" asked Memphis. "Surely it's not necessary."

"Vakha say what is necessary."

"Madam Chairman, how are you?"

"Tell the man how well I am treating my guests, darling," said Vakha.

"The cuisine is superb, the room service some-what lacking," she said.

"Ha ha," said Vakha. "She is funny girl. I like."

"All right, let's get to it, Mr. Shishani," said Nick.

"Oh, so you know my name? American police, very smart."

"We know everything. About the drugs stolen from the Russians, about the Russians now hunting you. About your need to get out of town before their hit men track you down."

"Then my demands should not surprise you. In fact, maybe you have already started to prepare. Listen good. Take notes," advised Vakha.

"It's all being recorded," said Nick.

"First, I repeat. No attack. Everybody die in attack. Nobody on roof. No bombs blow holes in wall. No grenades go pop! No sleeping gas.

Nobody approach. We have machine guns, we have no hesitation, we get what we want or there are consequences."

"I understand."

"Second, must be fast. Not Beslan, not Moscow theater. It doesn't go on for days and days while you bring in tanks or two more armies. That was mistake of Beslan. Russians had too much time. I don't make that mistake."

"There are certain limits to what we can do. Not of will, but of logistics," said Nick.

"Fuck logistics. Darling, say to them, 'Fuck logistics!'"

"Fuck logistics, motherfuckers," said the congresswoman.

"Stay on schedule or we start executing people one at a time. Every time you hear a shot, another pretty girl or boy has been executed. Is that what you want? Do I have to shoot one to show you I mean business?"

"No, no, but we can only do what is possible."

"*Make* it possible that at seven a.m. tomorrow, right after dawn, helicopter lands on roof. It is from Reynolds Air Force Base in Colorado. Of type called Black Hawk, UH-10. It carries thirteen, I know, I checked. I am not stupid. One pilot, in underpants and shoes. He lands on roof just behind us. Roof of theater, it has steps up to it and doorway, I know.

"When he lands, immediately we board. Thirteen of us. That is, my boys, myself, and these eight old people, your congressmen. This lady and her friends. They will circle us as we move to helicopter. No snipers, no fancy moves. One slip, all of us fire machine guns, congressmen die, including this funny girl, in one second. We kill pilot, maybe blow up helicopter. Massacre, slaughter, what you want to call it. Makes no difference to us, we have killed, we are professional, we can kill, no problem. We can die like men. Understand?"

The two law officers listened stoically. As a professional necessity, they allowed not the faintest flicker of emotion to play on their stone faces.

Finally, Nick said, "As I say, we will try—"

"No try," said Vakha, the Yoda of Chechnya, "only do. Well within capacities."

"What is the helicopter destination?" said Nick.

"Boise Airport. Onto runway. There is 747 jet plane. Big one. Engines running, all fueled up. Door open, stairway in place. Otherwise airport is empty, shut down. No other planes, no landing, no activity. No people within a thousand yards, too far for snipers. Again, circle of thirteen goes to plane and up stairs. Nothing happens, nobody nowhere, just airplane. Once we are aboard, we push stairs back, close hatch. You understand?"

"Yes, of course," said Nick.

"Two pilots. Underpants, shoes. No socks. They

never leave seat except to shit in bathroom, door open. They take off. Sixteen hours, nonstop, to Grozny. We land there. Plane has range of twelve thousand miles, Grozny is eight thousand miles. Plenty good for fuel."

"And you release the hostages?"

"That is when hostages are released. Everybody safe, everybody happy. Plane gets refueled, pilots put on some pants, and fly everybody back to America. Big celebration. Old lady is hero. They make movies about her. But in Chechnya, they make movies about *us*."

"Is that all?"

"No. Two more things. Number one, on the plane, ten million dollars, cash or gold. Federal Reserve cash depot is in Portland, six hours away by car, no problem getting there in time. I have calculated all the distances, everything is possible."

"I don't know—"

"Bang!" said Vakha, for effect. Then he laughed. "Oh, so sorry, shot old lady in head."

"Money will be there," said Nick.

CHAPTER 35

Presser

Feeley finished the briefing in the parking lot, a few hundred feet behind the police lines, in a roped-off area near the incident command van. He'd read the statement, taken questions. He didn't give them much, just the identity of the hostage takers, their demands, the bad news about the congressional press captives and the government's standard no-comment policy.

"Bud," asked Banjax, assuming the prerogative of leader of the pack as the noted Swagger expert as well as the man from the *New York Times*, "is there any chance of an assault before the deadline? Isn't it our policy never to deal with hostage takers."

"David, I have no comment. You know I can't comment about an ongoing operation."

"Bud," said the vagina-face *Post* guy, "given that the president's archenemy, Congresswoman Venable, is one of the hostages, does that change anything?"

"The president, and all the police professionals I've spoken to, are adamant that politics shall not be a consideration. We will do what we determine is best."

"Bud, have plans to yield to the demands been set in motion? I mean, there's an awful lot of stuff to do and not much time." This was NBC's reporter, who was wearing a safari jacket. Feeley was surprised he hadn't camouflaged his face.

Why did they ask such stupidities? But of course he knew it was for the folks in NY or DC or the newsroom or control room wherever. It had no connection with actual reality; after all, it was journalism.

"Mike, I can only say that no decision has been reached, that this is a difficult, potentially tragic situation, that at least ten people are already dead, that everyone here is under the greatest pressure and doing their absolute best, even at jobs we never thought we'd have. Like me. But you, like everyone else, will have to wait and see."

It went on for a few minutes, and then he got a signal from a lieutenant colonel of some police force to wind it up.

"If there are any developments, I will let you know," and though the reporters screamed yet more q's at him, he gave no a's, and turned abruptly and headed back to the incident command van.

But not quite.

Somehow a presence was next to him, someone had gotten through, and of course it was Mr. Bob

Lee Swagger–expert himself, the newly silky, prosperous (book deal? movie sale? long-form narrative in the *New Yorker*?) David Banjax.

"What are you doing here, David?"

"I pulled rank on a twenty-two-year-old Boise police cadet," he said. "The *New York Times* usually gets what it wants."

"I can't give you any more. It's a tightly controlled situation, you know that."

"I'm not here to get," said Banjax. "I'm here to manipulate."

"Meaning what?"

"Meaning this. The *Times*, I have been not only informed but asked to share with you, will not editorially support any attack. It is our collective wisdom that such a thing would be a slaughter, and if Mother Death got a friendly-fire round between the eyes, the *Times* would look upon it with horror and anger."

"Nobody's going to shoot her, for God's sake."

"I don't mean purposely, no one's saying that. But in a gunfight with a lot of machine guns, a lot of innocent people can die. *Her* death would be particularly upsetting. The *Times* suggests that the president and all these gun-crazy police commandos proceed with that in mind."

"What eleven-year-old editorial writer thought that up?"

"And," said Banjax, "there's one other thing. We realize that Bob Lee Swagger is still inside."

"In a wheelchair, unable to move."

"Whatever. See, given the intellectual thrust of Congressman Baker's argument and the universal endorsement of its meaning and further implication by millions of Americans, we want to see it used as a guide for solving this situation."

"Meaning?"

"Meaning conciliation, meaning negotiation, meaning consideration, meaning empathy. Meaning reaching out with open hand, not steel fist. Not, especially, with lead bullets of the nine-millimeter variety. Meaning no gunfights. Meaning no Bob Lee Swagger. No Earl, no Charles. No Patrick Ferguson. Meaning no heroes. Just passing it along, for what it's worth. But that's what we believe is the moral force of the argument, here in spades. No heroes. The day of the heroes is over."

CHAPTER 36

The Toys

They were under a blanket. Niner illuminated the proceedings with a small SureFire.

"Okay," said Delta. "What have you got for me?"

Niner had been in the foot space of the back seat of the cab for a couple of hours now, while Delta had merely rested. He'd been busily diddling away, and the energy of his preps sometimes generated a gently rocking motion on the vehicle's interior, as it jiggled on the shocks.

"Here's the star of the show."

It was a backpack of no particular singularity, black nylon, straps hanging off, familiar from a million malls and high schools.

"In here, I've got six pounds of C-4 plastic explosive molded about an inch thick into a ceramic funnel. I carry the funnels in different sizes as part of my kit, because you never know. This one's medium. At its base the detonator pierces the explosive and is wired to a relay switch which is in turn wired to a throwaway phone from Target. God bless Target, you couldn't blow up shit without it. Right now the system's dead, meaning safe. So here's the play.

284

"When you get to the wall, you lay the pack down, bottom pointing toward the wall and as close to it as you can set it. That way, the funnel faces the wall. When it goes, that configuration will channel maximum blast into a very small area of the wall. It's the way you kill Tiger tanks or fracture a granite substrata for the drill bit six thousand feet below Texas. I could explain the physics, but at this moment, who cares? It should blow right through the brick, opening a hole big enough—"

"What happens inside?"

"There will be a considerable energy dump, and a lot of supersonic crap in the air, shrapnel, dust, and shock, lots of shock. Plus some flash. It should blow all the fuses inside, so no lights. It should excavate a hole about six feet by six feet. I don't care what's there, drywall, masonry, brickwork, cinder block, cast iron, that much C-4 directed into that small an area is going to open it up, certainly wide enough for you to scurry through. On top of that if there are any plasterboard walls it should blow them into confetti. Anyone inside will feel it big-time."

"What does that mean?"

"If they happen to be standing on the other side of the wall from the C-4, they will be shredded. The pathology of the destruction diminishes as the energy expands and decreases. The next fifty feet, and actors are blown significantly off their feet, with attendant concussive, abrasive, or lacerational damage. There may be some fatalities, depending on the breaks. Beyond that, it gets trickier and again the breaks play into it. Maybe the shrapnel kills somebody or cuts them up bad, certainly the hearing damage will be extensive. Bruises, contusions, sprains, deep cuts, possibly arterial, falling debris, broken limbs. Not fun but in most cases survivable."

"I'm talking about their heads. What'll it do to the bad guys, in particular?"

"Everyone goes to goofytown. Hand-eye coordination shot, mental function zero, hearing destroyed, dancing elephants in pink dresses everywhere, cause and effect suspended, everybody has lost at least fifty IQ points. Nobody will resist you. Nobody will recognize you. Many won't even see you because of the dancing pink elephants. However, the recovery rate will differ significantly."

"Bet I know who's first out of the blocks."

"You got it. It's your bad actors. They've been in combat and are to some degree used to the shock and have been schooled to resist it or die. Or possibly it's because people attracted to that kind of work are self-selected for hardiness, risk-taking, lack of fear, strength, lack of self-awareness, and general malevolence. Being psycho is probably an advantage. They also have hard ego structures, maybe driven by narcissism, high self-regard, low empathy for others—that means the sight of people with their limbs blown off or heads smashed open won't cost them a beat—and high-order survival and task-completion impulses. Also, they kind of enjoy mayhem, smoke, death, danger. It's their idea of fun."

Delta nodded.

"If I take down the most active, I'm probably going to do okay, is that what you're saying?"

"Yes."

"Where's my NV package?"

Niner held out what looked like a poorly engineered set of binoculars, whose two eyepiece tubes connected to one larger tube. The thing also had what looked like a jockstrap hanging off it.

Delta took it, played with it, pushed it on, examined the green, green depthless world it conjured.

"It's like looking through a filthy aquarium."

"Here, you use this to shoot."

He handed over a Glock Long Slide, with six inches of Gemtech cylinder extending beyond the barrel, meaning it was suppressed, meaning that its *krak!* now became a pop. But the bigger news was another optical device, this one a kind of cup mounted to a plate at the rear sight dovetail, offering a concave lens in metal or plastic constriction, clearly meant to be accessed over the gun barrel. Delta knew it to be a red dot sight, a gizmo he didn't quite trust because the dot could be difficult to find when you were going hard and fast. But this seemed to be a situation made for such a thing.

He looked and noted the dot in the center of what appeared to be a two-inch 1952 television set mounted on the pistol. He went to the same view with the night vision, and the red became yellow and the details all but vanished, but shootable shapes were visible.

"That's a Trijicon SRO sight, 5 MOA. Their biggest dot. Nice big lens. If you stay on your fundamentals, you can't miss."

"Turn on/turn off?"

"No, that's the genius of Trijicon. It's always on. Thousands of hours of battery life. I just put a new battery in it, so it's good till at least 2025."

"Okay, it seems all here. What's your distraction device?"

"Just a movie pyrotechnic. About ten ounces of smokeless powder in a toilet paper roll. A half-ounce of C-4 to make it real loud. The C-4 goes bang, the powder burns like the Fourth of July, and you'll get flare as tall as a ten-story building. But it's only show. You could stand next to it and the only thing it would harm is your dignity. It's a definite pants-wetter."

A few details remained. Niner showed him how to insert the phone interface into the slot on the relay switch for the big boomer in the backpack.

Then it was just holding the phone's On switch down to come alive, and clicking a certain number already entered in the phone's Contacts menu.

"Remember, you plant it, then edge away. You have to be far enough around the curve from the blast so you're not in the shock-wave path. If you are, you're in goofytown as much as anybody else."

"Got it."

They checked watches, went over the sked, and suddenly there was nothing left to do.

"You sure you want to do this, bro? One on five, even in the dark with night-v, it's not good. Plus lots of pedestrians running around shrieking 'The sky is falling' just because the sky is falling. I mean, these bad guys will be good and gone tomorrow and forgotten about by the day after."

"Not by the people I work for. A contract's a contract and a reputation's a reputation, guy. I am thanking you and hope to see you on the other side."

"You are a goddamn Delta-ass cowboy, that's for sure," Niner said. "Here's to the other side."

They shook hands.

CHAPTER 37

Bestseller

Feeley and Banjax knew each other from the paper, and newsroom friendships are perdurable. So are newsroom hatreds, but that's another story.

Now in a quiet moment they took a separate peace from the world capital of crazy and lounged next to the incident van.

There was a little career update—who got Moscow? was it true the kids were all in charge? was what's-her-face, the horse-faced Irish bitch, still a bitch? that sort of thing—and then as is their eternal tendency, they turned to the central absurdity of their position and of news-covering in general.

"All these people dead," said Feeley, "the truly insane nature of the world and the utter frailty of human control over events revealed—"

"—the stupidity of leadership," Banjax continued, "the utter disruption of lives for months, maybe years, the immense expenditure of public funds—"

"—it goes on and on. But for us—" Feeley paused.

"I know. It's a once-in-a-lifetime shot."

"I don't know about you, but as soon as it's over, I'm hitting the keyboard. First guy out of the gate gets the bucks."

"You'll have to race me, friend. And I'm a very fast typist."

"Oink-oink! I smell a big payout coming. No more getting butt-raped by Mother Death twice a day."

"No more sucking up to deplorables four times a day."

"This is our big break. The magic words are 'movie money,' 'bestseller list,' and 'getting laid a lot.' "

"The story will write itself. It's got everything!"

"There's only one person who could fuck all this up," said Banjax.

"Who's that?" said Feeley. "I don't— Oh, yeah."

"Yeah," said Banjax. "That fucking Swagger."

The call came within an hour.

Someone yelled to him, "Agent Memphis, DC on the line."

"Here we go," said Nick to the senior cadre around him. "Got it," he said, picking up a dedicated line off the incident command van panel.

"Memphis," he said.

"Nick," said the director, "it's time to decide.

I need your best thinking. I've seen the building from aerial recon photos. Sort of round?"

"Yes, sir. Adjacent to the school, accessed from the school by a corridor now locked and rendered unassailable by virtue of hostages handcuffed to the door handles. There are other entrances to the structure, fire exits required by code, all also inaccessible by hostage placement. If you blew the doors, even with mild charges, anything strong enough to take down the steel would surely kill the hostages. And even then, access to the interior would be through a choke point, slow and inefficient, giving the Chechens ample time to carry out their threat."

"Any other ways in and out? Tunnels, vents, through the roof, anything like that?"

"No, sir. We've gone over the engineering plans and blueprints. If someone were building an assault-proof structure, they'd come up with this one."

"In similar situations, the Russians tried both gas and armored incursion," said the director. "Both 'worked' but produced casualty figures unacceptable in this country. What about blowing a hole in the wall?"

"If we had a first-rate guy on-site and access to engineering consultants, he might be able to put together a charge that could breach a wall without killing everybody inside, and stun the bad guys into stupor. But we don't, and if he's on the way, he won't get here in time. It's that time factor that's the genius part of their operation."

"Do you yourself have a plan?"

"No guarantees. I see a flying squad of snipers, infiltrated close as possible to the entrance. At a given moment, another sniper shooting suppressed takes out their sentinel at that site. Head shot. The other four slide into the building, set up, acquire targets fast, and on a radio command, fire simultaneously, downing the remaining four. Just like the SEALS on the *Maersk Alabama*."

"Downside?"

"Big. Possibly the Chechens see their guy go down. They open fire. Or, the snipers can't find clear shots once inside. We're not certain as to the layout, and the presence of the wrecked bus may completely screw up the fields of fire. Maybe one of the snipers can only take a body shot, and though he scores a fatal, the dying guy has enough time to dump a mag."

"Chances of working?"

"I'd say one in five."

"You think they'd kill our people?"

"Sir, I saw the boss man up close. Named Vakha Shishani, midfifties, a psycho thug. Yes, I think he would. Killing doesn't seem to mean much, as they've already killed at least ten, including three state troopers."

"All right, Nick. Make your call. Tell me straight."

"I wouldn't go, sir. Too big a risk. Lots of ways lots of people here can die. Doesn't matter to me if they're representatives or janitors. It's not strictly speaking necessary. I'd pay up and let 'em go. Get our people home."

CHAPTER 38
No Fun

Fuck.
  Girl.
Now.

The three concepts entwined and would not leave. He tried, he tried, he tried, but it was Uncle Vakha himself who had brought it up, and by the way, was it not the eternal right of the conqueror to enjoy the women of those defeated? Had it not been so for centuries?

Ibragim chose carefully. The younger ones frightened him a little. They had no knowledge of the world, and being pretty, they were used to having their way. No one had ever defied them, and to have his way with them would necessarily involve violence, ruckus, and a great deal of attention. This would not do, as even he understood.

But that knowledge made him even madder. He was always angry, always ready to fight or scream, whichever. This seemed to be rooted in one of his singular defects—he wasn't at ease with women. It happens that way. He had never joined in the carousing, the whoring, the drinking. It just wasn't him. He was too busy fulminating on insults, nurturing grudges, imagining smashing his oppressors in the mouth with a crowbar, and in all that mayhem sex was not much of a lure. Getting even was so much more fun, even in fantasy.

And now, unwillingly and unknown to Uncle Vakha, he was in a mess. He was in no mood to rape. In fact, he'd never been in a mood to rape in his life. His sexual experience was limited to a gentle village girl, and that was five years ago. This was neither the time nor the place to add to that slender accumulation of data.

But the other part of the equation had to do with that force which has brought many a poor man to ruin. He could not lose face with his brother or his cousins or his uncle by not taking advantage of what he perceived to be a laissez-faire market in women. That none of the others had so partaken meant nothing; he knew he and his twisted ideas of masculinity were on the line, like it or not. If he failed, it would open him to years of ribbing, and ensure his placement at the butt end of all jokes, jests, jibes, and jabs in the time to come, be it long or short. His anger would increase exponentially, and he would become a living, breathing bag of angst and self-loathing, all of it outer-directed to the innocent, the vulnerable, the shy.

He chose Ginger Brooks, a good ten years older

than he, and extremely glamorous and knowing in a TV-correspondent kind of way. Her beauty—he did not know this—was really a function of skillfully applied cosmetics, plus some nose and lip work, done discreetly seven years earlier. It had gotten her to a network, not the best, but several rungs above weekend weather girl, where she had started out too many years before in Green Bay, Wisconsin. She made mid six figures. Not too shabby, in the end.

"You," he said nervously, "you come with me."

The nervousness was his first mistake. She had a keen eye for weakness, honed in the elbow-throwing festival that was advancement in the television news profession, and a perhaps elevated anger at several opportunities she had, she felt, been cheated out of, because she was not pretty enough or she hadn't slept with the news director or because she was a woman, whatever.

Now being under the command of terrorists from some godforsaken spot simply added to her frustrations and her grievances. The fact that she wasn't making enough money to justify the danger was another part of it; the guilt that she should be doing something still another. And the ultimate insult, that she had somehow been separated from her purse and that meant her makeup, which she felt was truly important to her for camera readiness and career advance, had put her in a psycho-bitch-from-hell mood.

So they were two angries facing each other, not exactly raw material for a tender night.

"No way, Junior," she said.

Immediately she felt the circle of colleagues and competitors on the floor with her shift, tighten, maybe squeeze away from her. She felt their anxiety: Why is she making trouble? She'll just get us killed.

"No. Come. Must come," the man said. He was about twenty-two, not unattractive in a kind of Eastern European brute-monkey way. He had the face and hair and body of a hockey player, tattoos running up over his jumpsuit collar, and a pistol, which he carried too non-chalantly.

"In a pig's eye," she said.

This baffled him, as it would most people under thirty-five, being an old midwestern farm retort, and she wasn't even sure where she'd learned it. It probably outdated her by several decades. She wasn't even sure what it meant, other than, generally, "Go fuck yourself," which she didn't want to say, as it was uncouth, and uncouth women never got anywhere.

Finally, figuring it out, the man put the gun into her face, though his hand was shaking.

"Must come. No die here. Die for what? For nothing. Come, now, goddamn you, American girl."

"Honey, I haven't been a girl in fifteen years. Go away. Go back to your boyfriends. If you want a piece, get it off of them."

He was too unsure of his English to read the homosexual innuendo in this, for among other things, the very concept of homosexuality was not anywhere near the front of his brain.

"I will shoot."

"You haven't the grit for that. Punch a woman, be a big man, maybe, but up-front, close-in killing, not for you. Not cold-bloodedly. You're not that psycho."

Again, he was utterly baffled. But he was also near fainting. The pressure building inside him was almost too much. What on earth could he do? Smash her in the head? Yes, but at the same time he had no urge to wreck what to him and the camera was great beauty. He could not make himself do that. Argue with her? For how long? And what if the others saw him? Old Chechen saying: to argue with bitch is to have already lost. Well, no, it's not an old Chechen saying, but it could have been. What was authentic was what trouble this unexpected issue might cause him: Poor Ibragim cannot even rape a woman. What is wrong with him?

"Ginger, for God's sake," said someone. "You're going to get us all killed."

"Ginger, don't be a dead hero. It's nothing, you'll have forgotten in a week."

"Please, Ginger. Don't set him off. He looks like he's about to shoot."

"Ah, you losers," she said. Then standing, she said, "The shit I go through for Fox!"

"You'll get a medal," someone said.

"I just want a vodka and a cigarette."

But at that point, the stern Old Testament figure of the big boss loomed across the confrontation.

"What? What is?" demanded Vakha.

"I take woman," said Ibragim.

"Who say?"

"Is war. Is what happens in war."

"You do nothing without permission. I have given no permission."

"Uncle, I need a woman."

He didn't. If he got one, he wasn't sure what to do with her. But now he saw his colleagues at full stop, their scrutiny deflected toward his little melodrama.

"You can wait."

"I cannot wait. Tomorrow, maybe dead."

"If you force her, she screams. It will happen. It always happens. Someone here with phone makes call. 'Help, help, they are raping our women!' Outside, the boss is holding his people under tight control, but maybe that's the thing that breaks them. On their own, they come crashing in, shooting, to save the women from rape by the hairy Russians. They have been dreaming of saving women from hairy Russians in this country for seventy years. Then we have big gun battle. Everybody die. I die, your brother and cousins die, most of these people die. You die. And for what? A little piece of pussy. In Grozny, you can have all pussy you want. Better pussy than her."

"Thanks, mac," said Ginger.

"Ibragim," said Anzor, who had come over, "Uncle Vakha knows. Put it back in your pants, if you can find it. Take it out in Grozny with all your new girlfriends."

"Gahhh," said Ibragim, signifying defeat. He let Ginger go, she spun away and sat down on the gym floor.

"Good fellow," said Vakha. "Now forget. Concentrate on task ahead. This business with the woman, it is nothing."

And it was nothing. Except that it explained why Ibragim became even angrier.

CHAPTER 39
The Word

R eports came in. The sniper gambit that Nick had plotted as Plan B was setting itself up, even if he wasn't sure of the quality. The idea was that if shooting started, a squad of snipers would hit the door fast, after someone dropped the sentry. They'd spread and immediately look to take down guys in orange, maybe preventing the start-up of the hostage massacre. Two of the shooters would be FBI agents out of Boise, SWAT-qualified, and two state policemen. No long guns, as they might prove difficult to manipulate in the helter-skelter of the auditorium. Each had an M4 and a quality red-dot optic. It was just a matter of finding a fundamentally sound position, acquiring the target by placing the red dot on the center of the face, thumbing off the safety, and firing.

Nick allowed himself the fantasy of believing it would work. He imagined the sound of the four rifles going off simultaneously, and imaged the four remaining Chechens dropping as if their knees had suddenly melted, straight down into a puddle of dead guy on the floor. Hip hip hooray for our team.

But it couldn't happen that way. It never did, or at least only once, under certain unusual circumstances aboard the *Maersk Alabama*. It was always sordid, messy, uncool. No fight choreographer had worked it out in advance, so nobody would be where they should be and only half of what had been planned was possible. Maybe there would be enough chaos that only a few hostages got whacked—say ten out of thirty-five. Technically, given the circumstances, that would be ruled a "success" even if nobody in the known world would share the assessment.

It killed him how everything had so far broken well for the Chechens. They pick a site almost impregnable, many of their hostages are so old that no gas warfare was allowed, there was no easy ingress, the distances were too far. Time was the ene—

"Agent Memphis?"

"Yes?"

"DC again."

Nick went to the console, picked up the phone.

"Memphis," he said.

"Okay, Nick," said the director, "here's the decision. It's a no-go. I've decided to give them what they want and take the consequences. It's okay by the White House as long as I own it."

"Yes, sir. Everyone here will agree, except the Idaho State Police people, who are gung ho for action."

"Understandable, can't be helped. Maybe tell their colonel privately so he'll feel special and know his concerns were considered."

"Good idea, sir."

"So we'd like to suggest you stand the men down, you all go to safety on the firearms, you withdraw the snipers, maybe decrease the perimeter presence by a third or a half, and you see yourselves now as responsible for assuring a smooth transfer to the airport. We've got an Air Force Black Hawk inbound. He's on the network now. Are you there, Major Burgess?"

"Yes, sir, call sign Whiskey 7, under your command, sir. I'm holding about twenty miles north of Boise. I have enough fuel to orbit over the target for several hours. Just give me the go sign and I can be there in five minutes."

"Good man. Did you get that, Nick?"

"I did."

"Agent Memphis, Whiskey 7. Can you brief me on how you see this working? How will they egress?"

"Looking at the blueprints, they'll go up several flights of backstage metal stairways to get to the highest level, which is a catwalk to provide access to the lighting fixtures for various shows and things. At the end of the catwalk, there's another short stairway up to a metal door that, by fire regs, has to be openable from the inside. That puts them on the roof of the auditorium. I think, from the photos I've seen, the roof is clear for a landing."

"Our information confirms that, Whiskey 7," said the director. "It ought to take a minute or so to get them aboard. Then straight to Boise Airport. Delta is flying in a 747, and they'll refuel it and place it at the end of the Alpha runway, engines on, ready to go. The money is on its way from Denver and in fact may even be at the airport now. So I'm hoping there are no complications of a logistical variety."

"Got it, sir," said Whiskey 7.

CHAPTER 40

Perimeter

6:00 A.M.

He didn't like this one. You can always tell. Sometimes in the chopper before insert, you just got a feeling in your gut that something had been missed, some possibility overlooked, someone wasn't up to the mission. But it was too late: you were airborne, draped in camo, ammo, and firepower, committed, on the clock. What happened happened. Epic screwup, max wipeout, or the kind of operator's glory that consisted entirely of a nod from your squad mates. You just did what you had to do.

Delta was prone in some bushes across the street from the police perimeter running around the back of the Frank Church auditorium. He'd snugged up to a modest suburban house that had been evacuated. The Glock was in his duty holster, but the suppressor hadn't been applied to its muzzle yet. As for the night vision, he'd mounted it, and now experienced the world of infrared light. Though set entirely in the green-yellow-gray area of the spectrum, the images still yielded some detail. Every twenty yards or so, a squad car. At each car, two officers, usually (but not exclusively) in SWAT gear, usually (but not exclusively) men, all with M4s or short-barreled pump guns. No night vision, no lights on, but a lot of contact between the units, as guys got bored looking at the auditorium's rear, a blank brick wall two hundred yards out, and wandered over to talk to buddies, make new friends (different municipalities at this far end of the siege), complain about overtime, boast about planned Caribbean cruises, and catch up on gossip. Now and then a supervisor's SUV, lights flashing, would ease around the perimeter road, stopping here and there to tell the guys to buck up and stay alert. It was necessary because the nature of police emergencies means that many of the men involved will be deep into second or even third shifts and thus deep into fatigue. Their main enemy was drowsiness.

From where he was, Delta could rotate to the left and see the beginning of the heavy assault positions at the front of the building, before they disappeared behind the curvature. Not much going on there either.

He plotted his best move. He'd wait until a supervisor's vehicle came along, and as it slowed, he'd crouch on the approach and fall in behind it. Then as it pulled out, he'd peel off and wedge himself against the curb of the street. Nobody would see because their orientation was totally toward the building. From that position he'd call Niner a few hundred yards farther down the orbit road, similarly indexed to the perimeter security, to blow the pyrotechnic.

When that sucker lit up, it would of course galvanize the cops. Squawking, panic, radio confusion. Some would rush to the explosion, some would hunker down behind their rifles and go to off-safety. He would count to thirty, waiting for all the movers to get by and all the hunkers to hunker, and then he would squirm over the curb and low-crawl between the vehicles. It should be easy going, and once inside the perimeter, it was a straight belly-swim to the building, exhausting but easily doable.

But always the doubts. The brain said yes, the lower colon said no. So many little things had to go just right, but what if they didn't? He didn't like this one, but he could figure no other way.

What if they got nervous and swept the area with lights?

They wouldn't.

What if they had night vision that he had missed?

They didn't.

What if they were smart instead of dumb?

They weren't.

This was the part he hated. You could tick off the attributes and convince yourself it was brilliant. It was well planned for an ad hoc op, it made tactical and psychological sense, it was in concordance with police behavior as he understood it, and it was within his physical capacities. But still, the gut wouldn't shut up.

The unknown, the unforeseeable, the accidental. It was the nature of the special operation. All the planning goes out the window. Extortion 17, with twenty-four of the best trained operators in the world, takes off on a rescue mission in Afghanistan, and there just happens to be a camel-fucker on a ridge with an RPG. He just happens to understand deflection—most of them had no fucking idea what that was—and he holds ahead of the rising chopper and doesn't jerk the trigger. All those guys—he knew several, as sometimes SEALs and Delta folks hung together in various hellhole watering troughs the world over—were gone. It still seemed grotesque and unfair, but it was neither. It was just the nature of the special operation.

He looked and saw a supervisor's car coming along.

He checked his watch. The next few minutes would tell.

He took out his throwaway from Target, pushed the button, and knew the vibes alerted Niner.

"Yo?"

"Guy has just passed you. Should be here in a couple. When he arrives, I'll call again, but don't answer. Just blow the movie explosion."

"You sure you want to do this?"

"If I get nabbed, just leave town fast. Don't fall into the net yourself."

"Guy, in my opinion you are way above and beyond."

"I have a rep to maintain."

"You must be made out of the hardest steel on the planet."

"Then why do my knees hurt? Why do I dread that long crawl? Why am I so fucking scared?"

"You're pretending to be human is all."

"Okay, out. Get settled."

He was now alone with his fear. It would unfold in pre-op time, which was different from any time in the world. It was the same for paratroopers waiting in their C-47s for green over Normandy, Marines fighting seasickness as the LCIs fought through the surf for Iwo, the ball-turret gunner seeing swarms of nightmare fighters rising from Schweinfurt. Didn't have to be World War II. Could be inside the big horse on the Trojan plain, in the fishhook at Gettysburg, wondering how it could get colder and darker at Inchon, swearing at the Phantoms for not putting the napalm on the ridgeline at Khe Sanh—

He watched as the supervisor's Ford, black and white for Ada County, finally arrived, pulled in, and the sergeant leaned out his window as one of the cops got out of the car to join him for a brief confab. He'd wait until they were engaged, the coast was clear, and then he'd—

Vibration.

What the fuck?

Vibration.

Not in plans. It was on him to call Niner when he was tucked flat against the curb, not the other way around.

"Yeah?"

"Something's happening."

"Are they assaulting?"

"No, just the opposite."

"No follow."

"It's like they're standing down."

"What?"

"They're calling most of the guys in. I see cops leaving their positions and pulling out."

"Can you check the Web on your phone? Maybe there's news."

"Wilco and back at you."

Delta looked. Yes, something was happening. The sergeant had just abandoned the chitchat and gone to his radio. He spoke as if to request clarification, then turned to the officer and spoke with him, even as the second officer got out of the car and came over, just to make sure they'd all gotten the same message, even if it was hard to believe.

Then the sergeant geared up, hung a swift U-turn, and headed back to the command location. The two cops departed also, and suddenly the road was almost jammed with police vehicles from the greater Boise area.

Vibration.

"Got it?"

"Yeah, the president has agreed to their demands. The perimeter cops are being recalled and moved to a holding area a few blocks away. All firearms put in Condition Three. All snipers to case their rifles."

"Holy shit," said Delta. "It's wide open. I could walk in dressed like Bugs Bunny."

CHAPTER 41
Yippee-Ki-Yay

6:10 A.M.

Suddenly it was almost a party.

"You people," Vakha announced, "we will not have to kill you. The FBI has announced he will accept our demands. Boys and girls, free at seven. Soon, eh? Old men and ladies, ride to Chechnya first, then fly home free. Or maybe see sights in Grozny. Beautiful city. See, not so bad."

So, except for the ten dead, no, not so bad. Human behavior being what it is—that is, low, base, squalid, and utterly self-interested—the youngish captured journalists and technicians began to cheer with relief. Hugs were universal, and even high-end network correspondents squeezed on scruffy camera techies.

Among the eight geezer congressmen and -women, the joy was somewhat more restrained, but just as genuine. Old bones were not as spry as once, and sitting on the floor so long had calcified many of them. Still, their mood soared, hand-gripping was exchanged, and all looked toward Committee Chairwoman Venable as the hero of the event.

"Madam Representative," gushed Matson (D-IL, 7th District), "you got us through. Your dignity, your strength, your refusal to panic, all were inspirational."

"Representative Venable," said Lincoln (D-MA, 13th District), "we'll all remember your composure and leadership. It's your finest hour."

The huzzahs were bipartisan.

"Charlotte," said Douglas (R-OH, 3rd District), an old friend, "I don't know what we would have done without your example. This is the capstone of a magnificent career."

Mother Death accepted their gratitude, feeling she had earned it, and herself felt the immense relief of a *Titanic* lifeboater who'd just spotted the approach of RMS *Carpathia*. Career concerns had gone away, as had political goals. She just wanted a massage, then two baths, one in hot steamy water with lots of bubbles, the other in cold steam-less vodka with no bubbles.

Baker, a few feet away from her, looked around the room, could see the circle of journos squeezing one another livid, and believed he even saw the radiance of survival lighting the eyes of the Chechen gunmen. He honestly had never felt so happy in his life. It was better than the birth of his children, the time he got into Café Milano without a res, his first network exposure, all the *Times* editorials supporting him and singing of his brilliance.

I made it, he thought.

Then it all changed.

Everybody happy. Everybody full of joy, the urge to dance, squeeze flesh, sing, drink. Everybody except Ibragim.

He sat in the bleachers by himself, remote, embittered, seething. All the good feelings made him angrier. All these fucking Americans going back to their plush, soft, pointless lives, while he, Ibragim, the strongest and best, a true Chechen warrior, carried the stain of failure and malfunction. No one had let him down but himself, but that was not how he saw it. He saw it as an affront. Their American self-love had somehow cursed him, given him the fucking heebie-jeebies, kept him from enjoying a man's right to conquest and the smooth, moist pleasures of the beautiful woman's body. He had never seen such a beauty!

Now, when he thought of her, it enraged him! An hour too late! Nothing to be done! A lost opportunity! Massive shame!

I should kill her, he thought.

He had the knife. He had taken it from one of the dead policemen before the bodies were removed. It was a black folder, thin, metallic, and with a flick of the wrist it unleashed three inches of black steel, sharpened to a killer point. He had already mastered the snap that made such magic possible.

I should ram it between her ribs and into her heart and watch her bleed out in oceans of red roaring from her wound, as her face grows pale and her eyes dim.

Yes, why not?

We can do anything we want.

We can—

He felt the spooky pressure of observation and looked quickly, to see someone's demon eyes, like black diamonds on white satin, flashing off him after a period of uninterrupted study.

This made him even more insane with rage.

It was the balding American in the now-rumpled suit, evidently a big shot, for he was sitting next to the important old lady. He had no idea who this fool was, but there was something innately appalling about him. Those eyes, always darting, radiant with fear and suspicion, yet at the same time smug and well pleased in his little dark suit and his little red tie. He was a man of slightness in appearance, no matter what truth lay under his suit; there was something ephemeral about him, and in an instant he came to stand for everything Ibragim had been taught to hate: the manipulator, the polite thief who steals on guile, not strength, the man in the network, protected by an alliance of friends and tribal connections, always soft and pink, never a man of the gun or the knife but as much a brigand as he. With a thousand times less risk. He looked rich, content, assured of the bright future. He'd never be a torturer for the Russians or a killer or do time. He was just an errand boy, as Ibragim had been and was still resentful for being.

Ibragim stood, reached into his pocket, pulled out the knife, and with a snap of his wrist flicked the blade out.

A shadow fell across Baker's happiness. He turned and apprehended a dark figure towering over him. The face was a sullen mask of indifference, slack and stupid and unreasonable. But the dark eyes gleamed almost incandescent rage. They narrowed, focusing, becoming yet more intense. The man himself had the weight lifter's body and tattoos crawling up his neck and vivid on his bare, bulging arms. He looked like Old Testament death, here to deliver condemnation, disparagement, and inevitably genocide.

Baker swallowed a gulp of sand, breathed over the hot coals that suddenly filled his lungs, felt his bladder and sphincter knit, then loosen, almost to the point of letting go. The pit of his stomach opened like a gallows trap and he felt himself falling, falling, falling . . .

The chatter and giggles died instantly. The area filled with the charisma of the eternal confrontation, killer and victim. Everyone could read murder in the Chechen's posture, and knew that in seconds he would strike with an adder's instinct, the black blade would flash and the congressman would scream as the knife penetrated, ripped, and punctured. It would be no movie stabbing, polite and discreet, but a flood of black blood everywhere in seconds.

"W-what do you want?" Baker managed.

"You stare at me? Why you stare at me?"

Eye contact: signifier of death among so many vertebrates. Make eye contact with the Cape buffalo and you've just invited two tons of fury to fold, spindle, and mutilate you, no matter how many .470s you put into him. Do the same to the alpha wolf and he goes from yellow-eyed growler to Fang the Destroyer and brings his posse to the party. Any big cat, really—and sometimes even small cats, which is funny until you figure out what it means. It can happen—and does—on many city streets in any city in the world, where the wrong glance generates the year's 406th homicide.

"I wasn't," said Baker, through lips that were ticking like a Geiger counter laid up to an Atlas warhead.

"You look at me. You put curse on me!"

"No, no," said Baker. "Please, I was just looking around the room and noting how happy everybody was."

"Those are the eyes of a demon."

"No, they're just my eyes. That's the way they are. I can't help it. One of my uncles was the same way. It's genetic."

"Genetic! What this mean? Fancy, fancy. You smarter than me? Then how come I have knife and you have shit in your pants?"

"Sir, I meant you no disrespect. I swear, it was random, meaningless."

"You curse me. Now I cut eyes out. Then I cut face off. Demon is dead, I am free. I know the legends."

"Young man," said Representative Venable, next to Baker, "this is preposterous. This man is an American congressman. He is no demon, he means you no—"

"Shut up, old lady! I cut your fucking eyes out too. I cut all your eyes out, you pricks. You bastards!"

He was screaming, fully out of control, sending saliva like gun smoke from his mouth, face red, body getting tenser and tenser.

He knelt next to his victim, grabbed him by his sparse combed-over hair, and pulled his unresisting head back, raising the knife with the other hand for the deep plunge into the eye socket.

"Wander in hell forever, blind man!" he shouted.

Someone hooked him by the wrist and spun him to his ass.

He looked up in full Jack-the-Ripper insanity and made to leap at his antagonist.

It was the man in the wheelchair.

With one hand—the other flex-cuffed to the

arm of the device—he had rolled himself from his isolation to the confrontation.

"You want to fight, motherfucker? Fight me! In a wheelchair I'll whip your ass and make you eat that blade, you little butt-monkey!"

CHAPTER 42
English Channel

Delta reacquainted himself with a hard truth of the infantry lifestyle, something he'd learned in basic training but long ago forgotten: low-crawling is only intellectually defensible when someone is shooting at you. Under those circumstances, but one body outpost is signaling headquarters, and with only one message. It's your ass, and it's saying over and over, louder and louder, "Don't let me die out here in this shithole." No other transmissions are permitted, and the urgency of the situation fills the body with abundant hormone therapies which prevent pain, discomfort, fatigue, or even boredom from making a point. Absent incoming, as he was now, halfway across the playing fields of Frank Church High School, other stations were heard from.

The knees for example, demanded to know if this trip was really necessary. The elbows requested, angrily, to consult with the shop steward. The neck proved more strident than either, wondering sotto voce, "Why are you doing this to me? What have I ever done to you to deserve this?" There were a few more loud spots about his body—wounds, all of them—which didn't enjoy the transit either, and though they registered, the precise words of their communiqués were lost in the cacophony.

Would it ever end? Why had this seemed like such a good idea? Two hundred yards is a *long fucking way* when you are on your belly, propelled by a breaststroke of elbow and knee into rhythmic collision with hard earth, the grass offering less cushioning than one might think. It was like swimming in concrete, and though he was in superb physical shape, off daily workouts and three-mile runs when permitted, he hadn't used these muscles in this range of motion and sequence in years. Thus it was also like bathing in pain, while breathing sulfur fumes and listening to the collected insights of political analyst Stephen Colbert in stereo.

Now it was the small of his back that decided to join the chorus of anger and agony. "Soak me in bourbon!" it sang, loudly, while sending blades of icy-cold double-edge up to his shoulder blades.

One-two, one-two, one-two.

He paused, counted the sweat beads switchbacking down his rib cage, out of his hairline onto his face, off his nose, off his chin, down his neck, and to his junk. He rolled halfway over to give his back some off-duty time, sucked in some oxygen over the hot coals that turned his lungs all toasty, wished for water, which—duh! some commando!—he'd forgotten. Hydrate or die, the man said, and about now, he began to think about Death: the Good Part.

Then he rolled back over, and broke every vow he'd made to himself, and looked ahead to the fucking back wall of the auditorium. He couldn't see it. WTF! Where the hell had it gone? It was like that moment in everybody's English Channel swim, when you're out of sight of the coast you came from but not yet in sight of the coast you're aiming for. The horizon is empty a full 360, and no direction offers anything another direction doesn't. Fortunately, for both low-crawling in the dark and swimming the Channel, the Suunto watch offers among its dozens of features— it'll apply to an Ivy League college for you if you know the right buttons—a digital compass, which he quickly summoned and learned that he was still on azimuth 188 S, which was his calculated route and wouldn't deposit him in a McDonald's drive-thru lane the next town over. New issue: Should he go through the sweat and difficulty of unpacking his PVS-7 from his 659-pound knapsack, and go to the trouble of getting it on, all while laying prone and motionless in a sea of grass? But he saw the stupidity in that, and gave himself another few minutes off, craning his neck to catch a view of the vault of summer sky above.

Stars by the hundreds, a few pinwheels and planets, a supernova here and there, the red, steady tracer of a plane over Oregon, now and then the flicker of a firefly, enough of a breeze to energize the far-off trees into some kind of hushed rush or hiss. Oh, and cop cars, though far fewer of them, sending their pulsing red-blue Morse code. Summer in America. Nothing could be finer! Wouldn't it be nice to sit with a gal by a pond with a jug of wine and a loaf of bread, listening to the birds and the crickets? But then he remembered that the birds and the crickets weren't actually birds and crickets but tinnitus he'd picked up from too much shooting and blowing shit up without ear protection.

That in turn reminded him of what he did for a living, and what it was, exactly, he was there to do. And the funny thing: the long crawl wasn't even the hard part.

It was the easy part.

One-two, one-two, one-two.

CHAPTER 43

Fallback

6:12 A.M.

The reports came in quickly and all were good. The perimeter strength had been lessened by half, all snipers had cased their rifles and moved to the holding area at Wrigley Elementary four blocks away, as had all suited-up SWAT teams, and particularly Colonel Lhotske's State Police team, who were anxious to assault.

"You're sure on this, Nick?" asked Colonel Lhotske, Mike by name, who had become Nick's ad hoc second-in-command, in the absence of senior FBI executives.

"It's from the top, Mike. The director himself. I will say, it was my recommendation as well."

"If it falls apart, Nick, you know it'll be on you, not him."

"I get that. I've always gotten that. That's how they play ball in DC."

"You seem like a hell of a good guy," said Lhotske, who'd played linebacker for the Utes in the eighties and still looked like he could go both ways for a full sixty. "So speaking frankly, I can tell you I don't like it one bit. I've got three new

325

widows to answer to, and the idea of the guys who put their husbands down sailing off into the blue with ten million in U.S. taxpayers' money doesn't sit well with me."

"I do understand. I get it. But in this one, we have to look at the bigger picture. The metric isn't 'What is just?' The metric is 'What does the most good for the largest number of people?' That's our job too. I can't have thirty-five or so more deaths when the means of avoiding them are right before us, just a few hours away. How'd you like to have thirty-five more sets of grieving parents, children, and spouses to explain to? Plus all the national jackals screaming at you for murdering Congresswoman Venable as well. Not a happy outcome, I'm telling you."

"Okay, Nick, we're on sked, my people have stood down, and all the Boise and western Idaho departments are in place. But . . . ?"

"Go ahead. But?"

"But suppose something goes wrong? Suppose somebody accidentally fires, suppose a car back-fires, suppose one of the hostages gets heroic and they shoot him? All those things could happen. Then what's to stop the massacre? We don't have enough guys left here to do any good, plus they'll be hung up at the choke point of the entrance, and coming through they'll face heavy fire and go down like at the Battle of the Somme. We don't have enough firepower to suppress, we don't have flashbangs to disorient, we don't have any armored vehicles to advance against heavy fire. It's a roll of the dice I can't get behind."

"Unexpected consequences. I can't pretend they aren't a feature of something like this. But I have to play by the instructions. The director was explicit. He said no close-by tacticals. There's the same difficulty there, Mike. One of them, maybe not well trained state officers, but some underbudget low-trained suburban guy all excited about finally playing cowboy, maybe he's the one who fires. You'd have a lot of men of unknown training levels fumbling around with high-tech weapons in the dark, a lot of emotion, excitement, fear, confusion, all of it in the dark. A shot or a burst from one of them could bring it all down."

"Wilco, Nick. I had to give it a try."

"If it comes to it, I'll put you on the record for voicing doubts. You won't get burned. And I'll meet with the widows for as long as it takes, and they can vent on me."

"That's above and beyond, Nick."

"It goes with the job, which you must know I didn't want and had no idea would ever come my way six or so hours ago."

"Got it and—"

But suddenly there was a policewoman next to him, urgent in body language.

"Agent Memphis?"

"Yes, what is it?"

"Someone just called from inside on cell. They called Boise downtown and forwarded it."

"What is it?"

"Swagger's been killed."

INTERLUDE: 1780

11th October

By the time we got to the parade ground, dawn's gray had begun to color the eastern sky behind the mountains. A chilling drizzle had arrived to lower the temperature yet further, and it seemed to pelt our skin and turn our clothes sodden as we moved. As we approached, we sank into the earth, and felt the mud ooze about our boots. It was thoroughly dreary. The auspices were not good, I felt, but I said nothing.

Drawing nearer, I could see Major Winston and his clique of thugees. He had shed his tunic and now practiced muscle-loosening phantom thrusts and parries, opening his body to vigorous action. From the posture and precision, I divined immediately that he was a swordsman of high skill. Again, I felt a wave of regret pass over, as it seemed sure Lieutenant Grammercy was facing clear-eyed death.

Also under half-tent there was a party of observers, notably the Colonel and his daughter, the Colour Sergeant Stanley, the Sergeant at Arms, and a squad of foot at rest, though prepared with short-pattern Bess and bayonet mounted, ready to enforce by shot or thrust any decree of the Colonel, but more to act as bulwark against unruly behavior by witnesses. Tillotson of Infantry was there, as well as Sergeant Kirk, the escapee from the mountain, still bandaged in head. Dr. Makepeace, to whom I had not been introduced, his being absent at the dinner last night, sat as well, a satchelful of catgut, needles, and linen I hoped. And finally another sergeant, again not of acquaintance, with an array of hourglasses for timing events.

In the distance one could see rankers, some with their camp-following wives and children. They did not, could not, would not approach, knowing this to be a species of folly reserved for the officer rank. As for the young woman, I wondered, Why was she here? I could not countenance that she would witness her theoretical "champion's" death, but then it was said she was highly spirited and had many manly accomplishments that women were not by rule of society permitted. She claimed them nevertheless, was a noted rider, a huntress of both fox and bird, and had even, it was said, tried the falconer's game.

Indeed, she broke to us as we grew nearer.

"Robert," she said, the rain wet on her face, her hair piled up under bonnet, an old campaign tunic of her father's wrapped around her shoulders, "I cannot bear to lose you and Patrick in the same week."

"Madam, I have no plans on being dispatched."

"But tell me, please. This madness is on account of Patrick and the horsemen and their lonely fate atop the mountain. It has nothing to do, fundamentally, with Winston's disrespect to my person. My honor is certainly not worth a life, not worth yours in particular, after all you have contributed."

"I suppose it was a tool to bend the rules a bit. But when word of such reached Patrick, he was inflamed. So then was I. I cannot pretend there is nothing to it."

"Please, Robert. Do not be a fool. This man is so dangerous."

"Susanna, I have good Major Kavanagh here as my second, and I see that Colour Sergeant Stanley, a fair man, will serve as Master of Duel. I am therefore not without resources and shall well acquit myself."

"Don't let him die, Major Kavanagh."

"It is not my intention, Madam," I said, "but when blades emerge, as well does the ferocity of whimsy, and against that, one can only do so much."

CHAPTER 44

Death

6:25 A.M.

The boy squared to Swagger. He swallowed, gritted his teeth so hard the muscles along his jawbone danced like snakes on fire, his nostrils flared wide as his eyeballs, he took a deep breath, held it.

"Motherfucker!" he screamed, announcing the move, which followed thereafter, a headfirst lunge with the knife low beyond reach.

The two smashed together, and the wheelchair jolted backward in the struggle but not before Swagger drove his free palm hard into the oncoming temple, feeling the solid strike of flesh on bone. The blow, in micro-time, twisted Ibragim's orientation to the sitting, half-tethered man, and they collapsed in each other's arms. In the instantaneous campaign of slap-grasp-grab warfare between two of the arms that was the next event, Swagger won out, getting a firm grip on his opponent's wrist, freezing the knife before it achieved penetration. But it was not without penalty. The blade opened two inches of gash on his left arm, and the point bit three, maybe four times into the back of his hand and his wrist. All of these wounds shed black, deoxygenated blood, all delivered a memo of the penetration. The long one burned and bled the most profusely, and Swagger could feel it running down his arm, hot and wet, turning his shirt and coat sodden plum. But he was by no means incapacitated, and when the boy, meaning to pull away, separated from the embrace, Swagger drove his crown— where forehead met head—into the boy's nose, smashing it, unleashing torrents of Chechen blood.

But in the jack of pain that lit up within the boy, torrents of strength were also animated, and he went briefly superhuman and leaped back, tearing his wrist free. He stood, shook his head, and drops of blood sprayed off. Meanwhile the hostages squirmed backward from the violence as from other points, Vakha, Anzor, and Khasan rushed to gain control of the situation.

They were not fast enough. Ibragim gulped another three gallons of air, lowered his head into the rushing-bull attitude, and threw himself at Swagger. Swagger took the return head butt but knew that it was merely a distraction against the deadly work of the knife, and he tried a blind intercept of the fast-closing blade, only struck it slightly from inside to out, squirmed into instinctive rotation, but felt the point and then the whole length of the edge on his body.

He felt the wound searing in pain, cutting, cutting, cutting, and marveled that he had blood yet to give, but the wound gave and his shirt flooded with it, slipping, sliding everywhere, leaving its spreading stain as proof of its gravity.

They froze, embracing in the intimacy of mortal hand-to-hand combat. The work was done.

Swagger looked. Blood. Blood. Blood. The boy stood back as Swagger put a hand to stanch it, but found his clasped fingers had no absorptive powers, and the fluid flooded between them, now filling his lap with its ungodly color as it reddened from the black when it realized the atmosphere held oxygen. The boy had a look of triumph—but also pain and pride and stupidity, all features of victory.

"Swagger!" somebody yelled, and he knew it was the old lady, who rose to run to him when no one else did, but was shoved to her knees by Anzor rushing past her.

"You motherfucker," Ibragim shouted, then turned. "Uncle, the sniper attacked me, I show him what a Chechen is!"

"A great victory," said Vakha, staring at the carnage, the puddling on the floor, sniffing the rank stink of ultimate-energy sweat thick in the air, and if his comment was meant ironically, Ibragim neither noticed nor cared.

He had a last ceremony to attend to. He rushed

to the wheelchair, where Bob sagged, feeling more blood rush between his inefficient fingers, spun it and gave it a mighty shove, and it sped across the floor, leaking contrails of blood, until it hit the edge of the proscenium wall and toppled, spilling sideways. The man inside did not fall out, however; he was still pinned by the flex cuff to his right arm.

"Bleed out in gutter, Sniper. Alone and forgotten."

"You people," shouted Vakha, "you tighten up, get closer together. You cannot be spread about like you are at a picnic. This isn't game. You keep fucking mouths shut, get no ideas. You see what heroism gets? Your guts cut out, your blood in lakes everywhere."

He turned.

"Anzor, you are now in charge of hostages."

"I can do, Vakha," claimed Ibragim. "I am not hurt."

"Your eye is size of grapefruit. You have probably pissed up pants. You go rest, wait for head to stop hurting and heart to stop running away. Khasan, stay with him, clean him up."

"Yes, Uncle."

He turned, saw that Magomet, though not the most aggressive of them, had had the intelligence to stay at his post at the smashed entrance to the building.

"Where is gun?" Anzor asked.

"I—I think I dropped it."

They turned and looked, and there the M4 lay next to the circle of hostages, untouched. Anyone could have taken it up and turned it on their takers and killed them all. No one did.

America! thought Vakha. He felt an odd melancholy at the sniper's death. It was like the death of an old god.

America! You put your heroes on trial and everyone left behind is too soft to fight even for their own lives.

CHAPTER 45

All the News That's Fit to Print

His iPhone vibrated in his shirt pocket.

Banjax, smiling, moved away from the clot of elite reporters—the *Post*s, Washington and New York—the *LA Times*, NBC, CBS, hotshot LA and Denver TV locals, and the *Miami Herald*—and slipped the phone from his pocket, not wanting to make a big deal of it.

He recognized the number as Bud Feeley's right away, and tried to keep from jumping with anticipation. He kept moving.

"Yeah?"

"You alone?"

"Now I am."

"Scoop time, brother. Everybody'll have this but you might as well be first, because you ran with the Patrick Ferguson stuff."

"Go ahead," said Banjax, a little squeak halfway through, suggesting that despite the fact he was trying to be cool, his excitement was rising fast.

After Feeley laid it out, he asked "Confirmed?"

"From two sources inside, who called Boise Metro, which patched it through. Now others with cell phones are calling their bosses or their staff or whatever, so it's going to break soon. You'd best get that ass in gear."

"Got it," said Banjax, hitting the end-of-call icon, going next to Contacts and selecting National News Desk.

"David?" It was Mitch Goldstein, night national editor, recognizing the iPhone number.

"Get this online fast and into the first edition if you can. I'm only a little ahead of the others."

"Give me a second to set up a dictationist."

Banjax managed a casual glimpse back at the cluster he'd just left, and saw that it was still coherent, nobody had gotten all freaky and jumpy on the news. He scanned the others, farther back, afraid that some *Idaho Statesman* guy with contacts in the police had gotten the call, but that group too was still.

"Okay, David, she's on. Shoot."

"Dateline Boise, Utah," he began.

"*Idaho,* god dammit!"

"Sorry, sorry. Anyway, 'Bob Lee Swagger, the former Marine sniper who has been the key subject in a House subcommittee hearing here on lethal force, has been killed in the ongoing hostage crisis at Frank Church High School, the *Times* has learned.' "

"David, Jesus Christ, are you sure?"

"I got it from Feeley."

"Okay, go ahead. Suzie, you're getting this?"

"I'm on it, Mr. Goldstein," said the dictationist.

"Sources among the hostages have reported that Sergeant Swagger attempted to intervene in a confrontation between one of the Chechen hostage takers and Representative Ross C. Baker, party affiliation, district number, blah-blah."

"We'll get it," said Mitch.

"The altercation turned violent, then lethal, as the younger man stabbed Sergeant Swagger in the chest. Witnesses say Sergeant Swagger was bleeding heavily and appeared to have collapsed into the wheelchair which has been, er—"

"Too complicated," said Mitch. "Getting murky. New graf, Susie. Now the wheelchair, David."

"Sergeant Swagger had been confined to the wheelchair during the entire duration—during/ duration, no good—"

"Lose 'entire duration.' "

"During the hearings period. He was wounded seriously last—I forget the date—in an anti-terrorist operation in which he fired to allegedly prevent a murder attempt, though no hard evidence has been produced to support that contention. He was hit seriously—"

"Lose 'seriously.' He wouldn't be in a chair if it weren't serious."

"—by return fire. Yadda, yadda, yadda. You can boilerplate the back end. Get in how ironic it was that the crisis was all but finished and even as a helicopter orbited overhead—"

"It's there?"

"I can hear it. Any lower and I can let you talk to the pilot, 'orbited overhead awaiting enough daylight to land on the roof and take the hostage takers'—'terrorists' would be better—"

"No official 'act of terrorism' designation yet."

"Shit. Anyway, 'and eight congressmen to Boise Airport. There, yadda yadda more boilerplate, flight to Grozny, Chechnya, yadda, yadda and out.' Oh, another irony, 'Representative Baker had emerged as Sergeant Swagger's interrogator and primary antagonist as the hearings went into their second week.' Get that in somewhere."

"Great, David. It'll be online in two minutes."

"Put somebody good on the boilerplate."

"Jack Simmons, the best. Woo-hoo, deadline reporting, I smell a Pulitzer."

Banjax had never thought of himself as a Johnny Deadline guy, and in fact this had been his first shot at dictation. He was surprised how good he was at it. He was usually one of those who began his long, leisurely pieces with an anecdote lede, complete to weather information, something like "It was a cold day in November, Jack Brownleaf recalls, when he realized he had to get out of West Virginia's coal mines. If he didn't, he knew, they would kill him." That, actually, was not a bad lede, one of his better ones—

"David, now get out there and finish this story. We're all counting on you."

"I won't let you down," he said.

CHAPTER 46

Reax

6:15 A.M.

W ell, Congressman Baker," Mother Death said, "congratulations. You've done what several thousand armed men couldn't do. You've killed Bob Lee Swagger."

"I am so sorry," Baker moaned. Abjectly returned to his place on the floor next to her, he was still on the verge of internal collapse. Images of the knife cutting his eyeballs out—his hated eyeballs, the bane of his existence, betraying him once again, and no, it wasn't thyroid or Graves' disease, it was just who he happened to be—danced and flickered in his brain, his heart still beating hard, his hands still trembling, hyperventilation a distinct threat.

"I didn't *do* anything," he continued, feeling the need to justify, rationalize, explain, expunge, express contrition, receive absolution, what have you in the realm of human guilt, "it's just how I am. There were so many other factors. It's not my fault, I—"

"No, it *is* your fault, you little pipsqueak. If you

had stood up to that brute, he would have backed down and Swagger wouldn't have had to come to your rescue and gotten himself killed for your wormy eyeballs. By the way, did you wee-wee? I bet you did. I bet your jockeys are as sodden as a dishrag."

"Please, I—"

"At least he went out to a tune of glory, as befits. That should impress his tight little clique of admirers, otherwise known as the American people. He should be given a Viking funeral, sent to Valhalla in a flaming longship. When your turn comes, your pallbearers will be cartoon mice from the Mickey clan, and Donald Duck himself will give your funeral oration."

"Am I ruined?"

"That's the horrible thing. You should be, but probably not. Feeley can figure out a spin. You may even get a medal out of it. Who knows, it might be the thing that gets you the Senate."

"I want to be a senator *so bad!*"

"Whatever. By the way, nice groveling. You grovel beautifully."

There was nothing more he could say, as who could stand before Mother Death when she got on one of her demon-from-id toots? She continued, inspired by his weakness and vulnerability, along these same lines, mashing him into the floor and loving every single second of it. It was so much fun to destroy another human being.

But even she grew weary after a bit, and reluctantly gave it up. That meant she had to face the reality of the situation.

She said to him, "By the way, now that you've killed our only hope of staying alive, what do you plan to do next?"

"We're going free."

"Of course we're not. These nasty fucks will kill us on the plane, just to make the point that it isn't very nice to fool with Chechens. Their national honor and reputation for ruthless violence and terror mean far more to them than our lives, especially since you've demonstrated in spades and wee-wee what the American man has become."

CHAPTER 47

The Widow

6:21 A.M.

Sooner or later, he knew, he'd have to make the call. He didn't want to. It was the worst moment of his life. He knew she'd end up comforting him, instead of the other way around. He thought maybe Sally could do it, but he realized how terrible it would be to put that on her. Finally someone said, "The *Times* has it on its site. The dam is about to burst."

"Shit," he said.

To yell at someone just to forestall a bit, he chose Feeley.

"Feeley, god dammit, how do the newspapers have this already? Jesus Christ, did you *tell* your old buddies or something?"

"No, no," lied Feeley with the practiced aplomb of a diplomat, "all those hostages still have their cells, and the bad guys don't show any interest in stopping them from calling. Once it happened, they got busy. Agent Memphis, you should issue a statement. Do you want me to draft one?"

"Yeah, yeah. Succinct, unsentimental, dry. Like the guy."

"Got it."

So: now. Nothing else.

He took up his cell, went to Contacts, found her name in the menu, and clicked on it. He heard the phone buzz, once, twice, three—

"Nick?"

"Hi," he said. "You're okay?"

"I'm still at the hotel. I didn't see any point in coming down there. I'd just get in the way."

"Great."

"Nick, I'm watching the TV. I know already."

"Well, the news is, they may be a little ahead of themselves. It sounds bad, but there's still no actual forensic confirmation."

"What have you got?"

"They say he was stabbed. They say there was lots of blood. They say they dumped him out of the chair and he didn't move."

"Did they shoot him in the head after he was down?"

"No, because a shot might have set off the whole volatile contraption we have here. They want to get out, so they're not taking any chances now, so close."

"Is there any possibility? I mean, he's a hearty, strong man, full of stamina, he comes back fast from injury. On top of that there's a lot of empty space in the chest. An inch one way or the other, the heart isn't pierced, none of the arteries or veins are cut, you just never know."

"I'm praying."

"I am too."

Julie didn't say anything then.

Nick continued.

"The thing that's so repulsive about it all was that he died trying to save that little scumbag Baker, the one with the goo-goo eyes."

"I hate that guy. He's one of those toads who never get their hands wet or dirty but who sit in judgment of everyone else."

"I agree. But it's so Swagger that he made that move. That was so him. He played it hard to the end."

"That little shit goes home to wife and kids, but Bob doesn't get to the rocking chair ever again. It's so wrong."

Suddenly, something exploded not far off.

"Jesus Christ," Colonel Lhotske yelled, "somebody just detonated a bomb in the rear."

"Julie, I've got to go. Something's happening."

"Thanks for the call, Nick."

Nick turned.

"Get our assault teams back here. Now. It looks like somebody else decided to start the ball."

CHAPTER 48
The Big Boom

6:24 A.M.

S oon?" asked Niner when Delta answered the vibrating phone.

"Real soon."

"I see light in the east. I can hear the chopper. It's oh-six-three-nine. All the assault teams and snipers have been moved out, skeleton crew on duty. It'll never be a better time."

"Affirmative," said Delta.

"You know, it's not too late to rethink. Nobody will know. You just tell your people the opportunity didn't arise, and there would have been too much collateral if you forced it. They'll understand."

"Actually, they won't. 'Understanding' isn't what they do. But I signed up for this, I took the bucks, so it's on me, not them. And now it's go time."

"Let's run a last check. More for me than you."

"Go ahead, guy."

"You're behind the curve of the structure so no direct detonation shock wave or supersonic debris will hit you?"

"Totally. About fifty feet around. I can't see the pack from here."

"Pistol?"

"Round chambered, red dot strong."

"Night vision function checked?"

"Just now."

"Straps tight? You don't want to pull it down and have it crash to the floor."

"Good one. Hadn't thought of that. Give me a second."

He set the phone down and ran his fingers over the nexus of elasticity that held the PVS-7 to his skull. All straps seemed tight, all buckles firmly fastened. He worked the pivoting hinges of the thing, and it slipped down, its lenses perfectly indexed to his eye. He turned it on, saw the green of the infrared world before him, even the flashing reds of the perimeter police vehicles beaming emerald.

"Affirmative."

"Shoelaces tight? You don't want to fall."

In all his operational years, he'd never checked his shoelaces, just as he'd never low-crawled. It was a night of firsts.

"Solid."

"Ears cottoned up?"

"I haven't inserted it yet, but I've got it right here. As soon as I break contact, I'll stuff it in."

"It's going to be some kind of bull-goose motherfucking loud, so you better be ready for it. If you ain't, you're knocked into the wild blue yonder by the decibels themselves."

"I am set on that."

"Now I want you to curl up, knees up to chin, fingers in ears despite the cotton, and hunker in as close to the wall as possible. The universe changes radically when you det six pounds of C-4 in it, and you have to be ready."

"Got it."

"Tense every muscle. You do not want to be loose and floppy when the bang stuff goes bang."

"Reading you solid and clear."

"Then that's it. Can you think of anything else?"

"I'm good to go."

"This is insanely heroic."

"Just another day at the office."

"I'm signing off, then counting down from sixty. Then I light the cocksucker up."

"You've been a professional through this whole thing. Much appreciated. We'll laugh about it."

"I'll still be shaking."

He put the phone back in his shirt pocket, rolled to the wall, brought up his hands to his ears, plugging them with cotton. He pressed each index finger into the ear channel, pushing the cotton in deeper, until it would go no farther.

He had no idea where he was in the count. He should have paid attention. It would be any second now and—

The sound was unholy. Even with the fingers behind the cotton, his ears felt pierced by nine-inch nails. The ground beneath snapped as if it were ocean in hurricane, and in the crest of the wave, he was actually tossed airborne a few inches before gravity reclaimed him and he rejoined the planet with a thud.

He opened his eyes to see the whirlwind. Animated by the forces of the released energy, debris, vapor, a mist of atomized brick and mortar, shards of wood, smoke unfurling like Little Boy over Hiroshima, all blurring the starry sky, all chasing one another crazily in the atmosphere. The far-off lights of civilization were dimmed, and from at least two sources, car alarms began to bleed geese calls into the riot of disturbance.

Go time.

He clambered to his feet, pulled down his night-vis binocs, clicked on—hello green, my old friend—and followed the curve to the wound in the brick. It was, as predicted, awesome. Spread before it for yards were chunks of what had once been building, and the hole blasted into the brick was a jagged giant sucking chest wound. It didn't look terribly stable, and the closer he got, the less stable it seemed to become. Two cracks had sheared their way from the site of detonation, reaching up to the roofline, and a whole acre of brick seemed out of register with the demarcations in the mortar on either side.

He peeked into the opening and saw space, indicating a passageway; indeed the blast had penetrated. It was low, of course, because the pack had been placed so low, more a tunnel than a doorway, but the infrared of the electro-optics didn't pick up details, much less the landscape or the interior of the structure. Then he realized that the gas or smoke or vapor or whatever contaminating the air was too heavy for penetration. The infrared lit what was there; it was no X-ray.

He bent, now wishing he'd included kneepads and a face mask in his kit, and made uneasy progress through the opening, the air gritty, the feel of chalk dust in his mouth, the sense of his eyes tearing up. It was so dark it seemed as if he were in a coal mine, searching for lost miners. Again he had a thought of that continent of brick above him suddenly letting go, and falling, crushing his spine, burying him in its disassembled self where his body wouldn't be found till the spring.

But he kept going, and somehow he emerged on solid ground, actually the hard surface of a cement floor. Ahead of him, he saw a geometric structure, heavy enough not to have been turned to abstract sculpture by the blast. He realized he was looking at the underneath of bleachers as expanded onto the gym floor for more seating.

Through the gaps in the struts, he saw movement, obviously human. He rose, unholstered the long pistol, indexing the finger over the trigger guard, checked to make certain the red dot at the center of the tiny screen still glowed—still bright— and removed the Gemtech suppressor from his cargo pocket. He screwed it to the barrel, tight, no wobble. When it wouldn't move anymore, he began to make his way toward the sound of people, the occasional shout, something that sounded like a chorus of moaning.

CHAPTER 49
Mortal Consequences

6:27 A.M.

Though he wasn't standing square to it, the impact of the blast still smashed Vakha hard. He'd been taking it in, observing his little empire and reflecting on the excellence of the plan and in the next second he was no longer sure of who he was, where he was, or what was happening.

He had been lifted and tossed backward a good five feet, and now lay asprawl on the floor, looking up at the network of catwalks that lurked above the stage, to give access to a system of walkways, pullies, and ropes that specified theater. But why was he in a theater? Why did acrid fumes suddenly bite into his nose and throat? What was his name, his mission, his hope? Who were his allies?

Attempting to solve these mysteries, he turned outward as he struggled to rise, only to encounter more mysteries. Who had turned off the lights and filled the air with dust? Who had released the two basketball backboards and nets, so cleverly tucked away. They had both pivoted downward from their secured position, and though still a-thrum with a vibration that made their nets dance and shimmer in the weird light, they were fully deployed for a hard game of full-court five-on-five. A few banners on the walls had flopped and fallen loose. Everywhere, things that had been attached were unattached and hung or fell or scattered crazily across the floor. Most of the overhead lights, now dark, swayed and spiraled at the end of their tethers, while strangely two of them continued to function, throwing moving beams of radiance in whimsical patterns. A bin had shattered and, tilted and ruined, had liberated a dozen basketballs to roll and bounce randomly through the wreckage.

His eyes recognized, but his brain could not organize, the visions he encountered. Logic had fled the world, cause and effect gone on separate vacations, air replaced by dust and grit. It was a vision of hell, as re-created in a high school gym in Boise, Idaho.

But as far gone as he was, he was nevertheless the fastest back into his actual self, this as a consequence of much war-fighting where detonations were a commonplace and his system had made some acquaintanceship with them, perhaps even a provisional peace. It all began to make a sort of medieval sense, pieces locking in, data supporting certain conclusions, memories fighting their way up from the soup that filled his brain, all of it assembling itself mysteriously.

Raid!

That was it, and his mind assembled the blocks of information into more or less coherent sequence. The Americans had betrayed him. Despite the charade of helicopter, airport, flight to Grozny, $10 million, they had detonated a charge, blown in the wall, and now their commandos scrambled toward him to kill him before he could react.

At this game they would lose all they valued, all to wipe out the Shishani family. He stood, ready to repel, pistol in hand, but noted instantly that he was first to rise, and that before him it looked like the aftermath of an opium party. Among the mob of hostages, some squirmed, some writhed, some attempted without success to come to their feet. Most lay supine, as if asleep on the night before Christmas, unable to stir. The shock had clearly sucked thousands of IQ points from their brains, and even among the quickest to gain control of themselves, none of them had figured out the who, what, when, and why of the moment.

Though it was dark, enough illumination from the hole in the wall engineered by a bus at ramming speed got through to issue fragments and streaks of light at the far end of the gymnasium. Some beams deflected off the reflective surface of the dead vehicle's green gloss too, turning the whole vision riot-crazy. Vakha watched as his eyes adjusted and eventually made out Ibragim, also flattened by the wave, but also coming fast upright. Ibragim was too full of hate to stay out of the fight for long and was now pulsing with life. He had retrieved his automatic weapon, and though he had yet to appraise the situation, he was checking it out, even as he shook his head to drive out the pain, which so much noise could not but help insert into the deep brain. It would hurt for weeks, Vakha knew.

Magomet, on sentinel duty at the ragged hole and therefore least affected by the blast, stood in stupefaction, beholding the spectacle before him. Vakha only recognized him by silhouette against the strobing of police lights. Vakha knew he had to concentrate his firepower no matter what and that Magomet alone at the entranceway would attract snipers the way sugar attracts flies. He was actually surprised no one had shot Magomet yet.

He waved broadly. By the man's jump, he knew the communication had gotten through, given even the dust and smoke and darkness in the air, and Magomet began his mad dash across the gym floor of flattened, felled chairs and rolling basketballs toward his relatives, hungry for their comfort, clarity, and camaraderie.

Suddenly, next to him, young Anzor appeared— from who knew where? Khasan got there a second later.

"Uncle, for God's sake, what is happening?" Khasan yelped.

"The Americans have blown a hole in the wall. They will pour through it. They may also blow others."

"Kill these people now?"

"No, wait. Be calm. Still time for that. Set up position forward to left. Bring fire on Americans coming in from the breach in the wall. Determined resistance and calm marksmanship will stop them. They have already failed, and if we drive them back and make them suffer heavy casualties, they will retreat and know that our plan must not be interfered with. Both of you now go."

As dispatched, the boys left. Meanwhile, Vakha raced to Ibragim, now fully alert, and holding the assault rifle on the squirming, slower hostages.

"Kill them?" he asked as Vakha drew near.

"No, not yet. Wait for a signal. If we can drive the first wave back, all returns to normal. Hold them at gunpoint. Meanwhile, I take a hostage and we fall back to the steps up to the roof."

Ibragim turned, moved to place himself between the hostages and the way out, screaming, "You stay where you are, you are still hostages. I will kill any and all who try to escape."

The muzzle of the M4 was like some kind of magic wand, as whoever it crossed fell immediately back, chastened by its as-yet-unexpressed power, terrified by its promise of immediate death.

The new plan—which was really a way to recover the old plan—clarified itself in Vakha's mind. He knew exactly where to go.

He raced around the perimeter of the circle, pistol out, and kicked the mewling baby-man out of the way, and reached the crazy lady, the big power player among them. He leaned to her, grabbed her thin arm. She was nothing but frailties, thin bones, nearly weightless as a wisp. Yet, unlike the others, she was preternaturally alert, and clearly in command of her faculties.

"You come with me, crazy old woman. They will not shoot if we have you."

"For God's sake," she cried, "let the others go."

"Others must die. Your police have violated the agreement."

"I'm sure it's some kind of mistake. Look, nobody's attacking."

She was right. No raiders attacked. A moment of odd stillness suffused the space. The whole thing, with all its complex parts, its insane symmetries as contained by the rows of bleachers lining the gymnasium floor, the overarching roof, the still swinging lights, the two outliers still sending beams randomly about, catching in their rays the poisoned atmosphere thick with settling dust from the rafters.

The peace still held, fragile as it had become.

The only sign of movement was Magomet, running crazily at them from his post at the entrance.

He almost made it.

That it came from a suppressed weapon probably had no meaning, since nobody at all had ears at that moment for hearing anything that was not yelled at them, but in its noiseless lethality and singularity of purpose, the shot hit him center chest, and from the way his legs kept churning on brain electricity while his upper body went noodly limp and seemingly dragged him backward to the floor, where he hit and fell akimbo, beyond grace or care, it was clearly a well-aimed bullet. Magomet! Not a genius but an earnest boy! Two children and a loving wife back in Coney Island!

Vakha pulled the old lady with him.

"Back to me," he called to Anzor and Khasan, waiting to ambush any invading crew from the breached wall. He turned then to Ibragim.

"Kill them all!" he yelled.

CHAPTER 50
A New World

6:30 A.M.

It had an underwater feel to it. Not only had the night vision rendered it green, but the human activity he detected was in slow motion, as if impeded by the pressure of the fathoms. He half-expected fish to swim by, bubbles to blossom from the struggling humans and float upward, mermaids to appear and sea monsters to rise. It was partly the wild swirl of light, the thickness of shit in the air, the difficulty in breathing—cancer would surely be an outcome of this one—and the utter soundlessness of it all, because to his surprise, the sound had penetrated the double seal of cotton and fingers in each ear and replaced it with a ringing that sounded like Coronation Day.

But then it began to make sense. He realized he hadn't come in backstage as he and Niner had thought, but instead about three-quarters of the way in, relative to the location of the stage. He still had some distance to go to get beyond the shelter of the bleachers, then a right turn and another thirty yards or so to get to the stage, where the captors held their hostages.

The first catastrophe was that the night-vis didn't do much with the color spectrum. Nothing was rendered into enough vividness to be singular. How would he mark targets? Because all the information that arrived as he moved came in a kind of colorless non-color, a wan smear of green and yellow on each of the human specimens visible through the rows of the bleachers. The vision lacked clearness, sharpness, precision; it seemed like a colony of amoebae on a microscope slide.

But then motion, left peripheral, and he turned and caught up with a runner, clearly with a weapon, clearly not a police officer or SWAT operator, not in that shapeless one-piece pajama suit the color of mud. Delta did a number of professional things well and quickly. He dropped to a more stable kneeling position, resting his elbow on his left leg, drew his other elbow in tight to his body, and raised the pistol. The Glock came up, solidly locked between his two strong, practiced hands, and he acquired both the trigger with his finger and the red dot of the Trijicon sight with his dominant eye. The runner was now of course a blurry amber smear in this deracinated PVS-7 universe, but it was good enough. He tracked and computed angle of deflection, and when his brain was satisfied, it instructed his trigger finger to commence action, and again, perfection, a straight backward stroke, no torque or twist, no jerk, just the even application of pressure and the gun recoiled against his palms, leaping a bit under the energy of the Gold Dot +P load, the suppressor leaching the percussion of its sharpness, mellowing the harsh by about thirty-five decibels.

The target and the bullet attempted to occupy the same space, a definite no-can-do according to physics, and so the target was therefore penetrated on a forty-five-degree angle, the bullet nicking heart, deflating left lung, while opening up into the formation of a blossoming metal rose, its petals slicing and dicing any flesh they encountered, and the mid-chest was a flesh-rich environment. Internal blood loss was significant.

The man's still living feet ran out from his now-deceased upper body and, whacked from balance, he sprawled, his shotgun bouncing away. From an adulthood spent shooting people all over the world, Delta knew him to be gone. He pivoted in the hunt for more targets, knowing there to be only four left, but as he emerged farther from the bleacher pathway, he saw that the angles were wrong. He didn't have a straight-on view of the stage, which rose five feet above the floor, and he could only see—he now realized this is what he had seen through the bleachers—

shoulders and heads, again the movement unclear and ambiguous.

No shot. Get closer.

He hunched into the posture of the Texas running back he'd once been, and also the posture of the professional armed raider he still was, and began his run toward the drama onstage, knowing he had to get there fast or the killing would begin.

CHAPTER 51

A Walk in the Park

6:33 A.M.

T he kick into his spleen jerked Congressman Baker from his stupor. However, it did not quite, despite its bruising, elevate him into the sentient world. Instead it deposited him in that zone that Niner had once called "Goofytown."

Stuff had stopped making sense. The problems were too difficult to figure. Though extraordinarily bright—Harvard Law, number two, after all— the upper regions of his intelligence remained utterly sealed off. His conclusions were therefore dubious.

He did notice that the dragon bitch Madam Chairman, whom he loved, feared, hated, wanted to fuck and murder and worship, be mothered by, be suckled upon, paint a portrait of, found a new religion on behalf of, desecrate, humiliate, destroy, set afire, see canonized, and so forth, had been dragged off by the head Neanderthal. He felt a very deep, even profound, response to this. It was: Too fucking bad for you, bitch.

Next he noticed the man who had once almost

cut his eyeballs out approaching with the grim set of murder in his eyes, to place himself between this gaggle of sleepy hostages and the exit, and he concluded—credit must be given—correctly that the fellow was about to machine-gun them all to death, as had been promised. This was actually quite a leap in ratiocination as it meant he recalled the circumstances, the threat, and the immediate past, and astutely interpreted the blast as not an errant artillery shell or a gas tank in a far-off Mercedes exploding, but as prelude to a very dangerous event, that is a raid meant to free the hostages. He also reached the right conclusion: Get the hell out of Dodge, fast.

However, his solution was somewhat crazy.

He wobbled to his feet, among the first of the hostages to do so, and came to the conclusion that he could, somehow, walk away from it all. This made no sense tactically or even eschatologically, but it filled his urgent need to do something, anything, even the dopiest thing. Headshrinkers call it perseveration, meaning that under duress, one devolves to ingrained behaviors, no matter their appropriateness.

He began to walk. He further thought that if he walked *real slow* nobody would notice him. So his walk was more like a tippytoe creep, as a child charged with sneaking up on somebody might do. He had no particular destination or strategy. He just walked a few steps one way, then the other. His journey produced an intricate pattern across the stage, turning here, turning there, going back, going forward, utterly indifferent to what was happening around him.

That he was an easy target made no difference to him, and fortunately, to none of his possible killers. The walk was so minuet-like in its stylized meaninglessness that it immediately put out the universally recognizable message: I am no threat, I am a germ, a bug, a mouse embryo, a mote in the devil's eye. Thus the predator passed over him as he continued, and he did not reward his potential executioner with eye contact, as he knew eye contact meant death.

For a single moment it seemed that all would work out. Another of those strange moments of quiet befell the drama, which was unfolding in the loud silence of ringing ears, and the congressman continued his back and forth, back and forth. That a gunfight might erupt and fill the air with whizzing invitations to the hereafter also never occurred to him, and even if it had, it probably would not have changed his behavior. In motion, he perseveringly believed, was invisibility.

This way, that way, upstage, downstage, stage right, stage left, to the line that marked the proscenium, to the brick that marked the denuded back wall of the auditorium.

But it all changed when he heard a voice

he recognized as Vakha's break through the craziness with two words: "Kill them!"

He turned, and indeed the man who had tried to cut his eyeballs out was raising the machine gun to his shoulder in preparation for a massacre.

CHAPTER 52
Hi There

6:37 A.M.

As in everything, there was technique. It wasn't the sort of thing you could just do without thought, and hope that all would turn out. Thus Ibragim anticipated methodically.

Start low. That is, at the closest, so that they won't be herded by death toward the entrance, but backward, to nothingness. Pay no attention to optical thing with red dot in small TV screen. Do not worry about individual shots. The twists and shudders of the hit will instruct you as to bullet flow and placement. Do not become absorbed in detail. You can enjoy detail later. If a particular pretty girl catches one in the head, and her skull is rather dramatically deflated into the shape of a squashed gourd, do not dwell, particularly if it is the hated Ginger, who witnessed his disgrace and would otherwise have broadcast it to the world. Record, move on, savor afterward. Keep the gun moving. Lean hard into it. Row on row, like a word-processing program eating up a screen. Plunk-plunk-plunk-plunk, row by row, automatic new row by row. Most of all, have new magazine ready. When number one comes up dry, shoot trigger finger to mag release, stroke hard, feel the disconnect as the empty vessel drops to floor, but be ready with off hand to feed in new magazine until click. As these guns worked—they were more sophisticated than the AK—the bolt would lock back on empty, and there was another button—well, more of a finger-sculpted lever, on the left that was bolt release—and a stout tap there, and he imagined the incredibly satisfying sound of the bolt slamming forward, scooping a cartridge off the top of the mag, shoving it into the chamber, and locking, even as the same symphony of mechanicals cocked the hammer for the trigger's release, and then return to the trigger guard. Squirt, squirt, the bullets would again jet out in their relentless speed, guided by his strength and resolution, his vengeance, row by row.

Ah, the deliciousness of it. The smell of the powder, the insane glee of the empty shells dispatched by recoil impulse from the breech into a brass arc, all glinty and spastic in the weird lighting conditions, the blinding flash at the muzzle, a dance so blinding in its radiance that it would haunt his dreams forever. The lakes, the pools, the rivers, the floods, the lapping seas of blood. More blood than even the sniper, stabbed in the guts, had released.

Late development: the idiot whose eyeballs he almost cut out was weirdly walking back and forth on the stage, as if with dog on leash. He would save him for last. Maybe a new magazine. Imagine what thirty high-velocity rounds would do to that girlish frame and those dolly eyes.

He was ready. He was set. He would do it.

The call came, as Vakha screamed from backstage, pulling the old bitch along with him, "Kill them!"

It was exactly what he had been waiting for.

He raised the gun, shouldering it tightly, not sighting but guiding, seeing the fear and agony of the Ibragim-screaming world before him, and with his thumb made a thousandth check to make sure the fire-selector lever had been pushed to FULL AUTO, felt his finger caress the trigger, and—

He felt a presence next to him, and his peripheral vision signaled motion.

He managed to flick his eyes to the right just far enough and fast enough to realize it was the sniper.

CHAPTER 53
WTF?

6:40 A.M.

N ick, phone, the director!"

Christ, of course he had to call right in the *fucking middle of it!*

Most of the staff in the incident command van had left, to take charge of their various ready-to-go units, who were not of course ready-to-go, and in fact were not even ready-to-get-on-the-bus, but still loading up four blocks away. At least a minute had passed since the detonation, and two outlying cars had reported a high-intensity blast at halfway around the rear of the building but they had seen no activity.

Nor had anyone inside called in information, as had been the case previously. But neither had there been any gunshots.

"Yes, sir?"

"Nick, satellite picked up serious disturbance at the perimeter of the building, northwest quadrant just a few seconds ago. It looked like a detonation or an artillery or RPG strike. What the hell is going on?"

"It was a hard hit, origin as yet unknown. No action from inside."

"Could it have killed everybody?"

"Possible, but my sense is no. It's damaged, I'm guessing, maybe even penetrated, but the structure still stands, no collapse, no rubble."

"You didn't—no, Nick, you wouldn't. I know that."

"Even if I'd wanted to, I didn't have any demolition technicians to assemble a breaching charge appropriate to the strength and size of the structure, much less the explosives on hand to make it happen."

"Christ! Could they have done it themselves?"

"The perimeter guys say it was an outside blast, lots of flash, not much smoke. Set off car alarms all over the town."

"I know you're busy, but I need a fast sitrep for the White House."

"Right now I'm still holding. All our assault teams have been moved out and are remounting to get here. Maybe two, maybe three minutes out. I don't have enough ground force here to assault now."

"What's your call? Will you send them when they arrive?"

"If there's no action, affirmative. Get inside, take control of the situation, get medical teams in fast. Must have every ambulance in Idaho here, plus half the emergency trauma staffs."

"That's cool, that's good. One other thing. We're all here thinking Idaho. Maybe some screwball militia decided to act on their own?"

"They couldn't have gotten close enough to plant the package. That had to be a one-man job. Plus, I was getting intel from all the state investigative agencies who had militia, or any entity with paramilitary aspirations, on the scope. Nothing. It happened too fast. Nobody saw anything coming. Maybe the Russians somehow put something together that fast. Ex-Spetsnaz people."

"Nick, we have all our gang intelligence going here tonight and they're running their snitches and their taps hard. We also got negative on the Russians. I just don't know—you know, Nick, not knowing how it's going to turn out and who's responsible, I think it's time to button up. No comment for the press. No explanation, no speculation."

"I'll put that out."

"We just don't know which way it's going to bounce. We could be looking at the biggest massacre since Las Vegas and—"

But someone—it was the Idaho State Police superintendent lit up like a burning Christmas tree—was shouting.

"Nick," he said. "They're coming out! They're pouring out!"

"Who?" Nick said.

"The hostages. All of them."

CHAPTER 54
The Wheelchair

6:41 A.M.

Ibragim was fast, swinging the gun to bear on him, but he was behind the curve.

Swagger was already deep into it. The wheelchair, still flex-cuffed to his wrist, rode an arc over and above his head, then, beyond apogee, began a descent so fast it seemed to blur in time before its footrest plates smashed hard into the Chechen at zero-degree angle to his face.

The rifle falling from his hands, Ibragim went down at the strike, knowing his nose had been shattered, this time higher up the bridge, and he hit the floor, took a dead-cat bounce, and settled, but still had enough electricity left to make a tepid stab at rising. For him at least, there was no time—no yesterday, no tomorrow, nothing—only some genetic imperative to raise himself, but he saw the cumbersome apparatus, sustained only by the sniper's single arm, as it crushed down again, the edge of the steel footplate this time destroying his mouth, spattering teeth in all directions.

"No hit!" he heard himself saying.

But Swagger hit.

The third one landed laterally on the cheekbone, smashing it like a pie plate, damaging the eye above it. All blows opened lacerations to the bone level, and yet more blood erupted onto the stage, the most seen in a theater since the high years of Jacobean drama four centuries previous, only this time real.

Swagger hammered the prick three more times, to make sure. He was so into his work that he failed utterly to notice that when the gunman went this way and his gun went that way, the hostages went all ways.

They rose like zombies and began their exit, stage front, fleeing past the destruction-by-wheelchair scenario, leaping the stage and surging toward the ragged entrance at the other end of the darkened basketball court. Yet it was not blind panic. Nobody abandoned anybody. Nobody put ass before honor. The youngers helped the olders, who were too far toward feebleness to jump, and had to be eased down, and guided or stewarded on the way out. At last and if only for a little while and too bad it only happens at disaster sites: the perfect classless society. Young guiding old, poor guiding rich, powerless guiding powerful. Ginger ended up with both arms around sixty-six-year-old Madison (R-IA, 4th District), keeping him on track and moving efficiently. In seconds, it seemed, all had ejected. Beside the strugglers, only Baker remained on the stage, locked in a widening gyre, tracing a spiral vector this way and then that, unaware of anything happening as he slipped into temporary insanity.

Ibragim's face had the appearance of a burlap bag soaked in strawberry pop out of a soft drink cooler that hadn't existed since the thirties. There were valleys and hills where there should not have been valleys and hills. Lots of ballooning was clinically evident, one eye completely vanished under the mass of tissue that engulfed it.

Swagger didn't notice, didn't care. He knelt by the destroyed figure, looting his pockets for the knife that had cut him so badly. With his left hand, he found it, flicked it open, and inserted it between his right wrist—now badly cut itself because the friction against it in the swinging exercise had done its damage—and the flex cuffs and started to saw. They were not easy to get through, especially one-handed with no leverage. But ultimately, it seemed they'd begun to part, then yield, when a figure slid in next to him.

Swagger beheld a robot. One centralized eye gazed at him.

"Who the hell are you, R2-D2?"

A hand pivoted the binocular up to that level, revealing a rather prosaic American face that

Swagger had seen a thousand times: Hard NCO.

"I'm the reinforcements, Gunny," said the man, "all one of 'em. Say, you're cut up real bad."

"This dumb motherfucker thought he'd put the blade into my gut. I twisted and it just rode around my body, slicing as it went. Bled like a slaughterhouse."

"So you killed him with a *wheelchair?*"

"It was the only thing I had."

"Cool. That's gotta be a first. Anyway, you need medical attention, stitches and plasma. Better take the rest of the day off now that you've saved everybody's life."

"I'm okay. I squished my shirt and jacket hard against the cut, a sort of improvised tourniquet. We've still got work to do. I figure the last four—"

"The last two. I popped one running across the gym floor and a second"—he gestured to deep stage right, where someone lay facedown resembling Rosencrantz or Guildenstern—"when he was coming back to hose you for this one and another zeroing you as I approached."

"Two left, then," said Bob, reaching for the M4 that lay a foot away, then pulling another mag out of his victim's hip pocket. "They got the old lady. I figure they had to take the stairways to get to the catwalks up there, where there's got to be an exit."

"I thought you were crippled."

"I have an arthritic hip. I been sitting in this fucking chair for two weeks for the drama. It hurts but I'm so cut up, I won't even notice it. Let's roll, R2."

CHAPTER 55

Anzor

6:42 A.M.

They got into the dark wings, deep stage left, slid back to the wall against which a steel stairway zigzagged into the even greater darkness above.

"Old lady, take off shoes," Vakha said.

"Are you kidding?" she said. "These are Louboutins. Eight hundred bucks."

"Take off shoes, goddamn," said Vakha, shaking her roughly.

"Okay, okay," she said, kicking her way out of the elegant heels, red of course. "I better get these back."

"Up, goddamn, or I shoot you here."

He shoved her against the steep angle of the incline, and followed close behind, bullying her by the imposition of his strength against her frailty. The steps were not wide enough for double passage, so Anzor and Khasan followed.

"Uncle," said Khasan, "why is Ibragim not firing?"

"Ach," said Vakha. "I don't know. Go back

379

and help, then bring him. We will go up to the catwalks and then to the roof. If the helicopter pilot sees a gun to her head, he will land, and all will occur as I have foreseen. We will not leave until you join us."

"I will do it," said Anzor, the youngest, still consumed by the idea that it was his errant head shot at a gas station just off the Jersey Turnpike that had caused this whole thing, and eager to make up for it.

"Be careful, goddamn," said Vakha. He prodded the old lady with his knee, and she started to climb again.

Anzor peeled back, and intelligently chose not to simply blunder onstage when he didn't know what was happening and couldn't see much. Instead, he raced on a parallel course in the wings, monitoring the now-empty stage. Or seemingly empty, as it was dark and he had a sense that a movement flashed before him, then vanished, and he could make no sense of it.

He had gone fifty feet when he saw what had to be a struggle, though in the darkness it was again impossible to understand. He rushed out.

There he beheld an astonishment. In the dim light that made it to the stage, he realized it was empty; the hostages, he now saw, had fled toward the entrance and were a struggling, ever-diminishing mass that was jammed up to depart via that opening. Otherwise it was clear. There was no swarm of commandos, guns at the ready, hastening toward him, murder in their eyes. He saw his chance for glory.

Kill them! he thought, knowing he had the means to bring at least a dozen of the fleeing civilians down before anyone figured out who was shooting. But at that moment a strange presence inserted itself briefly into the space between him and his targets, moving irregularly, almost a ghost. He was fascinated, even as the apparition vanished.

He stepped out farther, and yet more activity compelled his vision, and he turned to encounter the dreadful spectacle of the sniper, no longer bound in his wheelchair, at full upright and smashing that contrivance over and over into a pitiful figure who had to be his brother Ibragim. He lost another second wondering how such a thing could have happened.

He threw the gun to shoulder, meaning to ventilate the villain, but again a strangeness presented itself. Now that he could see it, he understood a man was simply walking back and forth, to and fro, onstage, occasionally coming between Anzor and his victim. He was like a fool in a park on a Sunday, lost in the flowers and the glow of the sun.

Kill them all! Anzor thought, and again threw the gun to shoulder.

It was like a punch, savage and unyielding

to his midsection, and though he fought its influence, it nevertheless took command, ordered his knees to collapse, and as he tilted forward, accelerating in the pull of gravity, he realized he'd been hit. He crashed to the stage hard, and the gun and everything else slipped away. He hadn't even heard the shot.

CHAPTER 56

The Administrator

6:44 A.M.

Nick and Sally had moved to the wrecked entrance, trying to assert discipline on the chaos.

Next time I run an incident, Nick told himself, I *will* have a goddamn bullhorn!

Like refugees from the Russian front, the hostages came clambering out, some dragging others, some just scooting ahead, some bounding joyously, some nursing injuries or limping. The red and blue lights of all the emergency vehicles in Idaho and its four contiguous states strobed chaotically, each one sending its pulse of illumination onto the scene, which already didn't make any sense. Overhead, police, news, and emergency service choppers hummed and buzzed, many of them contributing cones of radiance to skip or focus over the area of crisis, of course making the crisis even crisis-ier.

"That's the Illinois guy!" said Sally. "And Wyoming, the Republican!"

"See any more? Oh, there's Massachusetts!"

They watched as the hostages were processed

and distributed by an ad hoc medical screening team that had set up shop right at the entrance, seeking to prioritize ambulance service to those most in need. They tried to keep the flow going, escorting folks farther into the yard, into which yet more medics, many with gurneys or stretchers, had migrated, eager for patients.

"Medics," Nick yelled, "spread 'em out in the field, there could be a suicide vest underneath, we don't want to lose anybody now."

Then turning to the municipal cops who had massed nearby but seemed to have nothing to do yet, he yelled, "Uniforms, you get over here and check out these people. Body search the young ones. The bad guys may have changed clothes with some of them. Make sure this isn't some kind of escape plan."

Radio buzz.

He took the unit off his belt, pressed receive.

"Steamroller, this is Alpha 8, we have reached the hole in the back now."

"Sitrep," Nick said.

"Okay, lots of bricks, a hole, man-sized, the entire thing looks kind of shaky, might collapse. Still, you want an entry team to move in?"

"Negative on that, not with structure problematic. Plus we'll have SWAT people moving in lateral to you in a few minutes. It's dark in there, I don't want any friendly fire incidents."

"Got it, Steamroller."

"You set up a barricade, and handle anyone seeking exit. I want safeties on, fingers off triggers, light beams maxed out. If anyone shows, it could be hostages or perps. Be careful, try not to hurt any congressmen."

"Affirmative, Steamroller."

Meanwhile, the first buses had arrived from the staging area and raiders all SWAT-ed up and eager to go poured toward the opening. "Hold up, you guys," he yelled, rushing to them. "Squad leaders, control your people, get 'em organized, talk to them, no wild man stuff, no heroes, most of all no go till you get the word. Form up to the left, FBI SWAT first, State Patrol SWAT second, other jurisdictions behind."

Nick grabbed two younger officers who'd somehow come up on him, ready to enter.

"You guys, you go among the hostages, talk to five or six as fast as possible, and get me intel. We have to know what's going on before we jump."

Both nodded, swelled with the joy of being useful, and headed out.

Colonel Lhotske arrived, and got in closer to the reorganizing SWAT raiders, using hands-on to enforce Nick's directives and push some sense into the testosterone levels of what had become a heavily armed and armored crowd.

The phone rang.

He looked, saw that it was DC. Goddamn them.

"I'll take it," Sally said.

She took the phone.

"Sally Elion."

"Sally, where's Nick?"

"Yelling at people. What do you need?"

"Everybody's freaking. Got anything?"

"Most of the hostages are free, no serious injuries, at least not in preliminary reports. It seems dark and quiet in there now, and Nick is just about to take SWAT in; he's holding off till I'm sure everybody is on the same page."

"News on Congresswoman Venable?"

"Nothing confirmed."

"Okay, Sally, get back to it, let us know as soon as you can."

She clicked off.

Meanwhile Nick was yelling, "Squad leaders on me," and several men detached themselves from the parade of raiders and hustled to him.

"You guys, I will lead the insert, the colonel will lead his people, you key on my speed, no rushing. You filter in low-profile in a vertical stack, FBI left, State Patrol right, and infiltrate down the edges of the auditorium. We keep our fingers off triggers, we have one designated man with a flash bang second in the stack. No lights on until you're in close, on my signal. No full automatic. Only shoot at clear, designated targets. No friendly fire incidents on this one, guys, or you will regret it for the rest of your life. The targets should be in orange jumpsuits, but maybe they switched clothes, so your prime target indicator is a weapon. They have shotguns and M4s, which should be easy to spot; look for anyone walking awkwardly, he may be concealing a long gun. As for pistols, look to the hands, if someone moves them fast, he's pulling something, you have to put him down. Watch muzzle discipline, take ten deep breaths to chill yourself out, and once calm, stay calm. Sally, anything from Justice these guys should know?"

"You guys, you are under the microscope on this one," she said. "Justice is obligated to look at it very carefully, more on you than the bad guys. So if you have to decide, step back, not forward. From a Justice Department standpoint, that's got to be your op procedure. No cop needs to go to jail."

Just then a young man in uniform came by, one of the two Nick had sent into the hostage crowd.

"Sir, they say that Swagger killed—"

"Swagger?"

"Don't ask me how. Anyway, after the blast, he smashed the shit out of one of the gunmen with his wheelchair."

"Jesus Christ."

"Others report another downed bad guy in the middle of the gym floor."

"Who hit him?"

"Nobody knows."

"Do they think it's clear yet?"

"Nobody bothered to look back, so I counted heads. Forty-two made it out, including six congressmen and a lot of staffers and journalists and their techs. Then there's kids still cuffed to the doors but other than that—"

"Good, good work."

He turned back to his raiders, now in coherent formations, ready to move out.

"Latest info, guys, listen up, take into account. I have info suggesting two congressmen are still inside. I have also heard that Swagger is active and may be already moving against the aggressors. There may be another operator in there as well, so now you have to be double certain you don't hit any friendlies. The good guys won't orient their muzzles to you, so that's an indicator. Swagger is in some kind of suit, probably all messed up now. I don't have anything confirmed on the mystery operator."

He turned to the young officer still standing next to him.

"I need your pistol."

"Yes, sir," said the man, unholstering a Glock .40 and handing it over pointed up, finger off trigger.

"Good," said Nick, press-checking to see the glint of brass in the narrow space opened by the slight slide movement, and verifying a round in the chamber.

Nick assumed his place at the head of the parade. "Okay," he said, "green light!"

CHAPTER 57

Moving In

6:44 A.M.

Swagger managed to get up without opening his wounds, even if it felt as if his hip were being roasted over Satan's pit, ran a fast check on the late Ibragim's rifle, moving the selector lever to SEMI-AUTO, and they headed through the dark to the wings to secure—

"Movement," whispered Delta suddenly, squaring into shooting position.

A specter flashed into view before them, and only professional discipline kept them from shooting. It was the mad Congressman Baker, still roaming, eyes haunted yet empty of IQ and reality contact. He did not acknowledge them but simply evaded collision and kept his pace up, veering back toward center stage and whatever he thought was there.

"PTS big-time," said Swagger. "Let the docs handle it."

Slipping by him through the dark, they reached the stage left wall with its steel staircase dog-legging steeply up toward the catwalks and kneeled there.

With his night vision, Delta examined the climb before them. He saw only geometry, the steel of the staircase and its railing showing green against the murk, defining the perspective of a progress upward, its two boundaries converging toward infinity the farther and higher they reached. He saw no blots of light suggesting human heat.

"First stage clear."

"Okay, we move up real slow like we're actual grown-ups who do this shit for a living," said Swagger. "How's that orange show up on your thing?"

"Not so bright but I'm used to it now."

"My theory, you spot, I'll shoot. You're on point, I'm just behind, rifle up. When you get a response, you say direction, left, right, whatever, and I acquire and fire. Seems faster that way than you acquiring sights and shooting."

"Got it," said Delta.

"Two of them, and the old gal. We cannot shoot the old gal. If it comes to it, I'll take the hit, you shoot on his flash, and we'll get her out of it."

"Is she that valuable?"

"It's to prove a point."

"No reason to die to make a point."

"This point is worth the fuss, believe me."

"What they got in their holsters?"

"If I count right, the first three guys had rifles and so that's out of play. We're looking, I think, at prison shotguns, short-barreled, probably number one buck, plus Glocks. Don't know if he'll have to work the pump before he fires. Probably, as I'm doubting these guys have much pump experience."

"You up for this, Gunny?"

"I'm not bleeding, just a little seepage. I'm at least a pint low, and I'm woozy and my hip hurts like holy hell, but I can handle it. This is the fun part. I wouldn't miss it for nothing."

They began their upward journey, crawling up the stairs.

Vakha shoved the old lady ahead of him.

"I'm tired," she said, stumbling to a halt.

"No rest for wicked witches," he said. "Keep going, almost there," and he nudged her scrawny back with his pistol muzzle.

"Uncle," said Khasan, "I thought I heard something."

"Anzor, I hope."

"No, quiet. I mean noise by someone not wanting to make noise.

"Damn," said Vakha. "Hear nothing of Anzor. Where is he?"

"I heard no shot, though maybe I wouldn't because my ears are still ringing."

"You would hear shot."

"Could he have surrendered?"

"Anzor? No. It's not in him."

Vakha put his hand to the railing, felt it.

"No tremble. If lots of men were coming, we'd feel."

"Maybe just one or two."

"They are not smart enough to send one or two. Or brave enough. Two men, up alone in the dark. Not their kind of war anymore. They would send a herd of water buffalo, with bulletproof shields. They would bang and bounce like the beast, flanks and shoulders crashing into railings, footsteps heavy as iron, the whole thing loud and stupid and inefficient."

"I will ambush."

"You are the last. Be careful. You know how to work gun?"

"Yes."

"I will continue with old lady. We take second catwalk across, leads to platform on other side of stage. There, three steps up to door, door is open, Anzor already saw to that. I can hear helicopter."

"I will join you soon," said Khasan.

Khasan: not the brightest but the toughest and the bravest. Would always do what had to be done. Plodding, maybe, halting, perhaps, but as solid as an oak and as dependable.

"God be with you, my boy," said Vakha, and pushed ahead.

At the third crank in the stairway, he shoved her again, as she had slowed.

"Go, you old bitch. Faster. This is not a game."

"Why not just shoot me here if I'm so slow? You're not getting out of here anyway. You're dead, they're coming for you, you've lost all your sons."

"Nephews. The Russians killed my sons at Beslan. I will shoot you."

"Go ahead. I'm not afraid to die. I'm seventy-eight years old and I've fought hard against bullies every day I've been alive. Shoot me so the FBI knows where you are and can fire their machine guns without worry. I'll get statues, you'll get an unmarked hole in the ground."

"Bah, oink, oink!" He pushed her again, harder, and she went down again.

She saw him turn when she hit the railing, and she slipped her hand to her hair. It was spilling sloppily everywhere and she had to tidy it up. And while she was pushing the iron-gray strands this way and that, she found something quite useful.

CHAPTER 58
Bump in the Night

6:45 A.M.

Nick led his team slowly down the length of the floor, right at the edge of the bleachers. They moved in commando ritual, hunched over weapons, eyes wide and checking the action sector ahead urgently, the weight of so much gear—armor, boots, flex ties, pistols, helmets, radio gear, even combat knives, Suunto watches the size of monster oysters, and various medical packages—unfelt in all the excitement. It was dark, quiet. The only glow came from behind, and one of the two remaining overheads had gone out, the last making a wan but essentially worthless contribution.

"Steamroller," came a call over his earphone, "this is Broken Hand."

"Roger," said Nick, knowing it was Mike Lhotske.

"I've got one tango down alongside the bus, he's got to be dead, he's totally flat and motionless. Should I have one of the boys with a suppressor put a round in his head, for make-sure purposes?"

"How confident are you that he is dead?"

"Highly," said the colonel. "I've seen a lot of it."

"Then take a pass on the head shot. Some newspaper prick will win a Pulitzer for revealing that you desecrated a corpse."

"Affirmative," said Lhotske.

Almost simultaneously both columns reached the edge of the stage, and Nick sent one of his people to creep up the steps and make recon.

"Nick," the agent said over headset, even though he was six feet away, "I've got one guy down up close, center stage, orange uniform, looks like somebody took a pile-driver to his head. Blood all over the place. Wheelchair on its side a few feet away."

Swagger!

"Anything else?"

"There's a guy here. He's just sort of walking around, in and out of the light. He's in a suit like a congressman or something. Looks nuts."

"Would he be armed?"

"I don't see a weapon. Plus he doesn't have the aspect of someone who'd be armed. Frankly, he looks batshit."

"Somebody's freaked," Nick said, not even having to guess at who it might be. It figured. "Okay, for now ignore him. When it's settled, someone get on him fast, and get him to medical attention. For now, nothing. He's not a part of the problem."

"Affirmative."

"Broken Hand?"

"Copy."

"We have some kind of nutcase walking around onstage. I'm calling it a no-threat. Ignore during operations."

"Clear on that."

"Now I want you to infiltrate your people into the wings, stay close to wall, circle around. But nobody goes onto stage at all. Your goal is the stairway to the rafters, over near my side. On my signal we'll all go to weapons lights. Then you peel around the wall. Sweep carefully before proceeding, try and get illumination into every deep shadow."

"Got it."

"Be careful of a tunnel or corridor just behind the stage. It's called a walk-through and it's how the actors get from one side to the other without being seen. You'll have to clear that, and as I say, total illumination, careful movement, no rushing, good communication skills, no heroes. Team, team, team."

"Affirmative, we are team."

"FBI team, listen up. We'll access the stairs to stage level here and bend hard left, back to the wall on this side. We go to lights on my command. Then we'll sweep under and curl around the wall. There's a stairwell—that's how I got out—and maybe a couple of kids flex-cuffed to the doors at the bottom of it. Last two guys in stack, you get to them, cut 'em free, and if they can walk, escort them out. If not, you just hunker there and wait until the building is secure enough for medical teams."

"Roger," came a crackly response.

"Okay, all teams, we're all heading to same spot, which is a stairway against the brick wall. It takes us up to what they call the flyway system. It's where they have catwalks over the stage and sets of pulleys and ropes on heavy rods or masts so they can lower and raise scenery. If we don't have 'em yet, that's where they'll have to be. No other way out. There's a doorway to the roof. I guess they think the helicopter gig is still on. So we'll move up, spread out, and simultaneously, with a base of fire behind us, move across the catwalks. Maybe go dark, I'll have to see it. If there's contact, it'll be on those catwalks and platforms. Are we cool?"

"Cool," many agents and officers responded more or less simultaneously.

"Let's be professional, people," Nick said and—
Gunfire from up above.

Three, fast and hot.

"Shots fired! Shots fired!" came a batch of reports.

"Hold fast," Nick shouted over them into his microphone. "Anybody see anything?"

"Sir," one of the Idaho State SWAT guys said, "I saw muzzle flashes, maybe three guns, up at the third bend in the stairway."

CHAPTER 59

Khasan

6:45 A.M.

Khasan slipped down into the darkness. If he looked to his left, he saw a geometric invitation to vertigo, a chiaroscuro of closing, contradictory perspectives, every law of geometry first evoked, then broken, then all of it embellished with ropes and pulleys on masts, like the rigging of a ghost schooner. He blinked, not letting himself be mesmerized into distraction as was distinctly possible, and instead focused on what lay ahead, which was in its own way even worse.

It was nothingness, just a too-steep incline down vibrational metal steps, only a rickety railing and his own sense of balance between himself and the height's claim on him, and nothing but space between him and the hard floor thirty-odd feet below. He crept, his rear end maintaining contact with the brick behind, like a sort of lifeline. It was no fun, and would have broken the mind of a man of lesser courage or more imagination. Down, down he went, into pure dark, held upright only by legs that wanted to give way and the tightness of muscles locked into cemented permanence in every sector of his body.

But he hit a flat, and squinting about he realized he'd made it to the platform where stairway two paused and offered a space where tuckered climbers, shaky from stairways one and two, could rest before veering upward again to stairway three.

He went to knees, then to prone, squirming ahead as silently as possible, not wanting to excite the tremors in the sleeping steel. He came then to an edge, and in the murk his eyes had adjusted enough to see the empty stairway extending downward at the same steep angle, really the whole fucking thing was as much an assembly of ladders as stairways.

He peered hard into the incline beneath him and could make out nothing. The only light came from the far right, light from the crashed entrance, so meek by this long-distance commute from its original source it hardly existed. But enough arrived to show him the stage beneath, and on its surface he now and then saw the strange American patrolling it.

He knew his hunters were coming to him. He knew he had the advantage. He was prone and set and had a good shooting platform, and from this distance the shotgun's buckshot would cling together in transit well enough to inflict fantastic damage.

Was the shotgun cocked?

Goddamn! He didn't know.

He rolled to his back, and ever so slightly tried to move the pump down. It wouldn't budge. That meant the last time he'd administered it, he'd thrown the pump, thus elevating a shell into the chamber, thus cocking the hammer. But maybe it was locked now because the safety was on, and that device closed the whole thing down and only pulling the trigger would free it.

He brought the gun close to his eyes and rolled as far as he could, hoping to bring as much light to bear as possible, and was rewarded—for though it was wan, it caught the red base ring exposed by the safety button's outward position, meaning the gun was ready to fire.

He rolled over again, silent as he could be, bringing his knees beneath him and the gun to shoulder, so that at the first sign of motion in the steps below, he could rise, fire, and kill.

Delta and Swagger reached the first platform. Clear. They squeezed onto it, took a rest for a second.

Too close to a theoretical enemy for conversation, even whispers. If he was there, he'd hear, since no ambient sound canceled or obscured them and the ringing of ears had muted after this much time.

Each took in a few sips of air, squirmed snake-like down the length of the platform, reached its end and the upward thrust of the next set of stairs.

Eye contact. The simple nod that eloquently expressed the idea that men on a dangerous mission must share: let's do it.

Wearing his night vision, Delta oozed to the steps, took a look up, and saw nothing he hadn't seen before, just the converging angles of railings left and right, the diminishing width of the rising steps, some blur to the right from the light of the crashed opening as it tried ineffectively to provide illumination, but no human form, no blur signifying heat, no green smear speaking of human presence.

One knee. Then the other. He had the rifle locked in the vise between arm and chest, right hand on the grip, left forward and stiff on the plastic forearm. He'd tested it, and through the night vision the Eotech hologram sight provided just a murky circle against nothingness. Any shot would have to be indexed by his read of a target's position.

Swagger had no night vision, so it was all gut for him. Through his optic, even though he'd cranked it as low as he could, the blur of the dot itself was enough to haze any detail from the image. He could shoot fast and accurately but only at a theoretical target, based on what he hoped would be input from Delta, who'd seen more.

They climbed in syncopation, Delta setting the pace, knee by knee, Swagger behind, on his haunches, the Glock in a solid two-handed grip, trigger finger indexed along the receiver, just above the guard.

Vakha and the crazy lady had made it to the top. The surreality of the theater's loft didn't much register with Vakha. He was too focused on his combat senses. Now, he waited, the woman close to him.

Sooner, later, Khasan would spring his ambush and win or die. Whichever, Vakha would drag the old bitch across the catwalk to the other wing, and there find another stairway, three, maybe four steps up to a fire door, which could be easily opened from inside.

But to Mother Death, the vast opening so high up and its weird piercing by catwalks, its ricketiness and the bounce to its tread, the profusion of what appeared to be S&M torture devices so close and yet so far, the grotesque geometry of the gestalt, was so early twentieth-century German expressionism it made her a little batty. She felt like she was actually in *The Cabinet of Dr. Caligari—the Remake*, and the Golem himself held her tight to his chest, his sweat making him rancid, his strength making him scary, his pistol making him lethal.

"You shut up, old lady. No noise. Let Khasan do his work. If you betray him, I toss you over. Long way down. Hit hard. Big splatter."

"Such a charmer," she said.

"Ha ha, with the jokes. You think I'm so stupid I don't get you play on me. Is no funny. Death is here, close by, maybe for me. But if for me, then for you too, I tell you that, and maybe you can make a fun joke when I put bullet in head."

"I think I'm out of material," she said.

Silence, only the two hearts beating, hers fast and shallow, his thunderous and slow as it was a characteristic of his profession never to get too excited about anything. The next few minutes would work themselves out not as they themselves wanted, not in accordance to agenda, but as God willed, if he existed, or as the universe's indifference insisted.

"You can't escape," she said.

"No," he said, "but I can die well. As can you. Or you can die screaming and begging."

"The only thing I've ever begged for in my life is ice cream, and that was seventy years ago."

Shots fired.

In night-vis, a Day-Glo wand swept out of the darkness fifteen feet ahead, and Delta barked, "Left, left!"

In that instant Swagger made out not even a shape through his sight but only a trace of new movement arising, and he triggered off a world-class double-tap in something like .04 seconds, the last so hard on the first that the pistol hadn't even had time to recoil fully, and so whatever it hit, it hit a mere two inches higher than the first. The sound was of a cough concealing a refrigerator door closing, because the suppressor stole thirty-five decibels from the percussion's declaration of intent, but the quiet went away in the next .02 seconds as Delta sent two 5.56s into the same general zone, which he, like Swagger, had read to be the chest of an antagonist elbowing his way up slightly from the prone to bring muzzle to bear on the interlopers.

Whether inflicted by death spasm or last heroic effort of will, the shotgun then joined the melee, a blast more ragged and thunderous than the ear-piercing, supersonic release of the rifle. But it went high.

At that point, roughly inside .55 seconds for all five shots, the shit happening fast as it always does, the mercy of silence returned to cloak them all.

"Hit?" asked Swagger.

"Negative," whispered Delta.

"See anything?"

"I see gun barrel projecting over the edge. I get no movement."

"I feel no vibration from movement."

"Negative on noise," said Delta.

"Let's move up slow, careful."

"These bastards are tricky as hell."

They moved on, and Swagger, lower to the ground, checking himself for balance on the stairs, felt his fingers hit something warm and thick, lots of it.

"I have blood," he said.

In another second they reached him. Without a message between them, Delta took the observer's job, looking upward into the spiderweb of steel steps and railing to the final platform.

Swagger did a quick check.

"Looks like two in throat, one in center face, the other just above the hairline. Lots of bad on the exit wounds. I don't think my 9s came out. He's gone."

"Four down," said Delta.

"Sniper," came the call from above. "You come now, watch me kill old lady. Then I kill you. Then myself. We all die. Ha ha, funny joke!"

INTERLUDE: 1780

11th October

They had been at it for some time and he was now a sloppy mockery of the graceful duelist he had once been. Exhaustion, made more extreme by blood loss from pricks, cuts, abrasions, slippage in mud, the constant pressure of cold rain and bitter wind, eroded his grace and left him naked but for will.

It was *quartam finali* of the dueling. It was killing time.

"Gentlemen," said the Master of Duel, "engage!"

Winston began his lunge not after the permission but during it, signifying his higher state of aggression. It launched half through the second syllable of the command, a near-foul. It was as a lightning flash, though of Toledo steel, not bolt, plunging toward the lieutenant's heart, and had the younger man not had some reserves of animal still left, he would have come to his end right there. The blade moved too swiftly, at the extension of one of Winston's superbly practiced, lubricant-smooth lunges, off his rooted back leg, the sword arm at full drive, the point reaching, reaching for the treasure of the heart, and it was only in the pivot that Robert avoided it. But it did open him, perhaps skimming across his chest to yield a gash that would leak yet more blood, lessening, over the next minutes, his energy and his resolve.

But in driving across the chest, the sword also took some delay, which enabled Robert to continue his pivot, and execute a graceful spin, presenting for a fraction of a second his naked back to his adversary, but safely so since the sword was well past. The spin carried him apart from the adversary, both from the sword and the left-hand dagger, and permitted him to put three paces between himself and the other man.

Instantly they fell to classical positions, points nicking against each other, each set to plunge a gap if it appeared, the daggers extended in the rearward aspect for balance on the slippery ground. Robert began his rightward wheel about to remain shy of the dagger.

It seemed that the astute Winston had learned much. Instead of rotating with Robert and thereby ceding the initiative and the advantage of the stronger leftward dagger, he moved laterally himself, keeping quarter-bladed to his man, sowing in Robert some confusion, which the major answered with another strike.

Again it was a close one, meaning to send Robert to voyage upon the River Styx, but again Robert evaded, though the parry with which he answered, while effective, was also a weak effort, signifying his fatigue. Clearly on the offensive, clearly full of confidence and fury, Major Winston drove onward again, his strategy being to occupy Robert with a flurry of initiatives, which Robert kept track of well enough, while subtly cajoling him from his quarter-blade aspect into a full-on frontal by which he would be vulnerable to the dagger for the killing stab.

"Watch the left! The left!" I almost shouted. But such advice during the combat from a second is regarded as bad form; by ancient tradition we are here to serve but not to advise.

Still, it was looking dark. The two faced each other in an ocean of mud, and each thrust and parry, each clang of steel against steel, sent a sleet of droplets a-fling from the source. Meanwhile, it seemed the rain had increased and now pelted slantwise from above, thick enough to obscure vision even from so intimate a distance. Yet in the whirl of the dervishes, I could make out that Robert was running lower on speed and grit, his purchase of the mud, in boots clogged with the stuff, had abated considerable, and the new gash across his chest was perhaps deeper than on first impression, and now bled steadily across his white shirtfront, filling that billowing sail with enough of its weight to deaden it, mooring it against the skin.

His only chance was to last until *quartam*

finali had extinguished by forgoing lunge and committing completely to parry, somehow staving off the lethal puncture, and thereby be satisfied with a draw, though all present would have to acknowledge he had only survived on luck. The rain had destroyed the other's footing and obscured his vision and perhaps made engagement with the weapons themselves somehow of question. But he would be alive.

At this point, feeling the advantage, Winston unleashed another storm of lunge, the subtlety of which was lost in the downpour to my eyes, but steadily advancing he controlled the rhythm of the exchange, and steadily navigating to his left he brought the dagger—now held in his hand like a pirate's tool—into fatal play. Somehow again Robert survived, but I felt that unless lightning struck them both, he was not looking at much future. I cursed bitterly, for it seemed so wrong, but then I reminded myself of the imperative of *quis erit, erit*, which rules destiny for all of us, meaning that it shall be as it shall be without the influence of the human vanities of the right or the just or the appropriate.

CHAPTER 60

Bad News

6:47 A.M.

The cops held the press people back, against squawks and whines and squeals of protest. The reporters could see it was going down from their holding pen a hundred or so yards behind police lines, right at the edge of the parking lot.

It was orchestrated chaos unfolding before their eyes: streaming, limping hostages pouring from the crash hole, to be intercepted by just as many med teams, which in two-man units would take escapees onto the grass, sit them down, perform a quick check, then abandon them to stretcher bearers, gurney pushers, and walk-helpers, and head back for another client.

Helicopters swirled overhead, kicking up funnels of dust and debris, filling the air with grit. Light beams shot down from the choppers, while at the same time all the flashers on the emergency service vehicles that ringed the site seemed to go nuts, and beams from parked squad cars also poured in randomly on the happening.

"What the fuck is going on?" in various iterations and dialects became the moan of the imprisoned press boys and girls, and even Banjax's *Times* press ID around his neck didn't have the power to part the formation of beefy young men who stood in his way. He quickly phoned National.

"David, what's going on?" Mitch said. "We have video from airborne, it looks like Mardi Gras."

"What exactly I don't know. Big blast, lots of hubbub everywhere, and—"

"Was there a raid?"

"Nobody's saying. I'm not clear. After the blast, which came from the rear, it seemed that for a few seconds the cops were as stupefied as we were. Then they moved up. A couple of moments ago, buses pulled up, and all the commandos poured out. They got organized and then went in. These guys are ready for war, but the whole thing has a loopy, improvisational vibe to it. Wouldn't they be here already and go in exactly on the blast? It wasn't like that. It was confusion."

"Maybe you ought to move around back."

"I don't think so. These cops are going here in the front, the hostages are—oh, shit, I just saw someone that had to be Representative Hastings being led to an ambulance. And there's Dillman too."

"What about Venable? She's the important one. And her puppy-boy Baker."

"No sign. Oh, wait, I see Feeley, I'll call him."

"Good work," said Mitch. "Remember, we do not want to lose our lead on this story."

"I got it."

Banjax wandered to the side of the mob, tried to squeeze closer—"Back off, pal," said a young linebacker with a Smokey the Bear hat over a Saturday game face—but settled on a spot where he could watch for Feeley's availability. When he saw it, he quickly hit his Feeley button, saw his friend take out his phone, read the number, and click on.

"What the hell is happening?" Banjax asked.

"We don't know yet. Someone blew a hole in the rear, maybe operators went in, the lights are out, the hostages rushed out, and we're getting confusing details from them. It's all a mess now."

"Was this—"

"David, I don't know a fucking thing yet. We'll have to sort it out."

"Sorry, I'll wait."

"I should tell you, there is one bit of news."

"What?"

"Two or three of the hostages said the same thing."

"What?"

"The hero thing."

"You're kidding."

"No, I'm not. They say they saw Swagger kicking the hell out of one of the bad guys."

"But you—"

"I know, I know."

Banjax felt a sickness buckle through him. His knees almost went, and a stroke of dizziness knocked his eyes out of focus. His scoop! His glory! His hard-news triumph! His newsroom legitimacy! The explaining he'd have to do!

"Swagger's not dead," said Feeley. "Not only that, he's gone all Patrick Ferguson."

CHAPTER 61

Reckoning

6:49 A.M.

Swagger whispered, "He don't know there's two of us. Give me the rifle, you take the pistol. I'll go up first, present myself, try and talk him out of anything. You're not at platform level, but just below. You listen to how it goes. If it's getting shaky, you poke your head up and shoot between my legs. Shut him down."

"Swagger, he'll kill you. He'll kill the old lady first, then he'll kill you. At that point it doesn't matter if I peg him."

"Matters to me."

"You are one crazy-ass bastard."

"You got a better plan?"

"Just use the red dot and go for the head."

"Too risky. I got skin in this game."

"Crazy bastard. Okay, it's your call."

Swagger turned.

"Let her go," he yelled. "She doesn't have to die, you don't have to die."

"Ha ha," cried Vakha. "Everybody comedian in America."

"DEA's going to want your cooperation. They'll offer you some kind of deal. They need you to go against the Russians. You have leverage. You'll be surprised what's possible."

"You think I rat? No rat! Russ is rats, not Chechens. Come, Sniper. Face me. We see who is bravest man."

"I know it's you, pal."

He rose, stepped up two steps, rifle lowered, and set himself on the platform, legs V-ed.

Vakha had his left arm clapped almost killing-tight around her neck, her eyes bulging at the limited oxygen intake, and in the other the pistol, shoved hard against her head, its muzzle but an inch above her ear. The trigger was at break point, all slack vanished. Yet he was carefully stationed behind her, so that, skinny and wren-boned as she was, only his edges were visible, and an edge shot wouldn't take this character down.

"Drop rifle, Sniper."

"You'll kill me sure, then."

"Sure, why not? All die. Go to bar in heaven, even this grandma, have a good laugh about it, drink too much beer. Lots of fun."

"I'm telling you this ain't your smart move. You can make it out alive, cut a deal, bully DEA into anything. Then they get you a new life somewhere."

"I sell cars? I cut hair? I polish shoes? I am Vakha Shishani, last of the Shishani clan, famous in Grozny, feared in Grozny, hero in Grozny! I sell women's underwear? Battle death for me please, and thank you very much."

Pause.

"And for you too."

He pulled the gun from her head and aimed it at Swagger.

He was crushing her. She smelled his hot breath in her ear. The oxygen wormed its way through her passages, a small percentage reaching her parched and desperate lungs. She could hear him yelling at Swagger, who stood like a blood-soaked zombie fifteen feet away. How could he have lost so much blood and still not only be alive but standing, and not only standing but fighting?

"And for you too," she made out.

Here it comes, she thought. She began to beg forgiveness in Latin, the language of God in her youth. So much undone, so much unfulfilled, so many hurt and battered by the world, and that had always been the point, to help them, the lost, the anonymous, the crushed and filthy, help them all, lift them up, somehow, it was a humble enough dream but it had gotten her as far as she could have hoped to get.

The gun came off her head and snapped out for Swagger, and she saw this Vakha's tendons ripple as he pulled the trigger, ahead of Swagger by a good second.

But not ahead of her.

She jabbed upward with the hairpin, driving its needle tip into his wrist right behind the hand, feeling it sink deep. Nothing had ever felt so good in her life.

He twisted in a spasm of pain, squealing at the suddenness of it, and in that loss of strength and concentration, she twisted sideways, feeling his grasp lessen—

Delta shot him twice, fast as light. The first was the heart shot, upper right ventricle, pulped by the steel magnolia of the opening hollow-point bullet, shredding, slicing, even dicing as it tore through at about thirteen hundred feet per second. The second was under the eye, straight into that baseball-sized and -shaped globe of cerebellum set at intersecting lines from the ears and the bridge of the nose, the lights-off-right-this-second hit. Engagement time: .1 second.

Uncle Vakha's hands relaxed in the instant-eternity crushing him, his joints surrendered, his respiration came up dry, his blood smeared and poured, and when he hit the steel beneath he was just carcass.

"Jesus Christ," she said.

Swagger was there, keeping her from falling.

"You okay, ma'am? You're not hit or nothing?"

She looked like she'd just come out of the spin cycle. Her true hair was an iron riot, her makeup had melted, her lips were pale as ice, her bright red dress was rumpled like a dishrag dragged behind a pickup. But her eyes still had that wicked sparkle.

"I think under the circumstances, you can call me Charlotte. I'm fine. Swagger, aren't you supposed to be dead?"

"I didn't have time."

She saw that another man had come up to the platform. He was a first-team all-star professional battle animal if ever there was one, all done up in camo, some kind of strange lens covering his face, muscular, lithe, improbably attractive even if bathed in sweat and caked with grime.

"Who is this?" she asked Swagger.

"I have no idea," Swagger said.

"Are you FBI, sir?"

He cranked up his cyclops eye to reveal the eternal face of the legionnaire, familiar from the world's nineteen thousand or so armies over its seven thousand years of war.

"Not exactly," he said.

"Then who are you?"

"It's complicated."

"Maybe he's just the guy that saved both our lives and we ought to let it go at that," said Swagger.

CHAPTER 62

Plasma

6:51 A.M.

They all heard it. Some saw it. Not a gunfight but two suppressed shots, half-snap, half-click, maybe two muted flash signatures, orange spearheads of radiance, all in super-time, way, way up there.

Both units had made their way around the circumference of the stage and were clustered in the raw dark at the stairway.

Nick put up his hand, fist clenched: universal tactical language for Hold Tight.

He waited. Possibly sounds of chitchat reached his ears. He looked at Colonel Lhotske, who returned the earnest stare of a subordinate, awaiting orders.

Nick turned, designated five of his Boise agents with light units under M4 barrel. He touched one light, to indicate that's what he wanted. He gestured them out a little farther so they could get a better angle. He held up three fingers, dropped one, dropped the next, and finally dropped the third.

The five lights spurted on, hunted briefly, and their circles of illumination clustered on human forms on the utmost platform.

"Hold your fire," came a call from above, possibly Swagger.

"Swagger?"

"Yeah, me. Nick? All tangos down. Last hostage secured."

"Do you need medical?"

"You'll never get it up these steep, narrow stairs. We are coming down. That's me, Representative Venable, and another operator. Three of us. We'll get down on our own. Keep those fingers off triggers."

"Got you." He spoke into his throat mike. "Stand down, all officers. We have friendlies coming down the steps. Get medical in here."

Then another call came from above. It was the congresswoman.

"Somebody find my goddamned shoes."

They were almost down. Swagger held his rumpled shirt and jacket against the gash, which seemed not to be issuing blood anymore, but it burned like a green motherfucker in hell's thirteenth circle. Next to him, or rather more just off his left shoulder, Commando X steadied him, guided him, supported him, and with his other hand had a firm grip on Mother Death's biceps, steadying her as well, keeping her safely pressed against the brick wall. The descent was made easier by the helpful beams from the SWAT teams below and by their own perfect cadence. They looked like the Yankee Doodle Dandy of modern war.

They reached, and eager hands came at them, more support.

"Where are my shoes?" said Madam Chairman.

"Here, ma'am," said a young SWAT guy, the designated shoe locator. He placed them before her, and she seemed to think they restored her as magically as the young prince's glass slipper had restored Cinderella. But before anyone could say anything, she had urgent business item number two.

"Baker, quit walking your goddamned dog and get over here and pitch in."

"Ma'am," said Colonel Lhotske, "you should sit down until we've called the building secured and can get you a gurney."

"Don't be silly," she said. "I walked in, I'll walk out. Get these boys some help, though. They need it."

Someone eased Swagger to the ground, and a SWAT guy cross-trained as a medic got a light on and examined the wound. He quickly pulled on rubber gloves and applied a few rudimentary measures, a fast clean with an antibiotic-treated wipe, a pack of TrueClot to seal the wound, and a gauze wrap to protect it from airborne pathogens.

"Man, he cut you bad. You need plasma, cleaning, stitches, and a week in bed."

Nick leaned over to Bob.

"I thought I said no Great-grandpa Ferguson bullshit."

"I forgot," said Bob.

A light came onto Commando X, who flinched, shrugged, looked away, then said, "I'm okay."

"Baker," said Madam Chairman, "walk this young officer out to medical attention. You can do that, can't you?"

"Yes, ma'am," said Baker, seemingly back in the human race.

She yanked his ear to her mouth.

"Listen, dummy. Do one thing right tonight. Do exactly what he wants. Keep others away by congressional authority. Take him where he wants and then let him go and wish him god-speed. If you fuck this up, I'll ream you so hard you'll wish that kid had put your eyeballs in his martini."

"Yes, ma'am," said Baker.

Meanwhile Nick peeled off and got on the horn to DC.

"Nick, what's the situation?"

"The five terrorists are all down. Four dead, one of them still breathing but just. All the hostages, I repeat, *all* the hostages have been accounted for, including eight boys flex-cuffed to the fire exits, all congressional staff, and we even found three prison guards on the floor of the bus, flexed to the chairs. No criticals among the hostages: sprains, abrasions, twists, bruises, some hyperventilation, no heart attacks among the older, all of them in medical by now, all should be out of the hospital in a day or so. Worst thing: wet pants."

"Mrs. Venable?"

"Spitting fire, taking no prisoners."

"Swagger?"

"Cut bad, blood loss, but plasma, stitches, antibiotics, and lemonade ought to have him walking around in a week."

"Nick, can you give me a quick tactical rundown?"

"Lots still to be determined. We'll need a total forensics workup. But for now, it appears someone detonated an entry charge to the rear, an extremely capable operator got in and linked up with Swagger, and they moved quickly to neutralize the bad actors while the hostages fled. All this time our SWAT was stacked up outside."

"Who the hell was the guy?"

"No idea, at this point. He's around here somewhere, I just saw him. I guess they took him out to medical. I'll find him. Sir, I'm going to have to make a statement."

"This is what we've settled on. Tell them highly classified assets using highly classified techniques operated brilliantly to raid and destroy the hostage takers, and that all hostages were released without serious harm. Tell them details may not be forthcoming because of the top-secret nature of the operation."

"Got it," said Nick. "I'll go get that guy now."

"Nick, you did great."

"Swagger did great. I was just the traffic cop."

He put the phone away, and turned to Colonel Lhotske.

"Where is he?"

"Where is who, Nick?"

"You know, the guy who came down with Swagger and the old lady?"

"I don't know, Nick. I never got a good look at him. I assumed he was one of your guys."

Nick looked around. Mother Death was sitting next to Swagger, holding his hand. SWAT teams crawled through the building, calling in all-clears from various sectors. Lhotske okayed the building as secure, and two medics raced across the floor with a gurney and lots of new blood for Swagger.

But where was the other guy?

CHAPTER 63
The Big Walk

6:53 A.M.

With a nod and thanks, Delta ditched the goofball dildo who'd pretended to be helping him, slid between two ambulances, and headed out through the jam of first responders and news vehicles, edged through a number of officers racing toward the crash hole wanting to get in on it, take part, tell their kids they'd been there for maybe the best special operation in history, certainly the cleanest, and made his way toward open road.

He slipped out his phone.

"Yo?"

"Come get me, bro. It's done."

"You got 'em all?"

"Stone-cold. All checks canceled."

"I'm on my way."

"I'm exiting the parking lot. Lots of shit here, trucks, ambulances. I'll continue walking toward the next intersection, where it looks clear. Pick me up there."

"Affirmative, Delta, and out."

He had made it another hundred or so yards, however, when disaster, in the shape of a Patrolman R. Lopez of the Kuna department, on outer perimeter security and one of the few guys who'd stayed at his duty station in the aftermath of the whole shebang, hit him square in the face with a SureFire light. Too bright.

Delta blinked, dropped his face.

"Excuse me, Agent," said the boy. "I have orders to check everyone going in or out."

"Sure," said Delta. He could see several other officers ambling casually toward him.

"You're FBI?"

"Yeah." He tapped his night vision still strapped to his head. "Late arrival. We borrowed this from a sporting goods shop on the other side of town. Only way we could get night vision into the game in time. Now I'm sworn to get it back to him at full speed. Guy let us have an eight-thousand-dollar piece of gear. The deal was, it came back as soon as possible."

"Sure, no problem. Can you just show me some ID? You know, I have to make a report, the sergeant will ask."

"Well, to tell you the truth, actually, the call-up was so fast I left my creds in my wallet, which is in our SWAT van on the other side of the parking lot. You want me to go get it?"

"I hate to ask you to do that, but I'm new on this and I don't want to screw up and get yelled at."

"Sure," said Delta. "Or maybe I could just have my supervisor call your supervisor and tell him one of his operators was stopped by a young cop while on official business at a crime scene." He smiled.

"Well," said the young man, getting it, "that's really not going to do anyone any good, least of all me. I hear you. You're a hero, I'm a kid, why fuck around? Cops are brothers after all. So just let me take your name and badge number and I'll check it later and when I see it's okay, I'll just report you showed me creds."

"Ah, yeah," said Delta, "good man," smiling but knowing that he wasn't sure of the nomenclature of FBI badge numbers. Did they do straight integers, did they have dashes or maybe even letters thrown in, were the numbers three-, four-, five-digit? Even more problematic, the kid could get an evasionary vibe off this little man-on-man, decide to go full game face. Worse, the other officers were almost there.

He had a second to make up his mind, if that.

INTERLUDE: 1780

Major Kavanagh," I heard a call.

I looked and through the rain saw that it was Major Hancock, Winston's reluctant second.

"I say," he said, "your man's hair is in his eyes, putting him at disadvantage. Let us call a brief halt. We vouch no opprobrium attached therein."

"Agreed," I said, thinking it odd that he would break the rhythm of the thing just now, when his man was so close to triumph and ours to tragedy.

We simultaneously shouted to the Master of Duel, who interrupted, saw a plaster of hair against Grammercy's forehead, and called a halt.

"Timekeeper," he shouted to the sergeant so charged, "two minutes please."

Yet at that point I felt an odd sensation. Was it a ray of sun through the thick? Was it the peal of a far-off bell? Was it a memory from another life, another time, another body? Was it one of young Mr. Blake's odd but powerful Westminster drawings come to nest in the forefront of my mind? I could not shake it, yet I did not understand it, and as Robert approached, I made ready to wind his hair back under the control of the ribbon that held uncertain sway over its unruly affect.

And then it struck me, clear as a bell, odd but true as Blake's unformed genius.

"I have your man," I whispered to Robert.

CHAPTER 64

Exeunt

My badge number is—"

It wasn't really an explosion, because it lacked the percussion, the shock wave, the pure energy riot of a genuine high-X release. The noise played softer, muted, even had an archaic sense to it. But there was nothing shy about the tower of radiance it released, a structure of roiling fire climbing high toward the heavens, amid a penumbra of sparks and burning shards and chunks, briefly throwing everything into high relief and, simultaneously, producing gallons of gas, seen as smoke, a thick, dense spew of it, gushing outward in waves from the epicenter.

"Holy crap," said Officer Lopez. And he was gone. And so were the others, all racing to the site of this nuclear blast.

Delta watched them go. Then he turned, continued his relaxed shuffle beyond the perimmeter, and saw Niner turn the corner ahead and aim straight onto him.

He climbed in.

"Great gag. You can blow shit up in my movie anytime."

"I saw the cop giving you attitude. I popped my unused pyrotechnic and made a big hole in nothing and there he went, on cue."

The truck pulled away.

It was almost light out. The sun was coming up.

INTERLUDE: 1780

11th October

have your man," I whispered to Robert.

"Alas, no," he said from his place in the citadel of surrender, "he has me, I fear."

"Listen hard, Robert," I beseeched, "for I have wisdom."

I dispatched my discoveries.

"He instructs his second to call on secret signal the brief truce here exactly as he did at Chatham seven years ago. It's a guise. It allows him to turn from all eyes. In that pose, he scrapes his finger along the inside of his rapier's basket, where he has smeared an unguent, a lotion, a salve perhaps. In that chemical there lurks some herb or pharmaceutical that has near-alchemical powers. I have heard of such, from the southern continent, the leaf of a tree called 'coco.' He then plunges it into his nostril, closest and fastest to his brain. It is subsumed interiorly and sends its message in seconds to the next station. There, it imparts great strength and confidence, it banishes fear, it recharges both body and mind, for a short duration. So fortified, as against your depletion, he closes the duel in showy Mayfair fashion,

433

faster, more violent, more to the attack, and destroys you first with the dagger, and as you pause in pain, with the rapier, and twice struck you are beyond recovery. I so saw at Chatham."

"Then, sir, I am damned. I have no strength left. Please tell Susanna how hard I fought, and my mother as well, and my first captain who secured for me this life I now must leave."

"No, no, Robert, you do not grasp it yet. Listen hard, boy!"

I saw him brought aback.

"Do you not see, he had no foreknowledge of which rapier you would choose, as the choice was yours. Therefore he would have so applied his magic unguent to them *both*. The magic lurks within your own basket."

He made to look, but I checked him.

"No, no, do not investigate. That would be to give the game away. Go now to the fight, but in the second before the master gives his command, that is when you apply the unguent to yourself. He must see. In seeing, he will collapse. Never before has he engaged in lethal struggle without his hundred-to-one advantage. His mind will scatter, palsy will afflict his limbs. That is where, before in seconds he regains, you must strike, fully fortified and revived. You cannot tarry, enjoy, or procrastinate. Strike and kill and be done with it."

"I hear you, sir."

"Gentlemen," came the call from good Sergeant Stanley.

And so again they faced each other. A smile etched itself upon Major Winston's face, his whole body alert with eagle's energy and strength, eying the prey in shallow waters, his for the simple skill in his talons.

"Last chance, simpleton. Kneel in surrender or I skewer your heart as if for roasting. Then to bed with Ferguson's whore, she being thus disgraced and destroyed by my action, then back to Mayfair and the political career my heroism has earned."

"Sir, you'll rather breakfast in hell, alone, this day," Robert replied.

"To sword," said the Colour Sergeant.

The tips came up and brushed in mock salute, in Winston's mind prelude to execution and triumph.

"No quarter, sir," he said.

At that moment Robert broke his position for a second to apply unguent to his own nostril and upon regaining, said merely, "No quarter then, sir!"

"Engage," said Stanley.

The swords jangled together, a sleet of steel on steel too fast for the eye to mark. But I caught then a glimpse of Winston's eyes, wide now in fear, his pupils like raisins upon fresh dairy, face itself tighter than a fist. He gave ground, he gave ground, he gave ground, his blade deprived in far by speed and precision, taking a prick high on arm, again near elbow, and finally a deeper penetration into high chest.

Seeing it lost, he banked all his coinage on a last attack, and fell hard to close on Robert, but though they came chest to chest in the melee, each weapon blocking the other, it was Robert who was speedier into recovery, found foundation, and went to unfiligreed lunge.

He drove the rapier full into his man.

Time seemed to embed in ambrose. The clock allowed no tick, the heart no beat, the sand no trickle. Is it my imagination or did a lightning strike nearby send illumination and clarity to the momentary composition? Robert fully extended, his blade sunk so deep in the Major that its excess, dark with gore, emerged like a serpent's tongue from underneath the shoulder blade as the man was well skewered as the so-recently evoked piece of meat on the fire, all transpiring in a mist of liquifaction beshrouding, as if some vaguely remembered scene from ancient times.

The Major's look betokened astonishment, then regret, and he made a feeble attempt with dagger to bring revenge to the table, but with his own dagger, Robert blocked and then administered coup de grâce in the form of a neck thrust, the broad dagger cutting on either side, sundering all as it plunged through muscle and artery and sinew and various sundries, and it too emerged on the obverse side, beneath the ear, a good five inches equally sheathed in gore.

Gore was general as other arteries caught up with the development in seemingly but a second, as the Major stood, punctured and grotesque, his blood deserting his body in full rout. Robert let both grips of his weapons go, stood back to give room, and watched the Major fall laterally into the mud, which turned crimson with deposit. By freak of whimsy—*quis erit, erit* after all—he did not yet go supine, but the tip of the dagger jammed on the firm ground beneath the mud and suspended the body at an odd angle to the ground. Again in memory, lightning struck, giving incandescence to the portraiture.

"The duel is hereby completed by all legal sanctions as just and within the bounds of Code Duello," proclaimed Colour Sergeant Stanley, delivering the final act of ceremony in still pelting rainfall.

All rushed to the victor.

I was closest and therefore first to grasp the man.

"By God, sir, I could not find the unguent," he said. "It was all on bluff. Here it is now," and he revealed the clottage of paste-like cream applied to the curve of the Toledo hilt—"untouched."

"Superb," I said.

Then Susanna arrived, giddy in the meaning of it.

"Robert, you have avenged Patrick and the Horse," she said, giving him support.

"Not alone, but rather with the shrewd Major's wisdom as my guide," he said.

The surgeon, having examined and declared *le mort de Bannister*, came next to the bleeding victor.

"Brandy in the wounds and the gullet and then ordeal by catgut," he said. "Get this man to the dispensary."

"Good show," said Colonel Bruxhall, supervising the assemblage. "You continue to astonish, Lieutenant Grammercy." Then he turned to the Sergeant at Arms and said, "After the setting of the stitches, this man is to be escorted under guard to the gaol and there under lock and key detained."

CHAPTER 65
After

I t was too cold to sit on the porch now. Late October had brought its bitter gusts, its burnt-out palette, its flocks of southward-headed honkers, and its sense of closing down. The dark air had a snap to it that old bones didn't welcome, and the whistle of the wind through the leafless branches had a melancholy meaning old bones didn't care to contemplate.

Bob sat in his living room, rocking back and forth, wrapped in a thick cardigan, not that it was cold in the house, only that he was always cold. He was surrounded by Navajo pottery and rugs, arts and crafts furniture, a few high-end Fred Remington bronze sculpture replicas, a painting that reminded him of a buck he'd called Old Tim many years back. No TV. No terminal. Nothing modern. He didn't much care for modern.

No pain today. He was 158 stitches into a pretty easy recovery. In fact, they'd never had to put him under, the medical attention mostly an exercise in sewing. He felt as if they could have made a nice sport coat of him after all the needle-and-thread work. His body added another scar to its collection, and shirtless, he was looking more like a science museum exhibit called "The Wonderful Zipper," from 1952, the last time he'd been in a science museum. New antibiotics had been added to the pills he was already taking, and the goddamned hip still hurt, but the replacement operation had been put off until after the new year.

Just back and forth, coffee. No incoming information. He spent his time reading on the Crimean War—fascinating as he'd known a few like Lord Cardigan, hell for leather just one side or the other of crazy. Maybe Vakha, for one. The rest of the time was invested in his one concession to modern: email with old friends checking in and checking up, this and that, nothing urgent, just enough to eat the time and justify the coffee.

He was still too famous for anybody's good. His Little Rock lawyer reported an endless tide of offers from various folks in every kind of media, all of which he turned down without entertaining. News choppers occasionally buzzed overhead; sometimes they sent drones for a look-see at the "hero" of Boise. Too bad for them. Admirers and hucksters alike were turned away by the gate team, which was costing him a fortune, the best money he'd ever spent.

Back and forth, back and forth. A sip, followed by another sip, and finally, a third sip. Coffee was life. Another log on the fire, another cup of coffee. Julie was due back soon, and despite the lull in attention the whole deal had cost him, she had to report that business was booming. He was not only sort of rich but getting sort of richer. Not bad.

A few bad tastes remained, as if he'd been sucking on a nickel. He'd spent a long, tiresome week being over-interviewed by the FBI and the Idaho State Police, and it turned him into a cranky old man. Every little detail, as if he remembered every little detail. What he remembered most was feeling helpless in that wheelchair, and the bite of the flex cuff into his wrist. They were all surprised that he was not terribly impressed by their assiduous investigation of the criminal Shishani Clan, Vakha and his four nephews.

And he was no help at all on the subject of the unknown operator.

"Wish I could help," his tale went. "Never got a good look at him. I just assumed he was Bureau. I mean, who else could he be? He didn't say much. Hell of a shot though. Through my legs, double tapped that guy into the next world in less than half a second, maybe faster, saved my bacon and old lady Venable's as well. Maybe she got a better look at him than I did."

Needless to say, she hadn't. Nor had anybody on the first responder team. It was dark, you know.

The government was going to issue a report

soon. He wondered how the "classified assets" story would hold up. Rumors were everywhere, some incredibly stupid. The Internet was nuts with them, but after a few brief glances, he passed on further examinations of the craziness. He wasn't going to let it touch him.

Nick and Sally were back from a trip to the Virgin Islands, where they had gone for two months to weather the storm. Plans were being made for a visit after the new year, if the newly voracious COVID would allow. Sally was now formally unemployed, since Mother Death had discreetly announced that the House Subcommittee Hearings on Use of Force were closed and she had no plans to reopen them. It made page nineteen of the *New York Times*, he'd been told.

But he knew the rhythms. Just when he thought it all over, and nothing but smooth sailing ahead, something always turned up. Maybe not this time. Maybe he'd have the sense to say no. He was onto seventy-five now, and that wasn't chicken feed. Creak-creak, rock-rock. More coffee.

Door opens. In comes—fate?

Not this time. Julie, home from the office a little early, with some stuff in hand. She was alight with smiles, meaning that the financials were still looking good. No worries, clear skies, too bad we can't have a nice drink except for the fact you'll end up in Shanghai in four days with a new wife, dragon tattoos front and rear, and six children.

He rose, they had a nicely casual old-pal husband-wife exchange, she reminded him of this and that and he reminded her of that and this, and soon it would be supper, something plain and simple without any work for either of them.

"Oh, and this," she said.

"Good lord," he said, seeing a manila envelope packed full with some kind of document that thought itself to be important.

"I would have tossed it but the return address was familiar. 'Neal Hughes, Northwestern University, Department of History, Evanston, Illinois,' blah blah."

Bob squinted, as if such machinations were the key to accessing memory.

"Yeah, from somewhere."

He took it, saw that it was addressed somewhat strangely—"Bob Lee Swagger, c/o Idaho State Police, Boise, Idaho"—meaning that whoever had sent it didn't know his actual address, but that some clerk at Boise HQ had done the necessary paperwork and sent it along.

He found the rocker and opened the envelope, pulling what appeared to be a manuscript of a few dozen pages from it, and at that exact moment remembered that Neal Hughes was the academic someone had paid to go to England and who had uncovered his link to Patrick Ferguson.

Dear Mr. Swagger,

I hope this package finds you. As a professor of history with a specialty in Eighteenth Century British military affairs, I was hired by a firm called Artex, which had determined that your DNA samples linked you to a British officer killed in 1780, the great Patrick Ferguson, soldier and inventor of the famous Ferguson rifle. They desired confirmation and context.

As you certainly know, the early results of my investigation were leaked to the *New York Times*. I had no idea such a thing would occur, and it wasn't until a few weeks later that I realized you were being more or less impeached by a House committee there in Boise, and that the information I provided might have been useful to your persecutors.

I believe that ordeal is over and trust that your subsequent actions gave you as much pride and pleasure as they did most Americans. I hope that you hold no ill feelings toward me. It seemed an ethical assignment when I accepted and the payment was helpful in getting my own children educated.

But now I have an actual "find" and no place to send it. Artex, it seems, has ceased to exist and left no forwarding address. I will not send it on to Representatives Baker and Venable without your permission. I did try and call the *New York Times* reporter David Banjax for his suggestions, but learned he is no longer employed there and the newspaper had no idea of his whereabouts. I may publish it, with commentary, but again, not without your permission.

I believe you will find it quite interesting, as it explains so much about not only who you are and where you got your talents from but how you came to be where you were when you were born.

It is part of the unfinished memoirs of a British colonel named Matthew Kavanagh, who was killed in 1793 during the siege of Toulon, defending his superior officer from capture by Bonaparte. In fact, as Bonaparte led the French forces in the ambush, it's possible Colonel Kavanagh died at his hand.

In any event, in 1779, after being severely wounded at the Battle of Monmouth in 1778, he was assigned, as part of his recuperation, as a Surveyor of the Board of Ordnance. This was the oversight entity that supported British military enterprises logistically, administering selection and distribution of all necessary items from stirrups to cannons. Small arms, obviously, were included in that mandate.

Thus then-major Kavanagh spent the remaining war years in the colonies "surveying"—inspecting, interviewing, auditing, and so forth, making certain that Her Majesty's troops had all the flour and tent pegs they needed where they needed them and when they needed them. But, as an infantry officer of much experience (he had previously served in the Seven Years' War and had many interesting postings between that event and his arrival in America) he had an abiding interest in small arms, notably the cumbersome British short-pattern musket called the "Brown Bess," which he abhorred.

Thus, when he finally found the time, he journeyed to the Waxhaw Cantonment, in North Carolina, from which location Patrick Ferguson was leading a Tory militia against the Patriot partisans, mainly the "Overmountain Boys" from Tennessee. He wanted a firsthand report from Ferguson on the success or failure of Ferguson's revolutionary breech-loading rifle, as well as an understanding of what politics had been involved in the Army's refusal to adapt it on a wide scale.

What follows is his account of his visit to that cantonment, Oct. 8–12, 1780.

One note on language: As you probably know, British prose in the Eighteenth Century was florid, flowery, adjective-crazed, given to roving far off topic with regard to overmuch in the way of detail and background and, in sum, hard on modern eyes. And this says nothing about its annoying protocols of capitalizing all nouns, scattering an abundance of semicolons about sentences that should have been paragraphs, even chapters, using the ampersand (&) instead of writing out "and," and most famously rendering the capital S as if it was a capital F.

I have taken the liberty not of "translating" the account but of at least "massaging" for modern tastes. I have removed some overly expository passages. I have changed nothing of substance, merely lowercased aggressively, declared death to semicolons and &s, and fixed those infernal big Fs. (They drive me crazy too!)

Best, Neal Hughes, PhD
Department of History
Northwestern University
Evanston, IL

"Okay, then," said Bob to nobody. "Let's see what we got."

He read the first pages quickly, finding the fancy language initially annoying, but soon he grew used to the rhythms, the oddly placed words, the Latinisms (meaningless), and saw that it was a story as old as time itself. Two men, fighting to the death.

"How is it?" Julie said.

"Well, interesting. But I don't see yet how it connects."

"I guess you'd better finish the last."

"I guess I'd better."

INTERLUDE: 1780

After too much port, I fell to sleep effortlessly for the rigorous day it had been. I had declined attendance to Major Winston's burial, as I felt the presence of his slayer's second would not be conducive to high morale among mourners comprised wholly of horsemen of Winston's Dragoons. I also turned down Colonel Bruxhall's invitation to stay on post as commander of that troop, as by nature I am of foot and not cavalry, even if I am a passing horseman. In addition, I felt it not a wise path to take on my career for the burden it might have placed on both commander and ranks. He would have to wait until Lord Cornwallis sent along another horseman to fill Winston's boots.

I made my provision to leave and forewarned my traveling party of three to make provision. All were pleased to escape this forlorn cantonment in the far mountains of the damp and melancholy Carolinas. I saw no glimpse, after the duel, of either Susanna or Robert. I did make opportunity to pass on unrequested advice to the Colonel, suggesting that whatever crimes he could conjure for Robert, adjudication should not be harsh. In its rough way, justice had been served, and on campaign, justice rough is better than justice unserved. That good man said he would think hard upon it.

So I slept, aiming for an early rise—that is, until a knock came to my door. It was high dark, and I judged it to be near unto four of the morning. I shook sleep from my body and a bit of pain—an old wound had stiffened, owing to exposure to the damp for a prolonged period—and answered. It was of course the indefatigable Colour Sergeant Stanley. Did the man never rest?

"Sir, Colonel requests your presence in his quarters."

"Of course," I said. "Can you pray tell of what meaning?"

"It is for him to enlighten."

It had stopped raining by now, though the mud would not abide for several dry weeks. In its place had come weather, telling of winter on the move, bitter and windy, making the trees rattle while it whistled through them. I made my way swiftly, forgoing ablutions, in full curiosity. Why was this meeting, if such it were, not in cantonment headquarters, rather than the Colonel's own quarters?

I arrived, knocked, and the Colour Sergeant admitted me. Present were both Robert and Susanna, as well as the surgeon, and a clerk whose name I did not know but whom I had observed in the office and took to be an able fellow.

I nodded to all, as military custom seemed unnecessary given the irregularity of the assemblage.

Robert appeared no worse for his ordeal. His cheek had been catgutted, yielding a row of Xs beneath his eye. His other wounds, presumably so strung shut and bandaged or patched, were invisible to me beneath the buckskin shirt he had resumed wearing. Susanna appeared nonplussed, for nothing could discourage so courageous a young woman. If I were to have a daughter, hers is the model I should choose.

"Major Kavanagh, thank you for attending. Brandy?"

"If you please, sir."

It was Stanley who poured and served.

"All about. Stanley, please join us."

"With pleasure, sir." Now *that* was unprecedented!

"And the clerk too. Enjoy, Corporal Baker."

"Much obliged, sir," said the man.

"Major, I have invited you to give counsel to Lieutenant Grammercy as to my proposals. He may require an experienced hand's thoughts."

"No better man for the task than the good Major," said Robert.

"I shall try, sir."

"Excellent."

He cleared his throat, took a sip of brandy, and addressed us all, standing next to the mantel and the fireplace, which crackled with flame. The pendulum clock on the mantel signified the hour of half four.

"Lieutenant Grammercy, you present me with difficult issues. It is, whatever course I may choose, imperative that you leave this post. Your presence can but enrage the Winston Dragoons to the point of mutiny over time. The wound will stay raw. I fear mutiny, I fear riot, I fear dereliction. And that is why I despise duels, as they are inevitably fractious to good military order. So, Lieutenant, you are gone, that is a done conclusion."

"Understood, sir."

"I have before me two alternatives. The correct one is to send you to Charlotte guarded by force of arms. That is as much for your protection as anything. There some feeble charges will be brought, and under General Cornwallis's influence, owing to my advisement, you will be found guilty of one thing or other, returned to England, and sent to military gaol at hard labor for five years, after a dishonorable discharge. Your prospects then would be nil at least as far as service is concerned. I doubt civilians would be much keener. The only possibility I see is leaving the home country and drifting off into servitude with some colonial military, where your talents might be put to good use. You would be, in short, a mercenary, a violent and insalubrious trade, as well as treacherous, a state of near banditry, living alone for loot and rape, completely expendable at a despot's whim."

"Father, that is so unjust."

"Just or not, it may be necessary."

"I have no interest in serving the Sultan of Buwami, sir. You said there was another possibility?"

"Perhaps you'll find this more to your liking. It solves another issue much before my mind. My daughter Susanna, whom I love more than anything in the world, has been dealt a cruel fate. Her husband is dead. Being a widow is not a graceful designation for a young woman in today's Britain. Even more to the point, she bears the child of Patrick Ferguson. That intensifies matters, for being the widow of a Scot, despised still by so many, and being the mother to his child, is no primrose path. She would persevere without complaint naturally, as is her character. But I would find it too heartbreaking to endure. It would enrage me. It would make shite of everything I have believed in and fought for."

The silence grew. One could hear the ticking of the clock, the rustling of the clerk's papers, the suppressed breathing of we few in the audience.

He turned to me.

"Major, I am about to make a proposal that

violates all law and tradition. I invite you to take notes for a report to Lord Cornwallis if it so pleases you. At this point I am beyond caring what Charlotte makes of me. We have lost too many fine young boys in a pointless slaughter. We are bled out. No empire is worth such sacrifice by its finest. I feel it is they who set us on this mad course who have made the initial betrayal."

I knew where this had to go.

"Sir, I make no report to Charlotte. I owe no allegiance to Charlotte. As a Surveyor of the Ordnance Board, I shall restrict my remarks to infantry riflery at the Tower of London. That is my ken, that is what I shall deliver, obedient to the letter."

"Here it is, then," said the Colonel. "In this hour, I shall officially join Robert and Susanna in marriage and issue them a safe transit through any British forces they should meet as they head west. Since the Overmountaineers have withdrawn north for the winter, there should be no interception. As Robert speaks Cherokee, I foresee no difficulty with the tribes. My recommendation is that they abjure Tennessee, as Robert has seen service there. Beyond is a territory called Ar-kan-saw, said to be fair and untouched, of industrious settlers, committed to the greatness of what they believe will become a great country, once this idiocy is finished. If you do not love each other now, perhaps you will in time. I speak here of expediency, not emotion."

"Sir, I have loved Susanna since the first second I saw her. And indeed when Patrick was slain, I confess with shame that I had evil thoughts of such a possibility. Perhaps I sought death at the hands of Major Winston as self-flagellation for my treason."

"I should say nothing," said Susanna, "but to confirm the same."

"There is no treason here," I said. "Only honor."

"Robert, you must promise to raise and love Patrick's child as your own, so that, in some way or fashion, known or unknown, his lineage will continue and perhaps his gifts will continue to serve us."

"It is sworn," Robert said.

"Is this agreeable to you, Major Kavanagh?"

"You are a wise commander, sir. I have never doubted it."

"Clerk, fill out the document of marriage and the safe passage."

"Yes sir. Sir, under what name?"

This was an interesting conundrum. No one had thought enough in advance to consider it.

"One of you, pick a name."

"I have no preferred name," said Robert. "Brown, Smith, Jones? Any will do."

"Sir," I said, "Robert has told me he had a name among the Chickamauga. I cannot remember it, as it was quite a tongue-twister. But perhaps it might serve as inspiration."

"Robert?"

"It was *Ani-ja Nigan-guvna.*"

"As you said, Major, a mouthful. What meaning has it?"

"Cherokee is difficult to translate directly into our tongue," said Robert. "It is as poetic as Shakespeare. This would be something along the lines of 'Walks Bold' or more properly, 'He Who Walks Boldly.' "

"Hmm," said the Colonel, "that's hardly helpful."

"Sir," I said, "there is a near synonym."

"Indeed?"

"Why not 'Swagger'?"

CHAPTER 66

List

The New York Times Best Sellers List
April 3, 2022

NONFICTION

1. *You Have to Ask Yourself: The Boise Incident and Extraterrestrial Intervention*, by David Banjax and David Childish. A reporter who covered the siege at Boise and a prominent ancient alien theorist make the case that the famous "mystery operator" was from another star system.

2. *The Rape That Wasn't*, by Ginger Brooks. NBC's new anchorwoman recalls her ordeal at the hands of Chechen criminals who threatened her with rape and worse, and embraces the feminist creed that got her through it.

3. *The Iron Wren*, by R. W. "Bud" Feeley. A biography of recently retired congressional icon Charlotte Venable, with an emphasis

on her heroism and leadership during the horrifying siege at Boise.

4. *I Walked the Walk*, by Senator Ross Baker with Robin DuhAngelo. Senator Baker, frequently cited as a 2024 presidential possibility after his heroism at Boise, recalls his ordeal by terror and maintains that it was such an anomaly that no meaningful lessons can be drawn from it.

5. *The Semiotic Rifle*, by Stephen Hunter. A thriller writer offers essays on the history, development, and purported "meaning" of several iconic firearms.

ACKNOWLEDGMENTS

First, apologies to Boise. In the past, it's been my practice to visit the towns in life that I visit in fiction. I have in fact been to Boise, but many years and many book tours ago. I have memories, but they could easily also be of Denver, St. Louis, Seattle, or any other spot where booksellers have let me peddle my wares. This time the travel was a no-go because of steel hips, prostate issues, stamina difficulties, and of course COVID. I hope people forgive any stupidities as derived from incorrect readings of Google Images—no malicious intent intended.

Second, thanks to so many of the usuals who helped out: Gary Goldberg, Lenne Miller, Dave Dunn, Bill Smart, Barrett Tillman, my brother Andy, Jeff Weber. Professionally, Mark Tavani was of great help, and special thanks to Emily Bestler, of Simon & Schuster, who took this book in a nanosecond when it became available. Made the old dog feel good. Esther Newberg, of course, agent extraordinaire, navigated a potentially awkward professional midstream horse change with grace and skill. To me, she's Mother Life. Then my wife, Jean Marbella, the Mother Reporter of the *Baltimore Sun*, kept me in coffee and good cheer. She would also be Mother

Caffeine. Thanks to all, and as usual any fault accrues to me, not them.

As for the book itself, I can only go Latin: *Res ipsa loquitur*. The thing itself speaks (from Jonathan Turley's fabulous blog). You buy it, you rent it, you find it in a bus station refuse can—you get to come to conclusions about its meanings. Your interpretations are as valid as mine. What do I know? I only wrote it.

I will say that the key moment arrived one day in Baltimore traffic. I'd been thinking about the idea—a use-of-force hearing with Bob Lee Swagger in the hot seat when it turns into a hostage situation—for some time with no luck whatsoever. I was sitting there, and suddenly the world went green. I looked to my right and saw myself next to a green Maryland Division of Corrections bus, armored up like a T-34 at Kursk, radiating existential bad news as its hue washed across everything. My apoplectic imagination instantly conjured: bus rams hearing, bad guys take over, don't think it's been done before. Then I figured out a way to bring in an untethered plot strain from my never-to-be-written novel of origins, which would have been called *Redcoats*. By the way, I have wanted to do a duel *a Florentine* in the mud and rain since then!

And a teaser: Next one, whether I'm here or not, Earl in WWII. No cell phones, no satellites, no Internet, plenty of tommy guns.

Center Point Large Print
600 Brooks Road / PO Box 1
Thorndike, ME 04986-0001 USA

(207) 568-3717

US & Canada:
1 800 929-9108
www.centerpointlargeprint.com